THE GRAND GAME
BOOK 2: WAY OF THE WOLF

THE GRAND GAME

BOOK 2: WAY OF THE WOLF

TOM ELLIOT

THE GRAND GAME

New Powers and Old.
A conflict millennia in the brewing.
And at the center of it, one man.

Michael has escaped the clutches of the Dark, if only temporarily. Surfacing in the world above, he finds matter no less complex than down below and survival as challenging as it had been in the dungeon.

Is the harder path the one you must forge on your own?
Many want Michael as their ally. Yet more want him dead, and the Dark is not done with him either. Can Michael find a way to navigate the treacherous waters of the Game and uncover the mysteries about himself?

Or will Michael bend to Powers greater than him?
Follow Michael on his epic journey of discovery and find out!

PRAISE FOR THE GRAND GAME:

"Interesting portal litrpg. Well-paced and the start of a new series. Curious to see where it goes..." —**Tao Wong on goodreads.com.**

"... Great action, great storyline and I honestly binge read it, start to end..." — **Alex Kozlowski on goodreads.com.**

"Smart MC. Great Tension. Full of Action." —**CookieCrumble on RoyalRoad.com.**

"Everything I look for in a LitRPG." —**CosmereCradleChris on RoyalRoad.com.**

"Oh I liked this very much!" —**The Enlightened Beard on amazon.com.**

"One of the best in this category this year." —**kindle customer on amazon.com.**

AUTHOR'S NOTE

Dear Readers,

Thank you for reading the Grand Game. This is a self-published book. Even though care has been given to the review and editing of this novel, some mistakes may have slipped through. If you spot any grammatical errors or typos, please get in touch with me via email.

This book also contains game-like elements. They are generally unintrusive and integrated into the story, but beware, they exist. Otherwise, I hope you enjoy Michael's story.

Happy reading!
Tom (**TomLitRPG.com**)
Support me on PATREON[1]

---

[1] https://www.patreon.com/grandgame

CONTENTS

MICHAEL'S EVOLUTION

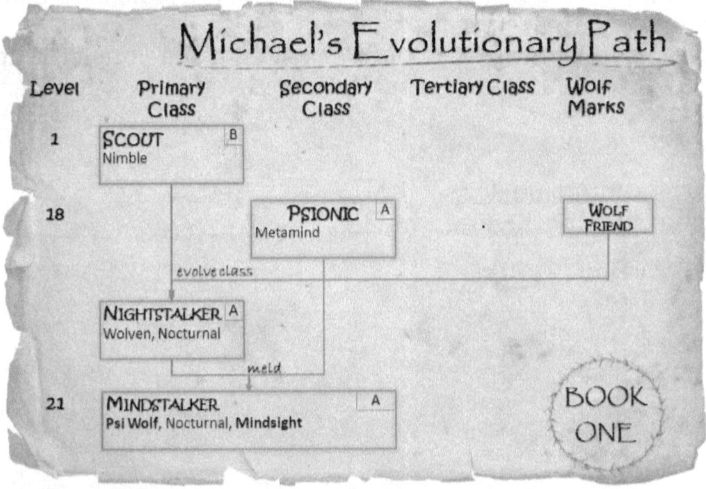

As always, Michael continues to grow during his adventures in the Forever Kingdom. The chart above only illustrates his latest achievements (as accomplished over the course of the last book). If you wish to view Michael's earlier evolutionary charts, please visit my site at the link below.

tomlitrpg.com/michael

The System of the Grand Game

The universe of the Grand Game continues to expand with every book in the series, and at this point, it no longer makes sense to include all the maps, charts, and diagrams in each new book.

If you wish to learn more about the world of the Forever Kingdom or understand the system of the Grand Game better, please visit my site at one of the links below.

tomlitrpg.com/game-lore
tomlitrpg.com/world-lore

tomlitrpg.com/glossary

Michael at the End of Book 1

<u>Player Profile: Michael</u>
Level: 23. Rank: 2. Current Health: 100%.
Stamina: 100%. Mana: 100%. Psi: 100%.
Species: Human. Lives Remaining: 2.
Marks: Wolf-friend, Lesser Shadow, Lesser Light, Lesser Dark.

Attributes

Available: 0 points.
Strength: 2. Constitution: 5. Dexterity: 13. Perception: 8. Mind: 5. Magic: 0.
Faith: 0.

Classes

Available: 1 point.
Primary-Secondary Bi-blend: Mindstalker.
Tertiary Class: None.

Traits

Psi wolf heritage: +2 Dexterity, +2 Strength, +4 Mind.
Beast tongue: can speak to beastkin.
Marked: can see spirit signatures.
Nocturnal: perfect night vision.

Skills

Available skill slots: 0.
Light armor (current: 22. max: 50. Constitution, basic).
Dodging (current: 31. max: 130. Dexterity, basic).
Sneaking (current: 42. max: 130. Dexterity, basic).
Shortswords (current: 38. max: 130. Dexterity, basic).
Two-weapon fighting (current: 33. max: 130. Dexterity, advanced).
Thieving (current: 1. max: 130. Dexterity, basic).
Chi (current: 20. max: 50. Mind, advanced).
Meditation (current: 31. max: 50. Mind, basic).
Telekinesis (current: 13. max: 50. Mind, advanced).
Telepathy (current: 16. max: 50. Mind, advanced).
Insight (current: 32. max: 80. Perception, basic).
Deception (current: 9. max: 80. Perception, master).

Abilities

Crippling blow (Dexterity, basic).
Minor backstab (Dexterity, basic).
Basic trap disarm (Dexterity, basic).
Simple lockpicking (Dexterity, basic).
Simple charm (Mind, basic).
Stunning slap (Mind, basic).
One-step (Mind, basic).
Minor reaction buff (Mind, basic).
Basic analyze (Perception, basic).
Lesser trap detect (Perception, basic).
Conceal small weapon (Perception, basic).

Simple mindsight (Class, basic).

Known Key Points
Sector 14,913 exit portal and safe zone.

Equipped
common thief's cloak (+3 sneaking).
spider's bite shortsword (+15% damage, webbed).
shortsword, +1 (+15% damage, +10 shortswords).
common fighter's sash (+3 shortswords).
enchanted leather armor set (+20% damage reduction, -35% Dexterity and Magic).
slotted potion belt (3 minor heal, 4 moderate heal, 3 full heal).

Backpack Contents
26 x field rations.
1 x flask of water.
2 x minor healing potions.
2 x iron daggers.
1 x bedroll.
7 x moderate healing potions.
1 x coin pouch.
1 x keyring.
1 x basic fire-starting kit.
1 x Catalog of Skills and Abilities.
1 x rank 1 priest's robe.
1 x blood siphon master Class stone.

Bank Contents
<u>Money</u>: 46 gold, 4 silver, and 9 copper.
2 x full healing potions.
2 x basic steel shortswords.

If you wish to view Michael's earlier player profiles, please visit my site at the link below.

tomlitrpg.com/michael

CHAPTER 89: THE OUTSIDE WORLD

Day One of Michael's Pact with Erebus.

I stumbled out of the portal and fell to my hands and knees, struggling to catch my balance.

I was blinded.

Light. White and brighter than anything I had yet felt in this world filled my vision. I squeezed my eyes shut. *Bloody hell, that's bright.*

I waited for a heartbeat or two to allow the dancing afterimages to fade. Then I opened my eyes to careful slits.

Green. Trees. Rocks.

That was what I saw. My heart thudded louder. I had done it. I had escaped Erebus's dungeon, and largely unscathed too.

I opened my eyes wider. The light, while still harsh and painful, was no longer blinding. I was standing at the mouth of a cave set high on the slope of a mountainside.

Below me was a verdant expanse of green, a forest of tall trees. Oaks, redwoods, sequoia, and many others for which I had no names filled the horizon. Beyond them, I saw more mountaintops in the far distance, cradling the forest on all sides.

I'm in a valley. This must be the dire wolves' home.

I had made it. I was safe. Or was I? Multiple messages from the Game were waiting for my attention. Turning my focus inward, I scrolled through them.

You have completed the task, <u>Escape the Dungeon,</u> and failed the task <u>Find your own way out</u>. Through your deeds, you have foiled Erebus' plans and earned his ire!

The Marks on your spirit signature have changed. You have escaped the dungeon using the exit crafted by the Dark, yet in a manner wholly of your own making. The Dark is pleased by your pursuit of self and your refusal to bind yourself to another. Your Dark Mark has deepened.

Shadow is satisfied that your actions have not disturbed the balance between the Forces. Your Shadow Mark remains unchanged.

Light is dissatisfied with the manner of your escape. You have scorned unity and pursuit of the greater good. Your Light Mark has weakened.

Wolf admires the strong. Wolf acknowledges the leader, but at the same time Wolf accepts no being as its master. You have refused to bow to any Power and held true to your lupine heritage. Wolf is pleased. Your Wolf Mark has deepened.

Congratulations, Michael! Your Wolf Mark has advanced. You now bear the Mark: <u>wolf-brethren</u>. Most wolfkind will react favorably to this Mark and welcome you as an honored guest, defending you as one of their own against outsiders but still considering you as separate from their pack.

I paused the flow of messages while I considered their implications. My Wolf Mark had been strengthened. I wasn't sure yet what this boded for me, but I was certain it was important. At the very least, it would ease my introduction to the dire wolves.

With a flick of my hand, I willed the messages to continue scrolling.

You have entered sector 12,560 of the Kingdoms. This area is part of the Forever Kingdom's wild borderlands. It is currently neutral territory, unclaimed by any faction or Force. No additional restrictions apply to this region.

You have accomplished the feat: <u>Novice Dungeoneer!</u> Requirement: complete your first dungeon. You have been awarded an additional life! Total lives: 3.

By the terms of your agreement with the Power Erebus, your non-aggression Pact with him has commenced. For the length of this Pact, neither you nor those bearing Erebus' Mark may take hostile action against each other. Remaining duration: 7 days.

I chewed over the alerts, especially the final one. So I wasn't safe. Not yet. And maybe I never would be.

Seven days, I thought. *That's how long I had before I could expect reprisals from Erebus. It was nice that I had gained another life, but I had no illusions that it would make much difference if the Power's people caught me after the Pact concluded.

I glanced over my shoulder. The shimmering curtain was still there, shining brightly in the darkness, and I was sure Stayne was still on the other side, straining against the Pact that leashed his actions.

He'll pursue me as soon as he can.

I had to conclude my business in the valley quickly and be long gone before then. Shouldering my backpack into a more comfortable position, I stepped onto the rocky slope leading downward in search of the dire wolves.

✳ ✳ ✳

The descent to the bottom of the valley was gradual enough to be manageable without climbing gear and easy enough to allow me time to think. As I made my way into the valley, I reviewed my plans for the immediate future. I intended on finding Aira and Oursk to see what more I could learn of the "Wolf," as the Adjudicator so often referred to it. I wasn't sure what the Wolf was yet. It could be a being—another Power perhaps—or it could be a metaphor for a path, a wolven way of life maybe.

Whatever it was, I knew I needed to find out. It was important, I sensed, and not just to my choice of tertiary Class. *It could determine my future in this world.*

By now I suspected I was different, apart even from other players. It was the only explanation I could come up with for the attention Erebus, Loken, and Ishita had paid me. *Why* I was different remained a mystery, but I was sure the Powers' interest wouldn't make my life easier.

I would have to play every angle I could to survive.

And that meant finding out about the Wolf and what it held in store for me. I only hoped the dire wolves would be able to enlighten me.

I skipped down the final stretch of the rocky slope, jumping lightly from boulder to boulder.

I had no actual destination in mind yet. I didn't know the wolves' precise location, only that this valley was their home. I wasn't worried about finding them though. I suspected they would find me if I ventured far enough into the valley.

I reached the bottom of the mountainside without incident. Standing on the forest's edge, I studied the trees arching high over me, then glanced left and right. The woods extended in both directions as far as the eye could see. From what I had seen from the cave mouth, I knew it filled the entire expanse of the valley too.

The forest was not silent either. Insects chirped, birds sang, strange hoots sounded, and eerie howls emanated from within. All in all, I preferred the mountains. Still, there was no going back. I sighed. *Onward, Michael,* I encouraged myself and took a tentative step forward.

A branch crackled underfoot.

I froze and glanced at the ground askance. Twigs and fallen leaves littered the forest floor. *Huh. Sneaking here isn't going to be easy.* Holding my pose, I stared into the forest depths. The longer I looked, the more uneasy I grew. I got the distinct feeling that whoever I'd been in my past life, I'd been no woodsman.

I sighed again. *No time like the present to learn.* After all, I couldn't very well follow the path of the Wolf and be afraid of a forest, now could I?

I'm not afraid, I thought stubbornly. Pulling the shadows around me, I stepped into the forest's depths.

✳ ✳ ✳

A hostile entity has detected you! You are no longer hidden.

I bit off a groan at the Game message. The hostile in question was a level one squirrel scolding me from the tree above. I glanced upward in a parting scowl before moving on.

Treading softly in the forest was even harder than I suspected. I didn't let it dissuade me though and kept at it. But even at my seemingly high skill level—rank four—I often dropped out of stealth almost as soon as I cloaked myself.

It has to be the light, I thought, squinting suspiciously up at the sunlight filtering down through the trees. But it was more than that, I knew. It was the environment itself.

The forest isn't as conducive to sneaking as dank, dark tunnels, I thought morosely.

The animals moving unseen through the foliage weren't helping either. I knew they were there. With simple mindsight, I was able to see the dozens of tiny minds scurrying through the underbrush, flitting through the trees overhead and even digging in the earth below.

I had even charmed a few. Not that it helped train my telepathy any. Most of the surrounding animals' levels were far below my own, netting me nearly no experience. And leaving my mindsight open drained my psi even faster than my single-cast abilities. Simple mindsight, I realized, was not an ability I could use for scouting, at least not for extended forays.

But as full of life as this bloody forest is, at least I won't go hungry, I thought grouchily and stomped deeper into the underbrush.

The leaves rustled overhead. I paid them no mind.

Probably another damn squirrel.

A heavy weight landed on my shoulders. Alarm flashed through me before instinct kicked in, and I fell forward into a somersault. Claws raked at me through my leather armor as my maneuver flung the attacker off. *Not a squirrel then,* I thought inanely.

I bounced back to my feet. Drawing both my blades, I spun around. A shape flashed through the air—a four-footed creature of some kind.

I ducked.

The beast sailed over. I was about to whip around when another blur of motion caught my attention.

A second attacker.

I crossed my blades in guard position a heartbeat before the creature's jaw snapped for my throat. Stymied, the beast dropped to the floor and darted forward to nip at my legs.

I kicked the creature in the mouth and thrust spider's bite downward. I still couldn't quite tell what the thing was. Its skin—scales really—were mottled shades of brown and green, perfect camouflage for the forest. The beast, whatever it was, seemed a weird combination of serpent and cat.

Webbed triggered! An unknown assailant has failed a physical resistance check! You have immobilized your target for 1 second.

As my enchanted sword made contact with my foe's skull, magical webs spun out of the blade to wreathe the creature.

I didn't waste the opportunity.

Leaping forward, I straddled the beast and plunged my second blade deep into the snake-cat's throat. Life drained out of it.

You have killed an unknown assailant.

I sensed movement on my flank—my original attacker rejoining the fray. The creature was sprinting toward me. Releasing the blade still buried in the dead beast, I flung up my left arm. The beast ignored my upraised hand and leaped through the air to bridge the distance between us.

I drew psi from my mind and sent it rippling down my hand and directly into the beast as it crashed into me. Paralyzing energy flooded the creature's muscles, locking it in place instantly.

An unknown assailant has failed a physical resistance check! You have stunned your target for 1 second.

The beast bowled me over, and I fell backward onto the soft earth. My breath was knocked out the next moment as the creature landed atop me. I had been expecting the collision though and managed to keep hold of spider's bite.

Before the dazed creature could recover, I slapped my left hand to its side again, freezing it with stunning slap once more. Then I stabbed into the scaled beast.

Once. Twice.

The beast's paralysis faded, and it mewed pitifully as it felt the bite of my sword. Weakly, it tried to clamp its jaws around my throat. I fended off the feeble attack with my left hand and slashed at it again with the sword in my right. I kept at it, stabbing repeatedly. With each fresh strike, I tore gaping holes through the creature. Finally, the Game notice I had been waiting for arrived.

You have killed an unknown assailant.

With a sigh, I abandoned my frenzied assault and let my head rest on the soft grass. Chest heaving, I stared up into the silently watching trees. It was over. More messages were waiting for my attention, and I perused them while my adrenaline subsided.

You have reached level 24!
Your shortswords has increased to level 39. Your two-weapon fighting has increased to level 34. Your light armor has increased to level 24. Your chi has increased to level 21.

Long seconds later, I felt recovered enough to move again and pushed the corpse of me. The thing was heavy, but eventually I freed my trapped legs and rested my back against a nearby tree trunk.

Looking down, I took stock of myself. I hadn't sustained any significant injuries, nothing more than a few scratches. Despite the suddenness of the ambush, I had weathered the attack surprisingly well.

Still, I was covered in blood and gore, and I was sure I stank too. I wiped the filth off my face, grimacing in distaste. Cleaning off was going to be a chore.

"Bloody hell," I muttered. "I hate this forest already."

CHAPTER 90: HUNTED

I cannibalized the priest's robe I'd looted from Saben's stash, cutting it into long pieces of cloth—I had no other use for it—and used the strips to clean my gear and weapons. Then I saw to my player progression and, after a moment's thought, invested my new attribute point.

Your Mind has increased to rank 6.

My Dexterity didn't need to increase yet, and I had only one Mind ability slot remaining. Given my growing dependence on my abilities in battle, I didn't want to find myself without enough available slots for crucial abilities in the future.

After that, I took the time to rest and recover my stamina. While I munched through my rations and sipped water from my flask, I reviewed the encounter.

I realized the woods had lulled me into a false sense of comfort. If anything, the forest was more dangerous than the dungeon. Here, I could be ambushed at any time and from any direction.

Worse yet, my senses would not serve me as well as they had underground. The abundance of life, the incessant noise, and the constant rustle of trees in the forest all worked to disguise the approach of any hostiles.

I'll have to be more vigilant here—not less.

I sighed and glanced up at the trunk I was resting against. The lowest branch was within grasp, with plenty more handholds further up. Rising to my feet, I deftly climbed into the tree's upper reaches. Even without ropes or climbing gear, it was easier than I expected.

Moderately secure, I closed my eyes and stilled my mind. It was perhaps slightly foolhardy to block out my awareness of my surroundings so soon after being ambushed, but I considered the risk of continuing the journey with insufficient psi even greater.

A few minutes later, I opened my eyes.

Meditation completed. Your psi is now at 100%. Your meditation has increased to level 32.

With my psi fully restored, it was time to get moving again. I dropped down lightly from the tree. My gaze fell to the dead creatures. I still didn't know what they were.

Kneeling beside the first, I inspected it more closely. The beast's torso was elongated, and from stubbed nose to whiplike tail it was covered in fine scales. Its head was flattened like a snake's but its powerful hind legs, slitted eyes, and long raking claws were reminiscent of a big cat.

Prying open the creature's mouth, I inspected the inside. There were only two fangs and a forked tongue within.

Weird, I thought.

Letting the head fall back down, I probed the body with basic analyze. The air around the corpse shimmered with strange symbols that my mind, remarkably, had no trouble decoding.

The target is a level 28 dead serline. Serlines are chimeras, part serpent, part feline. Expertly camouflaged, silent and quick-moving, they are stealth predators that are well-adapted to hunting down prey in woodland environments.

Your insight has increased to level 33.

Cat-snake chimeras. My lips twisted. That explained their strange appearance at least. More concerning, though, was the serline's level. It was higher than my own. Not since facing off against the goblin goliath—which felt like ages ago—had I found myself under-leveled during an encounter.

I guess I'm not the scariest thing around anymore.

I turned away from the creature with an unhappy grimace. Nothing about this forest was putting me at ease. *Maybe it would have been—*

My thoughts broke off as the hairs on the back of my neck rose. *Danger*, my mind screamed. I spun around, hands dropping to the blades at my sides.

You have detected a hidden entity!

Standing still and poised, with its left foot raised and less than two yards away, was a serline—a live one. Watching me with unblinking eyes, the creature slowly lowered its leg back to the ground and crouched down on all fours.

With my hands tightly gripping my sword hilts, I froze.

How long has it been there? And how the hell did it manage to creep so close undetected? We stared at each other for a drawn-out heartbeat, neither daring to break our standoff.

You have detected a hidden entity!

Motion in the corner of my eye drew my attention to the right. A second cat-snake was padding closer.

You have detected a hidden entity!

More movement. This time on my other side. My heartbeat quickened. I turned my head minutely to the left. A third serline was approaching from that direction. *Urgh. How many are there?*

I itched to draw my blades but stilled my hands, knowing the motion would likely impel the creatures to act.

Why haven't they attacked yet?

My gaze flitted to the two corpses. Perhaps their fellows' fate made the trio wary, but I suspected it was something else entirely. Sending psi rippling outward, I activated simple mindsight.

Tendrils of my will flooded the space around me, revealing every consciousness within ten yards. There were seven more minds, each resembling the three in my sights, hidden in the underbrush and the trees above. Moment by moment, they inched closer.

I swallowed. It was as I had feared. I was surrounded. An entire pack of the creatures was closing in on me. Closing my mindsight, I drew more psi and began a second casting. I wasn't going to win this encounter through a straight-up fight—*time to create some confusion.* Reaching out to the closest serline, I superimposed my will over its own.

A level 27 serline has failed a mental resistance check! You have charmed your target for 10 seconds. Your telepathy has increased to level 17.

The charmed creature rose from its crouch. Tilting its head to the side, it waited on my instruction. The predatory gaze of the other two serlines broke off from me to study their packmate. Their tails flicked uncertainly as they sensed something amiss.

"*Attack,*" I breathed through the mental leash I held around the bewitched creature's mind. Without hesitation, the serline spun around and toward its closest fellow.

The targeted creature snarled and swiped a paw threateningly through the air. My minion paid the warning no heed. Pouncing forward, it sank its fangs deep into its foe's throat. I didn't wait to observe the fight's outcome. Swiveling around, I raced away. The third serline pelted after me. I didn't think I could outrun it, but I didn't intend to. At least not on the ground.

I took three steps and risked a glance behind. The pursuing serline was closing in fast. I turned around and covered another yard. *Almost there,* I thought.

I sensed the creature behind me leap. I did too, launching myself upward at the nearby tree while weaving psi.

You have successfully one-stepped.

The serline's jaws snapped shut, missing me by a hairsbreadth. My right leg found solid footing in the air, and I vaulted higher, arms raised. With outstretched fingers, I grasped an overhanging branch.

The bough bent but held.

Using the momentum of my leap, I executed a backflip and landed neatly on the limb.

From beneath, the thwarted serline hissed in frustration. I smiled at the creature's annoyance before turning my attention upward. I knew I hadn't fully escaped the beast. The serline looked more than capable of climbing the tree, but it would take time to reach me.

Time I needed to deal with its packmate hiding in the canopy above.

My earlier casting of mindsight had revealed the other serline. I swung upward onto another branch, eyes warily scanning the foliage where I suspected it was hiding.

A leaf quivered. My gaze flew to the area.

You have detected a hidden entity!

Got you, I thought grimly and made my way closer. Below me, more serlines emerged from hiding. One braver—or more foolish—than its packmates attempted to leap onto my tree from an adjacent one.

Midway through its flight, I could tell the beast would fall short. I smiled tightly. I'd selected my refuge carefully, choosing an old oak tree set slightly apart from the rest. The creature howled as it plummeted to the ground. Sadly, though, it suffered no injury. Saved by its feline reflexes, the cat-snake somehow managed to land on its feet.

Curbing my disappointment, I banished the circling pack from my thoughts and gazed at my target—a half-seen shape crouched on a branch three yards away. The serline hadn't yet realized I was onto it. I drew closer. Rising slowly to its feet, the cat-snake readied itself to strike.

I kept advancing and drew my swords.

In a sudden explosion of motion, the beast leaped downward and burst through the foliage with its paws aimed at my torso. If I had been caught unawares, the attack would have been fatal. As it was, I was perfectly poised to repel the attack.

Twisting my torso, I ducked the outthrust limbs and slashed at the creature as it rushed by. My blades bit deep, cleaving the beast from forelegs to hindquarters.

You have killed a serline.

The corpse split, showering the pack below with blood and innards. *Perhaps that'll teach them.* I glanced down. Eight pairs of slitted eyes stared upward, indifferent to the gore that splattered their faces.

Only eight, I noted. My gaze flitted to another unmoving mound on the forest floor. It seemed my charmed minion had died too. The serline pack had already lost four of their number. But despite their losses, the group showed no sign of abandoning their hunt. *So be it,* I thought, my face hardening.

"Who's next?" I taunted.

✳   ✳   ✳

The serlines didn't respond to my challenge. Instead, they circled the tree, eyeing me with predatory patience, seemingly content to wait me out.

Bad choice, I thought. It would've served the pack better to have rushed me immediately. Then maybe they could've overwhelmed me by numbers alone.

As it was, the pack's delay only gave me time to prepare. Drawing on my psi again, I cast reaction buff. Energy coursed out from my mind and into my body, strengthening and enhancing my muscles.

Your Dexterity has increased by +2. Duration: 10 minutes.

On the tree bough, I bounced lightly on my haunches. My reflexes had quickened, and I felt marginally more agile. Not a lot, but every little bit counted.

Casting my gaze over the pack again, I analyzed each in turn and identified the one that appeared to be their leader. This cat-snake was bigger and meaner looking than its fellows. At level thirty-one, it was higher leveled than the rest too.

I smiled coldly and, reaching out to my target, cast simple charm.

A serline has passed a mental resistance check! You have failed to charm your target. Your mental intrusion has gone undetected!

The beast brushed aside the tendrils of psi I sent searching toward it, albeit unknowingly. My smile tightened, but I was undeterred. I tried again.

A serline has failed a mental resistance check! You have charmed your target for 10 seconds.

My mental leash slipped onto the beast without resistance on the second attempt. *"Attack,"* I ordered, directing my new minion toward its nearest packmate.

The bewitched serline didn't hesitate. Leaping onto its fellow, it drove the smaller creature to the ground and raked its claws through the startled cat-snake. With a pleased grin, I made myself more comfortable on my perch.

Until the pack wised up, there was nothing more for me to do but sit back and watch the fun.

✷ ✷ ✷

It took another three deaths before the serlines caught on. Clearly the beasts weren't the smartest.

Now only five strong, the pack charged up the tree en masse, their long, curved claws piercing the rough bark with ease.

I let them come.

My psi pool was about half-empty, and rather than spend what was left, I decided to keep it in reserve. I didn't think I would have too much trouble dealing with the rest of the pack.

Slipping onto the tree trunk I waited on, the first serline reached striking distance. Coiling back, it sprang toward me. My footing was sure on the tree bough, and I deftly sidestepped the beast. Its attack stymied, the serline spun in midair, claws scrambling to regain its hold onto the branch.

I wasn't about to let it.

Lunging forward with spider's bite, I slashed at the creature's limbs while at the same time channeling stamina through the blade.

A serline has failed a physical resistance check! You have crippled your target's foreleg for 3 seconds.

Energy gushed out of the sword's tip and into the beast. The creature's leg went abruptly slack, foiling its attempt to land back on the branch. With a startled hiss, the serline plummeted to the ground.

My eyes darted back to the remaining four members of the pack. Another shape was sailing through the air toward me, with a second following quickly on its heels. I ducked and the first creature flew over.

I wasn't able to avoid the second so easily.

Before I could attempt another evasion, the beast crashed into me. Its weight flung me off the branch, and realizing my peril, I threw myself backward, using the impetus of the collision to propel me further. Twisting through the air, I grabbed onto a lower branch—dropping both my blades in the process.

"Too damn close," I muttered as I pulled myself to safety. I glanced down. My blades glinted in the grass. The two beasts that had fallen were next to them. One appeared largely uninjured and only a slight limp marred its steps. The other, though, was severely hurt and crawled pitifully across the ground.

Movement drew my eyes upward. The other three serlines were pacing on my former perch and eying me hungrily. *I guess I underestimated the pack,* I thought sourly.

In tandem, the three snake-cats leaped down at me. Not waiting to meet them, I dropped onto a lower branch.

Then down to another.

I kept descending until, finally, I reached the lowest bough. Not pausing to consider my actions further, I flung myself off. Mid-leap, I solidified the air under me.

You have successfully one-stepped.

One of my windmilling legs found purchase, breaking what would otherwise have been a most unpleasant fall. I launched off the foot and directly at the less-injured serline.

The creature flung its head up and snarled in surprise. But caught off guard by my sudden change of direction, it was too slow to dodge as I landed on its back. Bones cracked beneath me, and with a mournful whine the beast sank to the ground.

You have crippled a serline!

I rolled off the beast and toward spider's bite. In a single motion, I grabbed its hilt and bounced to my feet.

I spun around in time to see the other three serlines land soft-footed behind me. I backstepped, ignoring the two downed creatures and my other sword. It was too far to reach.

The trio split to surround me in a half-circle. I set my stance and waited. The beast in front leaped. I swayed out of the way, slapping a hand to its side in passing.

You have stunned your target for 1 second.

The cat-snake on my left was airborne already. Dropping into a kneeling position, I thrust upward with spider's bite and skewered it through its soft underbelly.

You have critically injured a serline!

That, unfortunately, left the third creature free to attack unopposed. Rushing in, the beast clamped its jaws down on my neck. Twin fangs ripped through my flesh and blood gushed out.

I fell back and the creature landed on top me. Frantically, I slammed a hand against the serline, momentarily paralyzing it with stunning slap. Feeling the beast go slack, I shoved it away and rolled free.

I wasn't given time to recover. The first beast rushed at me again. Closing the distance, it leaped, and I staggered out of the way—barely. Even reeling from the blood pumping out of my throat, I retained enough presence of mind to strike at the creature and cast crippling blow.

You have injured a serline.

A serline has failed a physical resistance check! You have crippled your target's hind leg for 3 seconds.

Webbed triggered! A serline has failed a physical resistance check! You have immobilized your target for 1 second.

I smiled grimly as both abilities triggered simultaneously. The beast snarled in frustration as, for the second time during the encounter, it was disabled. Landing two yards away, it hobbled back toward me on three legs. I stumbled back and searched for my other foes.

Another beast was charging me.

With little time to prepare, I reacted instinctively. Taking a step to the side, I slapped my left hand on its torso as it sailed past.

You have stunned your target for 1 second.

The cat-snake crashed to a halt a few feet away. I dived forward with spider's bite outthrust. My aim was perfect, and the blade sank deep into the creature.

You have killed a serline.

Knowing I didn't have much time, I rolled off the corpse and quickly un-stoppered a healing potion, downing its contents without pause.

The effect was instantaneous.

Soothing ripples of energy flowed through my body, stemming the bleeding in my neck. I bounced back to my feet. The sole uninjured serline hobbled toward me, its hind leg still disabled.

I risked a quick glance at my foes. The other three serlines were out of the fight, moving pitifully or critically injured. I smiled grimly. The skirmish was nearly over. I turned back to my foe. The snake-cat leaped. Not bothering to dodge, I lunged forward.

Blade and beast met.

Sword triumphed.

The tip of my blade plunged into the creature's mouth, through the back of its throat, and out the rear of its skull.

You have killed a serline.

The creature crashed at my feet, yanking my arm downward. With a vicious grin, I withdrew my sword and turned to the injured pack members.

It was time to put them out of their misery.

CHAPTER 91: BIG GAME HUNTERS

DAY ONE OF MICHAEL'S PACT WITH EREBUS.

Not unexpectedly, after I killed the last serline, a slew of Game messages opened in my mind. I scanned through them quickly.

You have reached level 28!
Your shortswords has increased to level 40 and reached rank 4.
Your two-weapon fighting has increased to level 35. Your light armor has increased to level 26. Your dodging has increased to level 32.
Your chi has increased to level 23. Your telekinesis has increased to level 16. Your telepathy has increased to level 19.
Warning! The enchantment on spider's bite is running low and must be recharged.

"Wow," I murmured, studying my gains. *Four whole levels and a host of skill advances.*

I took stock of myself. I was healthy and uninjured, but my stamina was low and my psi even lower. The enchantments on my sword needed attending to as well. I needed to rest and recover. But I couldn't do it here. I was sure the dead serlines would attract other predators, ones I wasn't equipped to face right now.

It's time to get going.

Bending down, I cleaned my blades and sheathed them. Then reorienting myself, I headed deeper into the forest.

For the time being, I forsook further attempts at stealth. Jogging lightly, I traversed the woods as quickly as I dared while keeping a lookout for more ambushes. Distances in the forest were much harder to judge than in the tunnels underground. Still, when I staggered to a stop ten minutes later, I estimated I'd covered about half a mile.

Chest heaving, I studied the area. This patch of the forest looked little different from any other. I was surrounded by tall trees and thick underbrush. Anything could be lurking in the foliage, waiting to attack me. I shuddered. *Damnable forest.*

I was so tired I wanted nothing more than to sink down onto the ground and sleep, but I knew I couldn't do that. The forest floor was too vulnerable. I glanced upward. Even with the risk of falling, sleeping in the trees would be safer.

Groaning at the thought of further exertions, I dragged myself toward a large redwood tree and began climbing. This particular specimen was almost three hundred feet tall, and I scaled nearly two-thirds of its height before I felt secure enough to stop.

Bracing my back against the central trunk, I straddled a stout bough and looked down. The forest floor was almost invisible. *Good enough,* I decided.

I squinted up at the sky. I had no idea what time of day it was, but sunlight was still filtering down through the leaves. It was too early to sleep, and I knew I should see to my player growth before resting, but I was too tired to care.

Only taking the time to tie myself to the bough with strands of cloth scavenged from the priest's robe, I closed my eyes and surrendered to the call of sleep.

✳   ✳   ✳

"The tracks end here."

My eyes snapped open. My thoughts were muddled, and for a moment I wasn't sure where I was.

An owl hooted in the distance.

I'm in the forest, I remembered. I glanced upward. Between the swaying branches, I caught a glimpse of stars and a black sky. The night was well advanced then. How long had I been asleep?

"Are you sure?"

I started in surprise. I was still disoriented and had nearly forgotten about the voice below.

Get it together, Michael, I admonished myself. Shaking my head to clear it from the lingering strands of sleep, I peered down.

Directly beneath me was a half-giant and human. The human wore a green cloak and carried a longbow across his back, while his companion was outfitted in sleeveless leather armor, revealing bulging muscles.

A large broadsword was strapped on the half-giant's hip. Given his size, I wondered if he wielded it one-handed.

A scout and a fighter, I concluded. Both figures had their heads bent, studying something on the ground.

"Of course I'm bloody sure," the human said.

The half-giant scratched his head. "Then where is he?"

The scout growled. "How in hells should I know? We should've waited for morning."

"What? And let some other lucky sods claim the bounty?" The half-giant snorted. "Fat chance." He stroked his chin. "We should search the area," he suggested.

The scout chuckled. "What good will that do?" His cloaked head swiveled left and right. "I can't see a bloody thing beyond a few feet. Can you?" He shook his head a moment later, not seeming to expect an answer. "I told you we were wasting our time. This forest is too dark at night. I barely managed to follow the trail this far."

"Let's light some torches then," the fighter said.

"Are you mad?" his companion hissed. "The flames will only destroy what little night vision we have, and our quarry can see in the dark—or so the bounty notice claimed." He paused. "Who knows, maybe the bastard is watching us even now."

That seemed to worry the fighter. In a sudden fit of caution, he dropped a hand to the hilt of his blade and scanned the darkness.

I frowned, considering what I had overheard. It was obvious the pair were hunting me and, from the mention of a bounty, it was clear why. But where had the two come from?

I hadn't recognized either's voice, so it was doubtful they'd followed me from the dungeon. I studied them again.

A haze formed around the two. *They're Marked,* I realized, scanning their auras. *Which makes them players.* Reaching out with my will, I analyzed the pair.

The target is Henry, a level 22 human. He is a player and bears Marks of Minor Dark.

The target is Knorl, a level 21 half-giant. He is a player and bears a Mark of Lesser Dark.

My frown deepened. Both players had a decent number of levels. Given their relatively high ranks, I was certain they hadn't come from the dungeon but from somewhere else entirely. They didn't have any Marks identifying them as sworn followers of Erebus though.

Which means they aren't bound by our non-aggression Pact. My lips turned up. *But neither are they protected by it.* Moving carefully, I began untying the knots attaching me to the tree bough.

It was time to act.

✳ ✳ ✳

It only took a few moments to free myself. Rising to my haunches, I checked my internal reserves. Both my psi and stamina had recovered fully.

I didn't have time to ponder how to spend my new attribute points, but I didn't think it wise to leave them unspent before facing off against the two players. After a moment's consideration, I spread them evenly between my most important attributes.

Your Dexterity has increased to rank 14, your Mind to rank 7, and your Constitution to rank 7.

I glanced down once more. The pair had begun talking again, arguing about what to do next.

I smiled. Ambushing the two would be child's play, but I decided against it. After all, this was a perfect occasion to gain more information, and while attempting to do so would be risky, I didn't know when I would have a similar opportunity again. There was just one more preparation I needed to make.

Removing my secondary weapon and thief's cloak, I unclipped my sword belt from around my waist and retied it diagonally across my back so the hilt of spider's bite hung down and my slotted potions rested on my chest, within easy reach. The sword was short enough that neither its tip nor hilt stuck out. Reaching underhanded behind me, I tried drawing the blade. It came easily to hand.

Perfect.

Sticking my second sword into the fighter's sash still wrapped around my waist, I re-equipped my thief's cloak.

You have successfully concealed the small weapon, spider's bite.

I grinned. Now I was ready. Stepping forward into empty air, I dropped lithely to a lower branch. Then another. All the while, the arguing pair remained oblivious of my approach.

I cleared the last stretch to the ground, landing without a sound and less than two yards behind the scout. Neither reacted.

I rose silently to my feet. The half-giant was staring in my direction but still failed to see me.

A hostile entity has failed to detect you! Your sneaking has increased to level 43.

Huh. Guess his night vision is even worse than I thought.

"… should go back," Henry was saying.

"But we're already here," Knorl protested. "What will it hurt to search around for a bit?"

The scout shook his head. "Too dangerous. What if—"

I decided this had gone on long enough. It was time to intervene. "Good evening, gentlemen."

Henry spun about, fumbling for the sheathed dagger at his side. The half-giant reacted quicker, his massive sword almost seeming to leap into his hand.

So he does wield it one-handed, I noted.

Your hidden weapon has gone unnoticed!
Your deception has increased to level 10. Congratulations, Michael, your skill in deception has reached rank 1, increasing your chance of misleading your foes.

"Who are you?" the half-giant barked.

"Who do you think?" I said with an amused half-smile. "I'm the one you're looking for." The scout backed away quickly, but the fighter only laughed in delight, appearing unconcerned.

"Well now, isn't that handy," Knorl said, "you appearing so conveniently and all. Surrender yourself without a fuss, and we may just take you back alive."

I folded my arms. "Surrender? Now, why would I do that?"

"Because there's a bounty on your scalp, and we're here to claim it," the fighter said cheerfully.

"And there's two of us and only one of you," the scout chimed in.

I chuckled and faded back into the shadows.

You are hidden once more.

"Where'd he go?" Knorl shouted.

"Quiet!" Henry snapped. "I'm looking."

Either the scout's Perception simply wasn't high enough, or the darkness was too thick for his sight to penetrate. Whatever the case, he failed to spot me as I backed away and circled around the pair.

Two hostile entities have failed to detect you!

"He's gone!"

"He can't be," the half-giant snarled. "Find him!"

"As you can see," I said, emerging out of the shadows behind the fighter and continuing the conversation as if I had never left off, "numbers mean little."

Knorl spun around to face me. His eyes wide, the half-giant brandished his weapon and took a threatening step forward.

I glanced indifferently at the fighter's raised broadsword and didn't back away. "There could be a dozen of you, and it would make no difference." I held his gaze, my own hard. "I could've killed you before you even realized I was there."

My words were an exaggeration, but only slightly. Still, the half-giant took my point and stopped advancing. Though from his harsh breathing and livid stare, he didn't seem inclined to back down further.

The scout stepped up to his companion's side. "What do you want?"

"Information," I said succinctly.

Henry's eyes narrowed. "In exchange for?"

I smiled coldly. "Your lives."

Knorl growled and made to advance again, but the scout laid a restraining hand on him. "You seem very sure of yourself," he remarked.

I only shrugged in response. "What'll it be?" The scout didn't answer immediately. A second later, I realized why.

You have passed a mental resistance check! An analyze attempt by a hostile entity has failed. Your deception has increased to level 11.

"How'd you do that?" Henry asked, staring wide-eyed at me.

I grinned at his dumbfounded look. Already, my deception skill was coming in handy.

"Do what?" Knorl asked, perplexed.

The scout waved aside his companion's question. "What's your level?" he asked, not taking his eyes off me.

"High enough to kill you two without breaking a sweat," I lied.

Henry scowled at my response, but he must have known I wouldn't tell him. He glared at me a moment longer before seeming to come to a decision and turning to the half-giant. "Light a torch," he ordered.

"But I thought you said—"

"Just do it!" Henry hissed.

The fighter muttered under his breath but complied with the scout's orders.

A moment later, a torch flared to life. I eyed the flickering flames, thinking it was an unwise move on the part of the pair. If it came to it, the light wouldn't stop me from killing them, and it would only attract unwelcome attention from the forest's denizens. Still, if the torch made the pair comfortable and more inclined to talk, I wasn't about to object.

"Ready to talk now?" I asked.

Henry nodded grudgingly. "What do you want to know?"

"For starters, who are you two?"

The scout frowned. "My name is—"

I slashed my hand downward, cutting him off. "I know your names already. What I want to know is which faction you belong to and who sent you."

"Ah," he muttered. "We're bounty hunters." He paused. "Apprentices only."

I nodded. That was consistent with what I'd overheard. "Who put you on my trail?"

"No one sent us," Knorl growled. "We saw the bounty notice. One thousand gold for a mere rank two player? We couldn't believe it. And with us in the area already." He snorted. "We didn't have to think long before deciding to run you down."

I rubbed at my chin while I tried to make sense of his answer. "Where did you see the reward posted?"

"On the bounty noticeboard, of course," the half-giant snapped.

I frowned.

"Most safe zones have one," Henry added.

My ears perked up. "You've come from this sector's safe zone?"

He nodded.

"Where is it?" I asked.

The scout gestured behind him. "That way. At the southern end of the valley, at the foot of the mountain."

Now we were getting somewhere. "And where is the sector's exit portal?"

"Exit portal?" Knorl asked, his brows crinkling. "What do you mean, exit portal? This isn't a bloody dungeon." He squinted at me derisively. "What are you, a noob?"

His companion chuckled, seeming to grow more confident after my display of ignorance. "I think you've hit the nail on the head, Knorl." He shook his head. "I can't believe it. Who pays one thousand gold for a noob?"

I ignored their amusement. "So there isn't an exit portal?" I persisted.

Henry shook his head, still smiling. "There isn't. Only dungeons have exit portals, boyo. In case you didn't notice, there's open sky above us. We're on the surface. There aren't any ley lines for players to zip around between sectors."

My eyes narrowed. I hadn't understood everything he'd said, but rather than have them mock my ignorance, I focused on the one key piece of information he'd provided. "Then there are no portals on the surface?"

Henry shook his head. "I didn't say that. The Game doesn't provide any, sure. But there are other means of creating one."

I frowned. "But that's the same—" I broke off, realizing what he meant. "Players can create portals," I stated.

"Will you look at that, Knorl," Henry said. "The noob isn't as dumb as he looks after all."

I rested my hand casually on the sword at my hip. "You better put a pin on that sarcasm, friend, or I might just decide you're being uncooperative."

That wiped the amusement off his face.

"Better," I said softly. "Now, how do I leave this sector?" This time, Henry didn't smile, but I could see that he wanted to. "What's so funny?" I asked tersely. I was quickly losing patience with him.

"This sector is ringed on all sides by mountains that are colder than hell," the scout said, composing himself with admirable swiftness. Perhaps, he'd sensed my irritation. "But that isn't the worst of it. This is a closed sector, meaning nothing lies on the other side of those peaks. The only way you're getting out is through a portal."

My face turned grim. "I see." I didn't know if I could believe the scout, but there wasn't much point in pursuing that matter further with him. "What do you know about the wolves in this valley?" I asked instead.

"Wolves?" Knorl said. "There are no wolves in this sector." He spat. "Beasts and monsters of every other kind, that there are aplenty. Goblins even, but no wolves."

I opened my mouth to question him on this curious tidbit of information, but before I could a long, drawn-out howl cut through the forest.

My gaze flew to the right.

An immense creature stood there. A four-footed beast—built like a rhino and armored twice as heavily in scarred black plates—had appeared out of the foliage some twenty yards away. The single horn protruding from its snout was razor-sharp, and its uniform black eyes glinted with hate.

Lowering its head, the beast snorted and pawed at the ground.

"What in blazes is that?" Knorl whispered.

"A rhomodillo," the scout answered, licking his lips nervously.

I probed the creature with basic analyze and saw that he was right.

The target is a level 51 rhomodillo. Rhomodillos are lumbering behemoths, armored so heavily that even dragons struggle to pierce their hides and strong enough that they can uproot young trees. But despite their physical prowess, Rhomodillos are not the most cunning of predators. Easily enraged, they will keep fighting even when a smarter beast would flee.

My lips turned down. *Right, I don't want to tangle with that.* I backed away carefully. My movement drew Henry's gaze.

"Help us," he begged. The scout's face was pale and sweat beaded on his upper lip.

I paused. "Help you?" I asked, looking at him in surprise. "Now, why would I do that?"

He stared at me blankly for a moment. "You promised us our lives!" he squeaked.

The rhomodillo tossed its head and snorted again, not liking the sound of our voices.

"I did," I agreed. "And I'll keep my word too. *I* won't take your lives." I glanced at the beast. It was edging forward. *It'll charge soon*, I thought. "Make no mistake, you two are my enemies. I shan't kill you, but I won't help you either." I gestured at the approaching monster. "*Especially* not against that."

"Let the bastard flee, Henry," the half-giant growled. "We'll take care of this monster on our own." Without waiting for his companion's response, he spun around and charged the beast with a wild yell.

Shaking my head at his folly, I withdrew into the shadows and left the pair to their fate.

Chapter 92: In the Grip of Delirium

Day One. Night.

I didn't wait to see what became of the two bounty hunters. I suspected they wouldn't last long against the rhomodillo, and I didn't want to be around when the beast searched for a new target for its ire.

Journeying deeper into the forest, I adjusted my course to head farther south. If I didn't find the wolves, I intended to head for the sector's safe zone and see what I could learn from its inhabitants.

To my surprise, I found navigating the forest at night easier. Much of the wildlife was asleep—or in hiding. The darkness was a boon too, making it easier for me to slip in and out of the shadows.

Maybe I should stick to my new sleep schedule.

Napping during the day and traveling by night had a certain appeal. I chuckled in wry amusement. And, of course, it *was* the wolf thing to do.

As I walked, I reflected further on the two players' words. I was unsurprised to discover I was being hunted, though I'd hoped to have a bit more time before the chase began in earnest. But it seemed I couldn't count on such a luxury. I would have to remain on guard at all times, both in the wilds and among my fellow players.

I glanced behind me and spotted the deep indentations left by my boots in the forest's loamy soil. I could claim no skill in tracking, but even I would have no trouble following my trail.

Time to do something about that.

Vaulting upward, I leaped into the lower branches of a nearby oak and kept climbing until I was nearly thirty feet above the ground. The trees of this forest were ancient, and their boughs appeared sturdy and stout. More importantly, the branches overlapped closely enough that traveling by treetop would be no great hardship, especially not for someone with my high Dexterity.

Lithely balanced, I stepped from branch to branch and traversed the oak from one side to the other. Reaching the end, I jumped to the next tree—a redwood—and began my journey anew. I looked back and grinned at the lack of any visible trail.

I'd like to see anyone track me now.

Traveling by treetop was slower but more secure, and with practice I would only get faster. Smiling in satisfaction, I continued my journey south.

* * *

The next few hours passed pleasantly enough, and ever so gradually I found myself becoming more attuned to my new environment.

The forest was alive in a way the dungeon hadn't been, and while it took some getting used to, I began to believe that, eventually, I would become accustomed to its noisy depths.

Nearly four hours into my journey, just as I was contemplating resting, a splash of red on the forest floor drew my attention.

It was blood. Lots of blood.

I slowed to a halt and dropped down to a lower branch for a closer look. At an errant waft of air, I wrinkled my nose. The clearing below stank of death. Pinching my nostrils closed against the cloying smell of decay, I peered cautiously through the foliage.

A forest glade, some thirty yards in diameter, was below me. Nothing larger than an insect moved within it. From one end to the other, the clearing was littered with corpses, each fully obscured by the thousands of buzzing flies covering them.

My stomach heaved at the sight. Doing my best to ignore the sensation, I ran my gaze over the area again, searching for any hint of threat.

Finding nothing, I opened my mindsight and sent psi rippling outward. Tendrils of my will flooded the space around me.

Once more, I uncovered no threat.

In fact, there were *no* minds within ten yards of me. That in itself told me something. Whatever had happened in the glade, it had caused even the smallest of the forest's denizens to flee. Still, the forest floor looked safe to explore, and I dropped down.

The air turned black as the feeding flies swarmed upward. Closing my eyes, I shielded my face while I waited for the air to clear. When the flies' buzzing subsided, I opened my eyes again.

And found myself staring at a dead goblin.

Lifting my head, I took in the rest of the clearing. Every corpse within sight was uniformly green-skinned with sharpened teeth and black talons. My brows drew down. *What happened here?*

Padding softly around the glade, I paused every so often to inspect more of the bodies. Eventually, I returned to my starting point, sure now that my initial conclusion was correct.

They're all goblins.

There were a few dozen bodies in the clearing. A sizable force. Most of the corpses were five feet tall—the same size as the warriors I'd encountered in the dungeon. Some, though, were larger. Kneeling beside one such figure in the glade's center, I analyzed it.

The target is a level 25 dead goblin guerilla. Guerillas are a subset of the goblin warrior caste and, over time, have evolved to operate in the wildest and most remote regions of the Forever Kingdom. Nimble and quick, they make ideal scouts and, in a pinch, can also serve as light infantry troops.

Your insight has increased to level 34.

I pursed my lips. The goblin was a new type of foe and one higher-leveled than its fellows in the dungeon. As a rank two creature, a goblin guerilla wouldn't prove much of a challenge, at least not on its own. In numbers, though...

I shook my head. There was no reason to fear running into more of the creatures. *And besides, these are all dead.* Which brought me to my next question: what had killed the goblins?

I inspected the corpse in front of me once more. There was only a single wound on its body, a jagged hole torn through its throat. I brushed my fingers over the spot and found the end of a broken-off shaft buried beneath the congealed blood. Frowning, I turned the body over. On the other side, the tip of an arrow poked through. Grasping the projectile from behind the arrowhead, I pulled it free and turned it over in my hands.

It was a goblin arrow.

I rose to my feet, a suspicion forming in my mind as I studied the clearing with fresh eyes. Both the manner in which the goblins had fallen and the nature of their wounds suggested I wasn't looking at a single goblin force but two.

The goblins had killed each other.

Studying the corpses' attire more closely, I saw that most bore an insignia of sorts. There were two sets of symbols. One was a crudely drawn four-footed rodent... *a rat, perhaps?* The other was a snarling face.

That decides it. There are two tribes in the valley. I thought back to my encounter with the goblins in the dungeon. Their chief had named their tribe the Fangtooths. Neither symbol in front of me resembled a fang or tooth. *Maybe there are three tribes.*

I sighed. It seemed as if I had plenty of enemies in the sector. And as yet, my allies were nowhere to be found.

What do I do if—

I broke off as *all* the remaining flies in the glade rose abruptly into the air. *What—?* I spun around, sensing a menacing presence at my back.

You have detected a hidden entity!

An angry hiss erupted from the creature concealed in the foliage. *Another serline pack?* I wondered. A shape emerged, revealing green scales, powerful taloned feet, an elongated snout, and tightly furled wings.

I gulped and stepped back, my heart suddenly racing. I didn't know what the creature was, but it looked unsettlingly like a dragon.

God damnit! What is it with this forest? Can't I catch a break?

✳   ✳   ✳

Hands wrapped around the hilts of my swords, I watched my foe.

It observed me as carefully.

I would've spun around and turned tail as soon as I suspected the creature's nature, but after observing its graceful entrance into the clearing, I knew I stood no chance of outrunning the beast.

Better to die fighting.

Backstepping warily, I analyzed my foe.

The target is a level 44 green wyvern hatchling. Wyverns are the lesser cousins of dragons. Unlike those titans of dragonkin, wyverns do not

possess great intellect, wisdom, or magical abilities. Nonetheless, like all dragonkin, they are highly evolved physical specimens.

Green wyverns are well-suited to their forest homes and are usually the apex predator in any territory they occupy. Over time, their fire breathing abilities have atrophied, but in their place they have developed other equally powerful abilities.

Hatchlings are the youngest and weakest within any particular dragonkin species.

That's a hatchling? I thought disbelievingly. The beast stood a good two feet taller than me, and from nose to whiplike tail it had to be twice that length. If this was a baby, how big would a full-grown wyvern be? It didn't bear thinking upon.

Look on the bright side, Michael. At least it's not a dragon.

I snorted, disgusted by my own black humor.

At the sound, the hatchling paused in its languid advance. Tilting its head to the side, it studied me curiously.

"Bad joke," I murmured by way of response while enhancing my reflexes with minor reaction buff.

The hatchling slipped forward again, its movements smooth and sinuous. It looked like it was waiting for me to make the first move.

Preparing to do just that, I backed away once more and drew on my psi. The wyvern was about six yards into the glade now, and less than twenty yards separated us. While the creature's movements appeared unhurried, it was surely but slowly closing the distance to me.

It's now or never, I thought. Bracing myself, I sent tendrils of psi into the beast's mind and attempted to leash it to my will.

Green wyverns are immune to all forms of mental assaults! You have failed to charm your target. Your mental intrusion has been detected!

My mouth dropped open in shock. Immune to all mental assaults? *Bloody hell.*

The hatchling zipped three steps forward and hissed at me, making its displeasure evident.

"Don't worry," I muttered sourly. "I won't try that again." I retreated once more but didn't draw my blades. There was still a chance—a slim one admittedly—that the wyvern wouldn't attack.

I reached the end of the glade. As if that was the signal it had been waiting for, the hatchling charged forward, jaws opening.

I reacted instantly and dived to my left. The beast rushed by, its teeth snapping at me in passing. But I'd moved too fast, and its jaws closed only on empty air.

I rolled back to my feet and drew both my blades. Backing into the glade, I watched the hatchling spin around. Without any of my psi abilities, I was at a severe disadvantage.

But I still have one-step and stealth.

Experimentally, I tried fading into the shadows.

You have failed to conceal yourself from your foe.

I grunted unhappily. I'd expected as much. It seemed this skirmish was destined to be a straight-up fight. The wyvern snaked forward again.

I can beat this thing, I told myself. Its rank was the same as the goblin chieftain I'd defeated, and I had advanced significantly since that fight.

I stopped retreating.

Poised on the balls of my feet and with my weapons raised, I waited. The hatchling blurred through the air toward me. I sidestepped and thrust out my swords, casting crippling blow.

The sharpened tips of my blades bit into the creature's green scales, scoring twin lines across its left wing but failing to do anything else.

Green wyverns are immune to all forms of physical disabling abilities! You have failed to cripple your target.

I sighed. Somehow, the Game message came as no surprise.

Blood spurted, and the beast's hissing transformed into a snarl of rage. I smiled grimly. I'd hurt it, if only superficially. While my blades had pierced the wyvern's armored hide, they hadn't penetrated as deeply as I'd hoped. Spinning about, the hatchling leaped at me again.

I rolled out of the way. The beast pursued, not letting up on its attacks. I bounced back to my feet in time to see the creature's jaws darting toward my exposed throat.

There was no time to dodge. I flung out my left blade to block the blow. But the hatchling was too strong. Its snout brushed aside my sword, and the course of its attack altered only minimally.

Iron jaws clamped down on my shoulder but not my neck—I had managed to shift its attack that much at least. My leather armor was no match for the beast's razor-sharp teeth, and they dug deep into me.

Skin was torn and muscles were ripped apart.

I shrieked. I couldn't help myself; the pain was excruciating.

You have failed a physical resistance check! A green wyvern hatchling has infected you with an unknown toxin. Your health is degenerating by 1% per second.

Ignoring the oily sensation of the toxin dispersing into my body, I gritted my teeth and tried to wrench my shoulder free, but the hatchling refused to let go. Instead, it clamped down further with its jaws.

Flesh was mangled and bone was crushed.

My mind went numb with pain, and I felt myself fading. *No,* I protested, clinging desperately to consciousness.

You have failed a physical resistance check! Your left shoulder is crippled. You are bleeding. Ongoing damage sustained. Your health is at 60% and dropping.

I attempted tugging free again, but my movements had grown lackluster. I was weakening quickly from the toxin, blood loss, and the white-hot agony that was my left side.

It was hard to think, but with grim determination I clawed free of the pain. The wyvern wasn't going to let go, not unless I forced it to. *I have to make it let go.* That single thought burned through the fog of agony.

Raising spider's bite, I thrust it forward. Scales parted, and the blade dug deep into the wyvern's exposed throat.

You have critically injured a wyvern hatchling!

It wasn't a fatal strike, but it was enough to cause the hatchling to flinch. Whining in pain, the beast released its hold on my shoulder and retreated to the far end of the glade.

It didn't, alas, flee altogether.

Winding its body tightly about itself, the wyvern crooned softly while its tongue licked at the gaping wound in its neck.

I didn't have any more attention to spare the beast though. My left hand was useless and hung loosely. Falling to my knees, I dropped spider's bite and fumbled for a healing potion. One-handed, I unstoppered the flask and down its contents.

You have restored yourself with a full healing potion. Your health is now at 100%.

Almost instantaneously, the bones in my left arm mended themselves. I gasped in relief and bent down to pick up my dropped swords.

And nearly toppled over.

I thrust out my arms, managing to halt my fall in time. My legs were trembling and I was suddenly lightheaded.

What in the world?

I hung my head, trying to regain control of my shaking limbs. Another Game message dropped into my mind.

An unknown toxin has spread. Your health degeneration rate has increased to 2% per second.

My eyes rounded in shock.

I was still poisoned. Whatever was in the wyvern's venom, not even a full healing potion could counter it. Would the toxin keep spreading? I had no idea. All I knew was that I had to kill the beast. And I had to do it while not getting bitten again.

My dizziness subsided, and I flung up my head to find the hatchling. It was still crooning to itself, ignoring me altogether. I staggered to my feet. About to charge the beast, I paused as I noticed something else.

The wound in its neck was closing. The wyvern was healing!

A venomous bite and *regeneration,* I thought bitterly. *Can this fight get any more unfair?*

Stop whining, Michael, I chided myself.

I ran forward. I wasn't about to give up, no matter how forgone the battle's conclusion seemed. While I lived, there was hope yet. The wyvern sensed my approach before I reached striking distance. Uncoiling itself with startling speed, it hurtled forward.

I was prepared though.

Casting one-step, I catapulted myself over its reaching jaws and dived forward with both swords outstretched.

I landed hard on the creature's back and the air rushed out of me. The wyvern jerked to a halt, startled by my weight on its torso. Before the beast could spin around, I thrust downward with both my swords, burying spider's bite in the hatchling's right hind leg, then my second blade in its left one.

You have crippled your target's right hind leg.
You have crippled your target's left hind leg.

It was the wyvern's turn to shriek. Shuddering in agony, the beast whipped its head down to nip at me. I rolled away, leaving both my blades buried hilt-deep in the creature's haunches.

Let's see how well it heals now, with cold steel sunk into its body.

The wyvern darted forward again, trying to reach my fleeing form, but hampered by the blades in its rear, it was too slow.

Three yards away from the injured beast, I rose to my feet, a crooked smile on my face. I was weaponless but considerably cheered. The hatchling was dying, if slowly, from the wounds to its hindquarters.

I only need to—

I staggered, overcome by another wave of dizziness.

An unknown toxin has spread. Your health degeneration rate has increased to 3% per second.

This time I lost control of my limbs entirely. Quivering violently, I fell to the ground in a helpless heap.

The wyvern, meanwhile, was dragging itself closer.

No! No! No!

This time my shaking took longer to subside, and the beast was nearly upon me before I recovered. Delaying only to down another healing potion, I rolled away from the hatchling.

Its head dipped down, narrowly missing me.

I kept rolling, but only a few seconds later I started convulsing again.

An unknown toxin has spread. Your health degeneration rate has increased to 4% per second.

"Damnit!" I growled. "W-why won't thish t-t-toxin sstop!" My voice had begun slurring, and even my thoughts were growing incoherent.

The hatchling advanced on me again.

"Nooo!" I snarled. *I won't die like this. I won't. I refuse!*

Rage suffused me. My mind grew dark and my vision turned red. I glared at the hatchling with hate-filled eyes. Conscious thought fled entirely. And from somewhere deep within me, something rose up. Unbidden, a howl tore itself free from my throat.

Startled, the hatchling froze.

I howled again, a deep unending sound that gave vent to my fear and fury, to my rage and frustration.

It was a clarion cry for help.

A call to war.

And from somewhere in the forest, a wolf howled.

Then another.

A voice spoke in my mind. *"Hold on, brother. We come."*

It was Oursk. I sensed Aira join him in my mind and add her voice to his. But it had all become too much. I couldn't hold on anymore, not to conscious thought, and perhaps not to life either.

"Thank you," I breathed before finally succumbing to darkness.

Chapter 93: The Law of the Pack

Day Two.

"MICHAEL!"

The shout reverberated in my mind, reaching me even in the depths of oblivion.

"MICHAEL!"

The cry came again. Loud. Insistent. My mind was helpless to resist its call, and I was unceremoniously yanked out of the sea of unconsciousness I'd sunk into.

I surfaced back into awareness.

Who... is... that?

Thinking was hard. Pain riddled my every thought, and I wanted nothing more than to return to the comforting embrace of darkness. But something held me to consciousness. Some instinct warned me that letting the reins of myself slip again was dangerous.

"MICHAEL!"

It was Aira. This time I noticed the strained note in her voice. Images of the last few moments flashed through my mind. I was in the glade.

Dying.

"Aira...?" I tried to open my eyes and thought I had managed it, but I still couldn't see for some reason.

"Michael," the dire wolf replied, her relief palpable. *"Drink a potion."*

My thoughts flowed about as fast as molasses dripped, and I struggled to make sense of Aira's words. Why did I need to drink a potion? There was something I knew I should remember, something important.

My foe. *"Where... wyvern?"*

"Forget the dragonkin," Aira said. *"It has been dealt with. You must heal yourself. Sulan has slowed the toxin's spread, but she doesn't have the strength to defeat it entirely. You are still dying."*

The wyvern was dead. That was good. But who was Aira talking about? *"Sulan?"*

Another voice barged into my mind. Vast. Annoyed. *"Ignorant whelp,"* she snapped. *"Focus on the here and now. The rest is immaterial. Do as Aira commands, pup, or I will cease my efforts on your behalf."*

That was Sulan, I guessed. She was right too. My questions could wait for later. I brought up one hand slowly, blindly feeling for the potion belt strapped across my chest.

"Further to your right," Aira said helpfully.

My fingers clasped a flask. With some difficulty I unstoppered it, but even that small task drained me, and I wasn't sure if I had the energy to bring it to my mouth.

Jaws—Aira's, I sensed—clamped down on my hand and gently guided the flask to my lips. *"Thank you,"* I murmured as the potion's contents slipped down my throat.

New strength flooded me. My thoughts quickened and the haze around my mind dissipated.

You have restored yourself with a moderate healing potion. You are no longer blind. You are no longer dazed. Your health is at 35%.

"Well done, pup," Sulan said.

My eyes cleared slowly. I blinked, bringing the blurred shapes around me into focus. I was still in the glade and lying on my back. Light streamed down from the trees above. It was morning.

I turned my head to the right and saw a wolf sitting on her haunches. Aira. I met the dire wolf's eyes and nodded in greeting.

Turning the other way, I saw a second dire wolf on my other side. She was the same size as Aira, about four feet tall, but where Aira's coat was pitch black, hers was snow white. She was older too. Despite the startling color of her fur, it didn't hide the gray around her muzzle.

"Sulan?" I queried.

The wolf's mouth dropped open, revealing yellowing teeth. *"Well met, wolfkin."*

Her greeting had a ring of formality to it. I attempted to respond in kind. *"You have my thanks, lady."*

Sulan snorted. *"I'm no human lady, pup. You can address me as pack elder."*

I inclined my head in acknowledgment. Planting my elbows on the ground, I tried to get up but my body failed me. My limbs were as weak as a day-old babe's. I fell back down, chest heaving.

"Don't try to move," Aira said. *"The toxin has not released its hold on you yet."*

I glanced at her in surprise. *"It's still in me?"*

"I could not purge it entirely," Sulan answered. *"The venom was too strong. It was all I could do to slow it down. I will continue to keep the toxin at bay, but it is up to you to keep up your strength."*

I nodded.

"Drink another potion," the elder ordered.

I did as she bade, then turned my attention inward, querying the Adjudicator on my status.

Your health has increased to 60%. Current Debuffs: you are infected by an unknown toxin. Current Buffs: Sulan has cast helping hand on you, halting the toxin's spread by absorbing a portion of its damage.

Startled by the Game's response, my eyes flew back to the white wolf. Now that I looked closer, I noticed a minute trembling in her limbs. *"Stop,"* I protested. *"It's killing you. Let me fight the venom off on my own."*

Sulan snorted again. *"You would only fail. Besides, it is my duty, pup. The old must look after the young—even the foolish young. It is the way of the pack."*

Despite her words, there was a gleam in the ancient wolf's eyes. My words had pleased her, I thought. *"So, what do we do now?"*

"We wait for the toxin to run its course," Aira said. *"Sooner or later, your body will flush out the venom."*

I closed my eyes. It wasn't good news, but it was a damn sight better than being dead. Raising my head, I surveyed the glade and frowned. My foe's corpse was nowhere to be seen. *"Where is the wyvern?"*

"It fled at our approach," Sulan said. *"A hatchling is no match for the full might of the pack. Duggar and the rest of our warriors are chasing it down even now."*

If I had the energy, I would have howled in frustration. How was the damn wyvern still not dead? Biting back my disappointment, I asked instead, *"Who is Duggar?"*

"The pack's leader," Aira answered.

"Ah," I said, wondering where Oursk was.

Before I could question the pair further, Sulan growled. *"That's enough questions for now. Rest,"* she ordered, *"before you undo all our hard work."*

Well aware of the damage the elder wolf was sustaining on my behalf, I didn't argue. Letting my head fall back into the grass, I closed my eyes and entrusted myself to the dire wolves' care.

✳   ✳   ✳

It was only a little later that my slumber was disturbed by a slew of Game messages.

A green wyvern hatchling has died.
You have reached level 30!
Congratulations, Michael! You are now a rank 3 player. For achieving rank 3, you have been awarded 1 additional attribute point.
You are no longer infected by an unknown toxin.

My lips curved upward. The wyvern was finally dead and its horrifying toxin was defeated. Even better, I'd gained from the kill despite not striking the final blow myself. Keeping my eyes closed, I spent my attribute points and reviewed my player growth.

Your Dexterity has increased to rank 15, your Mind to rank 8, and your Constitution to rank 8.

<u>Player Profile: Michael</u>

Level: 30. Rank: 3. Current Health: 100%.
Stamina: 100%. Mana: 100%. Psi: 100%.
Species: Human. Lives Remaining: 3.
Marks: Wolf-brethren, Lesser Shadow, Lesser Light, Lesser Dark.

<u>Attributes</u>

Available: 0 points.
Strength: 2. Constitution: 8. Dexterity: 15. Perception: 8. Mind: 8. Magic: 0. Faith: 0.

<u>Classes</u>

Available: 1 point.
Primary-Secondary Bi-blend: Mindstalker.
Tertiary Class: None.

Traits

Psi wolf heritage: +2 Dexterity, +2 Strength, +4 Mind.
Beast tongue: can speak to beastkin.
Marked: can see spirit signatures.
Nocturnal: perfect night vision.

Skills

Available skill slots: 0.
Light armor (current: 28. max: 80. Constitution, basic).
Dodging (current: 33. max: 150. Dexterity, basic).
Sneaking (current: 43. max: 150. Dexterity, basic).
Shortswords (current: 41. max: 150. Dexterity, basic).
Two-weapon fighting (current: 36. max: 150. Dexterity, advanced).
Thieving (current: 1. max: 150. Dexterity, basic).
Chi (current: 23. max: 80. Mind, advanced).
Meditation (current: 32. max: 80. Mind, basic).
Telekinesis (current: 20. max: 80. Mind, advanced).
Telepathy (current: 19. max: 80. Mind, advanced).
Insight (current: 34. max: 80. Perception, basic).
Deception (current: 11. max: 80. Perception, master).

Abilities

Crippling blow (Dexterity, basic).
Minor backstab (Dexterity, basic).
Basic trap disarm (Dexterity, basic).
Simple lockpicking (Dexterity, basic).
Simple charm (Mind, basic).
Stunning slap (Mind, basic).
One-step (Mind, basic).
Minor reaction buff (Mind, basic).
Basic analyze (Perception, basic).
Lesser trap detect (Perception, basic).
Conceal small weapon (Perception, basic).
Simple mindsight (Class, basic).

Known Key Points

Sector 14,913 exit portal and safe zone.

Equipped

common thief's cloak (+3 sneaking).
spider's bite shortsword (+15% damage, webbed), concealed.
shortsword, +1 (+15% damage, +10 shortswords), in fighter's sash.
common fighter's sash (+3 shortswords).
enchanted leather armor set (+20% damage reduction, −35% Dexterity and Magic).
slotted potion belt (3 minor heal, 2 moderate heal, 1 full heal, 4 empty).

Backpack Contents

25 x field rations.
1 x flask of water.
2 x minor healing potions.
2 x iron daggers.
1 x bedroll.
3 x moderate healing potions.
1 x coin pouch.
1 x keyring.
1 x basic fire-starting kit.
1 x Catalog of Skills and Abilities.
1 x blood siphon master Class stone.
1 x woolen rags.

<u>Bank Contents</u>

<u>Money</u>: 46 gold, 4 silver, and 9 copper.
2 x full healing potions.
2 x basic steel shortswords.

I'd gained two more levels, and my skills had advanced again. As dangerous as the valley was, it was proving an excellent training ground. *Perhaps this forest isn't so bad after all,* I thought. *Especially if I have allies to call on for aid.* Sensing a presence by my side, I opened my eyes.

Aira and Sulan were gone.

In their place was the largest dire wolf I'd seen yet. Sitting on his haunches, the black-furred beast topped my own height. Standing, he would tower over even Oursk. *This has to be Duggar.* "Greetings, pack leader," I said pleasantly.

There was no response.

Still and unmoving, the large dire wolf stared down at me. His winter-gray eyes were cold and unwelcoming, and even though he made no threatening gesture, the beast exuded an air of menace.

I felt myself tense in response. If I had hackles, they would've been standing on their ends. *There's danger here.* Had I done something to offend the wolf? My eyes darted to the left and right, searching for Aira or even Sulan. Only now did it occur to me to wonder why they had left.

My gaze returned to the silent beast. I rose warily to my feet. If there was going to be a confrontation, I didn't want to face it lying down. The pack leader tracked my movements, his gaze disdainful.

"You have endangered my pack."

The words lanced into my mind, each a sharp spike of pain resonant with anger.

I winced and rubbed my temples. "It wasn't my intent," I said aloud.

"Intent matters little. Only actions count."

I couldn't argue with that, and I didn't try. "I beg the pack's forgiveness."

Duggar studied me for a moment longer before rising to his feet and turning away. *"You will leave now and never return."*

My heart sank. However I'd imagined this meeting going, it wasn't like this. Still, I couldn't let the pack leader just walk away. I needed the wolves' aid. More desperately than I was willing to admit. "Wait! Please."

Pausing, Duggar looked over his shoulder to stare at me.

"I need your help."

"I have already risked my kin once to aid you. I will not do so again. The hatchling's mother will hunt us now. Many will die."

I licked my lips, suddenly realizing the significance of Duggar's earlier words. Given the difficulty I'd had battling the hatchling, the damage a full-grown wyvern could do didn't bear thinking upon. The pack had sacrificed more than I'd suspected on my behalf. It was a debt I had to repay, I realized. "I will help against the wyvern mother."

"You?" Duggar snorted in disdain. *"You are barely more than a pup. You will not survive long against the dragonkin."*

"Nonetheless," I insisted stubbornly, "I will honor the debt I owe."

The dire wolf turned around fully and sat down on his haunches again. Tilting his head to the side, he studied me. *"You are a strange one, human. Tell me, how did you come to bear our Mark?"*

"I freed Aira, Oursk, and their pups." I waved my arms, gesturing to the sky above. "The Adjudicator granted me a Wolf Mark by way of reward."

"Oursk told me of that," Duggar said. *"Yet it could not have been that alone."* Raising his snout, the pack leader sniffed the air delicately. *"There is a scent of something familiar about you,"* he allowed. *"Something that smells of Wolf."*

The emphasis Duggar placed on "Wolf" was unmistakable. He knew something about my Mark. I bobbed my head in response, trying not to let my excitement show. "It's why I sought out your pack. I need your help finding out more about the Wolf and how I can travel further down his path."

Duggar didn't say anything for a moment, but I sensed that something about my words troubled him deeply. *"Were your earlier words true?"* he asked finally. *"Or were they little more than human platitudes?"*

I frowned. "Which words?"

"That you will repay your debt to the pack."

"Of course. I will help defend the pack when the wyvern mother—"

"No," Duggar said, cutting me off. *"I told you we do not need your help with the dragonkin. We will deal with her on our own. But there is another matter you can help us with."*

"Go on."

"There are goblins camped in the eastern reaches of the valley. The creatures hunt us for our fur and meat." Duggar bared his teeth, displaying his anger. *"They have already slain many of my brethren. Find them and put a stop to their vile practices. Will you do this?"*

I glanced at the goblin corpses strewn across the glade. "Goblins like these?"

"No. The Howlers and Red Rats are consumed by their own conflict. They have no attention to spare for the pack. It is the Long Fangs who plague us."

I scratched my chin. So, my assumption hadn't been misplaced. There were three goblin tribes in the valley. "Don't you mean Fangtooths?"

"Fangtooths? There is no such—" Duggar broke off and let his tongue hang out in what looked suspiciously like a lupine version of a laugh. *"Ah, you mean those pitiful exiles who captured young Oursk and Aira. They were no true tribe, human,"* he said with undisguised amusement. *"You will see."*

I didn't like the sound of that. Still, I wasn't about to refuse the pack leader's request. "I will do as you ask."

"*Good,*" Duggar said. "*Individually, the Long Fangs are no match for the wyvern, yet collectively they represent a much bigger threat—*" his gray eyes pierced me—"*and one you are more qualified to contend with than the pack. Deal with the goblins and you will earn my gratitude.*"

I nodded firmly. Duggar's words made it clear that taking care of the wolves' goblin problem was the price I'd have to pay to gain the information I wanted. Yet, it was a task I would gladly undertake if only to fulfill my obligation to the pack. At my acceptance, a Game message pinged for attention.

On behalf of Wolf, the Adjudicator has allocated you a new task: <u>Aid the Pack</u>! Help the dire wolves in sector 12,560. Objective: Stop the Long Fangs from hunting the dire wolves.

I stared at the alert in surprise. '*On behalf of Wolf?*' *That implies—*

"*Goodbye, human.*" Duggar rose to his feet and swung away.

I pulled my gaze away from the Adjudicator's message and turned back toward the retreating wolf. "Wait! How will I find you?"

I sensed more amusement coursing through the pack leader. "*Never fear. We will find you.*"

Chapter 94: The Green Triangle

Day Two. Midday.

I didn't leave the clearing immediately.

I spent a few minutes taking stock of myself and my supplies. My potion belt was half-empty, and I refilled it. I grimaced when I realized I only had ten potions left, just one of which was a full healing potion. Thankfully Sulan had restored me to full health, so I didn't need to drink another just yet, but at the rate I was consuming potions, I would quickly run out.

I need to find another source of healing soon.

Next, I drew spider's bite from the concealed scabbard across my back and, drawing on my mana, restored the sword's enchantments. Only then did I glance up at the sky through the trees. It was midday, I judged.

Time enough to travel further today.

I had two possible destinations. East to find the Long Fangs. Or south toward the safe zone. I couldn't forget my time limit either. An entire day had passed, and it was already the second day of my Pact with Erebus. I needed to finish my business in the valley quickly.

East it is then, I thought and swiveled in that direction.

As I reached the glade's edge, five shapes emerged from the foliage. My hand dropped to the blade on my hip, but a moment later I relaxed as I recognized the five figures.

It was Aira and her family.

The three pups gamboled forward, and I dropped to my knees to greet them. "Hi there, fellas," I murmured. The pups' coats shone and their stomachs bulged. They were doing well.

I glanced up as a shadow fell over me.

"*Well met, Michael,*" Oursk said.

I rose to my feet and inclined my head to the two dire wolf adults. Like the pups, they seemed to have fully recovered from their ordeal in the dungeon. "Oursk, Aira, I can't begin to thank you for heeding my call. If you hadn't answered when—"

"*Speak nothing more of it,*" Aira interrupted. "*It was a kindness we were glad to perform.*"

"But Duggar—"

"*Don't take the alpha's words to heart,*" Oursk said. "*He knows the Law of the Pack as well as any. A brethren's cry cannot be ignored. Even ignoring what we owe you, the pack was honor-bound to help you. Duggar is angry, but it is less to do with you and more with the straits in which the pack finds itself.*"

I nodded, relieved at least that I hadn't soured my relationship with Aira and Oursk.

"*He is still our pack's leader though,*" Aira added softly, "*and we are bound to follow his commands. Duggar has given us permission to bid you farewell, but he has ordered the pack to abstain from further contact until you complete his task. I'm sorry, Michael, but beyond this, we won't be able to aid you.*"

"I understand," I assured her. They had done enough for me already.

"We came to offer what advice we could," Oursk said. *"Be careful of the Long Fangs. The witch who leads their delegation has mighty magic at his command."*

"Delegation?" I asked, wondering at his choice of wording.

"The goblins gathered in the valley are but a small part of their respective tribes," Aira answered.

I nodded, understanding what she meant but uncertain about the reason for the delegations' presence. Still, not having to face off against a full tribe should at least make the task I'd been given easier to complete.

"You will do well to avoid the witch and his apprentices until you are stronger," Oursk continued.

That, unfortunately, wasn't a choice I had, given my time limit. But, I nodded agreeably nevertheless. "Thank you, Oursk," I said. Leaning down, I gently batted away one of the pups trying to climb up my leg. "What about the wyvern mother? Can the pack defeat her?"

"Not without huge losses," Aira admitted.

My heart sank at the thought.

"Do not fear, Michael," Oursk assured me. *"Duggar is both canny and wise. He has led the pack for years and knows as well as we do the consequences of facing the dragonkin in open battle."*

"Oursk is correct," Aira continued. *"I suspect Duggar will take the pack into hiding. We've done it before."*

"If you need to find us, search the cave network beneath the eastern valley slopes," Oursk said. *"Its tunnels are too small for the dragonkin. I'm sure the alpha will shelter the pack there."*

I bowed to the pair. "Thank you, Aira, Oursk. I'll do that once I've dealt with the goblins." I paused. "Speaking of the goblins, why are so many gathered in the valley?"

Oursk snarled in frustrated anger. *"The creatures are here at Erebus' behest."*

My brows furrowed. If that was the case, why weren't the goblins in the dungeon already?

Noticing my confusion, Aira explained further. *"The delegations are here to negotiate terms with the Power before joining his faction. The tribes themselves are vast, and the hordes they command are mighty. They know their own worth too and will not sell their allegiance to the Dark cheaply. Do not expect to overcome their representatives easily."*

"I see," I said. I kept my face smooth and unruffled, but I felt my concern mounting. From what the wolves had told me so far, I gathered that the goblins I'd been tasked to deal with would be nothing like the Fangtooths I'd faced off against in the dungeon.

What have I gotten myself into this time?

✳ ✳ ✳

Shortly after that, the wolves and I said our goodbyes.

The pair had given me much to think about, and before leaving the glade I pondered my next steps. I realized completing Duggar's task might be trickier than I'd originally assumed.

I don't know enough yet, I decided. Before I could plan my approach, I needed better information on the goblins' numbers and levels. Deciding to stick with my original plan, I slipped back into the trees and headed east through the forest.

The hours passed without incident as I traversed the forest through the treetops. From what the wolves had told me, I knew I'd been in the center of the valley when the wyvern had ambushed me. According to Aira, the area was a regular battleground of the warring goblin delegations and a popular hunting ground for the wyverns.

My journey eastward took the rest of the day. During that time, I wasn't attacked, nor did I spot any goblins. Despite this, I stayed alert. As the day progressed, the glimpses I caught of the mountain peaks grew more frequent. Each time they loomed larger until finally, as twilight fell, the trees failed to conceal the mountains entirely.

Knowing the valley's eastern rim couldn't be much farther, I slowed my advance and slipped silently from branch to branch while I kept my senses extended and periodically checked my mindsight for nearby hostiles.

Despite my care, I came up onto the outskirts of the goblin camp with a suddenness that nearly caused me to lose my perch.

Not a hundred yards in front of me, the trees gave way to a boulder-strewn slope before rising steeply to sheer mountain cliffs. Entrenched in the short stretch of barren ground between tree line and cliffs were the Long Fangs.

My gaze flitted over the camp. It had been established inside a natural half-moon formed by the sheer cliff walls. Only one side wasn't bordered by the looming mountain, and that side was closed off with a deep-looking trench. Sharpened stakes had been planted into the dug-out channel and angled to protrude outward. Within these defenses, dozens of tents were pitched, which, judging by their size, held about ten goblins each.

Duggar was right, I realized. The Fangtooths I had faced off against in the dungeon were a far cry from the goblins in the camp ahead.

Squads of goblin warriors patrolled the perimeter of the encampment. They were smartly dressed, and their gear shone and looked in good order. Hesitantly, I reached out and analyzed one of the goblins.

The target is a level 38 veteran goblin warrior. Goblin warriors are the mainstay of any goblin fighting force. Strong and agile, they make for both excellent infantry and cavalry soldiers.

Veterans are among the rarest of goblin warriors. Survivors of countless skirmishes and battles, they have advanced to heights not achieved by most warriors.

By my count, there were about two hundred goblins in the camp. I rubbed my chin. The Long Fangs weren't going to be pushovers. *Why does Duggar think I'll be able to rid him of this threat?* I wondered in disbelief. I couldn't see how I would go about it myself, but I wasn't about to give up just yet.

Staying crouched low on my branch, I continued to watch the camp. I was wary of getting too close. As yet, I had seen no sign of the witch the wolves had mentioned, and until I knew how powerful he was I wasn't going to risk a closer look.

As dusk turned to night and fires sprang up in the goblin camp, I maintained my silent vigil, analyzing the goblins and counting their numbers. If nothing else, the time would be well spent increasing my insight skill.

The target is a level 39 goblin veteran warrior.
The target is a level 27 goblin guerilla.
The target is ...

...

...

Your insight has increased to level 40 and reached rank 4.

After my lengthy observation, the true scale of the task I faced became apparent. It wasn't just the Long Fangs' levels I had to worry about, it was also their training. The goblins showed no signs of rowdiness or ill discipline that the Fangtooths had displayed. The patrols marched mechanically along their routes, not speaking or joking with each other. The guards at the camp's single entrance were alert too and scanned the tree line constantly for threats.

A direct assault won't be easy.

With the mountain range itself protecting the camp on three sides, any enemy would have difficulty penetrating the goblins' defenses. I kept scanning the camp, hoping to spot some weakness to exploit. But as time passed and I failed to find any, my concern mounted.

About an hour after full darkness had fallen, I noticed activity near the gate. A dozen torches were approaching, appearing from one of the large red tents inside the camp. There were three such tents, and I had marked each as a potential location for the tribe's witches. My gaze sharpened as the figures bearing the torches came into focus.

They weren't goblins.

Six were human. Three were elves, and the last one was a half-orc. Quickly, I analyzed the figure at the forefront of the group—the leader, by all appearances.

The target is Cecilia, a level 29 elf. She is a player and bears a Mark of Lesser Dark.

Players, I mused. Ignoring the incongruity of players in a goblin camp, I ran my gaze over the rest of the party and inspected each in turn. Sure enough, I discovered that all ten were players.

Accompanying the players were two tall, slim goblins. These goblins, unlike the warriors, were dressed in colorful robes and feathered trinkets. Suspecting what they would be, I analyzed them anyway.

The target is Grul, a level 41 goblin apprentice witch doctor.
The target is a Sstak, level 35 goblin apprentice witch doctor.

Witch doctors are tribal leaders amongst goblinkin and are widely feared for the strength of their life magic. Unlike most other life magic wielders, witch doctors use their life spells offensively to harm rather than heal.

I had discovered the goblins' magic users at last, and if the apprentices were this strong, I could only imagine the witch doctor's own level.

The strange party stopped at the gates. "You can't do this," Cecilia said. "It's night. Let us stay until morning at least."

Grul laughed. "Foolish elf. You chose to come here. It is not the Long Fangs' fault your proposal was found wanting. We will not shelter you, player scum."

"Our captain will not be pleased when he hears of this," Cecilia responded sharply.

Grul snarled derisively. "What care we for your captain?" he asked rhetorically.

"The Howlers won't take kindly to this rejection either," the half-orc interjected.

"The Howlers!" The other apprentice, Sstak, scowled. "The Howlers are not the Long Fangs' masters. If they wish for us to join their war against the Red Rats, they should make their own overtures to our tribe and not send players to do their bidding."

"But we have a writ of safe passage from Hyek himself," Cecilia protested. "You must honor it."

"And we have," Grul smirked. "You have been treated well in our camp." He gestured to the dark tree line. "What happens to you out there is none of our concern."

Cecilia opened her mouth to object again. The half-orc placed a hand on her. "It's no use. These fools have made up their minds. We should leave while we still have a chance of making it through the night."

Cecilia glanced from the grinning apprentices to her companions and jerked her head in grim agreement. She waved to the silent players behind her. "Let's go," she said, "and make sure to keep your eyes peeled for danger."

Frightened faces and determined glances were her only answer.

"Open the gates, you filth. We'll leave now," Cecilia said.

The witch doctor apprentice bowed mockingly and waved to the gate guards, who swung open the wooden gate. With Cecilia and the half-orc at their fore, the squad of players jogged out.

I watched the players draw closer to my own position, a thoughtful frown on my face.

I hadn't missed how well-spoken the two goblins were. By the manner of their speech, the goblins I'd faced in the dungeon seemed almost barbaric in comparison, which further reinforced the point: the Long Fangs were nothing like the Fangtooths.

Though at this point, the goblins concerned me less than the players did. I still couldn't figure out what they were doing.

Why try to parley with the goblin tribes, and who was this captain they referred to?

Narrowing my eyes, I studied the nearing players. All of them bore a Mark of Lesser or Minor Dark. *They're all Dark players,* I thought unhappily. It was likely then that they served Erebus or one of his fellow Powers.

More enemies, I groused.

I held myself tense as the squad passed under the tree sheltering me, but they didn't seem aware of my presence. My gaze flitted between the disappearing players and the goblins.

Did I stay and continue to watch the camp, or did I trail the players?

CHAPTER 95: A ROMP IN THE FOREST

DAY TWO. NIGHT.

After another long pause, I turned around and followed in the players' wake. Like the two bounty hunters I'd encountered before, this group was also afraid of the dark and kept their torches burning.

They were in a hurry too, scrambling through the forests on a southerly heading. But for all that, the players moved in a well-knit and coordinated unit that scanned the surroundings constantly. Still, their lack of night vision made it easy for me to track them undetected.

Multiple hostile entities have failed to detect you! Your sneaking has increased to level 45.

I followed the party closely through the forest, even while remaining uncertain of my own intent.

Considering the matter further, I realized that even though the players bore Dark Marks, there was no reason to believe they belonged to the Awakened Dead or owed allegiance to Erebus or any of his ilk. After all, I was also Dark-marked.

Still, I didn't think the group would be well disposed to me. They might not be bounty hunters out to claim my scalp, but I couldn't afford to think kindly of them. Revealing my presence wouldn't be wise.

A roar shook the forest. Below me, the player squad froze in place.

"What was that?" one of them whispered fearfully.

I also stiffened. The sound was familiar. It was from the same sort of creature I'd encountered yesterday. "Rhomodillo," I whispered.

The roar sounded again, much closer this time.

"Ready yourself," the half-orc, Ultack, barked. "Whatever it is, we're not going to outrun it." The players unhooked their weapons. Four of them wore shields and carried axes or spears.

Another four were archers, and they withdrew to the center of the party's formation. Two raised staffs. *Mages.* Cecilia was one of them.

Ultack glanced over his shoulder at his commander. "We'll hold it," he said. "Whatever it is. You and Sora damage it."

Cecilia jerked her head once in acknowledgment. Another roar split the air, this time from the edges of the clearing.

The rhomodillo had shown itself.

I was in a tree directly overhead the party, and for the second time in as many days, I got a close look at one of the brutish-looking creatures. Snorting in fury and pounding its forelegs against the ground was a beast as large as the wyvern had been, only stockier. Heavy black plates covered nearly every inch of its skin, and its horn, pointing upward in threat, glinted in the torchlight.

I frowned. By all appearances, the rhomodillo was the same one I'd encountered yesterday.

Damnation, has it been following me all this time?

With a snort of disdain at the party arrayed against it, the beast thundered across the glade, its hooves trampling grass and vegetation underfoot.

To the players' credit, they didn't flee. Closing ranks, Ultack and the other fighters prepared to meet the creature's charge.

They don't stand a chance, I thought, watching silently from above.

✳ ✳ ✳

I'm not sure what spurred me to act.

Maybe it was the suspicion that the rhomodillo *was* following me. Perhaps it was knowing that the party stood no chance, or maybe it was that despite believing it unlikely, I still held out hope of befriending the players.

Whatever the case, I chose not to ignore their plight.

As the rhomodillo closed in on the fighters' line, I dipped into the well of my consciousness and sent tendrils of psi racing toward the creature.

The beast was oblivious as I slipped into its mind and imposed my will upon it.

A level 51 rhomodillo has passed a mental resistance check! You have failed to charm your target. Your mental intrusion has gone undetected!

I growled in frustration as my spell failed. I only had a split second to decide my next move: to intervene more directly and in a riskier fashion or leave the players to their fate.

Quelling my doubts, I raced forward along the tree bough and, gauging the rhomodillo's speed, carefully dropped down.

My timing was impeccable.

A few yards before the beast crashed into the fighters, I landed on its back. Sensing my sudden weight, the creature dug its hooves into the ground and flung back its head.

It's going to try skewering me, I thought, eyeing the approach of its gleaming horn. But before the rhomodillo could stick me, I wrapped my hands around one of its hardened plates and cast stunning slap.

Psi coursed from my palm and directly into the creature, flooding its muscles and freezing it in place.

A rhomodillo has failed a physical resistance check! You have stunned your target for 1 second.

Locked motionless, the beast lost its stride and its limbs collapsed beneath it. The impetus of the rhomodillo's charge wasn't entirely spent however, and it slid headlong across the ground. Balancing atop the creature, I tried riding out the crash.

Unfortunately, a dead tree stump had other plans.

Midway to the line of fighters, the creature struck the wooden protrusion. Its body twisted, falling over. Realizing my danger, I flung myself free and escaped the overturning behemoth.

I hurtled through the air and toward the ground. With outstretched hands, I cushioned my fall and sprang back up a few feet from the dazed rhomodillo.

My gaze flew to the startled players. They stared at me, mouths agape. "Don't just stand there!" I snapped. "Attack!"

Not waiting on their response, I turned back to my foe. The beast was lumbering back to its feet, shaking its head to clear it of the dirt and debris that coated its face.

I sprang forward, blade in hand.

I didn't fancy facing the rhomodillo at close quarters once it recovered. I had to keep it on the back foot. Behind me, I heard the half-orc barking orders. *I hope those aren't to retreat,* I thought in a moment of dark humor. *Then I might just be in trouble.*

Closing to attack range, I focused on the task at hand. The rhomodillo still hadn't realized the danger.

Striking out with spider's bite, I whacked the beast on the right leg.

Blade met hardened hide and skidded off, doing little more than scratching the beast's armor. But I had expected that. Channeling stamina through the shortsword, I cast crippling blow. Energy gushed out of the blade's tip and into my foe.

To no effect.

A rhomodillo has passed a physical resistance check! You have failed to cripple your target.

I bit off a curse.

The beast swung around to pin me with a glare. We were barely a foot apart, and I thought I saw joy spark in the creature's beady eyes as it caught onto that fact.

With a snort of unmistakable delight, the rhomodillo charged. Lowering its head, it angled its horn to skewer me. I was not unprepared. Springing off my haunches, I leaped upward—not to evade, but to attack.

Somersaulting midair, I landed on my foe's back again. A shudder rippled through the beast beneath me. I grinned. *Didn't expect that, did you?* Before the rhomodillo could react, I slapped down my left hand.

You have stunned your target for 1 second.

I hissed in relief at the ability's success. I'd been half-expecting another failure. Beneath me, the beast stuttered and sank. I rode it to the ground and renewed my stun.

The tread of soft footfalls across the grass caught my attention. The Dark players were approaching, albeit with an abundance of caution.

"Attack already!" I yelled, "It's helpless, and I won't be able to keep it pinned forever!"

Right on cue, the beast beneath me stirred.

Oh no you don't, I thought. Renewing my stun-lock, I shoved spider's bite into the seams between the rhomodillo's ridge plates and tried to pry one free.

I failed dismally.

God damn, is there no way to injure this beast? Stunning the beast again, I tried to work my shortsword deeper.

"Here, let me," a voice said from my rear. It was Ultack.

Taking his axe in a two-handed grip, the half-orc raised it up high before smashing it downward in a devastating blow. The axe edge hit the rhomodillo with a resounding screech but otherwise didn't seem to fare any better than my shortsword.

I scowled up at the fighter. His blade had struck less than a few inches from my outstretched fingers.

The half-orc shrugged, "I didn't hit you, did I?"

I had no response to that.

"Did it work?" he asked a beat later.

Ready to ignore the near-miss, I squinted at the rhomodillo's hide and spotted a hairline crack. "It's working," I said. "Hit it again."

The half-orc did so. His fellows joined him, and soon the group was striking rhythmically at the rhomodillo's rear while I kept it stunned beneath me.

"Hurry," I urged, watching my depleting psi pool.

More cracks appeared on the beast's hide, but the fighters had yet to penetrate its armor. My psi was draining fast, and soon I knew I wouldn't be able to keep the behemoth contained. Ultack hit it once more, as did his companions.

Then they hit it again.

And again.

Eventually, a chunk of the rhomodillo's armor broke free, but the moment had come too late, just like I'd feared. My psi was down to its last dregs.

You have failed to stun your target. Insufficient psi.

The beast trembled, then began to clamber to its feet. "Damnit," I growled. "I can't hold it anymore." There was still one more thing I could do though. Taking spider's bite in a two-handed grip, I plunged its hilt deep into the vulnerable flesh beneath the destroyed chunk of hide.

You have critically injured a rhomodillo.

The beast roared and shook violently, tossing me airborne.

I was flung through the air and glimpsed the fighters beat a hasty retreat. Tucking in my limbs, I transformed my tumble into a controlled dive and rolled back to my feet as I hit the ground.

I took quick stock of the battle. Spider's bite was still embedded in the rhomodillo, and the beast was laying into the closest fighter, its horn spearing deep into his torso as it gorged him.

Jalin has died.

I winced and drew my remaining blade. Ultack was reforming his fighters into a defensive line while, from behind them, the four archers loosed their arrows at the rampaging beast. But the projectiles bounced off the creature's armor and failed to do more than annoy it.

"Aim for the shortsword, you idiots," Cecilia ordered. "Its armor is impervious." Lowering her own staff, the mage hurled a flaming missile at the beast. Her companion did the same, sending lightning crackling toward the creature.

Charged bolt and flaming dart struck the creature simultaneously. The rhomodillo grunted in surprise but appeared otherwise unaffected. The magical attacks had done little more than irritate it. Fixing its gaze on the two mages, the beast charged the fighters shielding them.

Blade in hand, I sprinted forward. Focusing on the other players, the rhomodillo had turned its back on me.

Now was my chance.

The beast crashed through Ultack's hastily drawn-up defensive line, trampling two other players underfoot.

Timothy has died.
Saul has died.

In seconds, the pairs' lives were snuffed out. And the rhomodillo wasn't done yet. Before Ultack or any of his companions could intervene, the beast charged the mage, Sora, and pinned her against the tree with its single sharpened horn.

Sora has died.

This thing is devilishly strong. In only a handful of seconds, the rhomodillo had killed four players—each with a single hit.

But the beast's last attack, as devastating as it had been, had stemmed its rampage, if only temporarily. Leaping forward, I activated one-step midair and, kicking off again, landed on the rhomodillo's back.

Its horn was buried in the tree, and while it struggled to free itself, I plunged my second shortsword next to spider's bite.

You have critically injured a rhomodillo.

With a bellow of rage and pain, the beast freed itself, ripping off a good chunk of tree in the process. Backflipping, I extricated myself from the creature as it swung around.

"Charging," Ultack shouted and flew forward, straight at the snorting beast. My mouth dropped open as I witnessed this display of amazingly stupid bravery. *He's a goner for sure.* But to my surprise, when the two collided, it was the beast that faltered.

A rhomodillo has failed a physical resistance check! Ultack has stunned his target for 3 seconds.

"Now!" Cecilia yelled.

The remaining fighters rushed in, thrusting their blades into the beast. The mage herself plunged the tip of her staff into the vulnerable flesh exposed by Ultack earlier and sent fire coursing directly into the beast.

Three seconds wasn't a lot of time, but it must have felt like forever to the rhomodillo beset by fire and iron from the surviving party members.

"Get back!" Ultack roared.

A moment later, burned, dazed, and bleeding profusely, the beast shrugged off its stun and peered at the players surrounding it.

How is it still alive? I wondered.

Scanning the glade quickly, I spotted a shortsword lying near one of the downed fighters. Gliding toward it, I picked it up.

Ultack stepped up beside me. "Can you stun it again?"

"No," I paused. "Can you?"

"I can," he muttered. "But I'll be useless for much else afterward." His eyes narrowed as he studied me intently. "Make sure you finish it."

I nodded.

With another roar, the half-orc charged, his form blurring as he activated his stun ability.

Ultack has stunned his target for 3 seconds.

Ignoring the rest of the group, I raced forward too. The other players were converging on the beast's rear to plunge in their own blades while Cecilia burned the creature again.

I, on the other hand, made straight for the rhomodillo's face and, before the creature could recover from Ultack's attack, plunged my sword into one of its eye sockets.

The blade went in without resistance.

I'd guessed right. The armor covering the beast's eyelids was nowhere near as dense as that over the rest of its body. Pulling out my sword, I plunged it into the beast's second eye.

You have permanently blinded a rhomodillo.
A rhomodillo is no longer stunned.

I completed my attack and leaped back as the beast's paralysis expired and it gave vent to its pain with an earsplitting scream.

Stumbling back to its feet, the rhomodillo swung about slowly. It was half-dead and blind to boot. But that didn't stop it from charging.

"Get back," Cecilia roared.

Her companions dashed out of the way as the creature crashed headlong into another tree. Dazed, it staggered back. It spun about, making no move to retreat, and hurled itself across the glade again, only to crash once more.

I retreated to the edge of the clearing. In my mind, the battle was already over. Without its sight, the rhomodillo was too impaired to be of much threat, and it was only a matter of time before the beast died.

I eyed the surviving party members.

Now, to wait and prepare for whatever comes next.

CHAPTER 96: IN A PICKLE

DAY TWO. NIGHT.

I sat down against a tree trunk and inspected the dead player's shortsword more closely. It was a plain blade and a poor substitute for my own weapons—both of which were still buried in the rhomodillo—but at least I wasn't unarmed.

I wasn't so foolish to believe that my fighting was done for the day. For all that the party of Dark players and I had cooperated in the battle, there was no telling how they would react once the rhomodillo was dead, and I needed to be ready for anything. Wiping the shortsword clean, I sheathed it in the hidden scabbard across my back.

You have successfully concealed a small weapon.

Having finished my preparations, I watched the party play tag with the dying creature. It was unnecessary. The creature's wounds were severe enough that it would perish soon, but I understood what drove the group.

The beast had killed four of their companions, and the players' anger and frustration were clearly written on their faces. While they fought, I re-examined each closely but still failed to recognize any. If they had been in the dungeon, they had left before I'd become entangled with Saben's gang.

Satisfied the players were of no immediate danger to me, I closed my eyes and took the opportunity to recover some psi.

You have replenished 3% of your psi. Your psi is now at 4%.
You have replenished 3% of your psi. Your psi is now at 7%.
…
Your psi is now at 67%. Your meditation has increased to level 33.

Midway through my meditation, the Game alerts I was waiting for arrived.

A level 51 rhomodillo has died.
You have reached level 32! Your dodging has increased to level 34. Your shortswords has increased to level 42. Your two-weapon fighting has increased to level 37.
Your chi has increased to level 25. Your telekinesis has increased to level 21.

A small smile stole across my face at the Adjudicator's messages. I was advancing steadily. Given my circumstances, I didn't waste any time spending my new attribute points.

Your Mind has increased to rank 9 and your Constitution to rank 9.

The players, meanwhile, were converging on me. Keeping my eyes closed, I leaned back further against the tree in feigned weariness. None of the party were scouts, and their footfalls on the soft earth were distinct and clear—to my ears at least.

At least they're not trying to sneak up on me, I thought wryly as the six formed a loose semi-circle about me. I waited to see if the players would take any further action, but when they didn't I opened my eyes and rose to my feet, arms folded and, to all appearances, weaponless.

Your hidden weapon has gone unnoticed! Your deception has increased to level 12.

I held back a snort. The Game message was no surprise. The group had retrieved a still-burning torch, abandoned at the start of the battle, and shone its light on me. Even so, the torch was doing a poor job of illuminating the area, and the players were struggling to see. *It's no wonder they failed to spot my sword.*

"Who are you?" one of the players demanded, bare blade in hand.

I said nothing, bristling at the undisguised threat.

"Where did you come from?" Cecilia asked, her tone only a touch less combative than the first player.

My gaze slid to her, noticing her tense grip on her staff, but I didn't break my silence.

Ultack folded his arms and scrutinized me carefully. Of the six, he seemed the most at ease. "It's him," the half-orc said.

"Him?" Cecilia asked, casting her companion a sharp glance. "Him who?"

"The one whose face is plastered on the bounty board," Ultack replied.

Silence fell at the half-orc's words, and I could almost feel the Dark players' scrutiny deepen.

An analyze attempt by a hostile entity has failed.
An analyze attempt by a hostile entity has failed.
An analyze attempt by a hostile entity has failed.
Your deception has increased to level 15.

I hid my grin as three of the analyze attempts against me failed, advancing my deception skill. *Useful.* Still, it wouldn't do to grow overconfident. I'd only sensed three failed attempts, which meant as many as three more could've succeeded. *I have to assume they know my level.*

"We should claim the bounty," one of the players muttered, edging forward a step.

"We'll be rich," another said, licking his lips in anticipation. "Not to mention we'll—"

"No," Ultack snapped.

Cecilia frowned at the half-orc, but she said nothing to object. Observing the dynamics of the group, I realized he was probably her second-in-command.

"Ultack is right," the elf said. "This player has helped us. If not for him, we'd probably all be dead."

I snorted. "Not probably. Certainly."

Cecilia's lips thinned at my response, but she didn't argue. I noticed, though, that she didn't unwrap her fingers from her staff or command the other players to stand down.

"Why did you help us?" Ultack asked, speaking into the renewed silence.

I shrugged. "You seemed to need it." I smiled. "Was I wrong?"

"You weren't," the half-orc said. Ignoring the sputtered protests of the others, he glanced at Cecilia.

Interpreting something in his look, the elven mage rolled her eyes, but a moment later she turned to me and said grudgingly, "Thank you."

I inclined my head. "You're welcome."

"We can't let you go though," she added quickly.

I stared at her with a face devoid of expression. "Oh? And what's to say you can hold me?"

Her face tightened at my words. "There's six of—" she began.

Ultack laid a restraining hand on her arm. "We won't do this," he said. "We owe him."

The two matched gazes for a drawn-out moment before Cecilia reluctantly jerked her chin in agreement and turned back to me. "It seems you are in luck today, *Michael.*"

I didn't miss the emphasis she'd placed on my name. She was letting me know she'd successfully analyzed me.

"We won't stop you from leaving," Cecilia went on. "But beyond today, don't expect further mercies from us." She paused, then sighed. "But I cannot ignore that we owe you a debt—a debt that cannot remain unfulfilled. How can we repay you?"

I eyed the mage, her abrupt change of heart catching me off guard. I had been sure we were about to come to blows. And for all her obvious reluctance in making it, Cecilia's offer appeared genuine. I didn't know how far I could trust her, but for a Dark player she was proving more honorable than I expected.

"You could give me that writ of safe passage you carry," I suggested, deciding to put the elf's words to the test.

Cecilia's eyes widened, then narrowed. "How do you—"

"The bastard has been spying on us!" one of the watching fighters yelled.

"Well, that much should have been obvious," I murmured.

"Let's kill him!" another cried.

The other players growled in agreement and raised their weapons. I sighed. It looked like I was in for another fight after all. I held myself ready but didn't draw my own blade just yet.

"Enough!" Ultack snapped, spinning around to glare at his companions. When the discontented whispers died, the half-orc turned back to me. "*Have you been following us?*"

I didn't shy away from his gaze. "I have, but only since you left the Long Fang's camp." Before this could ignite renewed protests, I added, "My business is not with you. It's with the goblins. I only followed you because I found your presence there... interesting."

Ultack nodded slowly, seeming to accept my words.

"What do you want with the writ?" Cecilia asked, still looking suspicious.

I glanced at her. "That's no concern of yours," I replied, my tone hardening. "If you wish to repay your debt, give it to me."

The mage said nothing for a moment, chewing over my words.

"I could have chosen not to help you," I prompted as I sensed her wavering. "And taken it off your corpse."

That drew more scowls and muttered imprecations, but no one disputed my assertion. They all knew I was right.

"Give it to him," Ultack said finally.

Cecilia glanced at her companion in exasperation.

"We have fulfilled our task," Ultack said, undaunted by her look. "And we have little further need for it. It is a small reward in exchange for our lives."

Cecilia still didn't look convinced.

"You know it's what the captain would want us to do," Ultack persisted.

The half-orc's words piqued my interest. This was the second time I'd heard the pair mention a superior. It implied they were part of a much larger group. Where was their captain?

Cecilia nodded reluctantly, swayed by Ultack's arguments. Reaching into the pouch at her side, she pulled out a rolled-up parchment and held it out to me. Curiously, I analyzed the object in her hand.

This is a goblin writ of safe passage. This item is inscribed with the personal signature of Shaman Hyek of the Howlers and guarantees the bearer's safety in sector 12,560. Any goblin who disrespects the shaman's writ will feel the wrath of the Howlers.

I smiled as I read the item's description. My instincts had been right. Acquiring the writ would put me one step closer to completing Duggar's task and, at the very least, would get me into the Long Fangs' camp. Of course, I still didn't know what to do once inside, but I was sure I'd think of something.

"Will this suffice?" Cecilia asked.

I nodded wordlessly, concealing my eagerness for the writ.

"You agree that, once I give you this, the debt between us will be settled?" she persisted.

"I do," I said and reached out to take the item from her fingers.

The elven mage pulled her hand back before I could do so. "I will give you the writ," she said. "But not quite yet."

I straightened. "Why not?" I asked sharply.

"We require it ourselves," Cecilia said.

I frowned, not understanding.

"To get through the Howlers' camp," she added. Seeing I remained unenlightened, she elaborated, "The Howlers are encamped around the safe zone."

"The safe zone?" I asked, perplexed. "Why would you need to go there?"

"It's the only place we can leave the sector," she said with a frown of her own.

I stared at her blankly.

"This is a closed sector," Ultack interjected. "You know what that means?"

"There's no way in or out?" I guessed, recalling the two bounty hunters' words.

"Almost right," Ultack conceded. "There are no *natural* means into this valley. The only way in or out is through the ley line leading to the dungeon or a player-made portal from one of the other Kingdom sectors."

I certainly didn't want to return to the dungeon. I glanced at the glistening snow-covered peaks, still visible above the trees in my night vision. "The mountains can't be crossed then?"

A player to Ultack's left snorted. "I'd like to see you try."

The half-orc smiled. "Jorge is right. The mountains are inhospitable, but it's not just that. Even if you manage to scale their peaks, you'll find only a gray void of nothingness beyond. There are no sectors adjacent to this one."

I pursed my lips, not sure I believed him. What he was describing sounded like an impossibility, but Ultack's information was consistent with what I'd learned from the bounty hunter, Henry, and I couldn't ignore the possibility that they were both telling the truth. I turned to Cecilia. "About the safe zone then?"

"It houses the sector's only portal," she said.

I scratched my head. "And that's important why? Can't you just create another?"

Cecilia's lips twitched, but she didn't laugh at my ignorance.

"Creating a portal is no easy undertaking," she began.

"Not to mention expensive," Jorge interjected.

The elven woman ignored the interruption. "Only one faction has gone to the trouble of creating and maintaining a gate to this sector."

I didn't have to think too hard to guess who that might be. "The Awakened Dead," I said sourly.

Unsurprisingly, Cecilia nodded.

Still, her answer confused me. If there was one thing I'd learned about the Awakened Dead, it was that they didn't look kindly on those who didn't belong to their faction. Narrowing my eyes, I studied the shimmer around the elf that signified her Marks. A Game message opened in my mind.

The target is Cecilia, a level 30 elf. She is a player and bears the Mark of Lesser Dark.

I hadn't been mistaken the first time I'd analyzed her. Cecilia wasn't bound to Erebus, Ishita, or any other Power.

So how did she and the others get here?

"I don't suppose the Awakened Dead are letting just anyone use their gate," I said finally. "How did your party end up in this sector?"

"We were sent," she replied.

I frowned. "Sent to do what?" *And by whom?*

"That's no concern of yours," Cecilia retorted.

I couldn't help but grin as she threw my own words back at me. I let the matter lie though and turned back to the subject at hand. "Alright, if the Awakened Dead let you use the gate to come in, I assume they'll let you leave by it too?"

"They will," Cecilia and Ultack said in unison.

Despite the firmness of the pair's response, I sensed an undercurrent of uncertainty in their words. I ignored it. "Then they'll let me use it too. I have a Mark of the Dark, and I'm sure I can pass for one of your party."

Ultack shook his head. "It won't be that easy." He removed his right glove, revealing a spider tattoo inscribed on the back of his hand. "Ishita's people strictly control access to the portal with these. You won't get through."

My lips twisted sourly at the mention of the spider goddess' name. So, I could expect to encounter more of her people here. Worse yet, they appeared to be in control of the sector.

They wouldn't be constrained by my agreement with Erebus either. I paused, struck by a thought. Was that why the Power had agreed so readily to the terms of our non-aggression Pact? He didn't need to hunt me down himself if his ally did the work. *Urgh.*

My gaze drifted to the dead players. I assumed they would revive in the safe zone, but would the tattoo Ultack showed me remain on their skin after death? "What about them?"

"Their markings won't fade," Cecilia said, confirming my fears. "The tattoos are magical in nature and will remain as long as we're in the sector."

Escaping the region was looking more and more complicated by the minute. "So what? Are you saying I'm stuck here?"

Cecilia and Ultack exchanged silent glances, not replying—which I suppose was answer enough. Another player wasn't so restrained.

"That's exactly what she's saying," Jorge chortled.

I scowled at him but didn't respond. I was certain now that this was why Erebus hadn't been overly concerned with the terms of our deal. If I couldn't escape the sector, abiding by the non-aggression Pact cost the Dark Power nothing.

The thought left a sick feeling in my stomach—anger at the Power and bitterness at myself for being duped.

"You should come with us to the safe zone anyway," Ultack said slowly. Perhaps he'd sensed my dark thoughts. "Someone there might be able to help you."

I sighed. I doubted help would be easy to come by—or freely given. But I refused to be discouraged.

I will escape.

Shrugging off my gloomy reflections, I considered the half-orc's words more objectively. There was merit to his suggestion.

Visiting the safe zone would be useful, though perhaps not for the reasons Ultack proposed. I needed to understand the full extent of my predicament—*just how trapped was I?*—and confirm the truth of the players' tale.

And I could only do that by visiting the safe zone.

I turned back to Cecilia. "We have a deal. I'll accompany you to the safe zone, and after we get there you'll give me the writ."

The elven mage nodded. "Agreed."

Chapter 97: A Fortified Mess

After I reclaimed my swords from the rhomodillo's corpse, I stood guard while Cecilia's party looted the bodies of their dead. They took their time, storing their companions' possessions in their backpacks with care—to pass on to them later, I supposed.

While I waited, I reflected on my new companions. Ultack was likable enough, and Cecilia didn't seem that bad either. As for the rest, I already knew I disliked Jorge, but I hadn't spent much time considering the others, and I analyzed each in turn again.

The target is Ultack, a level 30 half-orc.
The target is Jorge, a level 26 human.
The target is Luriel, a level 27 elf.
The target is Fogbear, a level 26 human.
The target is Mist, a level 28 elf.

Like Cecilia, the others had gained a level from the skirmish with the rhomodillo, and all were surprisingly high-leveled. But then, there was nothing to say that any of them was a new player like me, and I already knew they hadn't come from the dungeon.

So, where have they come from, and more importantly, what are they doing in this out-of-the-way sector?

I also wondered about my urge to help them. I'd felt no similar inclination with the bounty hunters. What had prompted me to act this time?

Maybe I'm just a sucker for damsels in distress, I thought wryly, my gaze drifting toward Cecilia. The elven mage was certainly attractive, but her beauty was the cold, haughty kind. *Not my type at all.* I snorted. Not that I could remember what my type was, or even if I had one.

Maybe it was only self-interest that had spurred me to intervene. The writ of safe passage was valuable, and if the Howlers were indeed blocking entry into the safe zone, it had even more uses than I had initially foreseen.

Will Cecilia keep her word? I wondered. *Or will her party betray me once they reach safety?*

My eyes darted to Ultack. Intuition told me I could depend on him. I pursed my lips. There it was again: an instinct within me prompting my actions. Despite the disquieting strangeness of the sensation, I felt myself inexplicably trusting it. I couldn't recall ever experiencing such a feeling before, and I found myself wondering what had given birth to it now.

Is this something 'of the Wolf'?

I wasn't sure, but it felt like it might be. I bit the inside of my cheek. It was beginning to feel like there was much more to my supposed wolven heritage than I'd originally assumed, and it left me wondering what I was becoming.

❋ ❋ ❋

Once the others were done, we headed south.

I forsook my treetop highway to join them on the forest floor. For one, I preferred to keep my means of traveling the forest a secret, and I was also curious about the party's origins.

Sadly, I managed to pry very little out of my new companions. They were tight-lipped and alert, eyes constantly roving across the encroaching trees to scan for danger. But while I found the group's discipline admirable, I was less than impressed by their powers of observation.

Time and again, it fell to me to warn the party of the approaching predators they failed to spot and to steer them clear of creature dens they somehow missed. Eventually, of course, they noticed my unusual perceptiveness.

"How are you doing that?" Jorge asked, the irritation in his voice undisguised.

"Doing what?" I asked innocently.

The human fighter scowled at me. From his gear, I took him to be a damage dealer. "Don't play stupid," he snapped. He peered at me suspiciously. "Are you drawing the beasts to us?"

I laughed. "What? You mean the forest isn't dangerous enough already?"

He glared at me but didn't retort as he turned away to futilely study the surroundings. From beside me, Ultack chuckled. "You shouldn't toy with Jorge like that."

I glanced up at him. "Why? Because he's so pleasant and helpful?"

The half-orc only laughed louder. "No," he said when his mirth subsided. "Because you're distracting him."

I eyed him sideways. "I notice you haven't asked how I'm managing to spot what the rest of you aren't."

Ultack shrugged. "It's obvious. You're a scout or rogue of some sort."

I nodded, not bothering to correct him. "How far to the safe zone?" I asked, changing the topic.

"We should get there before dawn," the half-orc replied. He paused. "Assuming nothing ambushes us."

I smiled. "I'll do my best to make sure that doesn't happen."

❋ ❋ ❋

We reached our destination without any major incidents, mostly due to my own efforts. We were attacked once by a pair of forest cats—but they were easily fended off—and twice more by a pack of hyenas. The ugly creatures were more persistent than the cats, but after Cecilia killed a half-dozen with a single casting, they saw reason and troubled us no more.

Just as Ultack predicted, we reached the southern edge of the valley as the sky brightened. Emerging from the tree line, we found ourselves standing at the foot of a rocky slope. I stumbled to a halt at the sight that greeted us: goblin fortifications.

Sitting tall and undisguised on the mountainside.

The Howlers' encampment was many times larger than the Long Fangs, and truthfully it was more of a fort than a camp, complete with guard towers, mud-brick walls, ramparts, and wooden gates.

There was an abundance of guards everywhere. Goblins in chainmail armor and wielding long spears marched atop the walls, manned the ballistae placed on the towers, and stood guard before the gates.

I whistled appreciatively, glad it wasn't the Howlers I had been tasked to deal with. It was clear now that the size and strength of the goblin delegations in the valley were unequal, and by comparison to the Howlers, the Long Fangs were primitive.

"Impressive, isn't it?" Cecilia said.

I glanced at the elf standing beside me. "Quite," I murmured. "How long have they been here?" *And are the Red Rats this strong too?*

The mage shrugged. "I have no idea. The Howlers got here long before we did and seem intent on staying."

It certainly looked that way. I ran my gaze over the fortifications again, picking out as many details as possible. The goblin stronghold was built on the side of the steeply rising mountainside, making its insides clearly visible. Within the outer wall was an inner wall, and within it was a village.

The settlement consisted of a group of log cabins. From the difference in their design and the lack of goblins inside the space, I took the village to be the safe zone.

So, Ultack and Cecilia didn't lie. The Howlers really do have control of the safe zone. To get to it, we would have to pass through both the goblin fort's outer and inner walls.

"Come on," Ultack said. "They've seen us already."

Taking point, the half-orc led the party up the slope and toward the fort's entrance. A dozen goblins carrying halberds and dressed in chainmail waited there. The guards raised their weapons threateningly as we drew closer, though they didn't appear concerned. Still unsure about my companions and their own intentions, I let my hands stray toward my blades.

Ultack had told me goblins despised players and oftentimes would attack on sight. The situation in the valley, however, was unusual. The goblins had been tempted here by Erebus' offer, and while the negotiations with the Power were ongoing, the three delegations had agreed to honor the writs of safe passage.

When we reached the gate, Cecilia stepped forward and waved the writ in the air.

"Approach," the goblin squad leader grunted, lowering his weapon.

"Just how many goblins are in this fort?" I asked Ultack in a low voice while we waited for the guards to examine Cecilia's writ.

"The shaman leading the Howler's delegation has an escort of one thousand goblin warriors, all elite warriors from their tribe," he answered. The half-orc eyed me carefully. "Make sure you behave. Writ or no, they will attack if we break the peace."

"I won't do anything to provoke them," I promised.

Ultack grunted in acknowledgment.

After a few minutes of inspecting the writ, the goblin squad leader waved us through. I followed in the party's wake, hands still hovering close to my blades.

The inside of the fort was just as orderly and heavily patrolled as the outer defenses. Long rectangular buildings—barracks, I supposed—were arranged in militarily precise rows. Looming over them was a central keep.

That must be where the shaman is, I guessed. The keep itself was at least three stories high and topped with towers and crenellations of its own. It loomed high over the inner wall and would be clearly visible everywhere in the safe zone, which I guessed was by design.

Clearly, the Howlers wanted the players within to be reminded of their presence.

We marched through the camp unmolested, down a central aisle that cut straight from the fort's northern gate to the inner one leading to the safe zone. I swiveled my head left and right. Goblins watched us from every direction, but none approached.

Picking out goblins at random, I analyzed them.

The target is a level 59 elite goblin warrior.

The target is a level 62 elite goblin warrior.

Elites are the pinnacle of the goblin warrior caste, stronger, faster, and more deadly than other goblins. Every elite is equipped with the best available goblin gear and has undergone rigorous training in group tactics. Individually they are a match for most players, but group fighting is where they truly excel. Working in tandem, goblin elites can take down even the strongest players.

Damn. Every goblin I examined was an elite, and all were almost twice my level. That left me wondering about the shaman himself.

"Will we see the shaman?" I asked.

Ultack snorted, "Unlikely. The Howlers' shaman doesn't deal with the likes of us. Besides, we have a writ already. We'll head straight for the safe zone."

I nodded thoughtfully and spent the rest of the short trip in silence. Soon we came to the gate set in the inner wall. Wordlessly, the guards there let us through, and we exited the fort.

A Game message dropped into my mind.

You have entered a safe zone.

I exhaled, some of my tension dissipating. We had made it in safely.

Now to find out what else awaits me in this sector.

And, more importantly, how to escape.

CHAPTER 98: A MUG OF ALE

Day Three. Dawn.

The gate slammed shut ominously behind us.

I paid it no mind though. I was sure I could scale the inner wall if I needed to—it was half as tall as the outer one. But getting past the fort's other defenses wouldn't be as easy.

Good thing I'll have a writ then.

Wordlessly, Cecilia's party dispersed, only the two leaders remaining behind. I ran my gaze along the walls encircling the safe zone. They, too, were heavily patrolled. The Howlers had gone to a lot of trouble to contain the players in the sector, and I couldn't help but wonder why. "What's the purpose of all this?" I asked, gesturing to the fortifications.

"Control," Ultack answered grimly.

I frowned at him. "Control of the players entering the sector, you mean? Why would the goblins want that? And why would the players even allow it?"

Cecilia snorted. "It's not the goblins who desire control."

I stared at her blankly, then took her meaning. "You mean the goblins did all this at the Awakened Dead's behest?"

She nodded. "More like Ishita gifted them the area and let them do as they pleased."

I scratched my chin. "Again, why? She already owns the portal coming here. Why does the Awakened Dead need additional control measures?"

The mage smiled. "Perhaps you'll find out," she added cryptically.

I opened my mouth to question her further, but before I could, Cecilia spoke over me. "This is where we must part ways. We must report to our superior."

I closed my mouth with a snap and held out my hand. Without objection, the elven mage placed the writ in my palm.

You have acquired a goblin writ of safe passage.

"Thank you," I said, breathing out slowly in relief. My instincts hadn't steered me wrong. The pair had kept their word.

Cecilia inclined her head and turned around. "Let's go, Ultack. The captain will be waiting to hear from us."

The half-orc paused to wave farewell. "Good luck, Michael."

"You too," I said and watched them go.

After the pair disappeared from view, I stored the writ in my backpack and, looking left and right, scanned the area. There were at least two dozen log cabins in the village. Their sizes varied from single one-bedroom homes to a few multistory buildings. I marked those for further investigation, assuming they were either shops or public buildings of some other kind.

The streets were empty, leaving the safe zone eerily quiet, but the day was still young. If not for the intruding presence of the goblins, the little village perched on the mountainside would have made for a tranquil scene. Stepping forward, I wandered through the settlement.

While I walked, I reviewed the tasks before me. This was the third day of my non-aggression Pact with Erebus, and I didn't have much time left to accomplish my goals. Before escaping the valley, I needed to fulfill Duggar's task. I owed the wolves a debt, and I had to do at least that much for them. Not to mention that ridding the valley of the Long Fangs would earn me Duggar's favor and get me the information I sought on my Wolf Mark.

I didn't have a plan yet though.

Oh, I had the makings of one, but it was still a long way from being complete, and there were still many unknowns. I had to plug the gaps in my knowledge fast or risk still being in the valley when my Pact with Erebus ran out. Being unprotected from Ishita's followers was bad enough. I didn't want to add Erebus' to the mix too.

Where to begin?

Orienting myself toward the largest structure in the village—a three-story building with two chimneys puffing out smoke—I headed its way.

✳　✳　✳

The building in question was elevated above ground level and had a short stairway leading up to its double doors. Before ascending, I paused to study the sign planted at the foot of the stairs. It read, "The Sleepy Inn."

The tavern's doors were closed and its windows shuttered but, from the smoke escaping the chimneys, I was certain it was open for business. Next to the sign was a wooden noticeboard. There were scraps of aged paper pinned all over its surface, but prominently displayed in the center were two recent posters.

The first contained a likeness of me.

I grimaced as I read the notice. It was Ishita's bounty—one thousand gold coins—and it described the torments the Power demanded I suffer in great detail. Ripping the page free, I shredded it and let the pieces scatter in the wind. Not that it mattered. By now, every player in the sector was likely on the lookout for me.

Interestingly enough, there was another bounty too. This one was for a beast—the wyvern mother. Leaning forward, I scanned the notice. It had been posted by a player called Gelar.

The reward wasn't named, nor was the reason for the bounty spelled out. It simply directed all inquiries to Gelar's shop. I pursed my lips as I wondered why any player would be foolish enough to attempt claiming the bounty.

Turning back to the tavern, I climbed the stairs and entered its murky interior. The double doors led into an open dining area with haphazardly scattered tables. On the left was a bar counter, and on the right was a small stage—currently empty.

Even at this early hour, the tavern was occupied. Four shapes sat in the darkest corner of the room. Two were slouched in their chairs, sipping slowly from their mugs, while the other pair rested their heads on the table, passed out by all appearances. I took a moment to examine the group.

The four were players but too drunk to be much of a threat. Ignoring them, I strode up to the bar. The man behind it studied me intently, his eyes narrowing as I drew closer. A moment later, he gasped. He had analyzed me, I assumed.

"You!" he hissed. "What are you doing here? Didn't you see the noticeboard?"

I smiled. "Isn't this a *safe* zone?"

"That doesn't make it safe," he retorted. "You'll never make it out alive." Picking up an empty mug, the barkeeper—which is who I assumed he was— began scrubbing energetically at it.

"Maybe," I agreed. "But in the meantime... can I get a drink?"

My request seemed to flummox the bartender for a second, but then he nodded grudgingly and asked, "What will you have?"

I shrugged. "Your best ale." I sat down on one of the bar stools, only to realize I had no money on me. "Oh wait, how much is it gonna cost?"

The barkeeper eyed me for a moment, then snorted. "Seeing as how you're not long for this world, it's on the house." He paused. "The first one only. The rest are on you."

I grinned. "Thanks."

While he poured, I studied the barkeeper. He was a wisp-thin man with graying hair and dressed in simple cotton clothes. He wore no armor and carried no weapons. Not at all what I expected of a player, even one in a safe zone. Curiously, I analyzed him.

The target is Benadean, a human. He is a player and bears Marks of Lesser Dark, Shadow, and Light.

Interestingly, the Game revealed no information regarding the barkeeper's level. "What level are you?" I asked, deciding to be blunt.

Benadean looked up, one eyebrow raised. "You analyzed me?"

I nodded.

He sighed. "How did a newbie like you ever manage to offend Ishita?"

I blinked, nonplussed by his reply.

Benadean shook his head at my confusion. "*Everyone* knows civilians don't have player levels. You must be pretty green to have not caught on to that fact."

My lips turned down sourly. "Give me a break, will you? Let's just say I didn't have the best of mentors when I entered the Game. And I'm still new to this world."

The barkeeper bit the inside of the lip. "And yet you've already reached rank three," he murmured, more to himself than to me.

"What's a civilian?" I asked, ignoring his comment and steering the conversation back on course.

"Not all Classes in the Game are combat ones," Benadean replied, happy enough to educate me. "Some players decide to follow a more peaceful path. Admittedly, there aren't very many of us."

He means merchants and barkeepers, I thought, considering his response. "You get to choose three Classes though," I pointed out. "Didn't you want to choose at least one combat class?"

"Civilian Classes aren't like combat ones. They fill all three slots."

"Really?" I said. "That's interesting. How do civilians progress or grow stronger then?"

"We don't. Or not in the way you mean."

I frowned, at a loss as to why anyone would pick such a path.

Benadean chuckled. "Being a civilian isn't entirely without benefits, you know. We don't get stronger, but we can still learn skills and abilities, and unlike you combatants, we aren't limited by our attributes. Most of the Powers don't especially care for us. Still, enough of us have become mighty artists and crafters that we're tolerated."

"I see," I said, realizing that every merchant I'd met had also been a civilian.

"So, your life is what? Traveling from sector to sector, running a tavern?"

He shrugged. "Something like that."

"Isn't that... boring?"

Benadean shrugged. "Excitement is overrated. And besides, I've yet to meet a wealthy adventurer. Now, rich merchants... those I've met aplenty." He smiled, not unpleasantly. "You fighters risk death daily and, more often than not, struggle to rub two coins together. I, on the other hand, live comfortably and will likely live to a ripe old age—if not indefinitely." He plonked down a mug of ale in front of me. "Now tell me, whose path is better?"

I didn't answer, not wanting to concede the point. Bowing my head, I sipped on my drink. "I like it," I said in what was an obvious change of topic.

The barkeeper grunted. "That warms my heart."

I drank in silence for a bit before plumbing the barkeeper for more information. "Is there a bank around here?" I asked.

"A bank?"

"Yeah."

"Didn't you know?" Benadean said, sounding surprised. "This sector's aether coordinates are hidden and known only to the mages who control the portal. There is no bank access here. Or Nexus access, for that matter."

I looked up to stare at the barkeeper in astonishment. No bank? That meant I really was broke, not to mention the lack of access to banks, and the Nexus markets had to be a major inconvenience to the players here, yet they were still here... what was it about this sector? Why was it so important?

"I see," I said at last. "Anywhere I can trade then?"

Benadean looked at me pityingly. "Most of the players here are either part of the Awakened Dead faction or bound to them somehow. With the bounty Ishita's placed on you, the village's merchants won't sell you anything—even if you had coin."

My lips tightened, but I said nothing. I'd known expecting to resupply in the safe zone was a long shot.

"Although," the barkeeper said, reflecting further on his answer, "you might try the dark druid."

"Who?"

"Mariga. She owns the shop on the southern end of the village." He paused. "Be careful around her though. She is a bit... odd."

"Odd," I could manage. "Thank you," I said gravely. Setting down my empty mug, I stood up.

"Oh," I said, pausing as something else occurred to me. I didn't have many good options, leaving me with less wise ones.

Perhaps it was time to be foolish.

"Can you direct me to Gelar's shop too?"

Chapter 99: Square of Surprise

Leaving the tavern, I headed southeast. The streets were still empty, and much of the town lay in shadow. Gelar's shop was the closer of the two destinations I had in mind.

According to Benadean, Gelar was a gnomish alchemist and one of the village's most prosperous merchants. His shop was in the main market square and supposedly impossible to miss.

I found the square easily enough. If Benadean's information was accurate, the alchemist's place was the garishly painted log cabin directly across from me. But I paid it only passing notice, my attention captured by something else entirely.

In the center of the square, beneath a translucent dome of crimson, was a portal.

Two red-cloaked figures stood on either side of the shimmering curtain of light, one toying lazily with the staff in his hands. *Mages.* My steps slowed, and unconsciously I dropped into a crouch, marking the pair as Awakened Dead players.

Reaching out, I analyzed both.

The target is Ishan, a level 96 human. He is a player and bears a Mark of Minor Dark and a Mark of Ishita.

The target is Worca, an elf of indeterminant level. She is a player and bears a Mark of Greater Dark and a Mark of Ishita.

Sure enough, analyze confirmed my suspicions. My gaze fixated on the elf as I slipped into the shadows and padded closer.

You are now hidden.

"Indeterminant level," I murmured, my pulse quickening. The only other player my insight had failed to work on was Stayne.

Is the elf as strong? Surely not.

The pair hadn't spotted me yet. Despite obviously standing watch over the portal, the two sworn followers of Ishita were far from alert. Maybe it was their high ranks that made them complacent, or maybe it was because we were in a safe zone, but whatever the case, the two failed to react as I crept up on their flank until I was within a dozen feet of them.

Two hostile entities have failed to detect you! You have failed to advance your sneaking: skills cannot be gained in this area.

Their perception must be greatly lacking, I thought with a small grin. Pausing just outside the translucent dome, I stilled. I didn't know the shield's purpose and suspected I would alert the mages if I attempted to pass through.

Crouched down low, I patiently observed my targets. The pair didn't speak. The elf stood with admirable stillness, her eyes closed and her body not twitching in the slightest. I wondered if she was asleep.

Her human companion was not as restrained. He constantly fidgeted, shifting from foot to foot, rubbing bleary eyes and covering his mouth with his hand as he yawned.

The minutes ticked by, and still I didn't move. I wasn't sure what I hoped to achieve, but I recognized this as an unanticipated opportunity to observe my foes, and I wasn't about to let it pass unheeded.

"Where are they?" Ishan burst out nearly thirty minutes later. "Our shift ended ages ago."

Worca's eyes snapped open.

So, she wasn't asleep.

"Patience. They'll be here soon," she said, sounding exasperated. "Something must be keeping them."

"Something is always keeping them," Ishan grumbled. "I don't see—"

He broke off as the light emanating from the portal intensified.

"See," Worca said. "I told you they'd come."

"About god damn time," Ishan muttered.

Two bubbles of light exploded outward from the portal only to dissipate into nothingness a moment later, leaving another pair of red-cloaked mages standing in front of the gate.

I cast analyze on the newcomers.

The target is Lutra, a human of indeterminant level. He is a player and bears a Mark of Greater Dark and a Mark of Ishita.

The target is Xrex, a lizardman of indeterminant level. He is a player and bears a Mark of Supreme Dark and a Mark of Ishita.

I grimaced at the Adjudicator's feedback. I now had four of Ishita's followers to contend with, all likely too powerful for me to take on—even individually.

The lizardman turned to the two mages standing guard. "Anything to report?"

"No," Ishan replied. "It's been another wasted night."

"He will come," Xrex hissed. "Ishita is certain of it."

Ishan snorted.

The lizardman's red eyes narrowed at his companion's disdain, and he angrily admonished him. Meanwhile, the other newcomer began to look around disinterestedly. By a stroke of ill-fortune more than anything else, his gaze fell on where I was crouched.

Lutra has detected you! You are no longer hidden.

I bit back the urge to curse as the shadows around me fell away, revealing my crouched form. The gig was up. *And just when things were getting interesting too.* My gaze locked on the mage, I rose slowly to my feet.

Lutra's eyes rounded in shock, and he clutched at Xrex's sleeve. The lizardman didn't notice, too intent on scolding Ishan. Lutra tugged harder. "Xrex..." he began.

"What?" the other mage snapped, not turning around.

"He's here," Lutra said.

Xrex spun about, followed a moment later by Worca and Ishan.

I grinned wolfishly at the group, not letting any hint of my true feelings show. "Hello."

Four staffs were lowered my way, and a welter of emotions passed over the mages' faces. *Is that fear I sense?* My smile widened. Folding my arms, I waited for one of them to do something stupid.

Alas, not even the talkative Ishan was so foolish as to attack. Despite their high levels, the group appeared unduly wary. Just what had Ishita told them?

For a drawn-out moment, our standoff held. Then, predictably, it was broken by Ishan. "He's a mindstalker as well!" the mage hissed. "How can that be?"

"Quiet!" Xrex snapped.

My gaze sharpened at the human's phrasing. *What else do they know about me?* Ishan had obviously just analyzed me and read my Class and level. He had to know I was too low-ranked to pose a danger to the group.

So why doesn't he look reassured?

Maintaining my facade of disinterest, I raised a hand to run my fingers along the sides of the dome shielding the four and the portal they'd created. Not unexpectedly, I was repelled.

Entry denied! You don't possess the necessary access key to pass through this shield.

Lutra sneered at me. "You won't get through that easily."

I tilted my head to the side. "Why not?" I asked conversationally.

He opened his mouth to reply, but Xrex stomped his staff onto the ground before his companion could speak. The lizardman was the group's leader, it seemed. "What are you doing here, human?" Xrex demanded.

"Just checking out the competition," I replied lightly.

"Competition," Ishan spat. "You're no match for us!"

Obviously, whatever uneasiness the group felt around me was dissipating. "Shall we take a stroll through the forest then?" I suggested, baring my teeth.

"Anytime," Ishan growled. But despite the mage's sneering reply, I sensed a resurgence of uncertainty in his voice.

My show of confidence was working. Deciding to play on their fears further, I strolled around the dome. The four pivoted on their heels, tracking me.

"You should turn yourself in," Worca said suddenly. "It will be easier on you."

I laughed. "I doubt that. Your boss doesn't seem the forgiving type."

"Ishita is a goddess," Lutra said, his fingers tightening around his staff. "You *will* show her respect."

I rolled my eyes at the mage and kept circling. "Where does this go?" I asked.

No one answered.

"Why do the Awakened Dead want this valley?"

More silence.

I sighed. As amusing as this standoff was, it was going nowhere. I'd learned all I was going to. I spun on my heel and sprinted away. "Bye," I called mockingly over my shoulder.

"Follow him!" Xrex snapped.

Two sets of boots pounded after me. From the heaviness of the footsteps, I judged it to be the two humans. I wasn't worried. Constrained by the safe zone rules from using any magic that could be considered hostile, there was little chance the pair would catch me.

Sure enough, I quickly outdistanced them, and once out of their immediate sight I dropped into the shadows again.

You have successfully concealed yourself. Two hostile entities have failed to detect you!

Wedged in the dark and damp space between two log cabins, I watched the two mages pass by.

"How do you think he got past the Howlers?" I heard Ishan whisper.

"Snuck by probably," Lutra replied with a shrug. "But Worca will find out," he promised.

"She will," Ishan agreed.

A moment of drawn-out silence, then Ishan added, "This is useless. We're not going to find him this way."

"I think you're right," Lutra said, turning around. "Let's rouse the village. With everyone hunting him, he won't escape detection for long."

"Good idea," Ishan said, swinging around to fall in step with his companion.

I grimaced as I watched the two retreat. I had learned less of value than I liked, and I'd exposed my own presence in the process. While Ishita's sworn couldn't harm me in the safe zone, if I gave them enough time they could make leaving difficult, if not impossible.

My gaze drifted to the brightly painted building nearby—Gelar's shop. I'd deliberately fled in this direction.

I better finish what I need to do and get out quickly.

Chapter 100: Wheeling and Dealing

After the mages disappeared from view, I crouched outside the door to the alchemist's shop and knocked. In the distance, I could hear the four roving the streets and calling out to other players.

I knew Ishita's sworn and I weren't done yet, and the next time we met I likely wouldn't have the safe zone to protect me. When the time came, I'd have to be ready to face them. Raising my hand to the door, I knocked impatiently again. "Where is he?" I muttered.

I wasn't left wondering long.

My keen hearing picked out the patter of light feet approaching the door, and a second later it was yanked back.

You are no longer hidden.

A piercing gaze found mine, having no trouble picking me out in the darkness. "What?" the gnome snapped.

I blinked. Taken aback by the abruptness of the shopkeeper's greeting, I took a moment to study him before replying.

Gelar was short, and even with me crouched down we were at eye level. The gnome had a shock of red hair and wore thin, gold-rimmed spectacles. His clothes were rumpled as if he'd slept in them, and his fingers were stained.

"I'm here about the bounty," I said at last.

Gelar's eyes flicked beyond me. He must have heard the mages' cries already and likely guessed I was the one they were searching for. "Get in," he said abruptly, stepping aside to let me through.

I didn't argue and darted through the door. In contrast to the alchemist's own appearance, the shop was immaculate. A long table was set along the back wall and various ingredients were stacked on it, all neatly labeled. The left wall was covered with shelves stretching from floor to ceiling and stacked with ceramic and glass jars.

On the right was what was clearly a workspace. It contained a series of tables laid out with the alchemist's tools of the trade: test tubes, a mortar and pestle, burners, and oversized glass bottles.

The center of the shop was the only area free of any sign of the alchemist's craft. Striding toward the two large couches positioned there, Gelar sat down on one and pulled out a pipe. "Explain yourself," he said laconically.

While the gnome fiddled with his pipe, I sat on the opposite couch and analyzed him.

The target is Gelar, a gnome. He is a player and bears a Mark of Greater Dark.

The alchemist possessed only a single Mark and was surprisingly steeped in the Dark. *How does a civilian manage to become so deeply ingrained by a Force?* I wondered.

"If you're quite done analyzing me," Gelar said, not looking up, "answer the question." He finished lighting his pipe and met my gaze. "Or I will throw you out."

I pursed my lips, wondering if I'd made a mistake by coming here. On first impression, the gnome was unaffable and humorless. Still, I'd come this far, and I had nothing else to lose by going on. "It's like I said. I'm here for the bounty."

Gelar grunted. "And what makes you think I want, or even need, help from the likes of you?"

I raised an eyebrow in polite disbelief at his air of disinterest. He'd let me in, after all. "Because I'm guessing none of the other players in this sector have managed to complete the task yet."

Closing his eyes, Gelar leaned back in his chair and took a long, deep pull from his pipe. "You think you can succeed where they have failed?"

"I do." I didn't actually know that, of course, but this wasn't the time for expressing doubts.

The gnome puffed out three perfect circles. "How?"

"I have an unusual Class—" I began.

"Your psi won't help you against the wyvern," the alchemist said, cutting me off. "The bitch will be immune to your mind tricks."

"I know," I said, even as I wondered how the shopkeeper knew I possessed psi.

My response seemed to give Gelar pause. "You do?"

I nodded. "I've run across her hatchling already." Deciding to stretch the truth a bit, I added, "and killed it."

The gnome's eyes snapped open to scrutinize me. "You lie," he said mildly.

I shook my head. "I don't."

Gelar's eyes narrowed. "Where are your scars? If you'd been in a fight with a wyvern—even a babe—you wouldn't have walked away unscathed."

I shook my head ruefully. "I didn't." Reaching into my potion belt, I removed my last full healing flask and held it up. "I bear no wounds because of these."

Gelar leaned forward and intently studied the item in my hand before grunting dismissively. "Bah, that wouldn't have stopped—"

"—the wyvern's toxins from killing me," I finished for him. "I know. I also have other resources at my disposal," I said, not elaborating.

The gnome sat back and, drumming his fingers on the side of his chair, considered me. "Even assuming I believe you," he said at last, "you're too low-leveled to tackle the wyvern mother."

I smiled. "I might surprise you. And besides, what do you have to lose?"

Unexpectedly, Gelar chuckled. "Good point. Very well, I accept. You have my permission to attempt the bounty." Reaching into his chest, the alchemist withdrew a piece of paper and handed it over to me.

I took it curiously, not sure of its purpose.

"Shut the door on your way out," the gnome said. Seeming to consider our business concluded, he rose to his feet and ambled over to his worktable.

Not moving from my seat, I scanned the slip of parchment Gelar had handed me.

You have acquired a bounty authorization letter. This bounty is for the death of the wyvern-mother, a level 198 beast in sector 12,560. This bounty has been registered with the bounty hunters' guild, and the bearer of this letter is an authorized agent of the bounty holder, Gelar.

Proof of death can be provided directly to the holder or any guild office, and payment is guaranteed by the guild. This bounty claim is open to both guild members and non-members.

The Adjudicator has allocated you a new task: <u>An Alchemist's Bounty</u>! The alchemist, Gelar, has granted you permission to hunt down the wyvern mother. Objective: kill the level 198 wyvern in sector 12,560.

Folding away the letter, I placed it in my pocket. It had almost no details regarding the beast other than its level—which was scary enough, admittedly—and while I found mention of the bounty hunter guild intriguing, it wasn't a matter I wanted to pursue just yet. "Why do you want the wyvern dead?" I asked slowly.

"That's no concern of yours," Gelar said, not turning around. I thought I detected a hint of tightness in his voice though.

I looked around the room. "Is it for the ingredients?"

"No," the alchemist replied curtly. "But now that you mention it, those will be useful." He turned around, eyeing me. "Do you have the poisoning skill?"

I shook my head.

"Pity," he said, sounding disappointed. "You could have extracted the wyvern's toxins then. It would have made for a nice bonus."

I pursed my lips. "How much does it sell for?"

"Wyvern toxin?"

I nodded.

"Depending on the purity and the amount you manage to extract, anywhere between ten and twenty gold."

I whistled appreciatively. "Why so much?"

"It's a versatile substance and a key ingredient in many elixirs, including some powerful antitoxins and, as you know already, it makes for a virulent toxin in its natural form."

I couldn't argue with that. "Is there any other way to extract the venom?"

"You could try extracting it without the skill, I suppose, but that would prove challenging and could prove fatal. Or..." He eyed me doubtfully.

"Or?" I prompted.

"Or you could employ an alchemy stone. It's a magical device experienced hunters use to harvest alchemy ingredients when no alchemist is available."

My eyes lit up. That sounded like just what I needed. "Do you have one?"

Gelar nodded. "I do." He paused. "But it's expensive."

"How much?"

"Fifty gold."

I winced at the cost. That was more than any single item I possessed.

Gelar sighed. "I can see from your expression that it's more than you can afford. Now, if you can stop disturbing me and let me get—"

"I don't have the money," I said, cutting him off, "but I may have something of equal value to trade."

The gnome eyed me curiously. "What?"

I hesitated. I only had two items that were possibly of comparable value... spider's bite and the blood siphon master Class stone. I was loath to part with either, but without access to a bank, I knew I'd have to part with something. *But which?*

The stone, I decided. Spider's bite's value was more than monetary at the moment. It was my best weapon and irreplaceable, especially if I planned on farming the forest for alchemy ingredients. The blood siphon Class stone, on the other hand, was a stone I still had no intention of using.

Removing the Class stone from my pocket, I placed it on the table next to the gnome. The blood siphon Class contained two master skills—leech and life resistance—which I knew from the purchase of my own deception skill had to be worth at least twenty gold each, and perhaps even more to some Dark players.

Gelar examined the item closely. "It's not enough," he pronounced a moment later.

I deflated.

"But," he allowed, "it's close enough." He held out a hand. "We have a deal, human."

✳ ✳ ✳

A few minutes later, Gelar held out a nondescript green cube for my inspection. It was no larger than the palm of my hand and seemed to have been cut from a greenish stone. "That's an alchemy stone?" I asked skeptically.

"Take it," Gelar said.

Reaching out, I did as he bade.

You have acquired a small alchemy stone. This item contains an enchantment to extract and store common, uncommon, and rare alchemical ingredients from slain creatures. This item only works on animal lifeforms and cannot be used to obtain materials from plant life.

The enchantment can be replenished with mana. Currently stored ingredients: 0 / 150.

"The stone's capacity is small, and it is limited in what ingredients it can harvest," Gelar said, confirming what I'd just learned, "but it will more than suffice for a player of your level."

"How do I use it?" I asked.

"You only need to place it on a dead beast, and the stone will collect what it can. It will harvest less than an alchemist is capable of, and it will not work on plant life, so don't try," he warned. "Even my apprentice—"

He broke off, and a look of fleeting pain crossed his face too quickly for me to be certain I'd seen it.

Unsure what the look meant, I simply nodded.

"Ingredients stored in the stone will last indefinitely, so there's no need to hurry back," Gelar went on, his face smooth and unruffled once more. "As for extracting the stored substances, any alchemist should be able to do that."

"Thank you," I said, hoping I'd chosen wisely in buying the stone.

"Now, if there's nothing else?" Gelar asked in what was clearly a dismissal.

"One last thing," I said, holding out the bounty letter. The gnome must know who I was, yet he still felt comfortable dealing with me. I had to understand why. "Aren't you afraid of running afoul of Ishita's sworn by giving me this?"

"Bah," Gelar spat. "What do I care for Ishita's servants? As for the Power herself, she understands well enough that business is business." His lips widened into a smile that didn't reach his eyes. "Besides, I haven't done anything to help you escape her clutches. The spider goddess will not fault me for pursuing my own goals, not if they don't harm her own interests."

An unpleasant glint appeared in his eyes. "No matter how much gold you have in your pocket, you are still stuck in this sector. Now go!"

CHAPTER 101: THE SECOND OFFER

I chewed over the alchemist's words as I slipped out of his cabin. I couldn't fault his logic, even if it left a bitter taste in my mouth. *He was only half-right,* I thought. Gold in and of itself wouldn't let me escape the region, but it would certainly make acquiring the means to do so easier.

Ducking into the shadows still around the square—there were noticeably fewer of them now—I surveyed the village.

More players were out and about. Most seemed to be searching for me in a lackluster fashion. Some, though, moved around in organized bands.

I hesitated, torn between leaving immediately or continuing onward to my next destination. But once I left, I was uncertain if I would be able to return. *Best to visit the dark druid now,* I thought. Moving cautiously, I made my way south through the village.

It took me longer than I liked and more than one detour, but eventually I reached the cabin Benadean had indicated. Thankfully it was on the outskirts of the village and in a less-trafficked region. Even the search parties were less numerous here.

✳ ✳ ✳

Outside the door, I paused.

Benadean's words had painted an interesting picture of the dark druid. Mariga's cabin, set far away from the rest of the village, almost as if shunned, gave further credence to the barkeeper's tale. Wondering what it was about the druid that perturbed the other players, I raised my hand and knocked softly.

There was no answer.

After a long minute, I knocked again. Again, no one answered.

Just as I began to wonder if I was wasting my time, the door opened.

"Go away," an unseen voice hissed from inside.

I frowned. My night vision was fully active, but I couldn't penetrate the gloom of the cabin. Squinting, I peered harder.

You have failed a Perception check! A veil of darkness has foiled your night vision. Your attempt has been detected!

There was a moment of startled silence during which I felt myself being re-examined—minutely.

"My, my, what a day it is for strange visitors," the voice chuckled. "Now you have me curious. Come on in."

Uh... I puzzled over the speaker's words but couldn't make sense of them.

"Well?" the voice prompted.

Warily, I stepped inside. "I can't see..." I began.

A veil of darkness has been lifted.

My words ran aground as the darkness receded, revealing a thin lizard woman standing in front of me. The Dark druid?

Unlike the other lizardmen players I'd encountered, Mariga's body and limbs were slimmer, almost shrunken by comparison. She lacked a tail too.

I frowned. Was the druid starved or crippled in some way?

Mariga's snout was shorter and her face flat. Her skin was also strange. Where the scales of someone like Xrex were dull and lifeless, hers glistened with an inner radiance.

Beginning to suspect my initial assessment was wrong, I reached out and analyzed the druid.

You have failed a Perception check and are unable to analyze your target. This entity bears a Mark of Greater Dark.

"And here I thought you were a polite boy," Mariga said, hissing in displeasure.

I bowed. "You'll have to forgive me, but you don't look like any lizardfolk I've encountered before. I was only trying to identify your species." I paused, then forged on bluntly, "What are you?"

"Rude and ignorant," Mariga remarked, ignoring my question entirely. But despite her words, the dark druid didn't kick me out as I half-expected. "Come sit," she said. "Let's talk."

I moved toward the chair she indicated, but as I was about to sit down, I paused as something else occurred to me. "You are Mariga, right? The dark druid?"

My host chuckled. "I am," she said, confirming her identity as she glided to a stop in front of me.

I couldn't see her feet, they were hidden by the voluminous black robes covering her form, but now I doubted she had any. *She's more snake than lizard,* I thought. *A snake-woman?*

"Now sit," she commanded.

I sat.

Mariga didn't join me in sitting, I noted. "So," she said after a long moment of silence spent examining me, "you are the one who's got them in such a bother."

I stared at her. "Who?"

She smiled. "The Powers. Erebus for one," she said, ticking off points on her fingers. "Ishita for another. Artem makes three and Loken four."

My eyes narrowed. "You seem well informed."

"Oh, I know lots of things," she said airily.

"So, which one do you serve?" I asked, casually dropping my hands.

The move didn't go unnoticed.

"Oh, you have no need of your weapons, dear boy," Mariga said. "I'm no enemy of yours. Trust me."

I didn't, not in the least. I smiled without conviction. "I don't."

The druid laughed, the sound a hissing gurgle. "I don't blame you. Trapped in Erebus' and Ishita's web all this time, it's a wonder you haven't been more deeply infected by the Dark." Before I could respond to that, she went on, "But as surprising as I find your presence here, I'm glad for it."

I eyed her suspiciously. "Glad?"

"I could use your help," she said. "As could my mistress."

"Your mistress?" I asked, feeling lost by the abrupt swings in the conversation.

"Haven't you guessed? I serve Artem."

"I see," I said, recalling that was the name of one of the Powers whose attention I had attracted in the dungeon.

"I'm here at her behest," the druid added.

I wasn't sure I believed her, but she knew more about me than she had any right to and seemed to practice deception nearly as effortlessly as Hamish. I could easily imagine her as an agent of Shadow. What I didn't know was why Shadow would seek me out after I had shunned it. "Why?" I asked.

"To look out for you, for one. And to halt the Awakened Dead's machinations."

"And what are those exactly?" I asked. "Why do Erebus and Ishita want this sector so badly?"

Mariga expelled a breath. "*That*, I don't know. Yet. But I intend on finding out, and with your help, maybe I can do that sooner."

"So, is this another recruiting attempt? I'll warn you, Loken failed at that already."

"Oh no, dear boy. I won't try that. I judge you to be too cynical for my mistress' taste, but I do have a task for you. It involves—"

"I'm not interested," I said, cutting in. "I'm only here to find out how to get out of the sector."

Mariga hissed again.

She was laughing, I realized. "What's so funny?"

"Well, it just so happens I have the means for you to escape." Pulling out a scroll, she said, "I managed to sneak this through the portal when I arrived."

Curiously, I analyzed the item in her hand.

This is a portal scroll. This item allows a spellcaster to open a portal for a single player to any sector's safe zone known by the caster. This item requires a minimum Magic of 20 to use.

My gaze flew up to meet Mariga's.

"Yes," she said, seeing understanding dawn in my eyes. "I can get you out."

But you'll only do that for a price. "Why do you need my help?" I asked. "You seem more than capable enough."

Mariga sighed. "Because I can't leave the safe zone."

I looked at her blankly.

"Only followers of the Awakened Dead Powers may come and go as they please in this sector. As for the rest of us, the goblins manning the fort have been instructed to allow only low-leveled players outside the village—writ or no writ—and whatever is going on in this sector, the answers won't be found here but out there."

"So that's why the Erebus and Ishita have allowed the Howlers to close off the village," I murmured.

She nodded.

"But why did they let you into the sector in the first place?"

"Because, as much as Erebus and those other Awakened Dead fools may pretend otherwise, they aren't the only Powers among the Dark. Others in the Dark grow suspicious of what the Awakened Dead do here. They have demanded access for our representatives and, for now, remain content with the limitations Erebus has imposed in granting that access."

"But you serve Shadow," I protested.

Mariga hissed in amusement. "The Awakened Dead do not know that. My deception is high enough to hide my true allegiances from their minions here."

"You have the deception skill?" I asked sharply.

Mariga laughed again. "Yes. Just like you. Congratulations on acquiring it, by the way. It is not easily obtainable. Loken helped you with that, did he?"

I nodded slowly, my head bursting with all the information Mariga had dumped on me. I still didn't trust her, but what she said made sense, and if she really had a way out of this sector for me, could I ignore it?

I sat back in my chair and folded my arms. "Why should I believe you?"

She shrugged. "Believe me or not, I don't care. But if you want my help getting out, then you will aid me with my own mission."

I sighed. It seemed like no one in this world did anything without expecting something in return. "What do you want?"

"I want you to get rid of the goblin tribes."

I blinked. "What? All of them?" I asked jokingly.

"Yes," she said.

I stared at her. There was no hint of mockery or amusement on her face. "You're serious? You want me to get rid of the Howlers, Long Fangs, *and* the Red Rats?"

She nodded.

"If the Red Rats are anything like the Howlers in size and—"

"They are," she interjected.

"Then how in hells do you expect me to get rid of two thousand goblins?"

The dark druid shrugged her delicate shoulders. "I don't know." She stroked her leathery chin with one long clawed hand and stared unblinkingly at me. "But I'm dying to find out. I've been told to expect great things from you, and I think this is a suitable challenge to test your mettle."

"Told? By whom?"

She waved aside my question. "Maybe I'll tell you *if* you do as I ask." She paused and looked down her snout at me. "Will you?"

I ground my teeth together. Dealing with the minions of Shadow seemed like nothing more than an exercise in frustration. "How does getting rid of the goblins help you figure out what Erebus is up to?"

"It doesn't, but I don't need to know what Erebus is after to stop him. It is obvious the Awakened Dead want—no need—the goblins here. And that is reason enough for me to want to make them go away."

She was asking for a lot more than for me to "make them go away." Still, I didn't think I had much choice in the matter. I stared at Mariga for a moment. "I will accept the task," I said finally, "but I can't promise I'll be able to fulfill it."

The druid nodded solemnly. "That will suffice for now."

On the tail end of her words, a message dropped in my mind.

The Adjudicator has allocated you a new task: <u>Goblin Wars</u>! Eradicate the delegations of all three goblin tribes in the sector. Objective 1: destroy the Howlers' delegation. Objective 2: destroy the Red Rats' delegation. Objective 3: destroy the Long Fangs' delegation.

"Now," I said. "Do you have anything to sell?"

✳   ✳   ✳

The dark druid didn't stock many items, and the ones she did keep were mostly magic-focused. However, she did have a few deception ability tomes on sale.

Facial disguise spellbook. Governing attribute: Perception. Tier: basic. Cost: 10 gold. Requirement: rank 1 deception.

Ventro spellbook. Governing attribute: Perception. Tier: basic. Cost: 10 gold. Requirement: rank 1 deception.

Simple Parrot spellbook. Governing attribute: Perception. Tier: basic. Cost: 10 gold. Requirement: rank 1 deception.

Lesser Imitate spellbook. Governing attribute: Perception. Tier: advanced. Cost: 20 gold. Requirement: rank 5 deception.

Reading the titles of the four spellbooks, I itched to pick them up and devour their knowledge, but they were so far out of my reach. "Why so expensive?" I asked.

"Expensive?" Mariga's forked tongue slipped out to lick her snout. "This sector is in the middle of nowhere. I had to travel through multiple portals to get here. Not to mention all the trouble I had to go through to lug around the damn books myself, which I was forced to do without access to the Nexus." She shrugged. "Sorry, but I have to cover my expenses somehow."

I sighed. "So you won't go cheaper?"

"I won't."

"What about a... loan?"

A derisive snort was my only response.

Regretfully, I turned away from the books. *Perhaps I shouldn't have traded the siphon Class stone so quickly.* "Well then, I better be going."

"I look forward to your return," she called after me as I headed for the door. "And to the success of your mission."

I didn't respond.

CHAPTER 102: THE TARTAN LEGION

DAY THREE. MORNING.

Outside the door of Mariga's cabin, I dropped back into stealth, concealing myself in the porch's dimness.

Benadean had been right.

The dark druid was odd, and although I didn't trust her entirely, I thought she'd been honest about her aims. She had been hard to read, but I was sure she hadn't lied about wanting to rid the valley of the goblin tribes.

If I give her what she wants, maybe I'll get what I need in return.

Either way, it was time for me to leave the safe zone. I'd done what I'd come here for and still had lots to do before my Pact with Erebus expired in the next five days. I didn't have a concrete plan to escape the sector yet—or to rid it of one goblin tribe, much less three—but I had learned all I could in the safe zone, and it was time to get started on my tasks.

Turning my attention outward, I scanned the empty streets. This village quarter was still quiet, but the surroundings had brightened considerably. Once I left the porch, I wouldn't be able to stay hidden. And if I moved through the more trafficked areas of the settlement, I was sure to be spotted.

So what?

The players hunting me couldn't harm me in the village, and once I was through the Howler's fort, I was confident I could lose anyone still on my trail.

I slipped off Mariga's porch, and immediately the shadows concealing me fell away.

Two neutral entities have detected you! You are no longer hidden.

My gaze whipped to my left, sensing two figures watching me from that direction. A moment later, my tension dissipated as I recognized the pair.

It was Ultack and Cecilia.

I rose slowly from my crouch and padded softly toward the pair. "What are you doing here?"

"Looking for you," Cecilia said.

"The captain wants to speak to you," Ultack added.

My face expressionless, I studied him. "And why would I want to see your captain?"

Ultack opened his mouth to respond, but before he could speak, Cecilia interrupted. "It's not safe here," she said, her eyes darting left and right. "We can talk back at our base."

Still, I hesitated.

"We mean you no harm," Ultack said. "And the captain won't keep you long, I promise."

I jerked my head. "Alright. I'll come. Lead on."

                                 *   *   *

The pair cut a snaking path through the village, taking pains to avoid the main routes through the settlement. They weren't alone in their efforts to shepherd me either.

On multiple occasions, I spotted other players waving them on or warning them off. Some I remembered from the party I had rescued in the forest. Others were completely unrecognizable.

Eventually, we halted outside a long, low-lying building on the western end of the village. It was a barracks of some kind, I thought. Without pausing, Cecilia ducked in through the door. Ultack and I followed on her heels.

Inside, I found myself in an open hall. The room was full of players. Most stood to attention and looked alert, gripping their weapons.

Cecilia made for the center of the room and the most commanding figure in the hall. My own gaze was drawn to him too.

The player in question was a weather-beaten man dressed in full plate mail. His armor was scratched and worn in places but cared for nonetheless, like a favorite coat. He was well-groomed with a neat beard and closely cropped hair. His right hand rested on the hilt of a jeweled sword, and his left toyed with a piece of parchment.

This must be the captain. He appeared to be a man who spent more time on the battlefield than of it.

Three yards away from the waiting officer, Ultack and Cecilia stopped. The elven mage glanced at me and gestured for me to go on. My audience with the captain was to be a private one, it seemed.

The officer's gaze never left my own as I strode closer. Curious, I reached out and analyzed him.

The target is Talon, a human of indeterminant level. He is a player and bears a Mark of Supreme Dark and a Mark of Tartar.

I clenched my jaw to disguise my unease. Like Ishita's sworn, the captain's level was hidden. More worryingly, he bore an unexpected Mark.

Tartar. Who was that? It seemed likely he was another Dark Power. *Is he hunting me too?* Probably.

"Michael," Talon said. "We meet at last." Like the rest of him, the captain's voice was gravelly and well-worn.

I drew to a halt in front of the captain but didn't return his greeting. "What do you want?"

Talon ignored my brusqueness and continued speaking with a mildness that was in itself a rebuke. "When I heard Erebus was hunting a novice player, I thought the rumors false." He opened his clenched fist, revealing Ishita's bounty notice. "Then I read this and my curiosity grew. What, I wondered, could the two Powers want with you?"

He smiled. "But seeing you now, I begin to divine the source of their interest." His gaze roved over me. "A mindstalker. How fascinating."

I fought to keep my face smooth and unruffled, but I couldn't stop my eyes darting sideways, wondering who else had overheard the captain's words.

Talon looked amused by my reaction. "Don't worry," he said. "We are surrounded by a privacy shield. No one can hear us."

I concealed my relief and turned my attention back to the captain. "How do you know my Class?" That he had a superior form of my own analyze was obvious, but I wasn't certain which one he'd used on me.

Talon's lips turned upward. "You are still untutored in the Game, I see."

I scowled.

"I don't mean that as an insult," he said before I could speak. "It's simply the truth." He paused, then answered my question without any trace of animosity. "Any player with improved analyze can perceive your Class."

"Improved analyze?"

"It's a rank five ability," the captain said.

I pursed my lips. "I see." That put the captain's level much higher than my own. Once again, it seemed I was outclassed. I eyed him again. He watched, patiently waiting for me to go on.

For whatever reason, the Dark player appeared receptive to my questions. "What do you know about mindstalkers?" I asked, seeing no reason not to take advantage of his willingness to answer my queries.

The captain shrugged. "Not as much as I'd like," he admitted. "It's an advanced Class, and not one achievable without a bloodline."

My ears perked up, noticing the curious emphasis he placed on the word "bloodline."

He tilted his head and looked at me curiously. "Which one do you possess?"

I was certain I knew the answer to that already, but I wasn't about to share the information with him, no matter how helpful he was being. I gave him a shrug of my own and changed the topic. "Why can't I see your level?"

Talon's smile widened at my evasion, but he didn't remark on it, nor did he refuse to answer my question. "You used basic analyze on me?"

I nodded.

"Then the answer is simple. Basic analyze is limited to discerning entities below rank ten. It won't work on anyone of higher rank."

So he's more than three times my level.

I grimaced as I grasped the full implications of that. "Why am I here?" I asked finally, voicing my most burning question.

"I brought you here to warn you," Talon said.

"Warn me?"

"Ishita's people are hunting—"

I waved my hand negligently through the air. "I know that already."

Talon held my gaze. "And did you know they are in the Howlers' fort right now, planning to ambush you?"

I stilled. "You're sure?"

He nodded.

I cursed softly. I should have left when I had the chance. My mind raced, wondering what awaited me in the fort. How many players had Ishita's mages gathered for their ambush? And where exactly had they positioned themselves?

The players, though, weren't my biggest concern. The goblins were.

I'd already proven I could hide from Ishita's mages, but the Howlers' soldiers were too vigilant for my liking, and if the tribe had been placed on alert, there was no way I was going to sneak through the fort.

"The Howlers will not interfere," Talon said, seeming to follow the direction of my thoughts.

I broke off from my musings and scrutinized him intently. "Why not?"

"You bear a writ of safe passage," Talon said. "The Howlers are bound to honor it." He smiled. "And I've taken the liberty of reiterating to their shaman the consequences of not doing so. The Dark Powers do not look kindly upon those who fail to hold to their bargains, regardless of extenuating circumstances."

I blinked. "Thank you," I said grudgingly. "Not that I'm ungrateful, but why would—"

"Because you interest me," the captain said, interrupting me. "And because... I want something from you," he admitted.

CHAPTER 103: WHAT THE DARK WANTS

"I see," I said, unsurprised. Given all the trouble Talon had gone to, the least I could do was to hear him out. "Go on."

The captain did not respond immediately. Placing his hands behind his back, the Dark player paced back and forth. From the length of his laps, I gathered the privacy ward surrounding us was less than two yards in diameter.

Curiously, I looked around, trying to catch a glimpse of the shield itself but failed to spot any sign of it. Beyond the captain, I saw Ultack, Cecilia, and the other players watching us avidly.

"The Dark is not united."

I turned back to see that Talon had come to a halt before me, his brown eyes serious.

Seeing he had my attention, the captain went on, "There are many factions within the Dark. Erebus' faction, the Awakened Dead, is one. My master, the god-emperor, leads another."

I nodded slowly, beginning to realize where he was going with this.

"This valley was discovered years ago by scouts of a minor Dark faction," Talon continued. "The Awakened Dead requested rights to the region which, given the rumored remoteness of the valley, the other Powers in the Dark did not hesitate to agree to."

The captain sighed. "That decision proved shortsighted. Soon after gaining access to the valley, Erebus' people discovered it held an entrance— the very same nether portal you emerged from—to an unexplored region of the Nethersphere, one that connects with our other underground sectors." He snapped his fingers. "That quickly, the importance of this valley was elevated."

"I'm not sure I understand," I said slowly.

"This sector has the potential to become one of the Dark's main arteries into the Nethersphere, providing as it does a safe supply route."

I frowned. "Safe how?"

"Simply put, this valley is a closed sector, making recapturing it once it is claimed supremely difficult. Even better, the valley's location is presently hidden. It can't remain that way forever, naturally, but while it is we don't need to fear someone ambushing our supply lines," Talon explained. "And given how paranoid Ishita is about protecting the valley's location, it is likely to remain hidden for much longer," he grimaced. "Currently, the sector's aether coordinates are unknown not just to the Forces of the Light and Shadow, but also to anyone in the Dark not belonging to the Awakened Dead."

"How's that possible?" I interjected. "Didn't you say another faction found it?"

The captain's lips turned down. "The original faction that discovered the valley was wiped out soon thereafter—supposedly by a faction of Light, but no evidence of that was ever found, nor incidentally any record of the valley's coordinates."

I digested that, suspecting foul play as Talon clearly did. "Why does the Dark need to use the Game's portals to teleport supplies into the Nethersphere anyway? Surely you can create a player portal to do that more efficiently?"

"Ah," the captain breathed. "That's where you're wrong. While the aether and nether realms appear to be a singular whole that is the Forever Kingdom, they are in many ways *two* separate worlds—ones that even the Powers struggle to bridge."

My face scrunched up in confusion, having difficulty following the captain's explanation.

Seeing this, the captain tried again. "Let me try putting it another way. Player-made portals cannot be opened between Nethersphere and Kingdom sectors. Only nether portals provide direct access between the two, the only exception being the conduit merchants used to transport goods to and from the Nexus and its banks—and those are limited in capacity and what they can convey." He paused. "Do you understand the valley's importance now?"

I nodded. I thought I did. All along, I'd believed the same set of rules governed the Nethersphere and Kingdoms, but the reality seemed more complicated than that.

If this valley really is one of the few connections between the Nethersphere and Kingdoms, I can see why the Awakened Dead want it so much.

"Needless to say," Talon continued, "owning one of the Dark's supply routes into the Nethersphere has increased the prestige of the Awakened Dead, and in recent years Erebus' power has grown by leaps and bounds. So when it came to the matter of how to claim and secure this sector, it was only natural that the Awakened Dead were the ones appointed to head up the task."

I stared at him. "Let me guess... it was another mistake?"

Talon nodded sadly. "It was Erebus' idea to use the wild goblin tribes as the mainstay of the forces fortifying the valley. That wasn't a bad idea in and of itself," the captain admitted. "But the wild tribes have always been notoriously willful, which is why they've been largely ignored by the organized armies of Light and Dark. But when the Awakened Dead managed to convince two of the biggest tribes to send delegations to the valley, things looked promising. Sadly though, even after years, negotiations with the Howlers, the Red Rats, and more recently the Long Fangs have come to nothing."

"And you believe what? That Erebus is deliberately stalling the negotiations?" I asked.

The captain nodded slowly, displaying the first signs of uncertainty I'd seen.

"Why?" I asked, frowning. "How would that serve him?"

"That's what I don't know."

"But you don't trust Erebus?" I asked—not that I blamed him, knowing what I knew of the Power.

The captain snorted. "My master does not," he said bluntly. "Erebus is unscrupulous. Tartar and others among the Dark worry that the Awakened Dead plan on betraying them somehow."

"So, what's stopping you from finding out?" I glanced around the full hall. "It doesn't seem like your master lacks power of his own."

Talon laughed. "Oh, the god-emperor's legions are vast. The Awakened Dead will not last long against us if it comes to open war. Erebus knows this too." The captain sighed again. "But matters are rarely so simply resolved. If Tartar moves against Erebus without evidence, there will be consequences." He glanced at me. "While the threat of my master's wrath was enough to gain us access to this sector, I can only push so far. Neither I nor my people can investigate this matter as freely as I wish."

"And that's why you need my help?"

"It is," the captain agreed. "My company is confined to the safe zone. Erebus will not let us out, and I cannot force him to do so. Yet."

My gaze flickered to Cecilia and Ultack. They had been outside the safe zone and clearly were under Talon's command.

Following the direction of my gaze, the captain answered my unvoiced question. "Cecilia's squad are recruits for the Tartan legion. As yet, they are unsworn and unmarked by the god-emperor. That is the only reason they have been allowed out of the safe zone."

He grimaced. "I've been forced to rely on mere recruits, and you've seen for yourself how well that has gone." He pierced me with his gaze. "You, on the other hand, seem more capable of moving through the wilds and are, shall we say, less restrained in how you can tackle the problem."

He obviously didn't know about my non-aggression Pact with Erebus, and I didn't see a need to inform him about it. "Tell me what you want from me." I paused. "And what's in it for me."

Talon smiled. "I want you to secure the allegiance of the Howlers and the Red Rats. Failing that, I'll settle for you uncovering Erebus' motives."

My brows furrowed. "What about the Long Fangs?"

The captain snorted dismissively. "The Long Fangs are a minor tribe and of little value to the Dark. I have no idea why Erebus brought them here. I do not care about them, and neither does my master."

I nodded. "Assuming by some miracle I can achieve what you ask for, what do I receive in return?"

Talon's grin widened. "You want out of the sector, don't you?"

I just stared at him, neither denying nor agreeing with his statement.

When I failed to respond, the captain went on. "Regretfully, I don't have the means to smuggle you out, not directly. *But* I can offer you something better." He paused. "Will the god-emperor's protection do?"

"Protection?" I asked sharply. "What need do I have of your master's protection?"

Talon's grin faded. "You need it more than you know," he said softly. "Ishita is vindictive. She will not stop pursuing you even if you escape the sector. If you wish to survive, you'll grasp this opportunity while it exists. Only Tartar can stop Ishita from hunting you. No one else possesses that power."

"And your master will go to all the trouble? For me?"

"You will have to swear yourself to him," Talon conceded. "But unlike Erebus, Tartar is particular about those he allows to serve him. It's a great privilege. If you succeed at the task I've set you, he will permit you that honor." He glanced searchingly at me. "Will you do it?"

I said nothing for a moment. I had two tasks already, and this one directly contradicted the dark druid's mission. Still, there was no upside to rejecting the captain's offer. Meeting his gaze, I gave him the same noncommittal response I had Mariga. "I can't promise anything, but I will investigate further."

"That's all I ask," he said. "Thank you."

Tartar has allocated you a new task: <u>Forging Dark Alliances</u>! The Power has tasked you with assisting his representatives in establishing an alliance with the goblin tribes. Objective one: conclude an alliance between the Dark and the Howlers. Objective two: conclude an alliance between the Dark and the Red Rats. Optional objective: uncover the Awakened Dead's plans.

I gasped as I read the message's contents. At my sharp intake of breath, the captain looked at me inquiringly.

"I received a task," I explained. I paused before going on. "It says it's directly from Tartar...?" I left the question hanging in the air.

"That's correct," the captain said, nodding.

"How is that possible?" I exclaimed, my eyes widening. "The only way I could receive a task directly from Tartar is if you were—"

The captain laughed, interrupting me. "Forgive my amusement, but no, I am not Tartar. I am his envoy."

I blinked. "What's an envoy?"

Talon smiled. "An envoy is a trusted representative of a Power, one who speaks with their voice. As such, I can grant some tasks and even accept minor Pacts on my master's behalf."

"I see," I said, not knowing what else to say. I turned around. I had wasted enough time in the safe zone, and it was time to leave.

"Oh, one more thing," the captain said, stopping me. "Two, actually."

I raised one eyebrow in silent inquiry.

"Cecilia's squad wasn't the only one I sent into the valley," he said. "I dispatched another team north to the Red Rats. They still haven't returned. If you happen to spot any sign of them on your travels, I would be grateful."

I nodded. "I'll do what I can."

Talon hesitated, then added. "Please, this is important. The squad leader, Sturm... is my son."

My brows rose. "Your son? How is that possible?"

The captain chuckled. "What? You don't think players can have children?"

I shook my head. "No, I mean—"

Talon waved a hand, cutting me off. "I understand what you mean. Sturm is a player too. Not all players enter the Game from elsewhere, you know. Some—albeit very few—are born in this world. Sometimes the offspring of two players will be transformed into a player by the Adjudicator when they reach adulthood. It doesn't always happen though. But, when it does, the family considers themselves blessed."

I nodded thoughtfully. There was more of a future for players in this world than I'd first realized. "I'll keep an eye out for him," I assured the captain.

"Thank you. Sturm *is* a player, so I'm sure he's fine. Still, his absence is... troubling." Talon shook himself, dismissing his worries. "Now, to the last matter. The nature of your reward."

I stared at him in confusion. "Reward?"

He smiled. "For saving Cecilia's squad."

"I don't need—"

"I insist," the captain said. "What will it be? I have knives, swords, weapons aplenty, but sadly no spellbooks. I also have—"

"Money," I said, cutting him off.

The captain frowned at me. "Money?"

I bobbed my head. "Gold. As much as you're willing to give." I smiled. "Or as much as you value the lives of your people."

Talon's frown deepened. "Money," he muttered. "I didn't take you for a mercenary." Despite his words though, the captain reached into his pocket and pulled out a pouch. "Here, take it. It's all I have." He threw it at me with more force than strictly necessary.

You have acquired a coin pouch.

I caught it deftly and inclined my head gratefully. "Thank you," I said gravely and, without bothering to count the coin, turned around and dashed out of the room.

CHAPTER 104: A HOWLIN MESS

After leaving the Tartan legion's barracks, I retraced my steps to the dark druid's cabin. On the way there, I counted the coin in the money pouch. There was over twenty gold in it.

You have acquired 24 gold, 0 silver, and 9 copper coins.

I could barely contain my elation. It was enough to buy two of the ability tomes I had seen in Mariga's shop.

Reaching her cabin, I knocked furiously until she let me in. "Did you forget something?" she hissed.

Ignoring the sarcasm lacing her voice, I shook my head. "I'm here to buy one of your spellbooks."

Mariga's forked tongue darted out in irritation. "I told you I won't loan—"

Opening my palm, I showed her the gold in it. "I can pay."

The druid fell silent for a moment, then seemed to sigh. "Well, what are you waiting for then? Go have a look," she said and waved me to the display shelf.

Not needing a second invitation, I pulled out the three books I had in mind: ventro, simple parrot, and facial disguise. Sadly I wasn't skilled enough for lesser imitate, but for now acquiring two of three basic abilities would suffice.

Laying out the tomes on a nearby table, I considered them in more detail. Which two did I choose?

* * *

Simple parrot was a spell that allowed me to imitate another's voice. Facial disguise was similar in that it let me assume another's face, while ventro allowed me to conceal the source of my voice.

All three deception abilities had combat potential, and while they would do nothing for my raw damage output or defensive strength, they could, if properly used, change the outcome of an encounter.

I spent some time contemplating my options, much to the disgust of the impatient druid, but I refused to be rushed. In the end, I went with ventro and facial disguise, deciding ventro and simple parrot were too similar to choose both.

After handing over the gold to Mariga, I eagerly absorbed the spellbooks' knowledge.

You have bought a facial disguise spellbook and a ventro spellbook. You have lost: 20 gold.

You have acquired the basic ability: facial disguise. This ability overlays your face with an illusion, allowing you to assume the guise of another. Facial disguise only changes your face; it does not affect your voice or the rest of your body. The ability creates a light-based illusion that can be uncovered by a successful Perception check.

The illusion will remain in place for 1 hour or until dispelled. It consumes stamina and can be upgraded. Its activation time is very slow. You have 4 of 8 Perception ability slots remaining.

You have acquired the basic ability: ventro. This ability conceals the source of your voice, projecting it to anywhere within a 10-yard radius of yourself. The ability creates a sound-based illusion that can be uncovered by a successful Perception check.

The illusion will remain in place for 1 minute or until dispelled. It consumes stamina and can be upgraded. Its activation time is slow. You have 3 of 8 Perception ability slots remaining.

Exiting the druid's shop, I headed toward the goblin walls encircling the safe zone.

I had the makings of a plan, if only a rough one. My biggest concern, though, was time. I was uncertain if I would be able to complete everything I needed to do before my remaining five days ran out.

Both the dark druid and legion captain had offered me a way out of the sector, although both had set conditions that were onerous or impossible to achieve. As yet, I was disinclined to fulfill either's mission.

Still, the pair had revealed crucial information. I now knew why the sector was important, and unlike the other interested parties, it seemed I was less constrained in what I did.

I wasn't sure just yet how I would act, but both Talon and Mariga's information had strongly implied the goblins were the key to the valley, and it was with them that I would start my own investigations.

If I played my cards right, I thought I could escape the sector without compromising my independence. It wouldn't be easy, and much would depend on matters outside of my control. But I was determined to try.

First, though, I had to get out of the safe zone.

I reached the northern perimeter of the village without incident. There was only one gate set in the inner wall of the goblin fort, and it was the same one I'd come through earlier.

Skulking in the shadows of a cabin, I scanned the area. A short stretch of open space separated me from the looming wall. Goblins marched atop the ramparts, and a crowd of players was gathered before the sealed gate.

The moment I left the safety of the shadows, I would be spotted, both by the goblins above and the players below. If Talon's information could be trusted—and I thought it could—then the goblins would be no obstacle. The players, though... they could be problematic.

Time to move.

Rising to my feet, I strolled toward the gate. Faces turned in my direction, and the air filled with cries of alarm. I ignored it all and kept advancing.

The gathered players rushed toward me—some two dozen of them. Mobbing me, they screamed insults and threats but didn't lay hands on me. They dared not. The Game was not forgiving of those who broke its rules.

I maintained my steady advance, forcing the players ahead of me to retreat.

It was slow going, but eventually my "escorts" and I reached the gate. Walking up to it, I banged loudly with my fist. "Open up!" I yelled.

"Running away won't save you," one of the players behind me scoffed.

"You don't want to go out there," another sniggered.

Ignoring both, I pounded on the gate again when it didn't immediately open. This time I drew a reaction. A screen across a letterbox opening was pulled back, and two red-rimmed eyes glared at me from beyond. "Waddaya want?"

Reaching into my pocket, I pulled out the writ of safe passage and waved it in front of the goblin. "Let me through."

The goblin eyed the piece of paper in my hand and then the crowd of players behind me. "You the one they're after?"

I nodded.

He grunted. "On your head be it then," he muttered. He disappeared, and I heard a bar being withdrawn. A moment later, the gates began moving outward.

I stepped back and out of the way, giving myself space. Through the opening, I saw another gathering of players inside the fort. Their weapons were drawn, and they looked tense and eager to do battle.

"Ha!" the joker behind me chortled. "I bet he doesn't last ten seconds!"

"I give him less than five," another chipped in.

I didn't bother replying. The gates were halfway open, and it was time to move. I rushed forward. One step. Two. Then I leaped, hands outstretched.

My fingers wrapped around the top of the still-moving gate. Heaving myself up, I crouched down and balanced gingerly on the thin strip of metal.

"What's he doing?"

"Running!"

I scanned the top of the fort's inner wall. From my perch, it was reachable without any climbing aids. Shifting my balance, I waited for the gate to move closer.

When it was a double handspan away from the wall, I pushed off, hurtling forward again. Mid-leap, I cast one-step. My right foot landed on solid air and, kicking off, I threw myself higher. My reaching fingers found stone.

I'd made it.

Wrapping my hands around the rampart's edge, I pulled myself up. Below me, I heard the cries of consternation from the players on the ground. *Ten seconds, eh?* I grinned, reckoning I would have won the bet.

More voices rang out from below. This time they were goblin ones, shouting orders to seal the gate from the other side of the wall.

Good, I thought. At least I wouldn't have to worry about any other players besides those already inside the fort.

I took a step forward toward the center of the ramparts, then dropped quickly into a crouch as a Game message opened in my mind.

You have left a safe zone.

Bent nearly double, I was out of sight of the players in the Howlers' fort, but I knew I wouldn't remain that way for long. Already I could hear their feet pounding along the wall, heading for the stairs.

From my right, I spied one of the goblin squads that patrolled the wall hurrying in my direction. I pulled out the writ again, waving it in the air. Seeing it, the Howler warriors skidded to a halt.

The squad leader scowled at me. "Get out of here," he barked. "And take your fight elsewhere!"

"It'll be my pleasure," I replied with a tight-lipped smile. "But those players below aren't going to let me leave." I paused. "Will you get your fellows to open the outer gate?"

For a heartbeat, the squad leader studied me in silence, then he jerked his head in acknowledgment and snarled something to a goblin behind him. The warrior ran off.

I inclined my head in thanks and, drawing up along the inside lip of the ramparts, peered over cautiously. The immediate area below was free of players. Now was my chance. Swinging myself over the edge, I hung along the top of the wall for a second.

Then let go.

I dropped straight down. Gauging the distance carefully, I cast one-step mid-fall and formed a cushion of air beneath my feet, temporarily halting my descent. A moment later, the ledge of air vanished and my fall resumed.

Landing lightly on the ground, I rose to my feet and scanned the area. Goblins were watching me from every direction, their beady eyes fixed attentively on my slim form. But word seemed to have spread that I carried a writ, and none of the Howlers moved toward me.

More importantly, I spied no players close by. The fools hadn't thought to leave anyone on watch while they hurried to the nearest stairs.

A mistake I'll make them pay dearly for.

I had two choices. Run for the gate or... fight. Despite my adamant refusal to engage with the hecklers earlier, their insults had grated. The prudent course now would be to flee, but then again, the one thing I had learned about myself in this world was that I was *not* prudent.

If I had been, I would've sworn allegiance to Erebus a long time ago. Or to Loken.

Yet here I was, treading my own path.

It's time the Awakened Dead players learned fear. My lips turned up in a hungry smile.

It's time I taught them what it means to hunt a wolf.

Chapter 105: On the Hunt

Day Three. Morning.

After a few minutes, the watching goblins grew bored and moved about their business, deciding to ignore my presence entirely—which suited me just fine.

I needed less than a minute after that to hide.

Then I waited.

And waited.

Amazingly, the searching players still hadn't caught on that I was no longer on the wall. It took them five more minutes to reach that conclusion, and by the time they did, I was bored to bits. A little later, they gathered near the gate to confer. Sneaking closer, I stretched out flat on the roof of a nearby barracks and listened in. I couldn't see the players, but I didn't need to.

Multiple hostile entities have failed to detect you! Your sneaking has increased to level 46.

"Did you find him?"

"Has he fled?"

"The bloody wretch!" another swore. "He must have. No one's foolish enough—"

"No," a different voice declared. "He's still in the fort. I have the shaman's word on it."

"Then where is he?" a player whined.

"The shaman wouldn't tell me," the same commanding voice said again, and I marked him as their leader.

While the players speculated on my whereabouts, I considered what I'd overheard. The Howlers weren't being completely neutral, but on the other hand, they were being careful about what help they extended to the hunters.

Best I avoid the shaman.

The players were still talking, the one in charge rattling off orders for the others to search the fort. Listening with half an ear, I cast mindsight.

Psi rippled outward from me, flooding the space around me to reveal every consciousness within ten yards. The minds of the nearby goblins and players burned more brightly than that of the simple animals I'd observed before and were easily identifiable.

My attention focused on the immediate area around the gate, taking a tally of my foes. There were twenty players. Reaching out to the bubbles of awareness hovering in my mindsight, I analyzed them, one by one.

The target is Mersey, a level 48 human. She is a player and bears a Mark of Lesser Dark and a Mark of Ishita.

The target is Forsyth, a level 67 human. He is a player and bears a Mark of Minor Dark and a Mark of Ishita.

The target is Tuxai, a level 59 lizardman. He is a...

...

Your insight has increased to level 42.

The players were between rank four and seven and marked by both the Dark and Ishita. None, though, bore a Mark of Erebus. I'd made doubly sure of that.

I rubbed my chin, measuring the odds. Thankfully none of the four red-robed mages who guarded the portal were present, but the group was both larger and more experienced than I expected. Taking them on wouldn't be easy. Still, it was... doable.

And besides, I need the money.

"Does everyone know what to do?" The speaker was Forsyth, the one I had identified as the group's leader.

The players were about to disperse, and if I was going to act, now was the time. Reaching a decision, I cast simple charm on the lowest-ranked player, a level forty-one dwarf. My psi flooded his mind, and I wrenched control of him.

Redbeard has failed a mental resistance check! You have charmed your target for 10 seconds.

Excellent. Ordering the dwarf forward, I directed him to attack his closest companion. Through the mental link binding us together, I sensed my minion unsheathe his axe and bury it into the gnome standing at his side.

Tencil has died.

Hidden on the roof, I grinned. Perhaps the encounter would be easier than I expected. Chaos ensued among the players and orders were shouted.

"God damnit, don't forget he's a mindstalker!"

I urged my minion toward his next target, but before he took a step toward the human on his right, something unexpected happened.

You have lost control over Redbeard. Forsyth has dispelled your casting.

Redbeard dropped to his knees and I heard him rage, "Where is he? Point me at him! I'll kill him!"

"He must be close by," Forsyth said, ignoring the dwarf as he addressed the rest of the group. "Remember, he needs line of sight to cast that charm spell," Forsyth said. "Go find him!"

My lips turned down. The players were well prepared and had reacted quicker than expected to counter my spell. They also knew about my abilities, but their knowledge thankfully seemed incomplete. With mindsight, I didn't need to see my targets to charm them.

Still, Forsyth wasn't wholly wrong: I *was* close by.

The group was moving to search the area, and once more I debated my next move. Did I try charming another or fleeing? But I suspected any charm I cast now would be countered even quicker than the first. Fleeing didn't seem like a good option either.

The players were spread out all around the barracks, and if I left the roof, I was certain to be spotted. What had seemed a secure haven was turning into a trap.

Now what?

✳   ✳   ✳

I decided to stay put.

There were other abilities I could try using to escape, but after the failure of my charm spell I was wary about using them, uncertain if the group had a counter ready. And who knew, with luck, no one would think to check the roof of the buildings.

Unfortunately, luck wasn't with me.

"You two," Forsyth ordered, "climb that building and check above!" He muttered something else under his breath, which my sharp ears easily picked up on. "The bastard climbs about as well as a monkey."

I ground my teeth in frustration. So much for hiding.

Moving with deliberate care, I drew both my blades. Then I readied my voice and cast ventro. Projecting my words to appear as if originating from a spot far to my left, I spoke, "You fools looking for me? Well, here I am. Come and get me!"

The hunters spun around, orienting themselves on the projected voice.

"There he is!"

"I don't see him, do you?"

"Yes! He's hiding behind that building!"

"After him!" Forsyth ordered.

I smiled. It was working. Straining my ears, I listened to the sounds of the players' receding footsteps. Not all of them went though. One pair of boots was approaching the barracks. I tightened my hands on my blades. I could handle one.

I heard another player pause. "Wizel, aren't you coming?"

"It will be easier to spot him from the barrack's roof," Wizel replied. "You go on, Carr. I'll keep an eye out from here."

Carr's footsteps faded away as she hurried after the others while Wizel, grunting with effort, began clambering up the sides of the barrack. Blades in hand, I crawled toward him.

I could have slipped down the other side of the building, of course, but this was too good an opportunity to pass by. Reaching the spot where I expected the player to appear, I waited.

A rash of red hair appeared above the edge of the roof. Not hesitating, I rose from my crouch and plunged my swords downward into the hapless player.

You have killed Wizel with a fatal blow.

The corpse dropped like a stone. I followed after it, landing lightly atop the body. Crouched down on my haunches, I scanned the area. None of the other players had noticed my kill. The goblins, though, watched curiously.

Ignoring them, I reached down and yanked a coin pouch off the corpse. There was no time for further looting.

Hurrying to the other dead player—the one Redbeard had killed—I patted him down and took his money too before turning right and disappearing into the surrounding buildings.

You have acquired 2 coin pouches.

✳ ✳ ✳

It didn't take the players long to realize they had been tricked. Their faces contorted in rage, my pursuers flooded back to the area around the gate, searching for me. Finding Wizel's corpse only infuriated them further.

From a much safer distance this time, within the shadows of a darkened entrance, I waited to see what they would do. Forsyth divided the others into groups of four, each accompanied by at least one mage. Then the teams of four spread out to search the fort. None headed in my immediate direction, and I felt secure enough to keep watching.

Only Forsyth and one other player remained near the gate. The pair approached the goblins guarding the exit to the safe zone and fell into an animated argument with them. I was too far away to hear what they were saying, but it sounded as if the players were trying to get the goblins to open the gate—which the guards steadfastly refused to do.

I'd seen enough. Slipping away and taking care to remain out of sight of the searching player parties, I made my way to the fort's outer gate.

Unfortunately, it too had been locked.

I cursed softly. One of the hunting parties was loitering near the outer gate. They were clearly waiting for me to show myself.

I wondered what had happened. Had the shaman countermanded the orders of the squad leader I had spoken to on the wall, or had the squad leader simply lied to me?

It didn't matter though. I had no intention of leaving the fort just yet. Slipping back into the shadows, I began a hunt of my own.

Chapter 106: A Dance of Blades

Day Three. Morning.

I tracked my first chosen targets for a full ten minutes, observing their behavior and identifying their weaknesses.

The team I followed was formed of two mages and two heavy fighters, all rank six players. Forsyth had allocated each group a different quadrant off the Howlers' fort to search. While this was an efficient search pattern, it did isolate the four teams from one another. I would be able to attack each with impunity, something that clearly hadn't occurred to the hunters.

They still underestimate me, I thought as I readied my ambush.

I didn't plan on using charm this time. I suspected the mages' were prepped and ready to dispel any casting of mine, and rather than give away the advantage of surprise, my opening gambit would be altogether different.

Concealed again on the roof of a barracks, I watched through my mindsight as the party of four strolled through my chosen ambush spot, a narrow avenue formed between two adjacent barracks. From my earlier observations, I knew the two fighters would be marching at the head of the group, presumably to shield the mages.

I waited until the team passed my own position, then leaped down, landing soundlessly on the ground behind them.

Four hostile entities have failed to detect you! You are hidden.

Padding forward, I closed the distance. The players remained oblivious. Picking out my target, I buried both my blades' hilts deep into his upper torso.

You have backstabbed your target for 50% more damage! You have killed Dorsk with a fatal blow.

I yanked out both swords and whipped them around to strike at the second mage.

"He's here—" she began to cry out.

The mage didn't get to finish her warning. With spider's bite, I drew a line of red across her neck, while with my other blade I disemboweled her.

You have killed Meera with a fatal blow.

A hammer whistled through the air toward me. That was the first fighter entering the fray. I threw myself backward, avoiding the blow. The second warrior charged, blurring through the short space separating us to crash into my midriff.

Zed has stunned you for 2 seconds.

Bloody hell! I cursed as I was laid out flat. The move had caught me entirely off guard. Helpless to do otherwise, I watched as my foe took up his sword in a two-handed grip and rammed it downward.

Zed has critically injured you! Your health is at 50%.

The tip of the blade plunged through my torso and, fortunately, was turned slightly off course by my armor, sparing me a fatal blow. Still, it hurt. It hurt a damn lot.

Zed's eyes glinted in satisfaction. Withdrawing his blade, he prepared to deliver the killing blow. He would have done better to leave it in me, keeping me pinned down.

A heartbeat later, my paralysis wore off. Ignoring the agony coursing through my midriff, I heaved forward and slapped a hand onto the fighter's leg.

You have stunned Zed for one second.

With his legs cut out from under him, Zed fell forward and onto the waiting tip of spider's bite.

You have critically injured Zed!

Gasping, the fighter collapsed in a heap on top of me.

"Ahh..." I exhaled, unable to fully stifle the roar of pain that threatened to rip free from my throat.

"Zed!" the other warrior cried, hurrying forward.

My hands were trapped beneath the downed Zed, and with every slight shift fresh torment spiked through me, but I couldn't afford to be still.

My doom was approaching with the second fighter. Clenching my jaw, I released the hilt of my blade and fumbled for a potion. My fingers closed on one of the flasks slotted on the belt strapped across my shoulder just as Zed was yanked off me.

Unwittingly, the second fighter's actions freed my arms, and in a surge of sudden motion, I flipped open the potion and downed its contents.

You have restored yourself with a full healing potion. Your health is now at 100%.

Immediately, new life raced through me and my wound closed. By good fortune or ill, I'd downed my last full healing potion.

A hammer crashed down.

I rolled out of the way. The hammer flew at me again. I kept rolling. A yard away from the warrior, I leaped to my feet, blade flashing out to turn away the next hammer strike bearing down on me.

You have blocked Khone's attack.

I leaped backward to open the distance between us and gain some breathing room. My foe, a human fighter clad only in furs—*a barbarian?*—pushed forward and cramped me for space.

Realizing I wouldn't be able to easily escape Khone, I stepped into his reach and slipped past his sweeping hammer to slap my right hand on his chest.

You have stunned Khone for 1 second.

The fighter turned to dead weight, but momentum kept him moving forward to crash into me. I toppled backward with him. As I fell, I twisted and managed to land on top of Khone instead of under. Pressing my right hand against the barbarian's torso, I kept him stun-locked while I drove my shortsword through his exposed neck.

You have killed Khone.

I sat back, chest heaving. The battle was nearly over and I had won. I scanned both ends of the alley but heard no cries of alarm. Rising to my feet, a dripping shortsword in my hand, I advanced on my last surviving foe—the warrior who had injured me.

Zed lay dazed on the floor, bleeding out. Unlike me, he had no potions at hand. Kneeling over him, I yanked off his helm and thrust my blade under the cleft of his chin.

"Well fought," I murmured as the last light of life drained from his eyes. Wiping my blades clean, I sheathed them before turning to the waiting Game messages.

You have reached level 37!
Your dodging has increased to level 35. Your shortswords has increased to level 43. Your two-weapon fighting has increased to level 38.
Your light armor has increased to level 30. Your skill in light armor has reached rank 3, decreasing your light armor penalty by 15%.
Your chi has increased to level 27. Your deception has increased to level 17.
Your telekinesis has increased to level 24. Your telepathy has increased to level 20. Your skill in telepathy has reached rank 2, further increasing your chance of succeeding with telepathic abilities.

I whistled soundlessly. I'd gained five levels from the six players I had killed—four in this alley and the other two at the gate. The skill gains weren't anything to sniff at either.

I grinned, wondering if Ishita realized how much benefit I was deriving from her bounty. *Probably not.*

Still chuckling, I set about looting the dead.

*　*　*

Your Dexterity has increased to rank 16, your Mind to rank 11, and your Constitution to rank 11.

A few minutes later, after taking care of my player progression, munching through some rations, meditating, and searching the corpses, I considered my booty.

You have acquired a pack of 6 field rations.
You have acquired a basic sword belt.
You have acquired 11 gold, 4 silver, and 0 copper.

You have acquired a common mage's cloak. This item increases your air magic skill by +3.

Of everything I'd salvaged, the gold was the most valuable. The dead players carried a lot more equipment than what I had taken, of course, but I didn't judge any of it as useful enough to lug around on my back. *Now to see if I can really do what I intend with this stuff.*

Removing my thief's cloak, I tied my new sword belt diagonally across my back with the hilt of my offhand weapon hanging down. The two belts wrapped around my torso and formed a cross on my back and chest. Reaching underhanded behind me, I tested the draw. Both blades came to hand easily.

After that, I stuffed my old thief's cloak in my backpack and equipped the dead mage's cloak.

You have successfully concealed the small weapons spider's bite and a +1 shortsword.

You have equipped a common mage's cloak. Warning: your magic attribute is at rank 0. Item skill bonus not received.

Excellent. Both my weapons were now hidden. The mage's cloak was a startling shade of purple and not at all practical for sneaking around in the dark. But I intended it for a different purpose entirely.

Striding over to the cloak's former owner, I studied the corpse's face, committing it to memory. Then, with a thoughtful whistle, I strolled away to resume my hunt.

CHAPTER 107: THE GREAT DECEIVER

Leaving the alley, I made my way anticlockwise through the fort. The goblins paid me no mind.

The hood of my mage's cloak was pulled over my head, and my shoulders were hunched slightly. The player I'd chosen to imitate was the one who most closely matched my size and build. Still, he had been somewhat shorter, not enough to give me away immediately, but there was no sense in taking chances.

I found the next party of hunters searching one of the Howlers' barracks. Pausing outside the door, I took a moment to cast facial disguise. Energy coursed through my body and rushed to my face, causing its lines to blur and my features to alter.

I had no mirror to check if the spell had worked as expected, but trusting that it had, I entered the building.

"Dorsk, what are you doing here?" a player demanded, spotting me.

You have passed a mental resistance check! Multiple hostile entities have failed to pierce your disguise. Your hidden weapons have gone unnoticed. Your deception has increased to level 19.

Dorsk was the name of the mage I was imitating. "We've found him," I gasped, clutching at my side in fake pain. "Hurry!"

I had no idea what Dorsk really sounded like, of course, hence the reason for my "injury." Hopefully, any strangeness the others picked up in my voice would be attributed to the pain I was feigning.

"Where's your team?" another player asked, a frown marring her forehead.

"Dead," I mumbled in a strangled voice. "He's killed them all!"

"Where is he?" the first one demanded.

"Somewhere behind me," I said, gesturing vaguely out the open door. "Tracking me down."

Lifting my eyes, I risked a quick survey of the four. Two of the players were looking at me quizzically, but before they could question me or my news, the group's leader intervened. "Let's go," he ordered.

The four rushed for the door. Obligingly I sidestepped out the way, straightening slightly in the process and shifting my hands closer to the hilt of my concealed blades.

When the last player passed by, I darted forward. Wrapping my left hand around my target's mouth, I drove spider's bite into his back, then upward and through his heart.

You have backstabbed your target for 100% more damage! You have killed Timone.

I stepped over the corpse and, drawing my second blade, plunged both weapons into my next victim's retreating back.

You have backstabbed your target for 100% more damage! You have killed Yarra.

Amazingly, both my kills went unnoticed. The party's other two players—both fighters of some kind—were too intent on their quarry to notice the fate of their companions. Rushing forward, I cast one-step.

My left foot found purchase in the air, and I launched off it, diving toward the leader with my blades outstretched.

With the sharpened tips of my swords leading the way, I slammed into my target. My blades buried themselves hilt deep into his torso, slicing through his hide armor and skin with ease.

You have backstabbed your target for 100% more damage! You have killed Marlon.

The corpse crumpled beneath me, and I rolled off, abandoning my weapons rather than sparing the time necessary to disentangle them from the body. I had another problem to deal with. The remaining player had finally noticed something was amiss and spun around.

"What the—" he began.

I bounced to my feet and threw myself forward. Before the fighter could do more than half-unsheathe his weapon, I'd wrapped my hands around his throat and cast stunning slap.

You have stunned Nyka for one second.

I shoved aside the player's suddenly inert hand and took up his own blade. Drawing the longsword, I thrust it toward the largest joint of his plate armor.

The blade, however, didn't go where I intended. Striking the solid metal of Nyka's breastplate, it skidded off.

Nyka's armor has blocked your attack.

I cursed foully at the mishap. I should have known. I was no good with longswords, but I'd had no choice. I had learned from my last fight with Zed and Khone. If I struck hard and fast while retaining the advantage of surprise, I could easily overcome my foes. But once my opponents got the chance to bring their own abilities into play, I was dead, or as good as dead. Which was why I'd abandoned my own shortswords rather than take the time to retrieve them.

Meanwhile, the fighter's stun had worn off. Fury sparkled in his gaze and his lips twisted into a snarl. Before he could cry out in warning, I slapped a hand over his mouth and recast my stun.

Then I slammed the hilt of the longsword through the eyeslit of his helm, using it as a club. Even without any skill, from this close I couldn't miss.

I kept at it, ignoring the spurting blood as I slowly but surely bashed my foe to death. Eventually, when the face beneath me was no longer recognizable and his body no longer twitched, I stopped.

You have killed Nyka.

Chest heaving and gore-spattered, I rose slowly to my feet. *Two down. Two more to go.*

✻ ✻ ✻

Killing the remaining two hunter teams went off without a hitch.

Each time I went in hard and without restraint, using deception and sneaking to close in on my foes and strike from their midst. By the time I was finished, I'd accumulated a sizable amount of money but little else.

Total money carried: 35 gold, 9 silver, and 0 copper.

In my rush to complete my ambushes, I left off more extensive looting. If I delayed too long, I knew the surviving players would notice something amiss, and acquiring a few more trinkets wasn't worth the trouble it would bring.

Besides, the loot itself was only a bonus. The experience I earned was far more beneficial than the coins gained.

You have reached level 46!

Congratulations, Michael! You are now a rank 4 player. Your experience gains have decreased further. For achieving rank 4, you have been awarded 1 additional attribute point and 1 Class point.

My player level had advanced significantly, but more importantly, two of my skills were within reaching distance of rank five, the minimum skill rank required for most tier-two abilities.

While I meditated to recover my lost psi, I took the opportunity to review my player profile and spend my new attribute points, investing in Dexterity, Mind, and Perception.

Player Profile: Michael

Level: 46. Rank: 4. Current Health: 100%.
Stamina: 65%. Mana: 100%. Psi: 40%.
Species: Human. Lives Remaining: 3.
Marks: Wolf-brethren, Lesser Shadow, Lesser Light, Lesser Dark.

Attributes

Available: 0 points.
Strength: 2. Constitution: 11. Dexterity: 20. Perception: 10. Mind: 15. Magic: 0. Faith: 0.

Classes

Available: 2 points.
Primary-Secondary Bi-blend: Mindstalker.
Tertiary Class: None.

Traits

Psi wolf heritage: +2 Dexterity, +2 Strength, +4 Mind.
Beast tongue: can speak to beastkin.
Marked: can see spirit signatures.
Nocturnal: perfect night vision.

Skills

Available skill slots: 0.
Light armor (current: 33. max: 110. Constitution, basic).
Dodging (current: 37. max: 200. Dexterity, basic).
Sneaking (current: 48. max: 200. Dexterity, basic).
Shortswords (current: 47. max: 200. Dexterity, basic).
Two-weapon fighting (current: 41. max: 200. Dexterity, advanced).
Thieving (current: 1. max: 200. Dexterity, basic).
Chi (current: 34. max: 110. Mind, advanced).
Meditation (current: 36. max: 150. Mind, basic).
Telekinesis (current: 28. max: 150. Mind, advanced).
Telepathy (current: 25. max: 150. Mind, advanced).
Insight (current: 42. max: 100. Perception, basic).
Deception (current: 25. max: 100. Perception, master).

Abilities

Crippling blow (Dexterity, basic, shortswords).
Minor backstab (Dexterity, basic, sneaking).
Basic trap disarm (Dexterity, basic, thieving).
Simple lockpicking (Dexterity, basic, thieving).
Simple charm (Mind, basic, telepathy).
Stunning slap (Mind, basic, chi).
One-step (Mind, basic, telekinesis).
Minor reaction buff (Mind, basic, chi).
Basic analyze (Perception, basic, insight).
Lesser trap detect (Perception, basic, thieving).
Conceal small weapon (Perception, basic, deception).
Facial disguise (Perception, basic, deception).
Ventro (Perception, basic, deception).
Simple mindsight (Class, basic).

Known Key Points

Sector 14,913 exit portal and safe zone.
Sector 12,560 nether portal and safe zone.

Equipped

spider's bite shortsword (+15% damage, webbed), concealed.
shortsword,+1 (+15% damage, +10 shortswords), concealed.
common fighter's sash (+3 shortswords).
enchanted leather armor set (+20% damage reduction, -35% Dexterity and Magic).
slotted potion belt (3 minor heal, 4 moderate heal, 3 empty).
common mage's cloak (+3 air magic).

Backpack Contents (Key Items)

Money: 35 gold, 9 silver, and 0 copper.
2 x iron daggers.

1 x goblin writ of safe passage.
1 x alchemy stone (0 / 150 ingredients).
1 x bounty letter.
1 x common thief's cloak (+3 sneaking).

<u>Bank Contents</u>

<u>Money</u>: 46 gold, 4 silver, and 9 copper.
2 x full healing potions.
2 x basic steel shortswords.

<u>Open Tasks</u>

Aid the Pack (Stop the Long Fangs hunting the dire wolves).
An Alchemist's Bounty (kill the wyvern mother).
Goblin Wars (destroy all 3 goblin tribes in the valley).
Forging Dark Alliances (secure the allegiance of the Howlers and Red Rats for the Dark).

Closing my player profile, I smiled in quiet satisfaction. At the rate I was advancing, the level disparity between me and Ishita's sworn—the ones in this sector at least—was quickly disappearing. Soon, I would be their match.

But you're not. Not just yet anyway, I thought, cautioning myself against overconfidence.

It was really time to move on. But there was still one more person I wanted to kill before leaving.

And him, at least, I was sure I could take.

Disguising myself again, I crept toward the gate leading to the safe zone.

✳   ✳   ✳

Forsyth was standing out in the open, in front of the still-closed gate. The human mage was accompanied by the dwarf, Redbeard. My brows flickered upward, surprised by Forsyth's choice of companions.

Redbeard was the lowest-ranked of the hunters. Perhaps that was why Forsyth had chosen to keep him near. Or perhaps it was because the dwarf had previously succumbed to my spell and the mage didn't trust him.

I approached the pair openly. Leaning heavily on a wizard's staff I'd claimed from my last victims, I limped toward the two. It didn't take long for me to be spotted.

"Dorsk, you have news?" Forsyth asked.

"Dead. He's dead," I mumbled in a low voice, deliberately mangling my words.

"What's that?" Forsyth asked, taking a few steps toward me.

"We got him," I whispered.

"Speak up!" Redbeard snapped irritably. He scowled, eyes dropping to my leg. "What's wrong with you?"

"Injured," I muttered, not taking my eyes off Forsyth, who was still advancing on me.

"Did I hear you say you got him?" Forsyth asked, his face giddy with delight.

I bobbed my head, saying nothing else. The mage was nearly in range now. Abruptly, he stopped, his face wrinkling in confusion.

He sensed something amiss. I couldn't delay further. Abandoning my subterfuge, I flew forward, unsheathing my blades as I went.

Forsyth's eyes widened in alarm, and his hand dropped to the hilt of the sword at his side. Before he could draw, I was upon him, spider's bite carving a line of red down his torso while with my second blade I attempted to skewer him through.

He proved equal to the challenge.

Despite his surprise, Forsyth twisted out of the way of my darting blade and turned what was meant to be a fatal strike into a graze across the shoulder.

You have injured Forsyth.

I'd misjudged him. He wasn't a pure mage but some combination of spellcaster and fighter. A spellsword, perhaps?

"Ye gods, it's him!" Forsyth exclaimed, backing away.

A few yards away, Redbeard cried out in a wordless howl of rage, approaching rapidly. I didn't take my eyes off Forsyth though. I needed to finish him off quickly before the angry dwarf reached me.

I dashed forward again, swords poised to strike. Forsyth was mumbling something under his breath.

Casting a spell? I wondered.

Rushing him before he could finish, I struck out in quick succession from both the left and right.

Once more, Forsyth's speed saved him. His own blade whipped forward, fending off spider's bite. But I'd anticipated his reaction, and before he could disengage, I advanced, crowding the human while I slashed at him with my second sword.

You have critically injured Forsyth!

He stumbled back, grimacing in pain and clutching his stomach.

I made to follow, then abruptly threw myself to the left, some sixth sense warning me of the axe hurtling down on the spot I'd just occupied.

You have evaded Redbeard's attack.

The dwarf screamed in frustration as his attack failed. A few yards away, I rolled to my feet, both blades at the ready.

The dwarf rushed me again.

From the corner of my eye, I spotted Forsyth backing away, his mouth moving rapidly as he incanted the words of some spell.

"Damn it," I growled. I had to get the spellsword before he finished his casting.

Making a split-second decision, I charged Redbeard in turn. The dwarf's eyes widened at my unexpected maneuver, and in sudden panic he rushed his next attack.

Tumbling forward, I rolled under the dwarf's whistling blade and leaped to my feet out of range of Redbeard's axe. Leaving the confused dwarf behind, I chased down the still-retreating human.

Forsyth was some sort of caster, I realized, and a bigger threat than the dwarf. Feet pounding on the ground, I flew toward him.

Across the distance of a few yards, our gazes met, and Forsyth's lips turned upward in a victorious smile as he finished his spell. I was still out of striking distance. Raising his hands, the caster released his spell.

I had no idea what to expect.

So I did what I hoped Forsyth would least expect.

Continuing my reckless charge, I one-stepped into the air and, finding solid footing, leaped upward.

Flames fanned out from Forsyth's outstretched hands, passing inches beneath my booted feet.

The mage's eyes grew round with shock.

Still airborne, I grinned back.

"How—" he began.

He didn't get to finish as I crashed into him, swords first.

You have killed Forsyth.

Disentangling myself from the corpse, I spun around in time to meet Redbeard's angry charge. Overcoming the dwarf was laughably easy. My left blade flickered outward and parried away the axe while spider's bite snaked forward to strike the dwarf across the shoulder.

You have injured Redbeard. Webbed triggered! Redbeard has failed a physical resistance check! You have immobilized your target for 1 second.

The outrage coloring the dwarf's face as he was wrenched to a halt was almost comical. But I knew better than to underestimate a foe. Dancing forward, I buried both my blades in his throat.

You have killed Redbeard.

The corpse fell lifelessly to the floor. "Maybe next time you'll have better luck," I whispered.

Chapter 108: The Sworn

Day Three. Morning.

Under the watchful gaze of the gate guards, I looted both corpses.

You have acquired 10 gold. Total money carried: 45 gold, 9 silver, and 0 copper.

After I took their coin pouches, I saw to my leveling, this time deciding to increase my health pool.

You have reached level 48!
Your dodging has increased to level 38. Your shortswords has increased to level 49. Your two-weapon fighting has increased to level 43.
Your chi has increased to level 35. Your meditation has increased to level 37. Your telekinesis has increased to level 29. Your deception has increased to level 27.
Your Constitution has increased to rank 13.

When I was done, I looked up to find the Howler warriors staring at me, their faces impassive but with an ugly gleam in their eyes.

What are they thinking?

Sheathing my weapons, I turned around, wondering if the goblins would attempt to stop me from leaving the fort. My hunters were dead, and I could see no reason now for their shaman to keep the gates closed. With my every sense extended and alert for an ambush, I strode toward the outer wall.

I didn't manage more than a dozen steps though before my attention was caught by the screech of metal on metal. I recognized the sound immediately.

It was the safe zone gate.

I spun about, hands dropping to the hilt of my blades. I hadn't been mistaken. The gates were opening. Tense and wary, I watched the heavy metal gate creak open. I was sure now that the Howler shaman's neutrality had ended and he meant to let in more players.

Two figures slipped through the gate. I recognized both.

The tension in me eased as Ultack and Cecilia hurried toward me. "What are you still doing here?" Ultack barked.

I stared back at him mutely, saying nothing.

Cecilia's gaze drifted to the two nearby corpses. "You killed them?" she asked, slightly disbelievingly.

I nodded curtly, not elaborating further. "Why are you here?"

"The captain sent us," Ultack said.

"Why?" I demanded.

"To warn you that the shaman is opening the gate," Cecilia replied.

I rolled my eyes, but she interrupted me before I could speak. "Players are gathering in the village square. In a few minutes, a horde of Ishita's followers will be coming through that gate—" her look turned grim— "including her sworn servants."

My ears perked up at that. "Really?" I murmured.

"Yes, really," Ultack confirmed. He stared at me for a heartbeat longer. "What are you still doing here? Go!"

"I'm going," I assured him. I glanced at Cecilia. "What's the difference?"

She looked at me in confusion. "What?"

"Between sworn and followers. Aren't they the same thing?" I asked.

"We don't have time for—" Ultack began.

Cecilia waved him to silence. "This is important, Ultack. He should know this." She turned back to me. "Followers are players who have pledged allegiance to a Power. Becoming a follower is only a matter of making an oath. The sworn, though, are much more. They are players who have already proven their loyalty to a Power by deepening their binding Marks." She bit her lip. "Somehow, each sworn is linked to their Power. I'm not quite sure how, but—" her gaze darted back to mine—"killing sworn is bad. Very bad. When you do, the Power knows and invariably seeks revenge." She paused. "As you should know."

I scratched my head. All along, I'd thought the two—follower and sworn—were one and the same. I'd just learned they weren't. Was that why Ishita's hatred for me hadn't increased when I'd killed Forsyth and his gang? "How do I tell the difference?"

"You don't," Ultack chimed in. "Not until you've killed one. Then you'll know," he finished in a mutter.

"Those red-robed mages guarding the portal in the safe zone," Cecilia said. "You've seen them?"

I nodded.

"*They* are Ishita's sworn servants," she said. "Avoid them at all costs."

I nodded again, though it wasn't in agreement with her advice.

"What did the captain ask you to do?" Cecilia asked abruptly.

I glanced at her. "Didn't he tell you?"

The elf didn't reply, but her frustrated expression was answer enough.

"Thanks for the heads up," I said, making no attempt to satisfy her curiosity. "Time for me to go."

I turned around. Then hesitated as something else occurred to me.

I wasn't sure if I would be able to return to the safe zone. My gaze drifted downward to the coin pouch at my waist. And if I couldn't, all the money I'd looted would go to waste...

Swinging back to the Tartan recruits, I unclipped my coin pouch and held it out to Ultack. "Here, take it."

The half-orc eyed the small bag in my hand. "What's in it?"

"Money."

He looked dubiously at me.

I smiled. "It's not a gift. I want you to do something for me." I paused. "If you're willing."

He didn't say anything.

Taking that as a positive sign, I explained further. "I need you to purchase a few items for me."

Ultack still made no move to take the pouch.

"Please," I added.

Looking reluctant, the half-orc took the coin pouch. On feeling its weight, his eyes widened. "Where did you get all this?"

I jerked a thumb at the corpses. "From them." I paused. "And their friends."

Ultack grunted. "Alright. What do you want me to buy?"

I told him, describing in detail the items I wanted.

"Where should we meet you?" Ultack asked when I was done. "If you're giving me this, I can only assume you won't be returning to the safe zone."

"Which is unexpectedly wise of you," Cecilia remarked.

"I'll meet you in the glade with the dead rhomodillo," I said, ignoring the elf's comment. "Tomorrow morning, if you can make it."

"We'll be there," he replied simply.

"Thank you." I turned to leave.

"One more thing before you go," Cecilia said, stopping me.

Halting, I raised a questioning eyebrow at her.

"I almost forgot. The captain wanted us to tell you something else."

I waited for her to go on.

"Mariga," she said.

"What about her?" I asked.

"You shouldn't trust her," Ultack said.

I glanced at him. "Don't worry," I said. "I don't trust anyone."

And on that note, I finally took leave of the pair.

*　*　*

I passed through the fort without incident. The Howler soldiers gathered in groups along my route but made no move to stop me, and reaching the outer gate, I found it open.

I exhaled in relief.

If the gates had been barred, I was unsure what I would have done. Attempting to take on the entire fort and fight my way out was too rash—even for me.

Letting my hands hover in plain sight, I strode toward the open gate. Without prompting, the guards on duty shifted out the way, not demanding to see my writ of safe passage. I pursed my lips. Clearly they'd been told to expect me.

Was I about to be betrayed? I feared so. I didn't let any of my concerns show though as I kept up my nonchalant advance.

A drawn-out minute later, I passed under the gate.

The hairs on the back of my neck prickled. If the goblins were going to attack, now would be a perfect time.

But they did nothing. Their gazes cold and inscrutable, they simply watched me leave.

The air whooshed out of me as I escaped the fort and beheld the forest's greenery. Whereas days ago I'd eyed the forest with dislike, now its tangled depths looked inviting. I increased my pace to a fast walk, then a jog, and then once more until, finally, I was sprinting toward the forest.

Reaching the tree line, I pulled the shadows around me.

Multiple hostile entities have failed to detect you! You are hidden.

At last, I breathed. *I'm safe.*
Almost, it felt like I was home.

✻ ✻ ✻

I considered my recent sojourn into the safe zone as I strolled deeper into the forest. It hadn't gone entirely as I'd expected.

I had discovered far more than I'd bargained for and gained multiple tasks in the process—notwithstanding how seemingly impossible they all were. Now, I also had an inkling of what was going on in the sector, if not yet a means of escaping. Rubbing my chin, I considered my next move.

Where to now?

North, I decided.

To the Red Rat encampment and almost all the way back from whence I'd come. I'd visited two of the three goblin tribes, and it was time I saw the third. But before I headed their way, there was a detour I needed to make.

✻ ✻ ✻

I cut northeast through the forest.

By now, I had traveled the length of the valley, journeying from its northernmost point with the dungeon entrance to the southern border where the safe zone was situated.

At my best guess, it would take me a day to traverse the sector's entire length again, which should leave me sufficient time to go everywhere I needed to in the five days remaining on my nonaggression Pact.

My first destination was the clearing where we'd slain the rhomodillo. I had it in my head to employ Gelar's gadget and see what alchemy ingredients I could harvest from the dead creature.

Assuming it was still there, of course.

The journey progressed without incident, and I spent the trip practicing my insight and deception skills. With so many creatures available to analyze in the forest, insight was easy enough to improve. Making the most of the opportunity, I targeted and identified every creature I encountered, employing mindsight when the animals were out of sight.

Deception was harder to train.

It seemed the skill only advanced when I was in close proximity to neutral or hostile entities. Nevertheless, I persisted in my attempts to trigger the skill as often as possible, sneaking up on the forest's denizens with my blades concealed and facial disguise cast.

Just before noon, I reached the clearing with the rhomodillo's corpse. I was tired and weary, less from the hike through the forest and more from the sleepless night before. Before entering the glade, I reviewed my skill gains from the journey.

Your insight has increased to level 53. Your deception has increased to level 33.

Congratulations, Michael, your skill in insight has reached rank 5, allowing you to learn tier-2 abilities.

I smiled at the Adjudicator's message. At last, I had my first rank five skill, and soon I hoped to have my first tier-two ability.

Returning my attention to the glade, I surveyed the area with both my mindsight and physical senses.

The clearing appeared free of danger. A pack of hyenas was feasting on the rhomodillo, but no larger beasts were around. Judging it safe, I slipped out of the shadows and into the glade. On spotting me, the scavengers fled.

I reached the corpse and crouched down over it. It smelled awful. Wrinkling my nose against the stench, I studied the carcass while I waved the buzzing insects away.

The body was more than half-eaten. Most of its entrails were strewn about the ground, and the ivory-white bones of its rib cage had been exposed.

Wondering if the journey to the clearing was a wasted trip, I placed the alchemy stone on the dead creature and waited.

A few seconds passed and nothing happened, leaving me feeling foolish.

Uhm... am I even using this thing the right way?

Gelar had said only to place the stone on my target and let the stone do the rest. Now I cursed myself for not questioning him in more detail.

I should have gotten more precise instructions. Maybe I should—

I broke off. Something was happening. I need not have worried. Of its own volition, the stone had activated, pulsing a furious emerald. With each pulse, the corpse shrunk, shriveling before my eyes.

In less than a minute, the rhomodillo was nothing but an empty husk.

The light emanating from the alchemy stone faded, its work done. Leaning forward, I picked up the object.

You have acquired 4 x vials of beast blood, 5 x heaps of ordinary bonedust, and 1 x rhomodillo tusk.

I grinned in pleasure. *It worked!*

While the ingredients I had harvested were nothing to shout about, I was satisfied the stone functioned in the manner I'd expected and that my purchase hadn't been made in vain.

My work in the glade done, I rose to my feet and oriented myself toward the valley's center. The wyvern hatchling's corpse lay somewhere in that direction, and after my success harvesting the rhomodillo, I saw no reason not to do the same with it.

I yawned. But first, I needed a nap.

CHAPTER 109: A DEADLY HARVEST

DAY THREE. AFTERNOON.

An hour later, stifling incessant yawns, I set off west through the valley. I hadn't dared to sleep any longer and had forced myself awake despite my body's protest. It took only a few hours to reach the glade where I had fought the hatchling, and once again I'd spent the journey training my skills.

Your insight has increased to level 56. Your deception has increased to level 38.

Arriving at the site of my defeat, I studied the trampled ground. It was hard to believe that my battle with the hatchling had occurred only two days ago. In that short span of time I had grown significantly, and if the encounter had to be reenacted, I was sure I would fare better a second time around against the wyvern.

I snorted in amusement. That was my injured pride talking. Leaving off further daydreaming, I hunted down the creature's tracks. The beast's footprints were easy enough to find. It had fled further west. Following the trail of broken branches, scratched bark, and heavy footprints, I came upon the creature's corpse suddenly.

In death, the hatchling looked much smaller. The creature lay heaped against the trunk of a large oak tree, where I guessed it had made its final stand against the dire wolves.

Strangely enough, the carcass was untouched.

Not stopping to question my good fortune, I hurried to the dead beast's side while taking pains to avoid any spots of burned-out vegetation. I suspected that, even in death, the wyvern's venom was still potent.

Crouching down, I placed the alchemy stone on the body and waited. A few seconds later, the stone began to pulse green and I leaned forward, almost dancing in anticipation of the ingredients it would harvest.

This time, the haul should be—

Crrr...ack!

My head whipped upward at the sound of breaking boughs and rustling leaves. *Danger!* my mind screamed. Letting instinct guide me, I leaped backward, abandoning both stone and corpse to flee into the safety of the closest shadows.

A hostile entity has failed to detect you! You are hidden.

Concealed in the shadows, I froze. Something was coming. Something... big.

A moment later, a heavy shape thudded onto the ground, sending fine tremors rippling outward.

A hostile entity has failed to detect you! Your sneaking has increased to level 49.

Heart in mouth, I gaped at the behemoth before me. It was the wyvern mother. Over three times larger than her dead hatchling, she was a menacing-looking specimen.

And angry. Oh so angry.

Fury sparked in her eyes, and her forked tongue flickered in and out as she scanned the surroundings. The big wyvern didn't so much as glance at her dead offspring. She had known the body was there, I realized, and must have been lying in wait.

No wonder the hatchling's corpse was untouched.

I swallowed painfully, torn between cursing myself as a fool for coming here and counting my thanks for escaping the beast.

I'm not out of danger yet though.

Stretching out her long neck, the serpentine creature sniffed at the air.

Uh-oh. Can she smell me?

Tucking in her wings, the beast took a single step forward—in my direction. Instinct screamed at me again, urging me to flee, to run.

This time I ignored it.

Running would only spell my doom. I was under no illusions: the wyvern mother was not a foe I had any chance of surviving. I kept still, not moving and not even considering using any of my abilities.

The beast took another step. Again, in my direction.

I gulped and stopped breathing. Less than a dozen feet separated us now.

"I c-can s-s-smell you, human," came a sibilant hiss.

My eyes widened. *Bloody hell! She can talk?*

"Jus-s-t like I s-smelt your s-s-scent on my hatchling," she continued. "It was you-u who killed her. You and thos-s-se wretched dogs."

My fear ratcheted upward. The wyvern was altogether more intelligent than I'd anticipated. Which made her equally more dangerous. Realizing if I did nothing I was as good as dead, I called upon my psi.

The wyvern mother took another step forward, head snaking back and forth. The gesture reassured me somewhat. She hadn't sniffed me out entirely yet. But it was only a matter of time before she found me.

Unless I distracted her.

The spell I was readying completed, and without hesitation, I cast.

Nine yards north of my position, a voice—my voice—cried out tauntingly, "I killed your spawn, beast, and I won't have any trouble doing the same to you. Best you flee!"

The wyvern mother spun about, and in the blink of an eye she was gone, tearing through the trees in the direction my voice had emerged from.

I wasted no time in acting myself.

The moment the beast was out of sight, I dashed forward and grabbed the alchemy stone from the pile of desiccated skin.

You have retrieved an alchemy stone. New ingredients acquired: 5 x vials of beast blood, 5 x heaps of ordinary bonedust, 3 x sacs of wyvern venom, 1 x set of wyvern fangs, and 18 x wyvern scales.

With stone in hand, I fled for dear life.

It wouldn't take the wyvern long to figure out she'd been tricked, and by then I needed to be long gone.

* * *

After fleeing from the wyvern mother, I hurried north, not slowing to train my skills. My reasons were twofold. One, I didn't want to risk another encounter with the beast, and two, I hoped to reach the Red Rats' encampment with the night still young.

While I traveled along my treetop highway, I reflected on the encounter with the wyvern mother. The creature had to be beastkin. It was my beast tongue trait that allowed me to understand her. In hindsight, I realized the creature hadn't just been lying in wait for any careless interloper.

She had been waiting there for me specifically.

It implied a frightening level of forethought and planning. If the wyvern was anywhere near as smart as the dire wolves, then none of the vague plans I had conceived to take her down would work.

Still, killing the wyvern mother wasn't my priority. Escaping the valley was. Banishing the creature from my thoughts—but unable to stop my gaze from turning upward to worriedly search the sky—I continued north.

Just after nightfall, I reached the northern rim of the valley. According to the information Captain Talon had provided, the Red Rats were located slightly west of the dungeon's exit portal. Traveling counterclockwise along the foot of the mountain, I slipped quietly between the trees in search of the goblins.

An hour later, I found the Red Rats.

The goblin delegation was in a crater-like hollow. Its sides were boulder-strewn, gently sloping and free of the forest's clutches. The tree line ended sharply at the hollow's edge, making the rim of the crater quite distinctive.

At the base of the hollow, spread out messily across its entire breadth, were the goblins. From my treetop lookout point, I could see the full camp. In stark contrast to the valley's other two tribes, the Red Rats' camp contained no fortifications.

None.

Staring down at the sea of campfires, I shook my head in amazement. It almost seemed as if the Red Rats deliberately scorned any defenses. It was a statement, I realized.

A statement of power.

And given the size of the encampment, one that was seemingly well-warranted. The Red Rats easily outnumbered the Howlers. On first impression, there seemed to be nearly two thousand goblins in the hollow.

This is a tribe that relies on numbers alone, I concluded.

There were no guard patrols or any walls ringing the camp. The tribe also lacked the rigid discipline displayed by their counterparts in the south. Goblins idly roamed the camp, in ones and twos and in larger groups, laughing, weaving drunkenly, and generally without purpose.

The Red Rats are aptly named.

Like their rodent namesakes, they were populous and chaotic. Sneaking into the camp would be easy. Although given the number of freely wandering goblins, I doubted I would remain undetected for long. I wasn't certain what I intended on doing in the camp, but at the very least, I needed to investigate the anomaly I'd spotted.

In the center of the camp, in an area conspicuously empty of tents, was a clump of wrought-iron cages.

The cages, raised up high, dangled on the end of stout wooden poles and were kept that way by the thick iron chains securely fastened to the ground. Ten scruffy-looking and half-starved individuals were inside the enclosures.

The captain's lost squad.

One after the other, I analyzed the distant captives. All ten were players of similar rank to Cecilia's squad.

The Tartans' plight intrigued me. They were clearly prisoners of the Red Rats, but why the goblins would bother imprisoning players was a mystery. *Let's find out, shall we*, I thought, dropping down from my treetop hideaway and slipping into the shadows. It was dark enough now that doing so was trivial.

Multiple hostile entities have failed to detect you! You are hidden.

None of the dozen or more goblins within sight range came close to spotting me. Leaving the concealment of the forest's vegetation, I edged closer to the camp, my gaze fixed on the closest Red Rats.

None showed the slightest interest in watching the surrounding foliage. Their attention was focused inward, on their companions and their own revelry.

Timing my movements carefully, I ducked out of the forest and slunk into the camp.

Multiple hostile entities have failed to detect you!

I didn't stop moving until I reached my target destination: a goblin tent that, after careful observation, I believed to be empty. Placing my arms behind my back, I wrapped my hands around the hilts of my blades and rushed into the tent.

It was unoccupied.

Relaxing my grip on my blades, I studied the interior. The tent was filthy. Bits of food were strewn about, and the owner's rumpled beddings had been left unattended. I grunted in disdain. There didn't appear to be anything useful in the mess, and I wasn't about to dig around in it.

Time to move on.

Closing my eyes, I opened my mindsight and probed the surroundings. Six goblins had wandered near and loitered close by. Creeping back to the tent flap, I waited patiently for them to leave.

Five minutes later, they ambled away and I slipped out of my refuge and into another nearby tent that mindsight also confirmed to be unoccupied.

I nearly gagged at the stench that wafted out.

Like the first tent, the second's state left much to be desired. Holding my nose, I rechecked my surroundings. Too many goblins were around. Fighting my impatience, I waited until the coast was clear before dashing out of the tent.

And into another.

For the next thirty minutes, I continued in this manner, leapfrogging from tent to tent and always edging closer to my goal.

Inevitably, the more deeply I penetrated the camp, the more risks I was forced to take. But both my sneaking skill and abundance of caution served me well, and despite the numerous goblins crawling about, I went unnoticed.

Multiple hostile entities have failed to detect you!

Your sneaking has increased to level 50. Congratulations, Michael, your skill in sneaking has reached rank 5, allowing you to learn tier-2 abilities.

Finally, I found what I was searching for: a tent with a single occupant. The goblin was asleep. From his loud snores and the strong odor of drink permeating the tent, he was likely drunk too.

Slinking closer to my target, I crouched down and inspected him closely.

The target is a level 39 veteran goblin warrior.

The warrior was nearly my own height and dressed in steel armor. A long sword was sheathed at his hip. Disappointingly, he had no helm—that would have made disguising myself easier.

Still, he'll do.

Drawing spider's bite slowly, I positioned it beneath the sleeping goblin's chin. I was poised and ready.

In a spurt of motion, I acted.

Clamping my left hand down on the warrior's mouth, I drove the tip of my blade under his chin and through the roof of his palate.

You have killed a goblin warrior.

He died instantly, eyelids not even flickering.

I turned the body on its side, taking care not to bloody the goblin's gear. Working swiftly, I stripped the corpse of its armor and weapons. When I was done, I studied the pile of equipment I'd assembled.

This is a rank 2 set of goblin banded mail armor. This item requires a minimum Constitution of 8 to equip.

This is a rank 2 longsword. This item requires a minimum Strength of 8 to equip.

The longsword was of no use to me, but the armor would serve my purpose nicely. Unequipping my own leather armor, I dressed in the goblin's smellier and heavier gear.

You have equipped a set of goblin banded mail armor. This item set reduces the physical damage you sustain by 30% and penalizes your Magic and Dexterity by 60%.

Warning: you do not have the necessary skill, medium armor, to use this item. Armor benefits not received. Penalties are in effect. Current

modifiers: -12 ranks in Dexterity. Dexterity skills and abilities have been limited to rank 8.

I grimaced at the Game's message. The armor was heavy and cumbersome, and fighting in it would be difficult at best. Still, it wasn't my intent to fight, at least not yet.

I packed my own armor and thief's cloak in my backpack. Neither would serve my disguise. Spider's bite, too, went into my pack. The sword was too distinctive, and I wouldn't risk a passing goblin's attention being captured by the sword's jeweled hilt and wondering how a lowly goblin warrior had obtained such a weapon.

My other short sword had a plain leather hilt, and I fastened it on my hip. To complete the look, I cast facial disguise, using the dead goblin's face as a template.

I was nearly ready.

Searching the tent, I found a discarded sack and shoved my backpack into it. While it would look odd for a warrior to be carrying a sack, it would have been even stranger for me to have been seen sporting a backpack, and I wasn't about to leave my gear behind. Lastly, I bent down and picked up one of the empty beer jugs lying about.

Now, my costume was complete.

Taking a deep breath, I stepped boldly out of the tent.

You have passed a mental resistance check! Three hostile entities have failed to pierce your disguise. Your deception has increased to level 39.

The tension eased out of me as my disguise held up to scrutiny. With my frame slouched, the sack across my left shoulder, and the beer jug in my right hand, I headed deeper into the Red Rat camp.

It was time to visit the prisoners.

CHAPTER 110: STRUNG UP LIKE RATS

DAY THREE. NIGHT.

I weaved through the camp, swaying drunkenly and raising the empty jug to my lips anytime a goblin came too close.

Some of the passing warriors inquired curiously about what was in the sack, but none of them cared enough to stop me and find out when I pretended not to hear. With every encounter, my deception skill ticked upward, a reassuring reminder of the success of my ploy, and as nerve-racking as the entire venture was, it went off smoothly.

In short order, I reached the center of the camp where the prisoners were being held. Stumbling about with what I hoped was convincing drunkenness, I surreptitiously studied the space before me.

Ten wooden poles had been planted in the soft earth, and an iron ring had been affixed atop each. Steel chains were looped through each ring, the lower ends of which were tied to stakes driven into the ground. It kept the chains taut and the cages connected on their other ends aloft.

It seemed a strange way to secure the prisoners, and I wondered at the reason.

There were no guards nearby either, making freeing the prisoners simplicity itself. All I needed to do was remove the stakes anchoring the chains. The cages would drop to the floor. And just like that, the prisoners would be free.

But not only would this cause a racket, it would also be clearly visible to the entire camp.

So not so simple after all.

No goblins roamed the immediate area below the cages and, curious to talk to the prisoners, I staggered forward, the picture of drunkenness. I had no plan for freeing the players yet, but perhaps I could still learn something from them.

I took one step, then another.

Almost there...

A glint, glimpsed out of the corner of my eye, drew my gaze. I frowned. *That's odd...* Tilting my head to the side, I peered at the half-seen shimmer more fully.

And jerked to a halt.

A heartbeat later, realizing my error, I resumed my swaying, although this time I headed the other way—*away* from the cages. From beneath my lowered head, I gazed quickly left and right to see if anyone had noticed my most un-drunken-like behavior.

No one had.

I sagged in relief and let my eyes drift back to what had attracted my notice: a barely perceptible shimmer around one of the stakes driven into the ground.

That's definitely not natural.

I fell backward onto my rump, feigning a drunken stupor—for anyone watching—while I ran my gaze more intently over the other nine stakes.

They, too, were surrounded by a half-seen haze.

They're booby trapped, I thought. *They have to be.* Drawing on my stamina, I cast lesser trap detect.

Energy rushed into my eyes, sharpening my gaze. From the edges of my vision, glowing dust particles swirled into being and, after a beat, coalesced around the ten stakes to outline them in red.

You have spotted a trap! Your thieving has increased to level 2.
You have spotted a trap! Your thieving has increased to level 3.

...

You have spotted a trap! Your thieving has increased to level 10.
Congratulations, Michael! Your skill in thieving has reached rank 1.

Well, damn. In that moment, there was nothing feigned about the stupefied expression on my face.

I'd received ten separate Game messages, and while the skill increase accompanying each was nice, each alert also denoted the presence of a different trap.

Ten traps. I smiled grimly. I had underestimated the cunning of the Red Rats. For all the apparent simplicity of their prison, their captives were well-guarded.

I raised my gaze, still enchanted to perceive traps, and scrutinized the cages themselves. Unsurprisingly, I found more traps.

You have spotted a trap!

...

...

You have spotted a trap! Your thieving has increased to level 20 and reached rank 2.

The cages' doors were trapped too. I sighed. Freeing the Tartans was going to be harder than I'd anticipated.

* * *

I took my time examining the prison area. I wasn't sure if I'd get such an opportunity again. But despite my extended surveillance, I spotted no further traps.

Satisfied there were none, or if there were that I wasn't going to spot them, I bowed my head and pretended to snore. It was time to carry out the next stage of my tentative plan.

I had already marked the cage containing the captain's son, and I thought it best to contact him first. Where the other Tartan soldiers could've been anywhere between twenty and thirty years old, Sturm was clearly much younger. I pegged his age at eighteen, if that. Still, he was in command of the squad. Was that nepotism at work or talent at play? I would find out soon, I guessed.

Readying my voice, I cast ventro, projecting my words—at barely above a whisper—to appear as if originating from within the player's cage. "Sturm, can you hear me?"

No response.

"Sturm!" I called louder.

Even from a few dozen yards away, my sharp hearing picked up his startled grunt. He had been asleep, I thought.

"What? Who's that?" he demanded loudly.

"Ssshh," I hissed. "Not so loud. You'll attract attention."

There was a moment of surprised silence, and I could almost sense him looking around wildly. "Who are you?" he whispered.

"That's better. Keep it quiet," I said. "Look to your left. Do you see the goblin snoring there?"

A drawn-out silence.

Guessing that Sturm had nodded or used some other non-verbal cue, I said, "Use your words, Sturm. I can't see you."

"Yes," he replied. "I can see the goblin."

"That's me."

There was another heartbeat of silence, then an interrogatory query rippled over me.

You have passed a mental resistance check! An analyze attempt by a neutral entity has failed. Your deception has increased to level 44.

"How did you do that?" Sturm asked in a strangled voice.

"Doesn't matter," I said. "Now, listen—"

"And how are you speaking to me from over there?" Sturm asked, his voice rising an octave.

"Keep it down!" I ordered. "Or you'll give us away."

"What are you?" Sturm persisted, ignoring my instructions.

"I'm a player," I said. "Now shut up and listen!" I growled in exasperation. "Your father sent me."

That finally got through to Sturm, and he quieted. "My father?" he asked in a hushed tone.

"Yes, your father," I said. "Captain Talon has sent me to discover what has become of you and your squad."

"But you're not one of his men," Sturm objected.

"I'm not," I agreed. Deciding I needed to share more information in order to gain the player's confidence, I offered, "I'm the one the Awakened Dead are hunting in this sector."

"I see," Sturm said after another contemplative moment of silence.

"I can't free you or your men just yet," I continued. "The Red Rats have fashioned your prison more cunningly than I expected."

"Oh," Sturm said with undisguised bitterness.

"Do you know why the goblins have taken you as prisoners?"

Sturm didn't answer immediately. "It's to stop us from passing on what we know to my father," he said eventually. "If the Rats kill us, we'll be reborn in the safe zone. Keeping us imprisoned is the only way they can keep their secret safe."

"Ah," I exhaled. "And what is their secret?"

"I will tell you," Sturm said. He paused. "On the condition you get the information to my father. Will you do that?"

"Of course."

Sturm weighed my words for a second, then said, "The Red Rats are already allied with the Awakened Dead, but Erebus is intent on keeping that knowledge secret."

I frowned. "Why would he want to do that?"

"I don't know," Sturm admitted. "But there's more."

"Go on."

"Not only are the Rats pledged to Erebus, but they've also been ordered to wage war on the Howlers."

My brows shot up, unable to make sense of any of the information Sturm was conveying. "Are you sure?"

"I am," he said. "My squad ambushed a messenger from Stayne himself to the Red Rat shaman before we were captured in turn."

"Stayne," I murmured. So, he was involved with matters in this sector too.

"What will you do now?" Sturm asked.

I took my time answering. "Leave," I said at last. If the Red Rats discovered me, I suspected they would do to me what they'd done to Sturm and his squad, and I couldn't afford that. "Sorry, I can't rescue you just yet," I added. "But I will be back."

"Thank you," he replied in a trembling voice. Still, he made no attempt to plead for his freedom. *Brave of him.*

I rose to my feet with affected grogginess, and another thought made me pause. "Do you know where the shamans' tents are?"

Sturm jerked his chin behind him. "That way. You can't miss them. The big red ones belong to the shaman and his apprentices." He paused. "What are you going to do?"

"Investigate," I said and swayed away.

✳ ✳ ✳

After leaving the prison area, I reviewed the latest message from the Adjudicator.

Your task, <u>Forging Dark Alliances</u>! has been updated. You have received word from a reliable source that the Reds Rats are already allied with a Dark Power. Objective two revised: inform Captain Talon or seek confirmation of your source's information.

My time in the camp was growing short. Sooner or later, the body of the dead veteran warrior would be discovered, but given the camp's lax discipline, I wasn't certain what would happen when that occurred. Nonetheless, I wanted to be long gone by then.

So what am I going to do?

The truth was, Sturm's information had piqued my curiosity. Erebus was playing some game, that much I was sure of, but with what end in mind, I didn't know. Still, I was desperate to find out.

It made no sense for the Awakened Dead to prolong their claim to the sector. They should be attempting to secure it as soon as possible. Why then was Erebus keeping his alliance with the Red Rats secret and, more puzzling still, ordering them to attack the Howlers, another group whose alliance he should also be seeking?

I shook my head, unable to understand the Power's motivations.

So, instead of exiting the camp immediately, which would've been the sensible thing to do, I delved deeper, heading toward the shamans' tents on the off chance I could discover more of the Awakened Dead's intent.

Sturm proved right. The shamans' tents were unmissable.

Painted a striking shade of red, the five tents were drawn up in a line like a crimson scar cut into the heart of the camp. I wandered nearby and, through half-lidded eyes, scanned the tents with mindsight.

Four of the tents were occupied. Only one, the one on the far right, was vacant. Seemingly by chance, I wandered closer toward it, and once I was certain no one was watching, I ducked inside.

Concealed within the tent, I stood unmoving at the entrance while I examined the interior with trap detection. Given what I'd seen in the prison area, I had to assume there would be more traps in the camp, especially around the shamans' possessions.

Almost immediately, a red haze superimposed itself over multiple objects in my vision.

You have spotted 5 traps! Your thieving has increased to level 22.

My lips turned down sourly. The Red Rat shamans certainly seemed to like their traps. Every chest, box, and bag I could see in the tent was trapped.

So much for finding a revealing slip of paper, I thought unhappily. Ducking back into the shadows, I readied myself to leave. I wasn't about to risk trying to disarm one of the traps while surrounded by two thousand hostiles.

Perhaps, I can—

My internal monologue broke, as through my mindsight I spied a goblin drawing closer. Reaching out, I analyzed him.

The target is Juxal, a level 43 goblin apprentice shaman.

The tent's owner was returning.

Damn it! Stepping to one side, I drew my blade and crouched down.

You are hidden.

The tent was too small for me to stay concealed long. My best chance now of escaping the camp was to slay the incoming apprentice before he could give the alarm. *At least it's only an apprentice.*

Poised for action, I waited.

A figure entered, dressed in a crimson robe the same shade of red as the tent. I uncoiled, left hand snaking out to wrap around the apprentice's mouth while the shortsword in my right hand drew a line of red across his throat.

You have killed Juxal with a fatal blow. You have reached level 49!
Your shortswords has increased to level 50. Congratulations, Michael! Your skill with shortswords has reached rank 5, allowing you to learn tier-2 abilities.

I lowered the corpse carefully to the ground, every sense extended for more signs of danger. When, after a few seconds, I heard nothing to warrant further alarm, I began to loot the tent quickly and efficiently.

You have acquired 4 trapped containers.

The traps around the containers were placed on their locking mechanisms, and they didn't prevent me from carrying them away while still fastened.

Only one chest was too large to fit in my sack. The rest, smaller pouches and bags, went in without further examination. After that, I stripped off the apprentice's robes. It, too, could come in handy in the future.

You have acquired a rank 1 crimson Red Rat shaman robe. This item requires a minimum Magic of 4 to equip.

Then I exited the tent, my drunken persona back in place.
It was time to flee.

CHAPTER 111: THIEVING WAYS

Day Three. Night.

I reached the camp boundary without incident, and once more my deception skill ticked upward.

Your deception has increased to level 47.

Ducking into a nearby empty tent, I stripped off the goblin armor and re-equipped my own gear before sneaking out of the crater.

No alarm followed on my heels.

Either the Red Rats hadn't discovered the two slain goblins, or they simply didn't care. Leaving the camp behind me, I hurried south through the forest.

I was tired and hungry but didn't dare rest so close to the hostile tribe. After two hours of hard travel, I finally drew to a stop and, tying myself to a tree, fell into a deep sleep.

✱ ✱ ✱

I awoke before dawn, rested and hale.

Yesterday had been a long and strenuous day, but I'd finally gotten some proper rest and felt better for it. Glancing about, I considered my surroundings.

The forest was still quiet. Pulling out a ration, I began to eat while I saw to my player progression. I had one attribute point to spend, and without dwelling on the matter, I used it to increase my health pool.

Your Constitution has increased to rank 14.

Next, I considered my plan for the day. Meeting Ultack and Cecilia came first, but how I proceeded after that... that I was no longer sure about.

Matters in the valley were tangled.

There were more interested parties than I expected, each with its own agenda. The Awakened Dead was hiding something—I wasn't certain what it was yet—but it couldn't be for nothing that Erebus was pushing the goblins to war.

The Tartans' goals seemed simpler. They wanted the valley claimed for the Dark to secure their supply routes into the Nethersphere. Mariga and the Shadow's objectives were no less straightforward: they wanted the Dark stopped.

The dire wolves sought their survival only, and for that they needed me to destroy the Long Fangs. What the goblins themselves wanted was anyone's guess.

And let's not forget the wyvern mother and Ishita's sworn. Both want me dead.

Somehow, I had to navigate through all these cross-purposes and threats and still find a way out of the valley in the next three days. I sighed.

How do you get yourself into these situations, Michael?

I dropped down from the tree. I wasn't going to find the answers sitting here, and if I didn't want to be late for my meeting with Ultack and Cecilia, I had to be on my way.

Summoning psi, I slipped through the forest, heading southeast. Along the way, I planned on training my skills further. If I could manage it, I wanted to reach rank five in deception before meeting the Tartans.

*　　*　　*

Your insight has increased to level 58. Your deception has increased to level 51.

I achieved my goal with time to spare.

Assuming Ultack had managed to get what I'd requested, I would soon add an advanced deception ability to my repertoire. A plan was slowly taking shape in my mind, and the ability would form a key component of it.

Reaching the meeting spot, I surveyed the clearing. It was as empty as I'd left it yesterday. The Tartans were late.

There was no point in just sitting around and waiting. I had a better use for my time. Sitting cross-legged, I pulled out the booby-trapped containers from my backpack and laid them out on the grass.

Chin in hands, I studied the items on the ground. One was a coin bag, kept closed with a simple drawstring, another was a lockbox, and the last two were thin leather sleeves.

All four objects were booby trapped, and given the nature of their former owner, I suspected the traps were magical in nature. Drawing on my reserves of stamina, I cast trap disarm.

Trap disarm was a strange ability. It didn't directly disable traps but instead gave me the tools necessary to do so. Where an ordinary thief was helpless without his lockpicks and disarming kits, a player-enhanced thief was less affected by the lack. Physical tools still helped, but with my abilities they weren't essential.

Energy rippled into my hands and eyes, transforming my sight and fingers.

I studied the simple coin bag anew, this time using eyes enhanced to spot concealed spells and hidden contraptions. Sure enough, I spied a coil of magic around the object.

A magic working had been wrapped around the bag in a replica of its physical drawstring. To disarm the trap, I would need to untie the spelled strands around the bag.

I reached out to the object with magicked hands. My fingers had been enchanted by the trap disarm ability, allowing them to interact with the spell wound around the bag. With nimble fingers, I deftly untangled the magic strands and disabled the spell.

You have successfully disarmed a trap. Your thieving has increased to level 23.

I grinned in satisfaction as I succeeded on my first attempt. Grabbing hold of the coin bag, I emptied its contents into the palm of my hand.

You have acquired 0 gold, 3 silver, and 0 copper.

I stared at the three silver coins in disappointment. "I guess it doesn't pay to be an apprentice," I muttered.

Putting away the money, I turned my attention to the lockbox. Recasting trap disarm, I examined it as meticulously as I had the coin bag.

This time, the trap was a physical one.

Peering into the keyhole, I spotted a thin strand of wire extending from the center of the keyhole to an unknown device within the lockbox itself. Drawing one of my daggers, I delicately pried at the tripwire and cut it.

You have successfully disarmed a trap. Your thieving has increased to level 24.

"Not too shabby," I said to myself with a small smile.

The lockbox was still locked, but I had another ability for that: simple lock picking. I activated it, enhancing my ears to discern the smallest clicks and turns of the lock.

Holding up the item to the side of my head, I jiggled my knife in the lock, noting the impact of every click and turn until, finally, I determined the correct combination and the lid of the lockbox sprang open.

You have successfully picked a lock. Your thieving has increased to level 25.

It had taken longer than I expected, but that was more a result of my poor tools than because of the complexity of the lock itself. "I need to find some lockpicks," I murmured.

Peering inside the open box, I found two items.

You have acquired an apprentice's ring, +2 Magic. This is a rank 1 ring and increases your Magic attribute by 2. This item has no requirements to equip.

You have acquired an acolyte's ring, +2 Faith. This is a rank 1 ring and increases your Faith attribute by 2. This item has no requirements to equip.

This is more like it. The two rings were the only items I'd found that directly affected my attributes. Given that, I suspected they were not only rare but expensive too.

Drawing off the glove on my left hand, I equipped both rings and felt my mana pool swell, a function of my increased Faith and Magic. While I had no real use for more mana, it was nice to feel the effect of the items.

You have equipped an apprentice's ring. Your Magic has increased to rank 2. You have equipped an acolyte's ring. Your Faith has increased to rank 2.

Finally, I turned to the slim, leatherbound sleeves. Pulling the first one onto my lap, I examined it carefully. At first glance, the trap woven about the object appeared as simple as the one I had just disarmed. A mechanical contraption was hidden in the small gold button that secured the sleeve's flap, and I disabled it without much trouble.

I was about to flip open the flap when a sharp prickle of unease shot through me. Having learned to pay close attention to such feelings, I withdrew my reaching fingers and cast trap detect.

The leather sleeve was still outlined in a shimmer of red. My brows drew down. Why was the pouch still booby trapped? Casting trap disarm again, I reexamined the item.

There was another trap.

It had been hiding in plain sight too—beneath the mechanical contraption—and was only revealed now because its counterpart had been disabled.

Bloody insidious, I thought, my admiration for the Red Rat apprentice shaman growing.

Tentatively, I picked at the spell, attempting to untangle the magical triggers set about the object.

You have failed to disarm a trap.

I frowned. This spell trap set on the leather sleeve was more complex than the one that had been woven around the coin bag, which accounted for my failure.

I tried again.

You have failed to disarm a trap.

...

You have failed to disarm a trap.

I ground my teeth in frustration. After ten attempts, I still hadn't managed to deconstruct the trap. Thankfully, though, my failures hadn't been so severe to trigger the spell itself.

I couldn't help wondering at the contents of the sleeve. What could it be? To be protected by *two* traps, one of which was devilishly complex, the contents had to be even more valuable than the lockbox's items.

With that in mind, I bent my head over the sleeve again. I wasn't giving up until I had it opened.

Renewing my focus, I began anew.

✳ ✳ ✳

More than a dozen attempts later, my perseverance was finally rewarded.

You have successfully disarmed a trap. Your thieving has increased to level 27.

About time, I thought, wiping the beading sweat off my brow. *Now to see my reward.* My anticipation mounting, I flipped open the leather sleeve and peered inside.

It was empty.

An involuntary bark of laughter escaped me. All that effort, and for what? Nothing.

Still chuckling, I drew the last item onto my lap and began to disarm its traps. If nothing else, it would help train my skill.

The second leather sleeve was trapped in the same manner as the first one, and this time around I had less trouble figuring out how to deconstruct them.

You have successfully disarmed a trap. Your thieving has increased to level 29.

Expecting nothing, I opened the sleeve. Much to my bemusement, it contained a single sheaf of paper. I withdrew the parchment and, holding it up to the light, read what was written on it.

This week's code words. Day 1: bedevil. Day 2: avatar. Day 3: sedition. Day 4: patriarch. Day 5: avalanche. Day 6: stigma. Day 7: deity.

I frowned. The words were scrawled untidily—by the apprentice's own hand, I suspected—but were still legible. What had a goblin shaman been doing with code words?

Was he a spy? And for whom?

I drummed the fingers of my hand on my thigh, thinking hard, but before I could make sense of my latest discovery, my sharp ears picked up the sound of an approaching party.

Cocking my head to the side, I listened intently. It was Ultack and Cecilia. The Tartans had arrived. Stashing the parchment into my pocket, I rose to my feet to greet them.

✳ ✳ ✳

The two recruits had come alone.

"Morning," I greeted, leaning against a tree trunk with my arms folded across my chest.

Elf and half-orc nodded in greeting as they hurried closer. "We have your items," Cecilia said without preamble.

"What, all of them?" I asked jokingly. I hadn't given them nearly enough money for that.

"Yes, all of them," she replied with no hint of a smile.

I straightened abruptly. She was being serious, I realized.

Ultack chuckled and, removing four books from his pack, held them out to me. "Surprised?"

"Very," I agreed. "I didn't think the money I gave you would be nearly enough."

"Ordinarily, it wouldn't have been," Ultack said.

"But the captain isn't without resources of his own," Cecilia said. "He has his own suppliers, and let's just say they can undercut the market."

I raised one eyebrow. "You went to the captain for this?"

"We had to," Ultack said seriously.

"We couldn't have helped you without his permission," Cecilia added, to which Ultack nodded in agreement.

"I see," I said, taking the items the half-orc held out.

You have acquired an advanced ability tome: lesser backstab. You have the necessary skills, rank 5 sneaking and a light weapon skill, to learn this ability.

You have acquired an advanced ability tome: improved analyze. You have the necessary skill, rank 5 insight, to learn this ability.

You have acquired an advanced ability tome: minor piercing strike. You have the necessary skill, any rank 5 light weapon skill, to learn this ability.

You have acquired an advanced ability tome: lesser imitate. You have the necessary skill, rank 5 deception, to learn this ability.

"Thank you," I said. "I'm grateful."

"You should be," Cecilia said. "The captain has gone to great lengths on your behalf." She eyed me carefully. "Why, I don't know. But be sure you do not disappoint him."

I inclined my head but said nothing, wondering myself what the captain's reasons were. Whatever he'd told me, I doubted he was helping me simply because of the task he needed completed. *He has to have an ulterior motive.*

"The captain wants to know if you have anything to report yet?" Ultack asked.

I hesitated. The Tartans had done me a great service, providing me with the ability tomes I needed and warning me of the ambush in the safe zone. I owed them, but I wasn't yet ready to repay the debt.

Until I knew better what was going on in the valley, I needed to play my cards close. "Not yet," I said finally. "I'm making progress, but I don't have anything definitive to report yet."

Ultack nodded, taking me at my word.

Cecilia, however, was not as accepting. She peered at me suspiciously. "Nothing? What have you been doing all this time?"

I stared at the elf. "When I know something, I'll let you know."

She opened her mouth, no doubt to admonish me again, but Ultack placed a restraining hand on her arm. "Let him be, Cecilia. The captain said to trust him."

The elven mage closed her mouth with a snap and nodded imperiously. "What will you do now?" she asked, still probing.

"I'm not sure," I answered less than truthfully. I had the bare bones of a plan, but I wasn't about to share it with her.

My answer didn't please her. Before she could speak, though, Ultack asked, "Shall we arrange to meet you at the same time tomorrow?"

I considered this for a moment before shaking my head. "No. It might take me longer than that to gather the information I need. I'll return to the safe zone when I have news."

I was sure now I had to return to the village, no matter the risk. I had too many unanswered questions, and the only ones who could answer them—Ishita's sworn, Talon and Mariga—were all in the safe zone.

The half-orc was surprised by my response but accepted it nonetheless. He held out his hand. "Good hunting then, Michael."

I shook his hand before turning around to disappear into the trees.

It was time to put my scheme into play.

DAY FOUR. MORNING.

I headed back north in the same direction from which I had just come. I still wasn't certain how I would accomplish all that I needed to, but I knew already that I had to begin with the Red Rats.

Sturm's information was the key.

If what he'd told me proved accurate, it would allow me to begin unlocking the puzzle that was this sector.

If my scheme was going to work though, I couldn't risk raising the Red Rats' suspicions. It was why I hadn't told Ultack and Cecilia about Sturm. I feared the knowledge that his son was a prisoner might spur Talon into attempting a rescue operation, thereby spelling disaster for my own plans.

It took me the better part of the day to complete the journey back to the goblin tribe, and by midafternoon I reached the outskirts of the crater. Before entering the camp, I stopped to ready myself and learn the abilities the Tartans had purchased for me.

Finding a comfortable perch on a tree branch, I opened the first book, the one containing the knowledge of the lesser imitate spell, and began reading.

You have acquired the advanced ability: lesser imitate. This ability allows you to imitate another similar-sized entity, including their apparel, voice, and appearance. It creates a light- and sound-based illusion that can be detected by a Perception check.

The illusion will remain in place for 1 hour or until dispelled. Warning: taking damage will cause the illusion to dissipate. This ability consumes stamina and can be upgraded. Its activation time is very slow.

Lesser imitate is an advanced ability and requires 5 Perception ability slots. You have 0 of 10 Perception ability slots remaining.

I blinked at the Game message in shock. *The ability took five slots?*

It was an unexpected and unwelcome surprise—not that knowledge of the new ability wasn't worth it, but I hadn't expected advanced abilities to require so many slots.

As a result, I didn't have enough Perception slots to also learn improved analyze, and I returned its tome to my backpack. Upgrading the ability would have to wait. *I'll have to reconsider how I invest my attribute points.*

I also wondered how much tier three and higher abilities would cost. *Too much,* I thought. I sighed. It was another complication. *But not one I can do anything about now.* Opening the next ability tome, I began to read.

You have upgraded your backstab ability to lesser backstab. This is a weapon-based ability that allows you to deal 2x more damage with a single blow. This ability can only be used when the target is unaware of your presence or is incapacitated.

The effects of this ability may be overcome by physical resistance. This ability consumes stamina and can be upgraded. Its activation time is near-

instantaneous. Lesser backstab is an advanced ability and requires 4 more Dexterity slots than its basic variant. You have 12 of 20 Dexterity ability slots remaining.

I grunted in satisfaction as my backstab ability morphed into a more powerful variant. Without further ado, I opened the last book and absorbed its knowledge.

You have acquired the advanced ability: minor piercing strike. This is a weapon-based ability that doubles the force of a single strike, increasing your chance to penetrate your foe's armor. This ability only works with piercing attacks from a bladed weapon.

This ability consumes stamina, and its activation time is near-instantaneous. Minor piercing strike is an advanced ability and requires 5 Dexterity ability slots. You have 7 of 20 Dexterity slots remaining.

I exhaled softly as knowledge of my new abilities settled into me. I was ready, or as ready as I could expect to be. Slipping off the tree branch, I dropped lightly to the ground.

Concealed by shadows, I crept to the edge of the tree line and peered into the crater. Little had changed since yesterday. Goblins still caroused and wandered freely, appearing no more alert today.

I couldn't ask for more perfect conditions. *Time to do this.*

Closing my eyes, I called on my newfound knowledge and cast lesser imitate. The ability was powerful but not without weaknesses. With it I could look like whomever I wished, but my false visage wouldn't stand up to close scrutiny. Most players would be able to easily penetrate it after prolonged contact.

But no players roamed the Red Rats' camp.

Holding my target image in my mind, I spun an illusion about myself. The lines of my body, clothes, and face began to blur as they were overlaid by a casting of light. My vocal cords too, I sensed, were altering.

Patiently, I waited for the illusion to settle into place. When it was done, I stared down at my hands. To my own eyes, they looked the same.

But to hostile eyes, I expected I would appear wholly different.

Taking a deep breath, I stepped out of cover and walked toward the crater. I was spotted quickly. Goblin soldiers turned my way, the cry of alarm on their lips stilling as they took in my appearance. Speaking to each other in hushed tones, they darted fearful looks at me.

I grinned to myself. *Looks like it's working.*

Reaching the crater's edge, I folded my arms across my chest and waited.

Multiple hostile entities have failed to pierce your disguise. Your deception has increased to level 53.

It took the goblins a full five minutes to work up the courage to approach me. When they did, it was to shove a sergeant my way while the rest hung fearfully back.

"H-halt," the sergeant stuttered, his fingers gripping his spear tightly.

The order was superfluous, of course. I was standing still already. But it wouldn't do to let a mere goblin command me. That wouldn't at all be in character for Erebus' undead henchman.

"You dare order me about, little goblin?" I hissed. To my own ears my voice sounded normal, but I could only imagine how the goblins perceived it.

The sergeant shrunk back fearfully. "N–n–no, sir. Of course not," he said before faltering to a halt.

I guess that means I sound like Stayne, I thought dryly.

"Then let me through." I strode forward boldly and straight toward the unfortunate goblin.

The sergeant didn't move, made of sterner stuff than I'd expected. "I can't," he whispered.

"Why not?" I demanded, coming to a halt less than a foot away from the hapless soldier.

"By your own orders, no one is allowed into the camp without the code, sir!"

"I see," I said. *So that's what they're for.* Displaying no hint of trepidation, I let my gaze rove menacingly over the watching goblins. "What day is it, sergeant?" I asked mildly.

"Sir?" the goblin squeaked.

"I can't very well give you the code if I don't know which day's code you require, can I?" I snapped, hoping I'd not misinterpreted how the code sheet worked.

The sergeant's face scrunched up in confusion. No doubt he was puzzled at my ignorance, but fear of the undead whose guise I'd stolen kept him from voicing his doubts. "It's day seven, sir."

I nodded curtly, then recited from memory, "Today's code word is 'deity.'" I puffed up my chest and let my lips curl up in amusement. "Appropriate, don't you think?"

"Yessir," the sergeant said meekly and stepped aside. "Go on ahead, and I'm sorry for delaying you."

I passed beyond him, then paused and pointed to a goblin at random. "You there! Take me to your shaman."

The unlucky soldier stared at me in shock, not moving.

"Now!" I barked.

The goblin scurried away and I followed on his heels, hiding a grin. *I could get used to this.*

✱   ✱   ✱

The soldier led me to the centermost of the red tents. "He's in there," the goblin stuttered. Not waiting for my response, he fled.

My gaze flitted over the surroundings. A score or more goblins were looking on from nearby, but when my eyes—or rather Stayne's pulsing red orbs—passed over them, they looked away. Satisfied that it was unlikely any of the goblins would interfere, I ducked into the tent.

The interior was more opulently furnished than the apprentice's I'd used yesterday. Thick fur rugs were spread across the floor, and trophies hung down from the roof. A gilded table sat in the tent's center, along with a throne-like chair.

Sitting in it was the largest goblin I'd seen yet.

His head was bent, reading something on the table. At my entrance, he looked up, eyes widening in recognition. "Stayne," he gasped. The shaman rose to his feet hastily. "What are you doing here, milord?"

I glared at him. "You expect me to answer to you for my movements?"

The goblin blanched. "No, of course not!" The shaman bowed deeply, hand over the hip. "Forgive me," he said, not rising from his bow.

I didn't say anything for a moment, using the opportunity to analyze the Red Rat leader.

The target is Klaxis, a level 71 goblin shaman.

Shamans, like witch doctors, are tribal leaders among goblinkin. They focus their energies almost purely on offensive magic and are particularly fond of fire-based spells.

Just as I feared, the shaman was a strong magic user. If my ploy failed and we came to blows, I couldn't afford to let the fight be drawn out. Casually, I strolled closer.

"Very well," I said at last. "You are forgiven." I paused. "This time. Now get up."

Klaxis unbent and gasped as I walked around the table.

"What is it now?" I snapped waspishly.

"I'm sorry, milord, but have you grown... smaller?" he asked, a hint of uncertainty and something else—suspicion?—in his voice.

Oops.

Stayne, I recalled belatedly, was a foot and a half taller than I was, and lesser imitate had done nothing to change my body size. *Perhaps I shouldn't have gotten so close.* But it was too late to back away now.

I drew to a halt two steps from Klaxis—within easy striking distance.

"I have," I said brusquely, showing no outward sign of fear of the goblin looming above me. *Let him make of that what he will.* "But that is no concern of yours either."

"As you say," Klaxis said, eyes narrowing slightly.

Damn it, I cursed. *He's still suspicious.* "Enough small talk. I'm here with orders."

"Orders?" the Red Rat leader asked, his gaze drifting to the table.

I kept my own eyes fixed on the shaman, not letting myself be distracted. "Yes, orders. You and your people are to attack the Long Fangs. Immediately."

"What? Why?" Klaxis asked, his eyes widening in surprise. "I thought the Master's orders were to leave that miserable little tribe alone? What's changed?"

I clenched my teeth in frustration. The shaman wasn't buying what I was selling. *This is about to go sideways,* I thought.

Placing my hands on my hips—and closer to my concealed weapons incidentally—I took another step forward and snarled, "You question me again?"

The goblin stared at me impassively, and a moment later I felt a tingle ripple over me, followed by the Game message I'd been dreading.

You have failed a mental resistance check! Klaxis has pierced your disguise.

DAY FOUR. EARLY AFTERNOON.

I didn't hesitate. Darting forward, I slapped my left hand on the goblin's cheek. In the same motion, I drew spider's bite and struck at the shaman's throat.

Klaxis has passed a physical resistance check! You have failed to stun your target.
Klaxis has evaded your blow.

Amazingly, stunning slap failed me. I didn't catch the shaman off guard by my sudden attack either. Moving nearly as quickly as I did, he sidestepped the blow meant to fell him.

The shaman's right hand came around, and out of the corner of my eye I saw a wand slip out of the sleeve of his robe and into his palm.

Flinging out my left arm, I stopped the shaman before he could point the wand at me and unleash whatever spell it contained.

You have blocked Klaxis' attack.

Still holding the shaman's hand, I lashed out with spider's bite, tearing a jagged line down his left shoulder.

You have struck Klaxis a glancing blow. Webbed triggered!
Webbed failed. Your target has passed a physical resistance check!

The shaman shrieked and, in a move that caught me by surprise, stepped forward and head-butted me on the forehead.

I staggered back, head ringing.

"You will die, impostor!" Klaxis screamed as he brought his freed right hand around again to point squarely at me.

Coils of roiling orange energy rippled down the wand and burst out toward me. I hurled myself to the side, narrowly evading the lance of fire.

The bar of blazing energy struck the tent behind me, setting it on fire alight. Ignoring the flames at my back, I rolled to my feet and threw myself forward again.

Muttering the words of another spell under his breath, the shaman recentered his wand on me. Another inferno fanned out. One-stepping, I leaped over the cone of flames.

You have evaded Klaxis' attack.

Midair, I somersaulted.

From above, I caught the flash of teeth as the shaman flung up his head to gape at me in surprise. Flipping end over end, I landed softly behind my foe and before he spun around sheathed spider's bite in his unprotected back.

You have critically injured Klaxis.

It was the goblin's turn to stagger. Blood pumped out of his wounds, streaking his already crimson robes a darker shade. "Guards!" Klaxis cried, finally calling for aid.

From beyond the now-burning tent, I sensed a rising commotion. Ignoring it, I advanced on the retreating shaman. I could still salvage this mess if I managed to finish him before the rest of the goblins intervened.

"Help," Klaxis gasped. "Help me kill the impos—"

He got no further. Charging forward, I crashed into the injured shaman's back and bowled him over. He fell to the ground with me on top of him.

Klaxis wasn't done fighting though. Heaving for breath, he strained to lift himself up. Brutally, I shoved his head back down into the dirt, and before he could twist out of the way I buried spider's bite in his neck.

You have killed Klaxis. You have reached level 50!
Congratulations, Michael! You are now a tier-2 and rank 5 player.

I rose shakily to my feet, barely in time to assume a nonchalant stance and verify lesser imitate was still active before two elite goblin warriors braved the flames to rush into the tent.

Mouths working soundlessly, the pair's eyes darted between the corpse at my feet and my implacable expression.

"What are you two idiots gaping at?" I demanded in the most imperious manner I could manage. I pointed a finger at one of the goblins. He flinched, then flushed at his display of fear.

"Put that out," I said, jerking my head toward the still-burning tent. I turned to the second goblin. "And you, take that away," I added, waving negligently at the dead shaman.

Neither goblin moved.

Striving to conceal my unease—if lesser imitate failed me again, I was dead—I took a threatening step toward the warriors. "Now!" I roared.

The two scurried into motion, and some of the tension eased out of me. A third goblin ran into the tent. Before he could open his mouth, I spun toward him. "Go and fetch the senior apprentice. And tell him to bloody hurry!"

The goblin's eyes flickered from me to his two companions busy doing my bidding. Bobbing his head in mute acknowledgment, the goblin pivoted around and ran out of the tent.

Given a moment alone, I exhaled sharply. My heart still thudded furiously in my chest, but slowly I was regaining control of the situation. I glanced at the two industriously working warriors. I had to tweak my original plan, I realized.

If I wanted to get out of this alive, I couldn't give the goblins further cause for suspicion. *Keep them guessing and too busy to think.*

With studied unconcern, I folded my hands behind my back and strolled toward the table. A letter lay there. Casually, I let my eyes drift over it.

Shaman Klaxis, your request to begin a major onslaught against the Howlers is denied. You are, however, still permitted to continue your raiding operations.

The Master is not yet ready to eradicate either of the other two tribes in the valley. Be patient. The time is fast approaching when we may move openly against them.

As to your second request, consider it granted. You and your people may freely kill any players not belonging to the Awakened Dead faction who you find in the valley—writ or no writ.

With regards to your last report, I find news of the assassinated apprentice disturbing. It appears your camp is no longer as secure as I'd thought. Transfer the prisoners immediately to the dungeon.

Yours truly,

Stayne.

With difficulty, I stopped myself from cursing as I read the note. Given its contents, Stayne must have penned it recently. I noticed too that the letter contradicted some of the "orders" I'd tried issuing.

No wonder Klaxis was suspicious.

Starkly aware of the nearby goblin warriors, I reached down to the table and deftly swiped the letter. It confirmed Sturm's information *and* proved the Awakened Dead's duplicity, making its worth incalculable.

You have acquired Stayne's letter.

Your task, <u>Forging Dark Alliances</u>! has been updated. You have acquired a damning note penned by a sworn servant of Erebus.

Optional objective revised: pass on Stayne's letter to Captain Talon. Objective two revised: inform Captain Talon that the Red Rats and the Dark are already allied.

I stowed away the letter just in time.

A moment after I folded my arms behind my back, a red-robed goblin burst into the tent. His gaze drifted over the half-destroyed tent and his dead master before locking on mine.

"What happened here, Lord Stayne?" the apprentice asked cautiously.

"Your shaman was foolish enough to question my orders." I smirked at him. "I hope you will not make the same mistake."

To his credit, the goblin didn't quake at my naked threat. "It will be my pleasure to serve, milord," he said, bowing smoothly from the waist. "The Red Rats have pledged our allegiance to the Awakened Dead. We will do whatever the Master requires."

"Excellent," I murmured. "You will prepare your forces for immediate departure."

Excitement danced in the apprentice's eyes. "At last," he breathed. "We are to move against the Howlers?"

I hesitated. It wasn't my intent to pit the Red Rats against the Howlers—there was too much that could go wrong with that—but seeing the eagerness in the apprentice's eyes, I realized he would be less likely to question my *other* orders if I gave him what he desired.

And besides, it will likely disrupt Erebus' own plans.

"Yes," I said finally. "But there is something else you must do first."

The apprentice quivered with joy at my confirmation but retained enough discipline to wait for me to finish before celebrating.

"The Long Fangs must be wiped out," I said.

The goblin frowned. "The Long Fangs? Why would—"

"What is your name, apprentice?" I asked, interrupting him. I could have analyzed him to find out of course, but this way was easier.

"Nyzack, my lord," he replied.

"Well, Nyzack," I said, leaning back against the table, "you are dangerously close to crossing the same line your fallen leader fell foul of. Do you understand?"

The goblin stiffened and bowed. "I do, master."

I let my smile deepen. "Flattering, but incorrect. There is only one Master."

The apprentice bowed again. "I stand corrected, milord."

"Now, will you heed my orders?" I asked.

"Yessir."

"Excellent," I said, pushing away from the table and straightening. "I expect the Long Fangs to be no more before noon tomorrow." I paused. "Then you may march on the Howlers."

Unmitigated joy spread across Nyzack's face at this prospect. "Thank you, milord," he said fervently.

"Good, see it done." Considering the matter closed, I strode toward the tent opening. Every second that I delayed my exit increased the chance of me being discovered.

"Sir..." Nyzack began.

Concealing a sigh, I turned around and looked at him inquiringly. "Yes?"

"What about the prisoners?" he asked.

I stroked my chin, pretending to consider his words. "Leave them here under guard." I would have preferred to order the apprentice to free the Tartans, but that might have raised his suspicions.

No point taking chances now.

"As you wish," the goblin replied.

Spinning around on my heels, I strode out of the tent. "Remember, noon tomorrow," I said over my shoulder. "By then, the Long Fangs must be vanquished."

Chapter 114: Adding to the Mayhem

I made it out of the Red Rat camp without incident. I didn't retreat far though. Finding a likely tree, I scaled its heights to observe the goblins. While I waited to see if the apprentice would do as I instructed, I reflected on the outcome of the encounter.

In the end, things had gone better than I'd had any right to expect. I barely had time to assess Klaxis, but he had seemed too wily for my taste. Having his apprentice in charge instead was a far more preferable outcome.

Nyzack will do what I want, I thought.

Sure enough, after a few minutes the camp began to stir to life. Orders were shouted, warriors hurried back and forth, and troops began to form. I smiled. The new Red Rat leader was faithfully following my commands.

I kept watching as the motley collection of goblins was transformed into something akin to a military force. In what was surprisingly short order, nearly all two thousand Red Rat warriors were assembled and set to march southeast through the forest.

I watched them go with a grin plastered on my face. If everything went as expected, then by this time tomorrow the dire wolves' goblin troubles would be over.

That's one problem taken care of.

My gaze returned to the crater. It was empty—or nearly so. The captives in their trapped cages remained. So did the two squads of goblin warriors Nyzack had set to guard them.

I pursed my lips as I considered the imprisoned players and what else I needed to do in the valley. Did I have enough time remaining to free them?

I do, I decided.

But they would have to wait a few more hours. I had another sleepless night ahead of me, and I needed to get some rest while I still could.

Before that, though, I had to see to my player progression. I'd earned two attribute points from killing Klaxis, and given what I'd learned about advanced abilities, I didn't ponder too long before investing in Perception.

Your Perception has increased to rank 12.

Then I closed my eyes and fell fast asleep.

* * *

I awoke in darkness, alert and rested. Glancing upward through the rustling oak leaves, I judged it to be less than an hour after nightfall.

Perfect, I thought. My gaze slid to the crater again. The darkness lay thicker in its hollowed depths, and the goblins guarding the prisoners had lit campfires to see by.

I smiled. It was time to hunt.

Pulling the shadows around me, I slipped into the welcoming night and crept down the boulder-strewn slope to my targets. Despite the lack of concealment in the crater, I reached the edge of the circle of light cast by the campfires without being spotted.

The goblins sat huddled around the two fires. Their backs were turned to the darkness, either overconfident in their own strength or ignorant of the forest's dangers.

Twenty hostile entities have failed to detect you!

Casting reaction buff, I took a moment to consider how to handle the guards. Nyzack hadn't skimped on the prisoners' protection detail. Analyze confirmed that all twenty goblins were rank six elite warriors and equipped in chainmail armor.

I wouldn't prevail in a direct confrontation, which left only more underhanded means of triumphing. After a further minute of silent contemplation, I formulated a plan.

Fixing my gaze on one of the goblins I suspected of being their leader, I cast simple charm. Slipping threads of psi into my target's mind, I overlaid my will upon his.

An elite goblin warrior has passed a mental resistance check! You have failed to charm your target. Your mental intrusion has gone undetected!

My lips turned down at the failure. It wasn't unexpected. The goblin was a rank six foe, and my telepathy was still at rank two. But my intrusion hadn't been detected, so I tried again.

It took three more attempts—all of which went unnoticed—before I succeeded.

You have charmed your target for 10 seconds.

My psi swamped the warrior's mind, and he finally fell under my thrall. I ordered the charmed goblin to his feet, and he rose smoothly in obedience to my will.

I didn't force him to attack his companions though.

I had something altogether different in mind.

Relaying my command through the mental link joining us together, I gave my minion his orders and watched as he pivoted around, striding determinedly away from the campfire.

"Hey, Risch," another goblin called out. "Where are you going? Get back here!"

Risch wasn't a squad leader, I realized. But the other goblin was. My minion, meanwhile, had kept walking, not answering.

"Risch, answer me!" the squad leader snapped.

A second goblin frowned. "What's he want with the prisoners?"

The squad leader rose to his feet, finally recognizing where my minion was going. "Stop!" he barked.

But it was too late to stop the charmed goblin.

Risch had reached his destination—the peg anchoring the chain keeping one of the prisoners' cages aloft. Bending down, he yanked it out.

Bedlam ensued.

The tension in the steel chain relaxed and the cage crashed downward.

"No!" the squad leader shrieked, racing toward Risch. Before he could reach him, spikes extruded from the peg in my thrall's hand, piercing his chainmail glove and the skin beneath.

Your minion has triggered a trap. Your minion has been poisoned.

The squad leader skidded to a stop, then backed away fearfully.

An elite goblin warrior has been killed.

I winced as Risch fell lifelessly to the ground. The trap had been powerful, and the hapless goblin had barely survived a handful of seconds after triggering it.

I turned my attention to the captives. The prisoner in the dropped cage—Sturm—had risen to his feet. He looked a little shaken but none the worse for his fall. He was still imprisoned but much closer to being freed.

The other prisoners, sensing something amiss, were muttering among themselves. The goblin warriors were on their feet too, looking around in confusion.

"Why'd he do that?"

"Damn. Risch go crazy."

"The fool!"

I smiled to myself. The Red Rats hadn't caught on to my presence yet. Seeing that they were distracted, I cast ventro while they debated their companion's fate.

"Sturm, it's me," I whispered a moment later, projecting my voice close to the Tartan's ear.

"You... again! Is... out... how... die. What... you want?" Sturm replied, but I had trouble hearing him over the ruckus the others were making.

"No questions, I can't talk," I replied brusquely. "I'm here to free you. While I'm working on that, I need you and the others to keep the goblins distracted."

Not waiting for his response—either he did as I asked or he didn't—I refocused my gaze on the warriors who had resumed their seats to huddle about the fire again. None of them had even bothered to check on their dead companion.

Shaking my head at the goblins' callousness, I recast charm. This time it took two attempts to subdue my target—the squad leader who had spoken up earlier.

An elite goblin warrior has failed a mental resistance check! You have charmed your target for 10 seconds.

Like I had with my first thrall, I ordered my second minion to pull out another peg. The charmed goblin slipped away unnoticed by his fellows and made his way obediently to the trapped area.

Your minion has triggered a trap. Your minion has been poisoned. An elite goblin warrior has been killed.

The squad leader didn't last any longer than Risch. At the death of the second of their companions, the guards' confusion transformed into fear.

"What going on?"

"This place cursed! Hok, we must go!"

"Let's get out of here!"

"It be evil forest spirits, I tell you!"

Another goblin, smaller and unassuming, rose to his feet. Unlike the other warriors, he retained his composure. With eyes narrowed in suspicion, he strode closer to the fallen soldiers to inspect them. Realizing this goblin had to be the second squad leader, I cast charm on him.

And failed. *Urgh.*

An elite goblin warrior has passed a mental resistance check! You have failed to charm your target. Your mental intrusion has been detected!

"Quiet!" the squad leader roared. "Unsheathe your weapons. We're under attack! Search the area!"

The warriors responded to the whip of command in their leader's voice. Drawing their weapons, they formed into the semblance of a formation and stared outward into the darkness.

Eighteen hostile entities have failed to detect you!

I sighed in disappointment, ignoring the warriors' searching gazes. It was a pity I hadn't managed to charm the second squad leader.

It didn't matter though.

Despite the guards' apparent alertness, they weren't equipped to deal with my mental assaults.

My gaze slid to the prisoners. They'd begun shouting, hurling insults at their guards. *Good,* I thought. Sturm had done as I'd asked.

Under cover of the racket the prisoners were making, I shifted position and chose my next target. From the safety of the shadows, I would pick the guards off one by one, and there was little they could do to stop me.

✳ ✳ ✳

Ten minutes later, another eight guards were dead. I'd used them to release the remaining chains, and now all ten cages were grounded.

I had tried but failed repeatedly to charm the remaining squad leader, and after a while I gave up. The other goblins were easy enough prey.

In response to my efforts, the squad leader had attempted everything he could think of to stop me. His guards, though, lacked the skills necessary to deal with a menace that lurked unseen in the dark.

Charging in random directions through the crater, the warriors had tried finding me, but I had melted away into the darkness each time.

Then they had attempted lighting the surroundings with torches, but the area in question was too large and I'd slipped easily between the pools of light.

The goblins had even gone so far as tying themselves together with rope, only for my minions to cut them.

Even when I failed to charm my targets, it mattered little. The goblins were unable to pinpoint me in the darkness, and after my failures, I simply repositioned and tried again until I succeeded.

The only thing left for the goblins to do was to disarm themselves completely or flee, and the Red Rat soldiers seemed unwilling to do either of those things.

I kept at my task, picking off the enemy one by one, but I didn't attempt to get any of the guards to open the grounded cages. I wasn't sure what traps had been placed on their doors, and I was afraid the prisoners might be killed if the traps were triggered.

It was safer to send my minions to attack their fellows. Killing the goblins this way was slow going but, more importantly, it didn't endanger either myself or the prisoners.

Nearly thirty minutes later, I had whittled down the guards to just the squad leader, all without lifting either of my blades even once.

It took me ten attempts to charm the squad leader, but once I did, I approached him openly, ignoring the onlooking prisoners. Stepping up behind the warrior, I yanked back his head and ripped open his throat with spider's bite.

You have killed an elite goblin warrior with a fatal blow.

Letting the corpse fall, I looked up, my face devoid of expression, at the now-silent prisoners. My bloody work for the night was done.

The prisoners were free. Or nearly so.

CHAPTER 115: INSTIGATING VIOLENCE

I strode around the crater, looting my victims of their valuables. From within their cages, the prisoners screamed at me to free them. I ignored them, not about to be rushed in my search. Disappointingly, none of the goblins had the keys to the trapped cages.

Through my scavenging efforts, I accumulated a tidy sum of coins but nothing else of value.

You have acquired 5 gold and 4 silver coins.

Only after I finished with the goblins did I approach the prisoners. "About time," Sturm ground out between clenched teeth.

Not bothering to reply, I cast trap disarm and inspected the convoluted spell strands wrapped around the lock of his cage.

"What are you waiting for?" a prisoner from an adjacent cage shouted. "Free him!"

Sturm, meanwhile, watched me from beneath lidded eyes. "What's wrong?"

"It's trapped," I murmured absently, my attention still fixed on the spell only I could see.

The nearby heckler began shouting again, but this time Sturm waved him to silence. Kneeling down so that I was at eye level with the lock, I set to work disarming it.

"You may want to step back," I said, glancing up at Sturm. I smiled wryly. "Just in case this goes wrong."

He said nothing but did as I bade.

In silence, I continued to work on unraveling the trap. Its nature was still unknown to me, but some half-understood bit of acquired knowledge made me suspect the trap was an explosive of some sort.

After a few minutes of intense concentration, I finally disabled the magical device.

You have successfully disarmed a trap.

I wiped off the beading sweat from my brow and smiled at the anxious Sturm. "I've deactivated it."

He stepped closer. "That's it? I'm free?"

"Not quite," I murmured. "I still need to unlock the cage."

It was only a matter of a few seconds to pick the lock. When I was done, I rose to my feet and stepped back. "*Now* you're free."

Sturm didn't need to be told twice. Whooping for joy, the Tartan rushed out of the cage. As he passed through the door, an alert from the Adjudicator arrived.

You have completed the hidden task: <u>Free the Captain's Son</u>! Your deeds have attracted the enmity of Erebus and the interest of Tartar. The Marks on your spirit signature have changed.

The Dark abhors those not strong enough to prevent themselves from falling prey to others. With your actions, you've allowed weakness to thrive. However, your efforts were tempered by self-interest. You made certain to free the prisoners in a manner that served your own ends. Dark is satisfied. Your Dark Mark remains unchanged.

Shadow is satisfied your actions have not impacted the balance of power in the sector. Your Shadow Mark remains unchanged.

Despite being deceitful with your intentions, you acted for the benefit of your allies in the sector and at great personal risk to yourself. Light approves. Your Light Mark has deepened.

The Wolf is both the protector and leader of the pack and, at all times, must act for its betterment. In freeing the prisoners, you have twisted the goals of others to remove a threat to the pack. Wolf is pleased. Your Wolf Mark has deepened.

"Well, well," I murmured to myself as I read the Game messages twice over. I'd completed another hidden task *and* strengthened my Wolf Mark.

This has been a truly successful venture.

Lost in contemplation as I reviewed the alert, it took me a moment to realize Sturm was speaking to me. I looked at him. "Sorry, I missed what you said. What was that?"

"I asked, just what in damnation are you?" Although he'd phrased it as a question, it sounded more like a demand.

"Let me see to the others first," I replied evenly, ignoring his tone. "Then we can talk."

✳ ✳ ✳

It didn't take me long to free the rest of the captives.

The traps placed around their cages were of the same design as the one on Sturm's, and with each prisoner I released, my thieving skill increased. When I was done, the eleven of us gathered around one of the goblins' campfires and I passed around some of my rations.

"Now," Sturm said, speaking for the group, "explain yourself."

Sitting down cross-legged before the fire, I eyed the young Tartan as I began to eat. He sat across me with his arms folded and his face expressionless. In that pose, he looked a lot like his father, and I suspected it wasn't by chance that he'd assumed it. But I wasn't deceived. Sturm was no Captain Talon.

"There's nothing to explain," I said with a shrug, ignoring his tone entirely. "Your father sent me to free you, and I did."

"There must be more to it than that," Sturm objected. "How did you get the Red Rats to abandon the crater?"

With effort, I stopped my exasperation from showing. Sturm was behaving more like the one in charge and less like a freed captive. "*That* you don't need to know."

Sturm's eyes narrowed. "What made the guards kill themselves?"

I shrugged indifferently, not answering.

The captain's son glared at me, and a heartbeat later I felt a prickle run across my skin. It was a sensation I was quickly coming to associate with failed analyze attempts. "Stop that," I said mildly.

Sturm clenched his teeth in frustration. "Why can't I see your level?" he demanded.

Smiling, I took another bite off my rations.

Another player spoke up. "He must have the deception skill."

"Is that right?" Sturm asked, his face scrunching up in disgust.

I shrugged and kept chewing.

"Why won't you answer any of my questions? I'm warning you—"

I'd had enough. Swallowing the last of my rations, I rose to my feet. "I'll be going now."

Alarm flickered across Sturm's face. "What? Why?"

I looked at him impassively. "You're free. My work here is done, and I have other things to do." I ran my gaze across the group. "You lot can make your way back to the safe zone on your own. The way is clear. If you leave now, you'll reach there before dawn."

Sturm blanched. "We can't. It's too dangerous to travel through the forest at night."

I nodded in belated realization. He was right. I had forgotten how much trouble other players had traveling at night. "Camp here then and leave at first light. The Red Rats will not be returning anytime soon." *If ever.*

"You won't stay?" Sturm asked. "My father will reward you if you escort us back to the town."

"He'll reward me anyway," I said matter-of-factly. "And like I said, I have things to do." Inclining my head, I bid them farewell. "Goodbye and good luck."

With that, I disappeared into the trees again.

✳   ✳   ✳

I hadn't lied to Sturm. I had a busy night ahead of me.

First on my agenda was a second visit to the Long Fangs' camp. Partly, this was to make certain the Red Rats were doing as they'd been told—I was confident they were, but I couldn't leave it to chance—and partly it was to even the odds somewhat.

I'd come to realize that even with the Long Fangs defeated, the other goblin delegations also posed a risk to the dire wolves, and while I doubted I could rid the sector of the goblins entirely, I would do what I could to minimize the threat to the wolves.

In this case, that meant making sure that as many Red Rats as possible died in their impending assault.

While I hurried southeast through the forest, I reviewed my gains from the battle and its immediate aftermath. I'd advanced eight player levels, less than I expected. My leveling rate had slowed again—*it seems I need to find higher-level foes*, I thought wryly—but eight levels was still a tidy handful.

Many of my skills had increased too, most notably telepathy.

After a moment's consideration, I invested all my attribute points in Perception. I needed to ensure I had enough open slots for future upgrades, and besides, in both Dexterity and Mind—the only other attributes for which I had abilities—I still had enough surplus slots.

Your Perception has increased to rank 20.

After I was done, I paused my journey to read the improved analyze ability tome.

You have upgraded your analyze ability to improved analyze. This ability allows you to inspect your foe's Class and overall health status in addition to their level. Beware, some targets may sense when this ability is used on them. The success of this ability is determined by the target's level and deception skill.

This ability consumes no energy and can be upgraded. Its activation time is near-instantaneous. Improved analyze is an advanced ability and requires 4 more Perception slots than its basic variant. You have 6 of 20 Perception ability slots remaining.

Finally, I called up my player profile to review my progress.

Player Profile: Michael

Level: 58. Rank: 5. Current Health: 100%.
Stamina: 100%. Mana: 100%. Psi: 100%.
Species: Human. Lives Remaining: 3.
Marks: Wolf-brethren, Lesser Shadow, Lesser Light, Lesser Dark.

Attributes

Available: 0 points.
Strength: 2. Constitution: 14. Dexterity: 16*. Perception: 20. Mind: 15. Magic: 2*. Faith: 2*.
* *denotes attributes affected by items.*

Classes

Available: 2 points.
Primary-Secondary Bi-blend: Mindstalker.
Tertiary Class: None.

Traits

Psi wolf heritage: +2 Dexterity, +2 Strength, +4 Mind.
Beast tongue: can speak to beastkin.
Marked: can see spirit signatures.
Nocturnal: perfect night vision.

Skills

Available skill slots: 0.
Light armor (current: 34. max: 140. Constitution, basic).
Dodging (current: 40. max: 200. Dexterity, basic).

Sneaking (current: 57. max: 200. Dexterity, basic).
Shortswords (current: 51. max: 200. Dexterity, basic).
Two-weapon fighting (current: 43. max: 200. Dexterity, advanced).
Thieving (current: 39. max: 200. Dexterity, basic).
Chi (current: 36. max: 150. Mind, advanced).
Meditation (current: 41. max: 150. Mind, basic).
Telekinesis (current: 30. max: 150. Mind, advanced).
Telepathy (current: 34. max: 150. Mind, advanced).
Insight (current: 59. max: 200. Perception, basic).
Deception (current: 53. max: 200. Perception, master).

Abilities

Dexterity ability slots used: 13 / 20.
crippling blow (Dexterity, basic, shortswords).
minor piercing strike (5 Dexterity, advanced, shortswords).
lesser backstab (5 Dexterity, advanced, sneaking).
basic trap disarm (Dexterity, basic, thieving).
simple lockpicking (Dexterity, basic, thieving).

Mind ability slots used: 4 / 15.
simple charm (Mind, basic, telepathy).
stunning slap (Mind, basic, chi).
one-step (Mind, basic, telekinesis).
minor reaction buff (Mind, basic, chi).

Perception ability slots used: 14 / 20.
improved analyze (5 Perception, advanced, insight).
lesser trap detect (Perception, basic, thieving).
conceal small weapon (Perception, basic, deception).
facial disguise (Perception, basic, deception).
ventro (Perception, basic, deception).
lesser imitate (5 Perception, advanced, deception).

Other abilities:
simple mindsight (Class, basic, telepathy).

Known Key Points

Sector 14,913 exit portal and safe zone.
Sector 12,560 nether portal and safe zone.

Equipped

spider's bite shortsword (+15% damage, webbed), concealed.
shortsword,+1 (+15% damage, +10 shortswords), concealed.
common fighter's sash (+3 shortswords).
enchanted leather armor set (+20% damage reduction, −35% Dexterity and Magic).
slotted potion belt (3 minor heal, 4 moderate heal, 0 full heal, 2 empty).
common thief's cloak (+3 sneaking).

apprentice's ring (+2 Magic).
acolyte's ring (+2 Faith).

Backpack Contents (Key Items)

Money: 5 gold, 7 silver, and 0 copper.
2 x iron daggers.
1 x goblin writ of safe passage.
1 x alchemy stone (42 / 150 ingredients).
1 x bounty letter.
1 x common mage's cloak (+3 air magic).
1 x code sheet.
1 x Stayne's letter.

Alchemy Stone Contents

9 x vials of beast blood.
10 x heaps of ordinary bonedust.
1 x rhomodillo tusk.
3 x sacs of wyvern venom.
1 x set of wyvern fangs.
18 x wyvern scales.

Bank Contents

Money: 46 gold, 4 silver, and 9 copper.
2 x full healing potions.
2 x basic steel shortswords.

Open Tasks

Aid the Pack (Stop the Long Fangs hunting the dire wolves).
An Alchemist's Bounty (kill the wyvern mother).
Goblin Wars (destroy all 3 goblin tribes in the valley).
Forging Dark Alliances (secure the allegiance of the Howlers and Red Rats for the Dark).

I smiled in satisfaction. The day's work had served me well.

I'd grown appreciably, and soon I would be able to upgrade my Mind abilities too. Given that I invariably found myself fighting against large groups of enemies, my Mind skills were of crucial importance.

If the rest of the night goes as planned, there will be more opportunities to advance further tonight.

Increasing my pace, I hurried southeast.

✳ ✳ ✳

I followed on the heels of the Red Rats' army. Their trail, marked by a wide swath of destruction in the forest, was easy to follow.

But as I covered mile after mile and still didn't catch up with them as I'd expected, my worry grew. *Nyzack must be pushing his people hard,* I thought.

The goblins had to have kept traveling well past dark to be so far ahead of me.

Increasingly troubling was the notion that the Red Rats might have chosen *not* to break for the night. I hoped that wasn't the case. Otherwise, I was making my run southeast in vain.

My concerns proved groundless, however.

An hour past midnight and a little more than a mile away from the Long Fangs' camp, I finally found the Red Rats' war camp. Staying concealed in the trees, I observed them.

The soldiers looked exhausted, and only a handful of guards had been posted to watch the camp. I shook my head at Nyzack's foolishness.

He had pushed his men too hard, and tomorrow when they met the Long Fangs in battle they'd still be feeling the effects of their march the day before.

It's better this way. More goblins were likely to die as a result.

Still shaking my head, I left the Red Rats behind me and made my way to the Long Fangs' encampment. Little had changed since my previous visit. The fortified camp was as well patrolled as before.

I frowned. I could see no sign of increased patrols. Which could only mean the Long Fangs weren't aware of the impending attack.

Time to warn them.

Given the disparity in numbers, there was no way the Long Fangs could triumph in battle against the Red Rats. But if I ensured they were forewarned, then they could give a good accounting of themselves and maybe make a sizable dent in the Red Rats' forces.

They wouldn't just listen to anything I had to say though. That meant getting creative again.

Delaying only long enough to cast lesser imitate, I stepped out of the trees and into plain sight. To all appearances I was the Red Rat shaman, Klaxis, if a notably smaller version. This time around though I would make sure not to approach my foes too closely.

Picking out one of the guards, I began casting simple charm. Before my spell was completed, I was spotted. But that was alright.

I meant to be seen.

Pointing my way, the guards sounded the alarm. I ignored them and kept casting. It didn't take the goblins long to decide how to respond.

Four of the guards hurried my way, while another two ran into the camp, no doubt to inform the witch doctors of my presence.

My spell completed, and one of the approaching goblins fell under my thrall. "Die, Long Fangs!" I roared in the former—and very dead—Red Rat shaman's voice. At the same time, I ordered my minion to attack his fellows.

Chaos ensued as a skirmish broke out among the guards.

"Tyga is bewitched! The Rat has bewitched him!" one of the goblins shouted.

Leaving one of their fellows to deal with my minion, the other two guards kept sprinting toward me which, while the right tactic to employ against a spellcaster, suited my own ends perfectly.

I grinned. Spinning around, I fled through the trees.

My sharp ears picked up the footfalls of the goblins racing after me, and not wanting to lose them, I kept my own pace measured. Leading the Long Fang guards on, I made straight for the Red Rats' camp.

I arrived at it without incident. Stopping short of its unpatrolled perimeter, I swung around and waited for the Long Fang soldiers to catch up. When I was sure they could see me, I laughed openly in their faces before fading into the shadows.

Two hostile entities have failed to detect you! You are hidden.

Wrapped in darkness, I waited patiently to see what happened next.

Huffing and cursing foully, the two goblins skidded to a halt where they had last seen me. "Where'd he go?" asked the first.

"Bloody shamans," swore the second, sheathing his bare blade. "He's vanished."

"Fool," hissed the first. "Keep your blade out. Shamans are tricky."

The second guard sneered. "Don't tell me you're scared? If the shaman could've slain us, he wouldn't have fled in the first place. Come on, let's head—"

The goblin broke off as his companion slapped a hand to his mouth.

"Listen!" the first hissed. With his hand still on his companion's mouth, the guard looked around fearfully. "Do you hear that?" he whispered in a low voice.

The second guard frowned, then a moment later his eyes widened as he heard the same thing his companion had.

About time, I groused.

The low murmur of sound from the two thousand goblins in the Red Rats' camp just a dozen yards away was unmissable. It was a wonder it had taken the pair so long to notice.

Moving with comical caution, the two goblins tiptoed forward and peered through the trees.

A moment later, they stared at each other, their faces pale.

"Back," the second goblin said, his voice trembling. "We must go back!" he all but shouted in a hushed whisper.

His companion didn't object, and a moment later the pair fled back to their camp. Watching from hiding, I chuckled in amusement.

My work here was done.

Chapter 116: Sowing Chaos

It was just before midnight when I left the Red Rat war camp. Hurrying south through the forest, I headed back to the safe zone to carry out the next part of my plan: causing more mayhem.

With the first of my primary goals—destroying the Long Fangs—seen to, my next task was to find a way out of the sector.

That, however, was easier said than done.

I didn't fancy depending on either the captain or the druid to escape. For one, I couldn't fathom a means of accomplishing Mariga's task, and certainly not in the time that remained to me. For another, I had no wish to bind myself to Talon's master, the god-emperor.

That left me with only one option: escaping the sector on my own.

To do that, I needed to draw Ishita's sworn out of the safe zone and somehow get them to drop the shield around the portal so I could use it to escape. I had a plan—of sorts—for accomplishing that, and it involved the Howlers.

But assuming my scheme failed, which admittedly was likely, I wanted the valley in as much turmoil as possible to make it harder for Erebus and Ishita's cronies to find me. Hence the chaos I sought to sow.

I sped south as fast as I could manage. To accomplish what I planned next, I needed to reach the goblin fort before sunrise.

* * *

I completed my journey with an hour to spare. Panting heavily from my long jog through the forest, I skidded to a halt at the edge of the tree line and allowed myself five minutes to recuperate. The clock was ticking.

When it no longer felt like my lungs were about to explode, I cast lesser imitate.

Energy rippled out of me to clothe me anew in illusion. One minute I was Michael, a human player. The next I was Xrex, the lizardman mage sworn to Ishita's service.

Leaving the safety of the trees, I marched toward the gate. The guards eyed me disinterestedly as I approached.

Multiple hostile entities have failed to pierce your disguise.

Stopping in front of them, I demanded, "Let me through."

The squad leader stifled a yawn. "What are you doing out here, Xrex?" he asked. His eyes drifted past me to study the dark outline of the forest. "I thought you sworn weren't supposed to leave the safe zone?"

Good, he knows who I'm supposed to be. What I intended wouldn't work otherwise.

"Where I've been is no concern of yours," I hissed. "Now open the damn gate!"

The squad leader's gaze snapped back to me, his bored air vanishing, and for a drawn-out moment he didn't say anything.

I stifled my trepidation. *Did I overplay my hand?*

But no, it didn't seem like I had.

"No need to be rude," the goblin said mildly a second later. Looking over his shoulder at his soldiers, he barked, "Open the gate!"

I inclined my head in thanks, softening my harsh demeanor. Perhaps, contrary to my prediction, Xrex was on more relaxed terms with the goblins than I thought. I doubted it though.

Feeling the squad leader's eyes on me, I strode through the gate, and the moment an opportunity presented itself I slipped behind an intervening building to cloak myself in shadows.

You are hidden.

Step one complete. I was safely in the fort, and my identity as Xrex was established. *Now, for some mayhem.*

Safe within the darkness, I scanned the area. Except for the guards patrolling the inner and outer walls, the fort appeared to be asleep—which was what I'd been hoping for.

Bent in a half-crouch, I crept toward the closest barracks. Bracing myself against the adjacent wall, I reached out and gently turned down the handle on the door.

It refused to budge. *Aargh.*

I ran my gaze along the length of the building. All its windows were shuttered as well. Not willing to rattle their locks and risk waking the soldiers within, I searched for another barracks.

It took me five tries before I found one that was open.

Slipping inside the building, I studied the interior. The barracks consisted of a single room many times longer than it was wide. A dozen bunks were set against each longer wall, forming two neat rows separated by a narrow walkway. Only half the beds were occupied though. I counted my targets.

Twenty elite goblin warriors. All sleeping.

Turning back to the door, I searched for a keyhole. There was none, but next to the door I found a stout iron rod that likely served as a means of locking the door from within.

Sloppy of them not to secure their barracks.

I lifted the bar carefully into place, slotting it through the two rings on either side of the door and barring the entrance. With the door attended to, I drew spider's bite and turned my attention to the occupants.

It was time to get killing.

✳ ✳ ✳

You have backstabbed your target for 100% more damage! You have killed an elite goblin warrior with a fatal blow.

You have backstabbed your target for 100% more damage! You have...
...

I slew my first ten victims silently and without fuss. Asleep and unarmed, the soldiers made for perfect targets.

My good fortune didn't last, of course.

As I tiptoed toward my next victim, things went awry.

For no good reason I could divine, my intended target groaned and sat up while I was still on the opposite side of the walkway separating the bunk rows.

Maybe he was an early riser or maybe he'd sensed something. Whatever the reason, it didn't matter. Things were about to get messy.

Fading back into the shadows, I watched the warrior as he rubbed his still-closed eyes. More than a dozen feet separated us, too far for me to rush the goblin without alerting the rest of the barracks. Cursing my misfortune, I crept closer. *Perhaps, he'll go back to sleep.*

Ten hostile entities have failed to detect you! You are hidden.

I closed the distance as rapidly as I dared.

The goblin yawned without opening his eyes. I relax slightly. It looked like he was about to go back to sleep.

Abruptly, the goblin's eyes snapped open to stare in my direction.

I froze in place. My target was more perceptive than his fellows, and somehow he'd sensed my approach. Squinting, the goblin searched the spot I occupied.

A hostile entity has failed to detect you.

The goblin's eyes narrowed further. He knew something was amiss, but not what. I began gathering psi. Charming my target was the only hope I had now of stopping his incipient outcry.

The warrior's gaze slid beyond me, his eyes widening in alarm as he caught sight of his dead bunk mates lying in pools of their own blood.

Damn, I thought. *Now that's done it.*

Abandoning both my casting and stealth, I charged forward. I was still too far away though.

"Wake up!" the warrior roared. "There's an intr—"

Lunging forward, I sank both my blades deep into the unarmed goblin. Blood bubbled out of his mouth and spurted from his mangled chest. He jerked once, then the light of life faded from his eyes.

You have killed an elite goblin warrior.

The damage, however, had already been done. The remaining nine goblins in the barracks had awoken. Cursing and shouting, they reached for their weapons.

All wasn't lost yet. If I moved quickly to contain the damage, there was still a chance that the alarm wouldn't spread outside the building.

Spinning away from the corpse, I sliced open the torso of the goblin in the adjacent bed. The warrior shrieked and tried to roll away. Darting forward, I plunged my second blade through his back.

You have killed an elite goblin warrior.

I dashed to the next rising warrior. He was fumbling for something beneath his bed, his weapons presumably. Without hesitation, I ran him through.

You have killed an elite goblin warrior.

A blade whistled past my ear. I spun around and spied a blur of motion. Raising spider's bite, I blocked the next incoming blow. My foe snarled in anger as his second attack was foiled. Darting forward, I pierced the warrior through the heart with the blade in my left hand.

You have killed an elite goblin warrior.

On my left, a goblin kneeled on his bed, equipping a quarrel to the crossbow he held. I flew forward, one-stepping through the air to close the distance in a single bound.

The goblin's head whipped upward to stare in horror. His mouth dropped open, but before he could plead for his life, I shoved spider's bite down his throat.

You have killed an elite goblin warrior.

Five down. Five to go.

My gaze darted around the barracks and picked out the remaining goblins gathering at the far end of the room. Unlike their fallen companions, the five had wisely retreated to regroup.

Two in the group were archers and were setting arrows to bows while the other three, melee weapons in hand, saw to their defense.

"Surrender, you double-crossing son of a whore," the goblin at the forefront of the five growled harshly. He hefted a broadsword in both his hands and looked to be in command of the group.

Ignoring him—there was no time to waste—I dashed forward, one-stepping to speed me on my way.

I was halfway to my targets when the two archers released in tandem. Throwing myself to the side, I narrowly evaded the first incoming projectile. The second grazed my cheek, scoring a deep furrow of red across it.

An elite goblin warrior has struck you with a glancing blow. A goblin's arrow has pierced your illusion! Your lesser imitate spell has dissipated.

I cursed softly.

I had no choice now but to make certain all the goblins in the barracks died. Otherwise, my plan to lay the blame for these killings on Ishita's sworn would come to naught. Disregarding the blood pulsing from the wound, I leaped back to my feet and resumed my charge.

Chapter 117: Deceitful Revelations

"Kill him!" the broadsword-wielding goblin screamed.

Before the archers could release their second volley, I was upon the goblins. The melee fighters moved to intercept me. I dodged the first warrior's attack and his broadsword swept harmlessly past.

The second lunged at me. I parried away his attack with my left blade and sent spider's bite snaking forward to land a crippling blow on his right forearm. The goblin dropped his spear from suddenly numb hands.

Spinning around, I lashed out at the last warrior approaching from my rear, causing him to beat a hasty retreat. I didn't pursue. The way to the archers was clear, and I rushed forward.

Their lines of fire suddenly clear, the two archers released their prepared shots from nearly point-blank range. I've been waiting for their attack though and wasn't caught by surprise. Diving forward, I rolled under the arrows.

Two meaty thuds marked the projectiles' impact as they collided with one of the warriors behind me. It was followed by a shriek of pain and then silence.

An elite goblin warrior has died.

Four to go, I thought grimly.

I bounced back to my feet in front of the archers. Dropping his bow, one slashed at me with a knife. I parried away the attack easily before skewering him with my own blade.

You have killed an elite goblin warrior.

Turning to the other archer, I lunged forward and clubbed him across the face with the hilt of my short sword, then drove spider's bite through his abdomen.

You have killed an elite goblin warrior.

I spun around, expecting to find more blades rushing at me. But that wasn't the case. The last two goblins were fleeing, one unarmed and the other still lugging his broadsword.

They were already halfway to the barred door. Racing forward, I easily overtook the second, the one bearing the broadsword, and slashed at the back of his legs in passing. The goblin yelped in pain and fell to the ground, moaning.

You have crippled an elite goblin warrior.

Not pausing to finish off the fallen warrior, I hurried after the last goblin. I caught up to him at the door. The warrior had his back turned to me while he fumbled with the bar. Without hesitation, I lunged forward and buried both my blades in his back.

You have killed an elite goblin warrior.

Withdrawing my blades, I let the corpse sink to the floor and turned around to face the only goblin still alive. Writhing on the floor, he moaned pitifully. I advanced on him, blades dripping blood.

It was time to end this.

✳ ✳ ✳

I kneeled over the injured goblin, preparing to deliver the final blow.

"W-w-who are... you?" the warrior asked, his pain-filled gaze locking on my own. "You are not Xrex."

I paused, surprised this goblin also knew the name of the leader of Ishita's sworn in the sector. "Perhaps I am," I said mildly, lowering my blade.

"Impossible!" the goblin gasped. "Y-you cannot be him. You *are* not him! We've done all the spider goddess has asked. There is no reason for her to punish us."

I stared at him. "What do you mean?" I asked slowly. I knew I was wasting time, but I found the goblin's words troubling, especially in light of what he had said earlier when he had still believed me to be Xrex. *"A double-crossing son of a whore."* Those were the exact words the goblin had shouted before.

The implications were startling...

"Do not pretend ignorance," the goblin said, unaware of my speculation. "You must know we are pledged to the goddess. Why else attack us?"

I stared at him, flabbergasted.

"It's revenge you want, isn't it?" The goblin's face contorted in fury. "But it is *us* who will be avenged. The Awakened Dead will see you slain."

I closed my eyes, hiding my confusion. What the goblin's words implied... was impossible. Could he really mean the Howlers were pledged in service to the Awakened Dead?

But then... why were the two tribes at war with each other?

It made little sense, but now wasn't the time to ponder the mystery. I turned back to the goblin. "Are you saying the Howlers and the Awakened Dead are allied?" I asked carefully, needing to be certain.

"Of course!" he hissed. "Give up this pretense. I know you—"

I stopped listening.

Someone was pounding furiously on the door. The ruckus in the barracks hadn't gone unnoticed, and more goblins had come to investigate. "Damn it," I growled. I was out of time.

My gaze darted back to the wounded goblin. "Thank you for the information," I said somberly and plunged my blade through his throat.

You have killed an elite goblin warrior.

160

Rising to my feet, I recast lesser imitate about myself, then hurried down to one of the shuttered windows farthest from the barracks' door. Unlocking the window, I slipped out and into a pool of darkness.

You are hidden.

I scanned the area. This side of the barracks was free of commotion, and no goblins were in sight. Momentarily secure, I paused to consider my options.

My original plan had been to keep killing until the toll of victims claimed by "Xrex" was high enough that the Howler shaman couldn't afford to ignore the deaths. When I was done, I'd hoped to leave the relationship between the Howlers and Awakened Dead irreparably shattered. Now though...

Now I wasn't sure what the best course was.

What the goblin had told me weighed on my mind. Had he been telling the truth? And if so, what should I make of it? Did it make what I planned easier or harder?

I didn't have the answers—yet.

Sighing, I turned toward the inner wall. I had a lot to think about, and before I acted again I needed to ponder what I knew. Or thought I knew.

* * *

I made it undetected to the inner wall. Remaining in the shadows, I took a moment to study the guards at the gate. They appeared no more alert than usual.

No fort-wide alarm had been raised then.

Deciding to risk an open approach rather than sneaking over the walls, I left the concealment of the shadows and strolled with affected indifference toward the gate.

The guards' attention fixed on me immediately, but none readied their weapons. Reassured somewhat, I stopped before them.

"Let me through," I said in a less belligerent tone than I'd used with the outer wall guards.

Silently, the pair did as I bade, swinging open the gate and gesturing me through. Without haste, I slipped past the guards and out of the fort.

The gate slammed shut behind me, and I let my shoulders sag, the tension in them easing. I took a step forward and the expected Game message dropped in my mind.

You have entered a safe zone.

Accompanying it, however, was another more unexpected one.

Lesser imitate dispelled. This spell cannot be maintained while within the bounds of a safe zone.

The illusion around me fell away, and I looked around quickly to see if anyone had noticed. Luckily, the day was still young and the village was quiet.

Striding unhurried into the village, I took cover within the shadows of a small cabin while I attended to the Game messages that awaited me in the aftermath of my recent encounter.

You have reached level 63!

Congratulations, Michael! You are now a rank 6 player. Your experience gains have decreased further. For achieving rank 6, you have been awarded 1 additional attribute point and 1 Class point.

Your dodging has increased to level 42. Your sneaking has increased to level 58. Your shortswords has increased to level 54. Your two-weapon fighting has increased to level 45. Your light armor has increased to level 37.

Your chi has increased to level 37. Your meditation has increased to level 42. Your telekinesis has increased to level 33.

Your insight has increased to level 60. Your deception has increased to level 55.

All my skills, with the exception of telepathy and thieving, had advanced again, and I'd gained another five player levels. My newly earned attribute points I invested in Mind.

Your Mind has increased to rank 21.

Soon I expected to upgrade all my mental abilities to the next tier, and for that I needed to raise the attribute much higher.

Next, I mulled over what I'd learned from the dead goblin and the alert it had prompted.

Your task, <u>Forging Dark Alliances</u>! has been updated. You have received word from a questionable source that the Howlers are already allied with a Dark Power. Objective one revised: inform Captain Talon or seek confirmation of your source's information.

I glanced askance at the Game message. For all that it described the goblin as a "questionable source," what he had said *felt* right.

I had no proof the goblin's words were true, of course, but at that moment, on the cusp of death, he'd had no reason to lie to me.

The goblin's outrage had been palpable and... authentic, and I found myself believing him.

What game is Erebus playing at?

It was becoming more and more evident that the self-proclaimed Master was involved in some nefarious scheme. What I couldn't figure out though was to what end.

Alright, let's review what I know—or suspect.

One: the Red Rats were pledged to Erebus.

Two: the Howlers were pledged to Ishita.

Three: both of these alliances were so secret that not even the other Dark factions were aware of them. In fact, given the war raging between the two tribes, I could safely assume the goblins themselves didn't know the other was allied with the Awakened Dead!

Four: Not only was Erebus allowing the tribes to fight each other, he seemed to be *encouraging* them to do so. Stayne had ordered the Red Rats to raid the Howlers, and it was a safe bet that Ishita's sworn had done the reverse, commanding the Howlers to attack the Red Rats.

For a long while, I pondered over my collection of facts and suspicions, trying to fit them in a manner that made sense, but no matter how hard I tried, I couldn't figure out what the Awakened Dead was about.

The only definitive conclusion I could draw was that Erebus *wanted* the valley in turmoil. Why this was the case, I didn't know, but it caused me to doubt my own plans to foment chaos.

I could still follow through with my scheme. However, now I was uncertain if, by doing so, I wouldn't only further Erebus' own ends.

I'm missing some crucial facts, something that completes the picture.

I pursed my lips in thought. I needed to speak to someone who hopefully knew more about what was going on.

Head bowed, I headed toward the Tartan barracks.

CHAPTER 118: A CONUNDRUM

DAY FIVE. DAWN.

I knocked on the door to the Tartan barracks for what felt like forever before someone answered. The door opened a smidge and an unknown player stared down at me from within.

"I need to speak to your captain," I said without preamble.

"Who—" he began.

"Now!" I demanded.

The player's mouth worked soundlessly and he looked ready to slam the door in my face, but before he could do that a voice called from within. "Let him in," Cecilia said.

Not waiting for the player's response, I barged in. I was being rude, I knew, but I was in a hurry and didn't have time for niceties.

It wouldn't take the Howlers long to muster a response to the killings in their fort, and before they did I wanted to be ready to act. Glancing around, I spotted Cecilia standing nearby.

"This way, Michael," she said.

I hurried to her side, and without saying anything the elf turned and headed deeper into the building.

"Where's Ultack?" I asked.

"Training," Cecilia replied, not elaborating further. She glanced at me sideways. "You look troubled. Is something wrong?"

"I'm not sure," I admitted. "I've uncovered some disconcerting facts. I'm hoping your captain can make more sense of it than me."

"He will," she replied unquestioningly as we drew to a halt in front of a closed door. "Go on in. The captain is inside."

I nodded in thanks and, opening the door, stepped within. The room was small, simply furnished, and configured as an office. Talon was seated behind a desk, writing something on a slip of paper.

At my entrance, he stood up. "Welcome, Michael," he said as if he had been expecting me. "Close the door and take a seat."

I did as he bade and opened my mouth to begin.

Talon raised a finger, stopping me. "One moment," he murmured. A moment later, he said, "Go ahead. We're shielded now."

I nodded, appreciating his precautions. "I found your son," I said, meeting the envoy's gaze.

Talon's face broke out in a grin, his delight and relief unmistakable. "Where is he?" he asked eagerly.

I shrugged. "Probably on his way south already by now. I left him and his squad at the Red Rats' camp last night."

The captain's smile faded. "So the squad made it to the camp? Why didn't they report back earlier?"

"They were being held as prisoners."

There was a heartbeat of silence as Talon digested this. "Prisoners?" he half growled. "Why were they bloody prisoners?"

I sighed. "It's a long story and one your son can tell you himself when he gets back. But the short of it is, the Red Rats have covertly pledged allegiance to Erebus. Sturm's squad found this out somehow, and to keep the matter secret, the tribe was ordered to hold your soldiers captive."

Your task, <u>Forging Dark Alliances</u>! has been updated. You have informed Captain Talon of the alliance between the Red Rats and the Awakened Dead. Objective 2 completed.

For another drawn-out moment the captain didn't say anything, but his gaze had seemed to flick inward in time with my own.

Had Talon received a quest update too?

"How did you free them?" he asked at last.

"I took advantage of the circumstances," I replied, sidestepping the truth. "The Red Rats have decamped." I held Talon's gaze. "They're marching south. To war."

I didn't elaborate further, letting the captain draw his own conclusions. I'd very deliberately not mentioned my own role in instigating the Red Rats' actions or the detour I'd ordered them to make.

I hadn't lied... not precisely, and I had shared the necessary facts. There was no reason for me to feel guilty. None.

Preoccupied with my tidings, the captain didn't seem to notice anything amiss. "They can only be moving against the Howlers." He cursed softly. "I can't say I'm surprised Erebus has lost control of his minions. But what is that idiot Red Rat shaman thinking? Waging war on the Howlers is one thing. Holding Tartan soldiers captive... is another matter entirely." He shook his head. "Rank foolishness."

"I don't understand all the whys of it myself," I confessed. "But you've got one thing wrong." I paused. "Erebus hasn't lost control of the goblins. The war the Red Rats are waging against the Howlers? That's at his behest."

Again, I wasn't telling the captain everything, but I didn't think I was stretching the truth too far. The gist of what I told Talon was true—Erebus *had* ordered the war between the goblins—the rest was... unnecessary detail.

The captain leaned across his table, pinning me with his gaze. "Let me get this straight. You're saying Erebus *ordered* the Red Rats to attack the Howlers?"

"I am."

"Are you certain of that?"

I nodded. "I learned it from your son himself."

"Sturm told you that?" Talon frowned. "But it makes no sense. I knew Erebus was stalling, but why attack the Howlers?" he murmured, more to himself than to me. "They hold the means to claiming the sector."

My ears perked up at that. "What does that mean?"

"Kingdom sectors aren't like dungeon sectors," the captain said absently, "they can be claimed."

My brows furrowed. We'd touched on this topic before, but I wasn't sure I understood the reference or how it answered what I'd just asked.

The captain's gaze drifted my way, and he noticed my confusion. "What do you know about sectors?"

I grimaced. "Other than what you told me before?"

He nodded.

"Not much," I admitted.

The captain smiled kindly. "Then you know more than most. Many players are unaware of how little they truly understand."

Talon paused, gathering his thoughts. "Remember what I told you before, that the Forever Kingdom is a world broken in two?"

"I do."

"One half, the aboveground world, resides in the aether, and the other, the world below, occupies the nether," Talon continued. "In a millennia-old cataclysmic event, each half was shattered into millions of smaller pieces—what we call sectors." He looked at me. "Still following?"

I nodded, fascinated by this bit of lore.

"Think of the sectors as little islands floating either in the void of the aether or in the darkness of the nether," the captain said. "Kingdom sectors—those in the aether—function differently from dungeon sectors—those in the nether. The most crucial difference between the two is the manner in which they are claimed." He held my gaze for a moment to stress the importance of his next point. "To establish ownership of a Kingdom sector, a faction has to *control* its safe zone."

I frowned for a moment, puzzled, then my eyes widened as I caught on. "Like what the Howlers are doing now?"

"Exactly," Talon exclaimed. "To control the safe zone of a sector this size requires a fort garrisoned by at least a thousand soldiers."

"That means—" I broke off, my frown deepening as something occurred to me. "Wait. If that's the case, shouldn't the Howlers already own this valley?"

Talon smiled. "The goblins aren't players. Only *player factions* can own a sector. But with the Howler fort already in control of the safe zone, the moment they join a faction—the Awakened Dead or Tartans—things in this valley will change drastically." He paused. "Do you understand what I'm getting at, Michael?"

"I think so," I replied absently, my thoughts churning furiously. "The Awakened Dead would be better served by coopting the Howlers into their faction—not going to war with them."

The captain nodded. "Correct. It's what makes your news so mystifying. I'd been assuming all along that the only reason Erebus allowed the Howlers to build their fort was so he could claim the sector immediately when they pledged allegiance to him." He shook his head. "Now I don't know what to believe."

I nodded wordlessly, my own confusion even greater than the captain's.

What the captain didn't know yet because I hadn't told him—and now I was no longer certain I *should* tell him—was that the Howlers were already allied with the Awakened Dead.

Which means what exactly?

With a heartfelt sigh, I bowed my head and rubbed my temples. Matters were refusing to make sense. If what the captain had told me was true, then the sector should already be under the Awakened Dead's control, shouldn't it?

Unless the captain is lying.

Or the dead goblin was.

I blew out a troubled breath. Instead of clarifying matters, my visit to the captain was only confusing me further.

The captain chuckled at my expression. "Perplexing, isn't it? The only way any of this makes sense is if the Howlers have refused the Awakened Dead's overtures."

I remained silent, saying nothing to disabuse him of this bit of speculation—even though I suspected he was wrong.

I wasn't being entirely forthcoming with the captain, but I couldn't forget he was an envoy of a Dark Power, one completely unknown to me. Talon's first loyalty would be to his master, and our goals weren't necessarily aligned.

"That must be it," Talon murmured after a moment of silent contemplation.

"What benefit does controlling a Kingdom sector confer?" I asked, steering the conversation to safer ground.

"Well, for one, the faction's players have free run of the sector, able to teleport into and out of the sector at will, anytime and anyplace. For another, the owning faction can brand players as criminals, making them easier to capture and identify. Lastly, the owner can also bar enemy and neutral players from teleporting into the safe zone. All of this, as you can imagine, makes capturing an *ordinary* Kingdom sector difficult. With a closed sector like this one? It's well-nigh impossible without overwhelming force."

I whistled appreciatively. Owning a sector was definitely advantageous. So why was Erebus delaying his claim to this one?

I had no answer.

"But all this speculation is fruitless and beside the point," the captain said, shaking his head. "What's important is having proof of what Erebus is doing." He eyed me searchingly. "Do you?"

I nodded. Withdrawing Stayne's letter from my pocket, I spread it out on the table for him to read.

Chapter 119: The Envoy's Envoy

An array of emotions flickered across the captain's face as he read Stayne's orders. First confusion, then anger, and finally satisfaction.

"Well done, Michael," Talon said, reaching out to take the note. "I don't know how you did it, but this is exactly what my master needs."

I placed my own hand on the note, blocking him. "Not so fast," I said. "We must discuss the matter of the price before I can hand this over to you."

Talon leaned back in his chair, his face transforming into an inscrutable mask. "Price?" he asked. "I thought we agreed on that already."

I shook my head. "I agreed to investigate." I paused. "And to find your son, but not as to the reward."

"I see," the captain said, steepling his fingers before him. "What do you want then for that?" he asked, his chin jerking downward.

"A portal scroll," I replied.

Talon blinked, caught off guard by my request. "A portal scroll?" he asked. "Why would you want that?"

I sat back in my own chair and, seeing no reason not to, explained. "I don't wish to be beholden to your master," I said bluntly. "I don't trust any Power that much."

The captain opened his mouth to reply, but before he could speak I went on, "Give me what I want, and I will leave the sector."

The captain said nothing for a moment, then, to my surprise, he chuckled. "So it's to escape the sector that you want the portal scroll?"

I nodded, confused by his sudden amusement.

"I'm almost tempted to agree to your terms," the captain said, lips still twitching, "but I value my own honor too much to deceive you so."

I stared at him uncomprehendingly.

"The truth, Michael," Talon went on, "is that a portal scroll won't help you escape the sector."

"Why not?" I asked sharply.

"For one, the sector is hidden—"

"I know that," I interrupted.

"—and for another, it's also shielded for good measure," the captain finished.

My brows drew down. "Shielded?"

The captain nodded. "Ishita's sworn have installed a shield generator somewhere in the sector. While it's running, I'm afraid only portals keyed to the shield can be opened from within or without."

I stared at the captain in dismay, unable to say anything for long moments.

"Well, isn't that just perfect," I managed finally.

✳ ✳ ✳

It took me some time to get over the news. Had all my scheming been for naught?

No.

The shield generator complicated matters, but I could still make my plan work. As my shock dissipated further, I realized another thing: someone was lying to me.

Mariga had all but said outright that I could escape with a portal scroll, while Talon had just told me the opposite. So who was lying?

Captain or druid. Which one is it?

I snuck a glance at Talon. He was watching me. I might not trust the captain enough to ally myself with his master, but I didn't think he was the kind to be deceitful—whereas Mariga positively reeked of it. I could well believe she'd lied to me.

So what do I do now?

Bowing my head, I pondered the matter further. Did I go back to the Howlers to continue my scheme? Confront the druid? Come clean with the captain? Or all of the above? I sighed. Escaping the sector unscathed was looking increasingly unlikely.

"... hear me, Michael?"

The captain had asked me something, I realized. I picked up my head. "Sorry, say that again."

"Will you accept my original proposal now?" he repeated patiently.

I rubbed at my chin, giving the matter serious thought. I still had three days—including today—and while my original idea of "convincing" Ishita's sworn to let me pass through the portal was looking less viable, I wasn't quite ready to throw in my lot with Tartar.

Maybe I can find the shield generator.

Destroying it would simplify matters. I turned back to Talon. "Do you know where the shield generator is?" I asked, ignoring his original question.

The captain shook his head. "No. Xrex has made sure it's well-hidden, but in order to function the device has to be somewhere within the sector itself."

"It must be in the safe zone then," I said, thinking out loud. It was the most obvious—and protected place—to keep the device.

But the captain was shaking his head. "No. It can't be. Shields don't work in the safe zone."

I nodded slowly. Then there was still hope I could find the generator and destroy it before my time was up. "In that case, I must decline your proposal."

Talon gazed at me searchingly. "Are you sure?"

"No," I admitted. "But it's the only choice I can make and retain my autonomy."

The captain nodded, seeming to accept my response without bitterness. He glanced down at Stayne's letter. "I still want that," he said. "If not the god-emperor's protection, what else can I give you in exchange?"

I deliberated for only a fraction of a second before stating boldly, "One thousand gold."

A bark of laughter escaped the captain.

He thinks I'm joking, I thought.

But as I continued to stare evenly at him, Talon's amusement faded. "You're serious?"

"I am."

"I don't have that kind of money in the sector," the captain said.

My lips turned down in disappointment.

"But I can get it," he finished.

I looked at him. "How long?"

Talon pursed his lips in thought. "Two days."

I shook my head. "That's too long. You must have the money in one."

The captain's eyes narrowed at my words. "Must?" He scrutinized me again. "What difference will one more day make?"

I hesitated, then seeing no reason to lie, told him the truth. "I have a non-aggression Pact with Erebus. It expires soon, after which time his minions will be hard on my heels. I need to be long gone from the sector by then."

"A non-aggression Pact?" the captain asked, his eyebrows raising. "How did you manage that?"

I smiled. "With some skillful negotiating."

That surprised another laugh from Talon. "I like you, Michael," he said. "I really do. Very well, I agree to your terms: one day. I will have your money by then. You have my word on it."

A Game message opened in my mind.

Envoy Talon, acting on behalf of Tartar, has offered you a Pact. If you accept, within one day Tartar will provide you with a sum of 1,000 gold. In return, you will hand over Stayne's letter. This Pact may be terminated at any time by either party.

Do you accept Captain Talon's offer?

"Are the terms acceptable to you?" Talon asked, seeing my eyes turn inward.

I nodded slowly.

You have sealed a Pact with Captain Talon.

The captain smiled. "Excellent. You'd do well, I think, in the Tartan legion."

I shrugged, deciding not to respond to that. Retrieving Stayne's letter, I rose from my chair. "Well, if that's all, I guess that concludes our—"

"You know," the captain said abruptly. "This only takes care of one part of the original task I gave you."

I paused. "Meaning?"

"Meaning that while the Red Rats may have been bound in service already, that still leaves the Howlers unaccounted for." The captain turned back to the unfinished letter still open on his desk. "One moment," he murmured and resumed writing.

When he was done, Talon withdrew an object from his pocket and pressed it down to the paper. Peering across the table, I saw that he had stamped a wax seal of some sort onto the parchment.

Talon folded up the letter and handed it to me. "I've been meaning to get Cecilia and Ultack to deliver this, but given your successes so far, I think you'd be more suited to the task."

I took the folded note from his hands and read the message it contained.

Shaman Hyek of the Howler tribe,

I am Talon, envoy of the god-emperor himself and captain commander of the Ebonguard, third-ranked among the Tartan legions.

In this sector, I act as the emperor's voice and have all necessary authority to conclude any alliances I see fit. I assure you Tartar has no ill intentions toward your people, and a partnership between your tribe and the god-emperor will serve both our ends well.

The bearer of this letter has been authorized to negotiate the terms of a treaty between us. It is my hope that one can be swiftly concluded between us.

Yours truly,

Captain Talon.

The wax seal beneath the captain's name bore the symbol of two crossed swords over a snorting bull.

"The seal is magical in nature and tamper-proof," Talon explained. "The shaman will recognize it for what it is, the symbol of one of the emperor's envoys."

I stared at the captain, not sure I understood him correctly. "You want me to secure the Howlers' allegiance?"

"I do," he said. "Convince them to forget about the Awakened Dead and to bind themselves instead to the god-emperor. If you can do that, I'll throw in another one thousand gold."

"Why trust me with this? Surely your own people are better suited to this task?"

"In truth, my people have already made multiple overtures to the goblin delegations in the valley." Talon shook his head wryly. "In all cases, the delegations' leaders have refused to even meet with my representatives." He smiled. "Somehow, I don't think you'll have trouble getting past the door. Will you try?"

Doing what Talon asked was tantamount to giving the Tartan legion the sector, and while that was better than the valley falling into the Awakened Dead's hands, I wasn't comfortable at the thought of any Dark faction owning the dire wolves' home.

Still, I saw no harm in at least accepting the task. I nodded. "I will."

Your task, <u>Forging Dark Alliances</u>! has been updated. Captain Talon has requested you secure the allegiance of the Howlers for the god-emperor. Objective one revised: negotiate an alliance between the Tartans and the Howlers.

You have sealed a Pact with the envoy Talon, acting on behalf of Tartar. If the Howlers' shaman pledges allegiance to the god-emperor, Tartar will deposit a sum of 1,000 gold into your Albion Bank account.

Day Five. Dawn.

Not wanting to linger—or be caught out by my half-truths—I left the Tartan barracks soon after the captain and I finalized the terms of our second Pact.

Pausing outside the barracks, I considered my next move. There was still much to do, and my plans were in flux. I hadn't learned as much as I'd wanted to during my visit with the captain, and much of what I had learned was confusing.

But as disheartening as it had been to find out about the shield generator, its existence did give me additional options—assuming I could find it, of course.

Discovering the generator's location was now a priority.

The sector dynamics were also an interesting twist and made me doubly grateful the valley wasn't already under the Awakened Dead's rule. But given that the Howlers were supposedly already allied with Ishita—something else I needed to confirm urgently—the sector could be claimed on short notice, which made it all the more imperative that I left quickly.

It was clear too that someone, or more than one someone, was lying to me. And it was time I confirmed my suspicions in that regard.

Ducking my head so I was more inconspicuous, I hurried toward the dark druid's cabin.

* * *

Mariga opened the door as soon as I knocked. Brushing past her dark-robed figure, I slipped into the room.

"Make yourself at home why don't you," she hissed in an amused tone.

Ignoring her words, I spun about in the center of the room to scrutinize her shrouded form. Frustratingly, her identity remained as opaque as ever. Reaching out with my will, I tried analyzing her.

You have failed a Perception check and are unable to analyze your target. This entity bears a Mark of Greater Dark.

Once more, the dark druid sensed my interrogatory spell. "Ah, you've gained improved analyze. The little player is growing up," she said, sounding approving.

"Enough games," I snapped. "What are you?"

She didn't answer. I attempted to analyze her again and failed once more.

"Stop that!" Mariga hissed in a sibilant voice. "I told you it's rude. As for what I am, you know that already. I'm an agent of Shadow."

Narrowing my eyes, I studied here carefully. "Are you? How can I trust anything you say when you've lied to me?"

Mariga spread her hands, flexing clawed fingers. "Me, lie to you? About what, pray tell?"

"About being able to use a portal scroll to escape this valley," I said, watching her closely.

"Oh, that," Mariga said, seating herself and making no attempt to deny the accusation. "You've learned a thing or two, have you?"

I sat down opposite her. "I have. Now I want an explanation."

"That sounds suspiciously like a demand," Mariga said, sounding amused again. "You don't get to demand anything from me, boy. I told you then, and I will tell you now, I don't care if you complete my task. Decide how you will." She hissed, displaying two prominent fangs. "Now go. I tire of this conversation already."

I didn't move. "You knew a portal scroll wouldn't work, didn't you?" I persisted.

"I did."

"And you know about the shield generator?"

"I do," she said in a bored voice.

"Where is it?" I asked, leaning forward slightly.

"If I knew that, boy, it would be destroyed already!" Mariga snapped. "Now I told you to go. This is your last chance to leave." The druid's snake-like eyes glittered. "I won't ask so nicely next time."

I ignored the naked threat in her words. "Give it to me," I demanded.

"Give you what?"

"The portal scroll," I said.

"Why would I do that?" she asked lazily.

"Because if you don't," I growled, "I'll tell Ishitia's sworn you are an agent of Shadow."

For a moment, my bald threat seemed to strike the druid speechless. A moment later, she recovered her equilibrium. "Are you threatening me?" she asked silkily.

"I am," I retorted bluntly.

She laughed delightfully. "My, my, you're growing indeed." Reaching into her robe, she pulled out the portal scroll and placed it in my hand.

You have acquired a portal scroll.

I stared disbelievingly at the parchment in my hand. Mariga had handed it over with less fuss than I'd expected. "You're just giving it to me?"

"Well, that's what you wanted, isn't it?" she asked with a chuckle.

My gaze narrowed. She was being awfully cooperative suddenly, and I distrusted her motives. "Why give me this?" I demanded again.

"Why not give it to you?" she rejoined. "And as we already established, it's useless to you."

"But *only* in this sector," I countered. "It's still worth a lot of money."

"Ah, money," she exclaimed. "What do I care for money?"

I snorted. Was this the same player who'd refused to negotiate the price of her spellbooks? Either she'd been toying with me then, or she was now. I ground my teeth in frustration. *What game is she playing?*

"If you don't want the scroll, hand it back over."

I made no move to do so.

Mariga laughed. "So you *do* want it?"

I nodded reluctantly.

"Good. Now, you've got what you came for. So go!" she hissed.

I rose to my feet, suspecting some form of trick but not knowing what. More troubling still, I was leaving the druid's cabin just as unenlightened as I'd been when I had entered.

My thoughts muddled, I headed slowly toward the door.

"Out of interest," the dark druid called out, stopping me on my way to the exit, "how far did you get with the task I set you?"

I paused and swung around. She was still seated and facing the other way. *Pretending disinterest?* I wondered. "Why?"

"Call it curiosity," she replied.

I was still being manipulated, I knew, but I decided to play along. Perhaps if I strung her along, I could find out what she was really after.

I shrugged with affected indifference, not that she could see it. "By midday, I expect the Long Fangs will be no more."

Was it my imagination, or had Mariga stilled at my last words?

When she said nothing, I went on, watching her carefully. "I also have the Howlers and Red Rats poised on the brink of open war."

This time, there was no mistaking the sudden tightening of the druid's fingers. I smiled to myself and kept her waiting for a drawn-out moment before adding casually, "It won't take much to push them over the edge."

Mariga still said nothing.

But I wasn't deceived anymore. My news *had* piqued her interest. I turned back toward the door. My hand was halfway to the latch when she finally spoke. "Can you do it?"

"Excuse me?" I asked, my face void of expression.

"Don't play the fool, boy!" she snapped irritably. "Can you force them into open war?"

"I can," I said simply.

"What will it take?" she demanded.

"One thousand gold," I said equably.

The druid snorted. "I don't carry around money like that, and in case you don't know, there's no bank here."

I let my lips turn down. "Oh well, that's disappointing. Maybe next time—"

"Perhaps we can come to some other sort of accommodation," she said, interrupting me. Rising to her feet, Mariga swung around to face me at last. "After you get the job done, we can—"

I shook my head with pretended sadness. "Oh no," I said. "I've learned my lesson. I won't believe your promises anymore." I held her gaze. "If you want me to do your dirty work for you, you'll give me the money I asked for—upfront."

"I wasn't lying," she hissed. "I don't have the money."

"That's a pity," I said and turned back to the door.

"Wait!" she screeched.

Interesting... she almost seems desperate. But were these her true emotions or another act?

Keeping my own face smooth, I turned around.

Mariga's tongue darted out to lick at her lips. "What if we form a Pact?"

I blinked. A Pact was the last thing I'd expected her to suggest. "How would we—"

"I'm an envoy," she said.

I stared at her, struggling to contain my shock.

From what Talon had told me, I knew being an envoy was no small thing, and here she was in what was surely enemy territory.

Mariga had taken a big chance by coming to this sector. While the Awakened Dead couldn't kill her in the safe zone, controlling as they did the only portal into and out of the valley, they could imprison her nearly indefinitely. *Whatever Mariga's true mission, it must be vitally important to risk all that.*

"Will you trust a Pact?" she asked, interrupting my musings.

"Maybe," I said cautiously. "What terms do you propose?"

"Exactly what you stated," she said. "You get the Red Rats and Howlers to meet in open battle, and I will see to it that one thousand gold is deposited into a bank of your choice." She paused. "I have one other minor request."

Ah, here it comes. "And that is?" I asked tersely.

"You promise to keep my identity a secret as part of the terms of the Pact. You can tell no one of my true nature."

That seemed reasonable, almost too reasonable. I rubbed at my chin while I considered her words from every conceivable angle, but I could see no unseen danger in accepting the druid's proposal. "Alright, we've got a deal."

"Excellent," Mariga said, her body swaying in what I interpreted as pleasure. "Place your hand in mine, and I will form the Pact between us."

I did as she bade, gingerly setting my gloved hand atop her scaled palm.

A Game message opened in my mind.

Initiating a Pact between the Envoy known as Mariga, acting on behalf of an unknown Power, and the player, Michael...

I squinted at the somewhat surprising wording of the Adjudicator's response.

Mariga waved at me, drawing my attention. "Go on," she said impatiently. "Let the Adjudicator know your requirements so we can get this done."

Refusing to be rushed, I reread the opening message. It suggested I knew less of the dark druid's true nature than I'd thought. "'...known as Mariga,'" I repeated aloud. "That's not your true name then?"

"Of course not," the druid said dismissively. She gestured down at her body. "This wouldn't be much of a disguise if I used my true name, now would it?"

I frowned. "You're not really a snake woman?"

A snort of disdain was my only response.

I walked a slow circle around Mariga, studying her in renewed fascination. "How do you manage to retain your disguise in the safe zone?" I asked, thinking of my own failure with lesser imitate.

"I use a master-tier deception spell, naturally," she replied.

"Naturally," I murmured, wondering what that said about her level. The ability she was using had to also be capable of fooling a player's analyze ability I realized. Otherwise, she would have roused the suspicions of Ishita's sworn.

"Now, can we get on with it?" she asked, getting more impatient.

I broke off from my fascinated study and gave her my attention again. "Not yet. Who is the 'unknown Power' you serve?"

That druid scowled. "I told you I am bound to the goddess of nature."

"You aren't," I stated firmly. "If you belonged to Artem, the Adjudicator wouldn't have labeled the Power you serve as 'unknown.'" I paused. "Now, will you be honest with me?" I asked, getting impatient myself.

The druid was silent for so long I thought she wouldn't answer. "I serve Arinna," she said at last.

I frowned, not recognizing the name. "Who?"

"She's a goddess of Light," Mariga said quietly.

"You're a *Light* player?" I asked in a strangled voice.

"Yes," she replied. "Does that bother you?"

It didn't, not in the sense she meant, but it did disturb me to discover another layer to her deceit. What else was she hiding? "Why does an envoy of the Light care about starting a war between two goblin tribes?"

"Isn't it obvious?" Mariga asked. "I'm here to curb the Dark's expansion. They can't be allowed to claim this sector. Once they do," she spread her arms, gesturing all around her, "the entirety of this valley will be heavily fortified and it could take months, if not years, to dislodge them. I've been sent here to stop that before it happens."

"What makes this valley so important?" I asked. I had Talon's view, but I wanted to hear her own. Would she tell me the truth?

"The Nethersphere entrance primarily," she replied. "Connections between the aether and nether are few and far between, and each one is dearly prized. What's more, this one is in a *closed* sector. That's almost unheard of."

She paused. "There is more to it though. There's something about this sector that draws the Awakened Dead in particular. In the months I've been here, I've spied many of their finest players passing through the valley. They've always been careful to hide their identities." She smiled. "But it's hard to hide one's true self from me." She glanced sideways at me from beneath lidded eyes.

Was her last comment directed at me too?

"And before you ask, I don't know what those players are up to," Mariga finished with an undercurrent of frustration. "But I intend to find out."

I hid my disappointment. It didn't seem like I was going to get all my answers neatly laid out.

"Will you still form the Pact?" Mariga asked.

I spent a moment considering my answer. "Yes," I said finally.

✳ ✳ ✳

You have sealed a Pact with the envoy known as Mariga, acting on behalf of Arinna. The Power will deposit a sum of 1,000 gold into your Albion Bank account if you push the Red Rats and Howlers into a pitched battle and keep Mariga's true nature secret from the sector's occupants.

Your task, <u>Goblin Wars</u>! has been updated. You sealed a Pact with Mariga, changing the terms of her original request. Revised objective: force the Red Rats and Howlers into a pitched battle.

I quickly retreated from Mariga's cabin once our Pact was concluded. Glancing up at the brightening sky, I stifled a yawn. Morning had arrived. In the end the druid's revelations had proved enlightening, and in the process my own path had solidified.

I was now certain what I needed to do next.

But it had been a long night, and I was tired. *I require sleep,* I decided. Pointing my feet in the direction of the tavern, I strode that way.

The village streets were no longer empty. Players strolled to and fro. Recognizing me, some cast me dark looks. I paid them no heed.

As I drew up to the tavern, I noticed fresh scraps of paper posted on the noticeboard. They were all the same: copies of the bounty Ishita had placed on me.

My lips turned down. Someone was making very certain my face didn't go unrecognized. Hurrying past the bounty noticeboard, I climbed the tavern's stairs and entered its darkened interior. It, too, was occupied by a smattering of players. They sat huddled around their tables, nursing their drinks. At my entrance, a few looked up and scowled.

Ignoring their angry mutters, I sat down at the bar. Benadean walked over. "Wow, you made it back." His eyes roved over my frame. "And with all your possessions intact. Impressive."

I threw him a wry grin. "I'm harder to kill than you think," I murmured and placed a silver coin down the bar counter's polished surface.

Benadean's eyes flickered to the coin. "What's that for?"

"For a mug of ale," I said. "And payment for the other day's freebie."

The barkeeper opened his mouth to protest, but I waved aside his objections. "Keep it, I insist."

Benadean pocketed the coin. "Thanks," he acknowledged and placed a brimming mug before me.

I took a sip, savoring the dark, earthy flavor of the brew. I sighed and leaned back on my stool. "How much for a room?"

The barkeeper's eyebrows lifted in surprise. "You're planning on staying in the village then?"

I nodded. "For a day, no more." Less, if I could help it.

Benadean shook his head, undoubtedly thinking me foolish for taking such risks, but this time he didn't voice his concerns. "It's one gold per day."

Wincing at the cost, I placed another coin on the counter and the barkeeper exchanged it for an iron key. "The room is up the stairs, the first door on your right," he said.

I nodded in thanks.

"So, what did you think of Mariga?" he asked suddenly.

I stared at him in consternation. *How does he know I visited the dark druid?*

Mistaking my expression for confusion, Benadean elaborated, "The last time you were here, it seemed like you were going to see her."

"Ah," I said, realizing it wasn't my most recent visit he was referring to. "You were right. She *is* odd."

The barkeeper nodded sagely. "I wouldn't have sent you her way, but given your circumstances... I didn't think anyone else would deal with you."

"No, you were right to direct me to her," I said, waving away his concern.

Benadean leaned forward and whispered in a tone too low for the others in the room to overhear, "Between you and me, I suspect she's not entirely of the Dark."

I looked up at him, my interest piqued. "What makes you say that?"

The barkeeper shrugged. "I don't know... for all that she bears all the trappings of a Dark player, she's shown little of the inclinations I've come to associate with those sworn to the Dark."

"Really?"

He nodded. "I've never known a Dark player to sit content in their home for weeks on end." He pursed his lips. "I'm not sure how to explain it, but in my experience, Dark players all bear one trait in common: ambition. They are always striving, always pushing to gain more. To advance. At the best of times, you lot are impatient."

I stroked my chin, ignoring his implication that I, too, belonged to the Dark—and that he didn't. "That's an interesting observation... are there any other players you suspect of not being Darksworn?" I asked casually.

Benadean laughed. "What? You mean one isn't enough? There aren't any others. Ishita's sworn have been too fanatical in rooting them out."

"What do you mean?"

"Only Dark Marked players *without* affiliation to any other Force have been allowed into the sector," he explained.

I cocked my head to the side and studied him. "But you bear Marks of Shadow and Light as well, don't you?"

Benadean snorted. "I do. And let me tell you, negotiating my way into the sector has proven to be more hassle than it's worth. Ishita's mages grilled me for hours before they let me through. The idiots suspected me of being a spy or something."

"Why did they let you in then?" I asked, generally curious.

He laughed—somewhat bitterly, I thought. "I'd like to think it's because I have a long history and solid reputation among the Darksworn, but the truth? It was probably because I was just a civilian and no threat." He paused, then added, "And though I didn't realize it at the time, they were likely desperate for merchants too."

I raised a questioning brow. "Why is that?"

He looked at me. "You've seen the valley. There's not much of value here. Business has been poor." He shook his head. "No, that's an understatement. Business has been abysmal. The gamble I took in coming here hasn't paid off. It's time to return home."

"You're leaving?"

He nodded. "I've been scraping by as it is, and I've made nowhere near the profit I've been expecting." He exhaled a heavy breath. "And with the way matters have been going, I suspect things are about to get a lot worse."

"When will you go?"

"I'm not sure yet." Benadean shrugged. "A month. A week. Maybe less." He sighed. "I'll need to find someone fool enough to buy this place first though."

I raised my glass. "Well, here's to you. May you find better fortune wherever you venture next."

* * *

Benadean left me to enjoy my drink in silence after that, and I sipped at it slowly, relishing the rare moment of quiet.

It didn't last long, of course.

Not five minutes after he'd left, the barkeeper hurried back over. "You better go," he whispered furtively. "I've just heard. A large group of Awakened Dead players is on their way here." He eyed me. "Looking for you."

"Thanks for the heads up," I said but made no move to leave.

Benadean stared at me in consternation for a moment, then, throwing up his hands, he left me to my fate.

Turning back to my ale, I nursed it, patiently waiting.

It didn't take long for the gang of Dark players to barge into the tavern. The one at the front of the group was immediately recognizable.

It was Forsyth.

His eyes simmering with hate, the spellsword advanced menacingly in my direction. I swung around on my chair and raised my mug in a casual toast. "Forsyth. Fancy meeting you here again."

Ishita's follower glared at me and, not unexpectedly, didn't return my greeting as he came to a halt less than two feet away. "What did you do?" he demanded.

"I have no idea what you mean," I said lazily. My gaze drifted beyond him to the players at his back. They had spread out to surround me in a loose half-circle.

"Don't play the fool," Forsyth grated from between clenched teeth. "I know it was you!"

"You're going to have to give me a bit more than that," I suggested, "if you expect a response."

The spellsword snarled in wordless rage and said nothing for a moment, chest heaving. "The Howlers have sealed the gates to the village," he finally ground out. "They're not letting anyone out!"

"Ah," I murmured and took another sip from my nearly empty mug. "That's a pity."

"What did you do?" he demanded again.

I looked at him innocently. "Me? I had nothing to do with it."

"You're lying!" he accused.

Of course I am. Maintaining my facade of innocence, I said nothing as I continued to stare at him blankly.

Our standoff lasted for less than a minute. The irate spellsword didn't have the patience to sustain his glare for any longer.

"You won't get away with this," he promised harshly. Not waiting for my response, he spun about and marched out the door, his troup following on his heels.

A small smile tugged at the corner of my lips. Finally, things were looking up.

CHAPTER 122: STIRRING UP A FUSS

Day Five. Early Morning.

I waited ten minutes before exiting the tavern myself. It wasn't that I feared Forsyth and his gang, but I could do without them dogging my heels as I went about my business.

I hadn't planned on leaving the safe zone so soon again, but matters were moving quicker than I'd anticipated and I couldn't risk delaying.

Somehow, Forsyth already knew enough to suspect me of being involved with the killings in the Howler fort. If I gave Ishita's sworn enough time, they might just manage to convince the Howlers' shaman they had nothing to do with the matter—which would be bad for me.

I had to strike now, while the shaman's outrage was still fresh and he harbored no doubts as to the perpetrator. Then I would have more chances of succeeding in what I aimed to accomplish next.

Ducking into the narrow alley between two buildings, I concealed myself in the shadows and crept toward the fort's inner gate. When I got there, I found a crowd of players had gathered before it. *Here we go again,* I thought. Leaving the shadows, I strolled boldly toward the gate.

The players attempted to bar my way, not obviously—the rules governing the safe zone precluded that—but with their mere presence. I was too quick for them though and slipped deftly under outstretched arms and around broad backs.

Deaf to the cries of "Stop!" and "Halt!" I slipped up to the gate and pounded on its solid surface with a closed fist. "Hey! You two in there, open up!"

There was no response.

"They're not going to let you through," a voice sneered from behind me.

Ignoring the heckler, I closed my eyes and reached out with mindsight, identifying the two goblins standing guard on the other side of the gate. "Ingu and Siltuk," I shouted, addressing the pair by name, "let me in! Your shaman will want to hear what I have to say."

A grate that served as a peephole was yanked back, and two scowling eyes scrutinized me. "Who are you?" the guard—Ingu—demanded.

"I'm Michael," I said evenly. I jerked my thumb to point at the players behind me. "And I'm no friend of theirs."

"Why should we believe you?" Ingu asked. "Or even care?"

"Because," I said, leaning in close to him so the players behind me couldn't overhear, "I have information your shaman will want to hear." I paused to make sure he focused on my next words. "It's about the Red Rats. They're on the move south."

Ingu's eyes flared at the mention of his tribe's hated enemies. "Wait there," he ordered peremptorily and slammed shut the grate.

"Of course," I murmured. "I don't plan on going anywhere."

*　*　*

The goblins kept me waiting for thirty minutes.

Closing my eyes and slouching against the gate, I affected indifference to the jeers and continued heckling of the nearby players. My pretense was so successful that I actually managed to doze off, awakening with a rude start at the sound of the locks being drawn back on the other side of the gate.

"What's going on?" someone asked from behind me.

"They're letting us through," another said.

Rubbing the sleep from my eyes, I folded my arms and waited.

The gate opened wide to reveal nearly one hundred goblins arrayed around the entrance. Their weapons were lowered and pointed toward the gate in unmistakable threat.

"Halt!" the goblin captain in charge roared to the players attempting to shove their way through. "We will slay whoever attempts to pass without permission."

The mob drew back fearfully.

The captain's gaze slid to my patiently waiting figure. "You! Come through. The shaman will see you now."

With a smile directed at the unhappy players at my back, I strode forward and followed on the captain's heels as the gate slammed shut behind me.

So far, so good, I thought to myself.

*　*　*

The shaman, of course, resided in the central keep. The goblin captain led me through its labyrinth interior to a large hall on the third floor. Nodding to the two guards on either side of the door, he waved me through, not entering himself.

Inside I found Shaman Hyek, leader of the Howlers' delegation, waiting.

Thick fur rugs covered the floor, and large banners with symbols and insignias I didn't recognize lined the hall's walls. Other than that, the room contained little in the way of decor.

The Howler leader was seated at a stone table in the center of the chamber. He was alone, unaccompanied by even a single guard. It was, I thought, a deliberate gesture, and one made to show how little the shaman feared me.

And from his physical appearance alone, Hyek's confidence seemed warranted.

The shaman was bigger than any other goblin I'd yet met. He was larger even than the long-dead leader of the Fangtooths. Even seated, Hyek towered over me. Standing, I estimated he would be at least two and a half times my height.

The shaman wore robes of startling white and a multicolored feathered headdress. The nails of his hands, which had been filed to points, drummed impatiently on the table as he waited for me.

As I drew closer, I cast insight upon him.

The target is Hyek, a level 85 goblin shaman and goliath.
Goliaths are a mutated and rare subspecies of goblins. They are thought to be blessed by the Forces with unusual size and strength.

"So," the shaman said, his eyes narrowed as he considered me, "you are the player who's been causing so much fuss."

I bowed slightly. "Guilty as charged."

"What do you want?" he demanded, moving straight to business.

"Like I told your guards, I have news to share about the Red Rats."

"That they have left that crater of theirs? Yes, I'm already aware," Hyek said mildly. "My scouts informed me yesterday that the scum march in force on the Long Fangs' encampment."

I scrutinized the goblin shaman. He was better informed than I expected. It didn't matter though. "And are you also aware that they plan on heading south to your own fort once the Long Fangs have been defeated?"

Hyek said nothing, but the slight stiffening of his face betrayed him.

I smiled. "I see that you were unaware. Consider the information—freely provided—a gift, a gesture of goodwill."

Hyek studied me for a drawn-out moment. "Even if what you say is true," he said slowly, "it is of little consequence. The Red Rats will shatter on these walls."

"Are you so sure of that?" I asked lightly. "They outnumber you two to one."

"Their numbers mean little," Hyek said unperturbed. "My men are better trained, and our defenses are strong."

Both true, sadly.

Strolling nonchalantly through the chamber, I seated myself without permission on the other side of the table. From the tightening of the shaman's lips, I could tell that doing so irritated him.

"Strong enough to repel an army of players too?" I asked, resuming the conversation.

The shaman leaned back in his chair. "What mischief are you trying to stir? I've been warned about you, you know. Do not think I am unaware of the bounty the spider goddess has placed on your head." He smiled toothily, revealing teeth filed as sharp as his fingertips. "I'm inclined to claim it myself."

I laughed, showing him how little his threat bothered me. "Oh, you won't do that."

"Why not?" the shaman asked, his eyes narrowing dangerously.

"Because right now you and your 'allies' aren't on the best of terms," I said evenly.

"'Allies?' What allies?" the shaman asked with pretended ignorance.

But he had waited a breath too long to make his denial. I had surprised him.

I smiled. "Don't bother with denials, Hyek. I already know that your tribe has pledged its allegiance to Ishita."

The shaman fell silent again, and this time the sense of menace in the air was palpable. "You play a dangerous game," he said softly. "I could kill you here and no one would care."

He hadn't denied my accusation, I noted. That was all the confirmation I needed. "Again, Hyek, I don't think you'll do that. If you did, you wouldn't learn of things vital to your tribe's survival."

"Go on," he said tightly. "Enlighten me then."

"I'm sure you're wondering why one of Ishita's sworn slew a barrack full of your men." I paused, waiting to see his response.

Hyek grunted, unimpressed. "They claim you did that."

So Ishita's followers had already got to him.

I chuckled, outwardly at ease. "And why would I do that?" I leaned forward across the table. "More importantly, how could I? You must know my level. Do you *really* believe me capable of slaying—what was it?—forty of your men?" I asked, deliberately getting the number wrong.

The shaman had himself under control now though, and he betrayed no reaction at my words.

I shook my head. "No, it wasn't me. Nor were the killings senseless. There was a reason Xrex did what he did." I held his gaze. "It is," I went on slowly, "because the Red Rats and the Awakened Dead have forged their own alliance. Stayne himself has pledged to gift the Red Rats this fort once your delegation has been destroyed."

I paused, then drove home the point. "Your alliance with the Awakened Dead is no more. You have been discarded, Hyek."

Unable to keep himself in check any longer, the shaman's face contorted in fury. "Lies!" he roared.

I held his gaze. "I have proof," I said evenly.

"Show me," he demanded, breathing harshly.

Silently, I extracted Stayne's letter and slid it across the table to the shaman. With trembling fingers, Hyek picked up the parchment and began to read.

I waited, striving to betray no sign of my own nerves. *Will he recognize the handwriting?* I wondered. I'd played my final card. Now, it all depended on what Hyek made of my "proof."

"No," the shaman whispered, his face paling. "No, No, NO!" he roared, his voice increasing in volume with each utterance.

The tension eased out of me. I hadn't been certain the shaman wouldn't reject the proof I presented him with or that he would draw the "right" conclusions. But my gamble seemed like it was paying off.

Bowing his head, Hyek rested it on the table, saying nothing further. Observing the shaman's despair, I felt guilt stir in me. I squashed it ruthlessly.

The Howlers were my enemies. As were the Red Rats and anyone else who called Erebus master. The Howlers may not have attacked me outright yet, but I was certain that if Erebus or Ishita ever commanded it, they wouldn't hesitate to do so.

I do what I have to.

I spoke quietly into the hushed silence. "*'The time to move openly'* that Stayne talks about? That time has come."

The shaman looked up at me, his face still ashen. "Why would Erebus and Ishita do this?"

I sighed. "I don't know, but it has been my experience that the Awakened Dead cannot be trusted."

Hyek laughed harshly. "You players. We are nothing more than pawns in your Game." He shook his head and looked at me bitterly. "You wouldn't have brought this information here if you didn't want something. What is it?" he demanded.

I looked over the goblin carefully. The moment had arrived for me to make a choice.

Chapter 123: A Difficult Choice

Two obvious choices lay before me: fulfill Mariga's task or Talon's.

The druid wanted the Howlers forced into a bloody war with the Red Rats, while the captain wished to secure their allegiance for Tartar. Of the two envoys, I trusted Talon more, and if the choice I faced was one between the pair, then my decision would have been simple.

But in truth, my loyalty belonged to neither envoy.

It was only to the dire wolves that I was truly beholden.

If I convinced Hyek to ally with the Tartan legion, then this sector would be claimed by the Dark, and while the Tartans seemed a better sort than the Awakened Dead, I suspected they would no more allow the wolves to roam freely in the valley than the Awakened Dead would.

It didn't matter that I felt a greater affinity to Talon and that there was something about Mariga that repulsed me. Nor did it matter that hundreds of the goblins would die. I had to see the wolves protected.

I had to convince the Howlers to go to war.

"You know already that I'm no friend of Ishita's sworn," I said slowly. "I need your help to lure them here."

"Why?" the shaman asked, his gaze fixed unerringly on me.

"To kill them," I stated baldly.

"And why should I help you?" Hyek asked.

I jerked my chin down to the parchment still lying between us on the table. "Because of that," I said softly, "and for revenge."

For a long moment, Hyek didn't say anything, then he shook his head. "My heart cries out to do as you ask, but my head says otherwise. The Awakened Dead may have abandoned my people and me and my soldiers will likely be dead soon, but I must consider the fate of the rest of my tribe too—those in our home sector."

The shaman sighed. "If I move openly against the spider goddess, she will wreak her own brand of justice. Not only will my people in this valley be killed, but the goddess will also see to it that my entire tribe is destroyed."

For a drawn-out moment, the shaman's response had me stumped.

I'd been hoping he'd be as bloodthirsty as the other goblins I'd met, but it seemed that to sway Hyek, I would have to dangle more than the prospect of revenge before him. It left me with fewer options.

"I do not ask you to move openly against Ishita," I said finally. "I only ask that you summon her delegates to a meeting here and leave the rest to me. You may lay the blame for the killings squarely on me."

Hyek chewed over this for a moment, still not looking convinced. "Then what?"

I exhaled soundlessly. I had no choice now but to play a card I'd been hoping not to.

I slid the second parchment in my possession across the table to the shaman. "Despite what you may think, there's hope for your people yet, Hyek."

Disinterestedly, the shaman picked up the letter Talon had penned and read it, only to inhale sharply a moment later when he digested its contents. "The god-emperor will extend his protection over my people?" he asked with barely disguised hope.

I nodded. "If you ask for it. But there is a condition."

The shaman blinked slowly, shuttering the emotions that had peeked through. "What does the Tartan envoy require?" he asked in a monotone voice.

"The god-emperor will not accept just anyone within his legions. You and your people must prove yourselves worthy first."

Hyek nodded, seeming to accept my assertion without question. "How?"

"You must march out of the fort and meet the Red Rats in open battle. The captain will see to it that no Awakened Dead players interfere. If you face the Red Rats and acquit yourselves well, the god-emperor will accept your tribe's pledge of allegiance."

For a long moment, Hyek didn't say anything. Then finally, he uttered the words I'd been waiting to hear. "I accept your terms, player."

Your task, <u>Forging Dark Alliances</u>! has been updated. Shaman Hyek has agreed to pledge allegiance to the god-emperor in exchange for the Tartans' aid in the Howlers' war against the Red Rats. Objective one revised: obtain Captain Talon's agreement to the terms of the alliance you've negotiated between the Tartans and the Howlers.

✳　✳　✳

Once Hyek agreed to my conditions, matters moved swiftly.

A guard was called and dispatched to the gate to summon Ishita's sworn. I was tired and impatient to complete my business at the fort, but resting would have to wait until matters here were seen to.

While the shaman and I waited for the guard to report back, I idly turned to the Howler leader and said, "There is one thing I still don't understand."

Hyek was pacing impatiently up and down across the floor. At my words, he swung around to face me. "What's that?"

"If you're already allied with the Awakened Dead, how is it they don't own the sector already?"

The shaman snorted. "So you don't know everything," he muttered. "Our alliance with Ishita is an informal one only. Erebus promised to finalize our agreement after his business in the Nethersphere has concluded."

"I see," I murmured, then asked casually, "and what business is that?"

Hyek threw me a sharp glance. "When can I expect the Tartan captain to formalize our alliance?" he asked, ignoring my own question entirely.

"As soon as you have defeated the Red Rats," I replied smoothly.

Hyek scowled. "What assurances do I have that your captain will not betray me like Erebus did?"

"None," I responded in a clipped tone. "But the captain is an honorable sort, nothing like Erebus. He will keep his end of the bargain if you do yours."

The shaman was not pleased with my answer, but he didn't have the luxury of other choices. Swallowing his displeasure, Hyek resumed his pacing.

"Although," I added after a moment, "you probably don't want to mention your dealings with Erebus when you meet the captain."

"Why not?" the shaman demanded, pinning me with a glare.

"I haven't told him about it," I said simply. "He might take a... dim view of your previous allegiance."

Hyek muttered something under his breath, too soft even for my sharp hearing to pick out. Whatever it was, I doubted it was complimentary to me.

Before we could resume our conversation, a guard stepped in. "They're on their way, sir," he said, saluting the shaman.

I rose to my feet and, sweeping my two letters off the table, stowed them back into my pocket. "I best be going then," I said. I glanced at Hyek. "Don't forget the plan."

His face still dark with anger, the shaman nodded mutely.

Knowing there was no time to extract further assurances from Hyek, I had to be satisfied with his response. Without saying anything more, I slipped out of the room.

He better not betray me.

✳ ✳ ✳

Concealing myself in a side room directly adjacent to the shaman's own chamber, I waited for the mages to arrive.

I was walking a dangerous path, one held up by little more than lies and mistruths. A single misstep and it could all come crashing down on me. But I could see no other way to accomplish the goals before me.

If matters went awry, the Tartans would number themselves among my enemies, and the god-emperor, I suspected, would be a much more difficult foe to elude than Erebus. But even if everything went according to plan, the Tartans might still be angered.

But there was no turning back now. I'd have to live with my choices.

Hearing that tread of footsteps, I broke off from my musings to open my mindsight and study the ones approaching. It didn't take me long to identify the pair.

It was Ishan and Worca.

I bit back my disappointment. I'd been hoping that Xrex, leader of Ishita's sworn, would come himself. If anyone was certain to know the location of the shield generator, it would be him. Nonetheless, I had to contend with the two who *had* come.

The two mages strode boldly into the shaman's audience chamber. With my ear pressed up against the wall, I listened intently.

"It is good of you to consent to see us," Worca said diplomatically, even though I knew it was the shaman who had demanded they meet.

"Ha," I heard Ishan mutter to himself. "Uppity bastard, summoning us like bloody commoners. Someone needs to teach him his place."

"Where is Xrex?" the shaman asked. "I requested that he come in person."

"Who in blazes do you think you are?" Ishan growled. "You don't get to demand—"

He broke off abruptly, and I guessed his companion must have restrained him. I smiled. What had possessed Xrex to send the volatile human as his representative?

"Given the accusations levied against him, Xrex decided it might be in everyone's best interest if he didn't come himself," Worca said. "Less chance of any... unfortunate accidents happening that way."

"Then the lizardman denies slaying my soldiers?" Hyek asked sharply.

"He does," Worca said. "Whoever did it, it was not—"

"And does he also deny that you are allied with my enemies, the Red Rats?" Hyek demanded.

The resulting silence was deafening.

Even Ishan had nothing to say this time.

"Where did you hear that?" Worca asked after the silence had drawn on too long.

"You do not deny it then," the shaman said heavily. I heard him walk away and mutter to himself in a low voice that I was sure the other two players didn't pick up. "So, it is true. We are betrayed."

Realizing she had erred in her response, Worca spoke up hurriedly again. "Forgive me, shaman. I was simply caught off guard by your words. Of course we deny it. Your tribe is important to our faction. Whoever has been telling you these lies is only trying to stir up trouble between us."

But Hyek was done listening. His footsteps had been the signal, and right on cue, a goblin warrior entered the room. "Sir!" he yelled in panic, "you must come immediately! One of the barracks is on fire!"

The shaman whipped about. "Lead on, soldier. I'm coming."

"We can help—" Worca began.

"No!" Hyek hissed. "I do not trust you two. You will both wait here, and when I return we will finish our discussion."

Not waiting for their response, Hyek and the goblin warrior strode out of the chamber, slamming the door behind them.

CHAPTER 124: THE SPIDER'S SPAWN

Day Five. Mid-Morning.

The shaman's hurried exit was part of the plan, of course.

The fire was real too and would give Hyek deniability for what was to come next. Before creeping back into the chamber, I spent another moment listening to the two mages.

"Damn, I don't think he bought it," Ishan said, stating the obvious.

Worca blew out a frustrated breath. "This hasn't occurred by happenchance. Someone is working against us."

"Forsyth was right. It must be that damn mindstalker," Ishan growled. "I told you and Xrex that we should never have let him go. We should track him down and kill him. Repeatedly."

"I'm beginning to think you're right," Worca said softly.

I'd heard enough. Slipping into the shadows, I padded softly into the room through a side door artfully concealed behind a tapestry.

Two hostile entities have failed to detect you! You are hidden.

The two mages had their backs to me. Both stood at one of the chamber's few window slits, observing the fire that raged in an emptied-out barracks below. They were unaware it was unoccupied, of course.

"That's no natural fire," Ishan remarked. "Who do you think started it?"

"I don't know," Worca murmured, "but I'm certain we'll be blamed."

I padded closer, hand on the hilts of my blades. Halfway to my targets, I analyzed both.

The target is Worca, a level 108 dark summoner and elf.
The target is Ishan, a level 96 spellweaver and human.

I knew nothing of either's Class, but based on both temperament and level, Worca was the bigger threat, and I angled my approach to come up behind the elven mage.

"What do we do next?" Ishan asked finally.

"We investigate *that*," Worca replied. She jerked her head downward towards the still-raging fire. "Then we prove to the shaman we weren't responsible for the killings."

Two hostile entities have failed to detect you!

I was two yards away and about to enter striking distance. I unsheathed my blades.

"And if we fail to do that?" Ishan asked, sounding more worried than I'd ever heard him. He shivered. "The goddess will not be pleased."

Three steps away. The mages remained oblivious. Coiling back, I prepared to attack.

"Let Xrex worry about—"

A hostile entity has detected you! You are no longer hidden.

The elven mage's words broke off as I lunged forward, the tip of both my blades heading straight toward her back. She had sensed my presence too late though.

Nothing could stop my attack now.

An inch from driving through my target's heart, my swords found resistance.

Worca's spell shield has triggered!
Your target's shield has blocked your attack, absorbing its damage.

No! I cursed as a bubble of shimmering black snapped into existence around Worca. The damnable mage was shielded.

Worca spun around, a pair of wands dropping into her waiting palms. Realizing her intent, I threw myself sideways.

A bar of liquid blackness scorched the air, missing me by inches. It was followed closely by a glistening arc of burning cold.

You have evaded Worca's wilting ray. You have evaded Worca's frost bolt.

Contorting wildly, I managed to avoid both attacks, but my evasive maneuvers had forced me farther back, giving my foes some much-needed space.

Three yards away, I rose to my feet.

"It's him!" Ishan shrieked.

"Shut up and kill him," his companion snapped.

At the human mage's outcry, my gaze jerked toward him. No similar shield surrounded his body. *That means he's vulnerable.* With my gaze fixed squarely on my new target, I raced forward.

Worca cast a second volley of ice and darkness my way. Not slowing my charge, I ducked beneath the first projectile and sidestepped the second.

You have evaded Worca's magical attacks.

"You missed him! How could you miss?" Ishan screamed. Fumbling for his own wand, the human mage launched his own attack. Dark flames of shimmering black and purple roared out at me.

I one-stepped, leaping over the fire and somersaulting through the air to land behind my target. In nearly the same motion, I thrust both my blades forward.

Ishan has trigger-cast dark repulsion. You have failed to resist the spell!

An instant before my blades made contact, a shockwave of air detonated outward from my target. The force of the casting was too immense to resist. Picked up as easily as a leaf in a storm, I was tossed away.

Flying clear across the chamber, I crashed into one of the chamber's unyielding stone walls and slid to the ground in a heap.

Ishan has injured you! You have failed a physical resistance check! You are dazed.

The wind had been knocked out of me, and my back felt like one bruised mass. But there was no time to acknowledge the pain. *Move, Michael!* I yelled at myself, knowing a follow-up attack was imminent.

Picking a direction at random, I rolled across the floor. An instant later, a barrage of magical fire scorched the spot I'd just occupied.

I kept rolling until the waves of nausea assaulting me receded. Then I lurched back to my feet and beheld another—larger—magical storm descending upon me.

Damnation.

For a fraction of a heartbeat, I froze. There were too many magical projectiles hurling toward me to count. *How am I going to get through all that?*

The full length of the room separated me and my targets. To get to them, I would have to wade through the onslaught of magic. It was impossible. The exit from the room beckoned. *It* was much closer than my targets. *Should I flee?*

For an instant, I almost did.

By god damn, no, I swore. There was no escape in retreat. If I fled now, I lost. Maybe forever.

I can do this. I have to do this.

Rushing forward, I dived into the hurricane of magic. Letting go of conscious thought entirely, I let instinct guide me. Twisting, leaping, ducking, and sliding, I danced through the onslaught.

You have evaded a wilting ray.
You have evaded a frost bolt.
You have evaded a flame dart.
You have evaded...

"How's he doing that?" Ishan screamed, his voice reedy with panic. "That's not possible! That *can't* be possible!"

"I don't know," Worca replied coolly. "Keep attacking," she continued, calm and unruffled. "I'm going to try something else."

I barely heard the two. All my senses and nearly every thought were trained on the maze that was the spell storm and weaving a path through.

An eternity later—or was it only a few seconds?—the hurricane petered out. I increased my pace. Avoiding the few magical projectiles still heading my way was almost trivial now.

My focus slid back to my foes.

Worca had stopped attacking. The elf had dropped her wands and closed her eyes. Her lips were moving, chanting the words to a spell. Whatever she was about, there was nothing I could do to stop her.

My gaze darted to Ishan, mapping a path to him. Weaving deftly through the flames he shot at me, I closed in quickly on the human.

You have evaded three magical attacks.

Five yards separated us. I rolled under another pair of spells.

You have evaded two magical attacks.

Two yards away. Springing off my hands, I leaped over the mage's latest projectile, the largest one he'd thrown at me yet—a fireball.

Ishan's head whipped upward, following the arc I cut through the air. I'd timed my move perfectly. If my flight continued uninterrupted, I would land squarely on the mage.

But I didn't expect that to happen.

Two feet away from my target, I cast one-step and threw myself higher. Then, exactly as I expected, and almost on cue, Ishan activated his spelled defenses.

Ishan has trigger-cast dark repulsion. You have evaded the spell!

A second wave of air exploded outward from the mage. But this time I was unaffected. My aerial maneuver had put me out of the spell's reach.

I fell back to the ground, eyes fixed on my target. In speechless disbelief, Ishan watched me. I landed softly on the balls of my feet and less than a foot from the mage.

"How did—" he began.

He got no further. Slashing out with both my blades, I ripped out his throat.

You have killed Ishan with a fatal blow. You have slain a sworn servant of Ishita, increasing her ire toward you!

I bared my teeth wolfishly. *One down, one to go.*

Whipping about, I faced my next foe. Worca had fallen silent, I realized belatedly. Whatever spell she had been casting was completed.

A tear appeared in the air.

And from within, something was stepping out.

CHAPTER 125: BORN FROM DARKNESS

Worca has cast summon giant stygian spider.

My mouth dropped open in shock. *Bloody hell, what now?* Images of the spider Saben had transformed into flashed through my mind.

I can't face something like that, not on my own.

Heart in mouth, I watched the emerging shape. Out of the corner of my eye, I saw Worca with her hands on her knees and gasping for breath. Whatever she had summoned, it had taken a lot out of her.

Two spindly legs appeared in the luminous slit of light hanging open midair in the chamber. It was quickly followed by six more.

A spider scuttled out.

The creature's form wavered in the air, indistinct and blurry. A dark miasma surrounded it, one that even my night vision had difficulty piercing. The little that I could see of the spider led me to believe it was covered in midnight-black chitin.

But as scary as my latest foe's appearance was, at only three feet tall it was small—at least as giant spiders went. The breath whooshed out of me in relief.

That doesn't look so bad.

Reaching out with my will, I analyzed the summoned creature.

The target is a level 51 giant stygian spider.

Contrary to conventional belief, the nether is not empty. The black void houses entities that, over time, have evolved to thrive in its depths. The stygian beasts are one such family of beings. The stygian spider is neither the largest nor most feared of its kind, but against foes from the physical realms, unprepared for its unique nature, it invariably provides a fatal challenge.

The Game's response was certainly ominous-sounding, but there was nothing that couldn't be killed. Bloodied blades in hand, I rushed forward to put an end to the spider. The creature scuttled forward, just as eager to meet me.

Raising a foreleg, the spider lashed out at me. I sidestepped the blow easily, noting in passing that it was slower than me. Lunging forward, I launched my own counterattack.

Both my swords sailed unopposed past the creature's guard. My eyes gleamed, imagining the moment of impact.

I struck.

My blades cut through the creature's chitin shell as if it wasn't there. My eyes widened.

There had been no impact.

It felt like I'd hit nothing but air.

A level 51 giant stygian spider is immune to physical damage! You have failed to injure your target.

What the—? Balance momentarily lost at the lack of contact, I stumbled forward and *through* the stygian spider's body myself. There was no resistance, or at least none of the type I'd expected. It felt as if I waded through a cloying ichor filled with gelatinous lumps. I emerged on the other end.

I was unharmed, but then so too was my foe.

Repressing a shiver at the strange sensation, I spun around. Two of the spider's rear legs were whipping downward to lash at me. Throwing my body into motion, I dodged the first, then parried the second.

I failed.

The end of the spider's shadowy—and immaterial—limb passed unheedingly through my blade, leather armor, and left forearm. But where my sword and armor were undamaged by the contact, my flesh wasn't so fortunate.

You have failed to block a giant stygian spider's attack. A giant stygian spider has injured you!

Gasping, I staggered backward, only then realizing the true nature of my foe. The spider had no true physical form, which meant I couldn't damage it or even block its attacks. The creature, though, as it had just demonstrated, could hurt me.

Its attacks are magical in nature.

In the wake of the spider's limb, the muscles and bone of my arm withered away. *A necrotic attack of some sort?*

I retreated further, clutching my suddenly weakened left arm to my body. The spider scuttled forward again. Turning around, I fled, using one-step to open the distance between us. I needed space to think.

A tired chuckle floated through the air. "You didn't think killing my pet was going to be easy, did you?"

From a safe distance away, I spun to face the elven mage. She was still encased in her shield, and even though some of the weariness had left her, she didn't look fully recovered from her spellcasting.

"What is that thing?" I hissed, one wary eye on the spider while it resumed its advance on me.

"It's a stygian spider from the depths of the abyss," Worca said, seeming to have no compunctions about sharing the information. "They are the perfect counter to fighters such as yourself. You can't hurt it." She paused. "The reverse doesn't apply though," the elf added drily, if unnecessarily.

The spider was drawing close again, and I fled to the far end of the room.

The perfect counter to fighters? I wondered, a sinking feeling in the pit of my stomach. I didn't want to take my foe's word for it, but I had ample evidence already that it was immune to my attacks.

How am I going to kill it?

Other than my mind spells, I had no magic of my own. And the mind spells I *did* have? None of them dealt damage. *Aargh.*

My gaze flitted back to the elf. She seemed content to let the spider do the work, not even bothering to attack with her wands anymore.

Catching my glance, Worca added, almost conversationally, "My pet won't stop. It will keep going, chasing you down until you're dead."

I guess that means it won't be unsummoned anytime soon. There was only one thing left to try.

Worca's assessment of me was mostly true, but she'd gotten one thing wrong: I wasn't just a fighter. I was a mindstalker. And while I didn't have many mind spells, I had one that had served me well time and again.

Keeping a careful eye on the spider to make sure it didn't interfere, I cast charm. Tendrils of my will expanded outward to Worca, slipping effortlessly through her shield and into her mind.

Where they were unceremoniously severed.

Worca is immune to tier-1 and tier-2 mental attacks! You have failed to charm your target. Your mental intrusion has been detected!

Really? I stifled a groan, not about to let the mage see my despair.

The elf's laughter rang out again. "Did you think we wouldn't prepare for you?" She languidly held out one hand for inspection as the spider hurried closer.

Forced to reposition again, I dashed across the room and closer to the mage. She seemed inclined to chat, and I saw no harm in listening to her. Because as much as I hated to admit it, I was out of ideas. Defeating Worca was looking more and more like it was beyond me.

"What are those?" I panted, studying the bejeweled fingers she held up.

"Rings of protection," Worca replied easily. She pointed to the large violet jewel on one of her fingers. "This one is the most useful. It stops mental attacks." The elf shook her head sadly. "I'm afraid you're outclassed. Now, why don't you surrender? It will please Ishita if I bring you to her on bended knees, maybe enough that she might even be merciful."

"No," I growled, not even needing to think about it.

Worca sighed. "Well then, I guess we're done talking. Time to die, human." Lowering both her wands, the elf pointed them at the floor and barked out a word I didn't understand.

Realizing I didn't want to feel the effects of whatever spell she was about to cast, I one-stepped through the air and onto the nearby stone table.

Worca has cast stygian web.

Dark silken web strands appeared in the center of the chamber and expanded rapidly outward to cover the entirety of the floor in a heaving mass of black silk.

This situation keeps getting better and better, I thought, eyeing the floor.

I was trapped on the table. If I stepped into the mess of webs, I was sure to be entangled. The stygian spider, though, was unaffected, gliding gracefully over the strands.

Worca's ploy with her latest casting was clear. Stuck in the web, I wouldn't be able to flee the creature whose only weakness seemed to be a lack of speed. I didn't have much time remaining. The spider would be on me soon, and this time I had nowhere to retreat.

My gaze flitted to the elf. Head down, she sagged against the wall. The second spell had drained her nearly as much as the first, but the gleaming black dome that protected her physical form looked as impervious as ever.

I couldn't kill her. Not as quickly as I needed to, and with the webs on the floor, I wasn't even certain I could get close to her.

There's only one thing left to try.

CHAPTER 126: BACK TO DARKNESS

Turning back toward the spider, I cast charm. It was the only thing I could think of trying. It was that—or flee.

Strands of energy extended from me to the creature, and where my blades had failed in their attacks, my mind spell did not. Finding purchase in the creature's consciousness, psi leashed it to my will.

A giant stygian spider has failed a mental resistance check! You have charmed your target for 10 seconds.

A few yards away from me, the spider froze mid-motion. A triumphant smile lit my face.

Bloody hell, it worked!

"What did you do!" the elf gasped, sensing the sudden change in her summoned pet's demeanor.

I grinned at her. "You're about to find out," I said, ordering the creature to advance on its former master.

Worca's eyes widened as the spider reversed course to dance across the floor toward her. Making use of the momentary lull in the battle, I extracted one of my healing potions and downed its contents.

You have restored 10% of your lost health with a minor healing potion. Your health is now at 100%.

Healing waves of energy pulsed through my body, restoring the flesh in my left arm and mending the bruises on my back. Straightening, I flexed my left hand. The weakness in it from the spider's attack had dissipated.

My minion, meanwhile, had completed its advance and hovered just outside the ebony bubble protecting the mage.

Let's see if this works, I thought and ordered the spider to attack.

My charmed pet passed as easily through the magical shield as it had through my own blades. My grin began to widen. *It's work—*

An instant before the spider's limbs could make contact with its former master, a Game message opened in my mind.

You have taken hostile action against your minion! Control of target lost.

Huh?

My brows furrowed, struggling to make sense of the perplexing development. The Game had interpreted the spider's attempted attack against Worca as a hostile action against the creature itself. Why had it done that?

It can only be because summoned creature and summoner are inextricably linked. Kill the summoner, kill the pet?

It was the only thing that made sense.

Freed of my compulsion, the spider had turned and was advancing on me again.

Worca was sputtering, convulsing with laughter, if of the somewhat hysterical kind. "I knew it," the elf whispered, her eyes shining. "I knew that wouldn't work!"

I didn't believe her. Her manner reeked of relief.

Nor was I despondent. After my initial dismay at the spider's failure, I'd realized something else. Even if I couldn't force the creature to harm its summoner, I could, at the very least, draw out the encounter into a stalemate.

Ignoring the mage's outburst, I focused my attention on the approaching spider again and recast charm.

You have charmed your target for 10 seconds.

This time, I didn't bother sending my minion to attack the elf. Ordering the creature to the furthest end of the room, I turned my gaze downward and studied the glistening web.

On closer inspection, I realized my earlier observation had been mistaken. As dense as the black silk was, it didn't cover every inch of the floor. There were random spots of emptiness, some no more than an inch across, others as much as a foot wide.

If I'm careful, I can reach the mage.

It would take time though. But it could be done. Mapping a route out in my mind, I set to it.

Gauging the distance carefully, I leaped off the edge of the table and landed lightly on one foot in the first safe spot I'd marked out. My hands flew out, breaking my forward motion.

For an instant I swayed precariously, then regained my balance. *Phew.* Still on one foot, I eyed the next spot—about two feet to my right. Casting one-step, I walked on air to touch down squarely on my target destination.

A look of sheer panic fluttered across Worca's face. Pushing off the wall, she raised a wand in a visibly trembling hand and directed it my way.

The sight heartened me. For one, the caster didn't attempt to flee, and for another she aimed only a single wand my way. It led me to hope her mana was nearly spent.

A bar of blackness burst out of Worca's wand and in my direction. I was prepared for the attack. Remaining stock-still until the last instant, I dropped down. The elf had targeted my chest, aiming high enough for me to duck beneath the magical projectile.

You have evaded Worca's magical attack.

I uncoiled slowly, careful not to move my feet so much as an inch while doing so.

Worca stared at me, mouth agape.

Staying in place, I threw the elf a feigned smile while I checked the remaining time on my charm spell. There were a few seconds left on it yet. I waited patiently.

Worca's gaze slid past me to the spider, which was standing idle at the far end of the room. Raising a shaky hand, the mage pointed her wand at me again.

I stood my ground, waiting.

Perhaps recognizing her chances of hitting me with a magic projectile was poor, the elf didn't cast. "What do you want?" she demanded harshly.

"Tell me where the shield generator is," I said evenly. "And I may just let you live."

While we spoke, I reached out to the spider with mindsight—my back was to the creature—and began recasting charm. The spell about it was about to expire.

I wasn't sure if Worca was simply playing for time—maybe she thought re-charming the spider would distract me long enough for her to get a shot in—but if she was, she was about to be sorely disappointed.

"I can't tell you that," she replied bitterly, still keeping her wand trained on me. "Nothing you can do to me will be as bad as what the goddess will do if I betray her."

You have lost control over a giant stygian spider.

Watching Worca carefully, I saw her lips twitch upward in a half-smile before she regained control of her expression. The mage had sensed the exact moment I lost control over my minion. And was waiting for her moment.

Without taking my eyes off Worca for an instant, I slipped a new leash about the spider's mind.

You have charmed your target for 10 seconds.

The expression of disappointment that flashed across the elf's face was almost comical. A second later, she sighed in resignation and released the spelled attack she held ready.

This time, she'd aimed low.

I sprang upward, flipped over in the air, and a heartbeat later landed in the exact same spot.

You have evaded Worca's magical attack.

The elf didn't react to her miss. She'd realized her chances of hitting me were slim. With another smile at her, I resumed my slow, torturous path through the maze at my feet and toward my target.

✳ ✳ ✳

With carefully timed leaps, steps, and lunges, I closed the distance between me and my foe, cutting a jagged path across the web. Worca, recognizing she couldn't stop my advance, had long since stopped trying.

Instead, hands at her sides, she waited.

A little later, I stood before the mage and, without pause, slashed down on the protective bubble encasing her.

Your target's shield has blocked your attacks, absorbing their damage.

"You won't get through," Worca jeered weakly.

She hadn't raised her wands again, I noted. Was her mana entirely spent? I suspected so.

"I will," I said with a mocking grin of my own. "It's only a matter of time."

I struck at her again, this time empowering both my attacks with piercing strikes.

Your target's shield has blocked your attacks, absorbing their damage.

Was it my imagination, or had the luminescent glow encircling the mage's shield dulled a touch at my last two blows?

I hit it again with twin piercing strikes.

This time, the change in the shield's intensity was unmistakable.

I smiled grimly. My attacks were having an effect, and no matter how long it took, I would break through.

✳   ✳   ✳

Worca's stygian shield has been destroyed!

The bubble of magic protecting Worca collapsed quicker than I'd expected.

Still, it had taken me a few minutes to break through, during which time I had to recast charm multiple times and avoid the occasional feeble attack from my trapped foe.

But at last, our standoff was at an end.

My left hand snaked out to wrap around the elf's throat and yank her up while the blade in my right flashed forward to stop an inch from her wide-open eyes.

"Last chance," I growled. "Tell me where the shield generator is."

"No," the elf replied stubbornly.

I gnashed my teeth in frustration. I couldn't sense an iota of fear in the mage at her impending death.

She's more afraid of Ishita than of death. I'm not going to find out what I need to know this way.

"Then die," I said, "and tell your fellows I'm coming for them too."

Not waiting for her response, I drove the tip of my shortsword forward, killing her instantly.

You have killed Worca with a fatal blow. You have slain a sworn servant of Ishita, increasing her ire toward you!

The moment the mage died, the charmed spider vanished, as did the stygian webs.

I barely noticed as I sank down onto the floor.

Despite my display of false bravado for Worca's benefit, I knew I was in trouble. I'd been banking on discovering the location of the shield generator from the mages, but with them now forewarned of my intentions, the chance of me catching any of them exposed and vulnerable was slim to non-existent.

Damn it all to hell! What did I do now?

Chapter 127: A Goblin's Revenge

The door to the chamber opened so quietly I almost failed to hear it.

My head jerked upward to see the Howler shaman and a squad of guards appear. My gaze slid from Hyek to the soldiers at his back. They looked tense.

I rose slowly to my feet, bare blades in hand and showing no sign of being intimidated by the shaman's show of force. "You've been observing all this time?" I asked casually. The goblin's reentry was too well-timed to be a coincidence.

Hyek nodded wordlessly as his eyes swept the chamber. "I underestimated you."

I jerked my chin toward the soldiers. "Is that why they're here?"

The shaman smiled. "I thought you might need the help."

I sheathed my blades. I had begun to fear he meant to betray me. "Thank you," I murmured. "I managed just fine."

"I see that." Hyek chuckled. "Not many can break through a mage shield so readily."

"What do you know about them?" I asked curiously. He sounded knowledgeable about the spell.

"Even the weakest mage shield requires a Magic skill of rank ten to cast," the shaman replied easily. He glanced at Ishan's dead body. "Which is why most players can't learn the skill until after they've reached level hundred. A few mages survive long enough to get to that point though." He kicked at the corpse and bared his sharpened teeth. "More's the pity."

I eyed the shaman askance. He appeared more at ease than when he had left the room not long ago, and interesting as his information was, I was more curious about why his mood had improved. "I take it you don't doubt my information anymore?" I guessed.

Hyek nodded. "The behavior of Ishita's dogs was enough to confirm your tale." He shook his head. "I should never have trusted them in the first place."

Before I could respond to that, the shaman went on. "I also took the liberty of contacting the god-emperor's envoy while you were... busy here." He met my gaze. "As a precaution, no more, you understand."

I stilled in sudden trepidation. "Oh?" I asked, readying myself for anything. "And what did you learn?"

"His response was most swift," Hyek replied, his eyes narrowing as if he sensed my renewed tension. "Captain Talon confirms that you have indeed been authorized to act as an intermediary on his behalf." The shaman paused, then added, "It seems you are trustworthy after all."

I snorted and folded my arms. "You shouldn't have disbelieved me in the first place."

The shaman inclined his head in acknowledgment. "And you should have told me what you were after. Then there would have been no need for this," he said, gesturing to the corpses. "Although, I suppose there is a certain satisfaction to be derived from their deaths."

I inhaled sharply, not missing his implication. "You have the shield generator?" I asked, my gaze fixed on Hyek.

The shaman shook his head. "No, I don't. But I know where it is. My people are the ones who helped the mages install it."

"Where?" I demanded tersely.

"In the last place anyone would think to look," Hyek said mildly. "In the lair of the wyvern mother."

Closing my eyes, I lowered my head into my hands, fighting off a sudden wave of despair.

Of course. Why would it be anywhere else but there?

✳ ✳ ✳

After he'd delivered his unwelcome news, the shaman and his escort rushed out of the chamber. Now that his tribe's survival seemed assured, Hyek was almost jovial.

And eager to go to war.

Whatever enmity lay between the two tribes, it was great enough to cause even the otherwise-rational shaman to become overcome. *He is a bloodthirsty bastard after all,* I thought, watching from the window slit as the gigantic goblin strode through the courtyard below, shouting out orders to the soldiers.

By Hyek's own estimation, his people would be ready to march out from the fort before noon. And if the shaman got his way, before day's end tomorrow, the Howlers and Red Rats would meet in battle—and the Rats crushed.

It was an attitude that suited me just fine.

I wanted the goblins gone quickly, in case the shaman took it upon himself to have a longer conversation with the Tartans. So far, it appeared my web of lies was holding up, but I wasn't sure how long that would last.

After the two tribes met in battle, I expected at least some of the mistruths I'd told to come to light. But by then, I hoped to be long gone.

Turning away from the window slit, I surveyed the chamber. It was a mess of half-burned banners, knocked-over ornaments, and of course, drying blood.

Examine the bodies first, I thought. Striding to the two corpses, I searched them thoroughly, stripping both of their valuables.

You have acquired 6 enchanted rings, 1 enchanted bracelet, 2 enchanted robes, and 3 spellcasters' wands.

It was a tidy haul. But somewhat lacking, I felt, for such high-leveled players. Other than the items I'd looted, the rest of the mages' gear was worthless trash. The pair hadn't even been carrying coin pouches.

Perhaps they feared being ambushed. Rightly so it turns out.

Further inspection of the loot revealed that only three of the items were usable by me. Before equipping them, I took the time to examine each more carefully.

This is a rank 3 bracelet of natural armor: troll's talisman. This item decreases the damage you sustain by 6% and stacks with any armor you may be wearing. This item has no requirements to equip.

This is a rank 2 ring: the gift of the unbound. This item has been enchanted to allow its user to resist tier-1 and tier-2 entanglement spells, these being spells that restrict motion. Its enchantment can be replenished with mana. This item requires a minimum Dexterity of 8 to use.

This is a rank 2 ring: the band of stillness. This item has been enchanted to allow its user to resist tier-1 and tier-2 mental spells. Its enchantment can be replenished with mana. This item requires a minimum Mind of 8 to use.

Surprisingly, it was only Ishan that had a ring of free motion. It explained why Worca had not tried to flee. Her own webbed field would have trapped her. Without further delay, I equipped all three items.

You have equipped the rank 3 bracelet, troll's talisman. Status effect added: troll skin.

You have equipped the rank 2 ring, gift of unbound. Status effect added: unbound.

You have equipped the rank 2 ring, the band of stillness. Status effect added: still mind.

After I stowed away the rest of the loot, I finally turned my attention inward and examined the waiting Game messages.

You have reached level 68!

Your dodging has increased to level 48. Your sneaking has increased to level 59. Your two-weapon fighting has increased to level 47.

Your light armor has increased to level 40. Your skill in light armor has reached rank 4, decreasing your light armor penalty by 20%.

Your chi has increased to level 39. Your telekinesis has increased to level 36. Your telepathy has increased to level 36.

I had profited greatly from the battle, acquiring five more levels and earning multiple skill gains. Deciding how to invest my new attribute points was easy.

If nothing else, the battle had shown me I couldn't rely only on my swords to inflict damage. I needed to increase my repertoire of Mind abilities—and soon.

Your Mind has increased to rank 26.

With my player progression seen to, I hurried out of the keep and back toward the safe zone.

After thinking the matter through, I realized while the shield generator's location complicated matters, it didn't make escape impossible. I knew where the device was now, *and* I knew what dangers I'd face to reach it.

I could still make it out of the sector with time to spare. I needed to make a few preparations first though, and before that I needed to find some rope.

∗   ∗   ∗

You have acquired a coil of rope.

The goblins had more than enough rope lying around, and I'd helped myself to a decent length of it.

As I approached the gate leading into the safe zone, I saw that it was still shut and that the goblin patrols atop the inner wall were still present. Hyek had told me they would be the last to abandon their post. Once the rest of the soldiers had finished mustering outside the fort, the inner wall guards would join.

The patrols had been instructed to let me pass, so with no more than a wave to the guards at the gate, I rushed up the steps leading to the ramparts.

Atop the wall, the complaints and angry shouts of the players gathered outside the sealed gate carried clearly to me in the crisp morning air. Crouched down low to make certain I wasn't spotted, I crept away to an isolated section of the wall that was free of passing players. *This'll do.*

Two nearby goblin warriors were watching me curiously. I waved one over. "You know who I am?" I whispered.

He nodded emphatically. "You're the one who convinced Hyek to let us wipe out those scummy Rats." He gave me a toothy grin. "Let me buy you a beer tonight."

I smiled. "Some other time maybe. Right now, I need your help."

The warrior's gaze slid from me to the rope looped about my arm. "You want me to let you down?"

"I can manage that well enough on my own, but when I'm down, I need you to throw the rope to me." I didn't want to leave it behind for some errant player to spot and use in turn. "Can you do that?"

He nodded vigorously. "I can."

∗   ∗   ∗

A short while later, I was back in the safe zone with the rope stowed away. My entrance had gone unnoticed, and if possible, I wanted to keep it that way.

Stuffing my thief's cloak into my backpack, I re-equipped the mage's cloak that I'd looted what felt like ages ago. As disguises went, it wasn't perfect but would serve in a pinch.

Pulling the cloak's hood low over my head, I strolled leisurely into the village. The streets were busier than I had seen before, but no one gave me a second glance.

I reached my destination without incident. Walking up to the closed door, I knocked softly. There was no answer. I kept knocking.

Eventually, the door was yanked back. "We're closed. Now, go—"

Gelar broke off as he got a close look at me. His gaze darted beyond me to the passing players. No one was paying us any attention. "Get in."

I slipped past the gnome and into the room, taking a slow look around. The alchemist's chamber was unchanged since my last visit.

Gelar closed the door behind him and, seating himself on one of his couches, glared at me. "What do you want?"

I sat down opposite him. "You seem more worried about my presence now than during my last visit," I said, deliberately avoiding his question.

The gnome's scowl deepened. "Did you have to go and kill so many of Ishita's followers the last time? Do you know how long her blasted sworn questioned me after that?"

At my blank expression, he waved irritably. "Bah! I see that you don't. Just tell me why you're here. You can't have slain the wyvern yet."

Removing the alchemy stone from my pocket, I placed it on the table between us.

Without prompting, Gelar picked up the object. "Ah. You've been busy at least," he said grudgingly. Pulling out his pipe, he puffed energetically on it as he inspected the stone. "For these ingredients, I'll give you—"

"I don't want money," I said, interrupting him.

Gelar lowered his head and peered at me over his spectacles. "What do you want then?"

"Antitoxin."

The gnome stared at me wordlessly for a moment. "To take on the wyvern, I suppose." He paused. "You really mean to try slaying the beast?"

"If I must, I will," I replied obliquely. "Can you make something that will cure her venom?"

He nodded. "With what you've given me, yes."

I exhaled in relief and waved at the stone. "Will the other ingredients in there cover the cost of making the antitoxin?"

"They will," he replied. After a moment, he added, "There will be a fair bit left over too. Do you want anything else?"

Whatever else the gnome was, he appeared fair. About to reply in the negative, I paused as something else occurred to me. "What about healing potions? Can you make any of those?"

Gelar snorted. "Not with the ingredients I have available in this sector." He chewed on the end of his pipe for a moment in thought. "But... I do have some in stock already. I'll warn you though, they are pricey."

I sat up in sudden excitement. "How much?"

"I have three full healing potions," he said. "Each will cost you fifty gold over and above what I'll give you for the ingredients in the alchemy stone."

I winced at the price, but it didn't matter. I needed the potions. "I don't have that much with me, but I'll get it," I assured him, wondering if there was somewhere I could sell my looted items. The Tartans would have been a good bet, but I wanted to avoid the captain until strictly necessary.

"You have at least a few hours to come up with the money. It will take me that long to brew the antitoxin." Gelar stared at me, his gaze unwelcoming. "I expect you have somewhere to wait?"

I stifled a yawn. Thus far, adrenaline alone had been keeping me going, but now that I'd sat down, the aches in my body were making themselves known again. I needed rest, I knew.

"I'll be at the tavern," I said. Rising to my feet, I waved farewell to the gnome and slipped out of the shop.

Chapter 128: An Unexpected Arrival

The tavern was packed, more crowded than I'd ever seen it before. Standing in the doorway, I scanned the room from under my lowered hood. No one had looked up at my entrance. They were all too consumed in their own discussions.

The topic on everyone's lips, of course, was the Howlers.

The reason for the goblins sealing the village's gates had become common knowledge, and speculation was rife among the players about why Ishita's sworn had committed the killings. It was telling that no one seemed to doubt they had.

Among the tavern's patrons, I spotted Jorge and a few other Tartan recruits. I looked away. Sooner or later I would have to deal with the captain and explain the deal I'd made with Hyek. When Talon found out what was going on, I expected he would try to prevent the Howlers from leaving or from engaging the Red Rats.

To tempt Hyek into open war, I'd been forced to dangle Talon's offer of the god-emperor's protection before the shaman. Unfortunately, that meant an alliance between the Tartans and Howlers was now all but inevitable. *If* it was concluded while the goblins remained garrisoned in the fort, the sector would almost instantly revert to Tartar's control.

I couldn't let that happen—both for the wolves' sake and my own—which was why I wanted to avoid Talon until it was too late for him to change the course of events.

Slipping through the crowd unnoticed, I crossed the floor and made my way to the stairs leading up. The upper level was quiet, and I found the room Benadean had allocated me without trouble.

The chamber was simply furnished, with only a single bunk, chest of drawers, and washbasin in evidence. The sight of the bed alone was enough to start me yawning again. Not bothering to clean up, I shrugged off my backpack and slumped down on the bunk.

In a matter of moments, I was fast asleep.

✳ ✳ ✳

I awoke with a groan.

My head was ringing—literally. Rubbing away the sleep from my eyes, I sat up. The buzzing was from Game notices calling for my attention.

"Alright, alright, I'm getting to it," I groused. Turning my attention inward, I let the messages scroll through my mind.

The Long Fang contingent in the sector has been destroyed, fulfilling all objectives of the task <u>Aid the Pack</u>!

You have completed a task! Your deeds have furthered the interest of Artem. The Marks on your spirit signature have changed.

In aiding the dire wolves, you have strayed from the pursuit of self. Once more you acted to protect the weak, but this time without any tangible benefit to yourself. The Dark disapproves. Your Dark Mark has lessened. In future, beware of such acts of generosity. Every such one weakens you.

Once again, you have acted selflessly, striving for the betterment of your allies, heedlessly endangering yourself on their behalf. Light approves. Your Light Mark has deepened.

You have begun redressing the imbalance in the sector and rectified a long-standing wrong against the valley's dire wolf pack. Shadow is pleased. Your Shadow Mark has deepened.

The wise Wolf knows that when it comes to defending one's own pack, there are no rules. To protect the pack, Wolf demands you to act ruthlessly, without mercy, and with every tool at your disposal. You have done that and more. Wolf is pleased. Your Wolf Mark has deepened.

A shiver of excitement rippled through me, banishing the last clinging tendrils of sleep.

The Red Rats have done it! They'd destroyed the Long Fangs. Without any goblins hunting the pack, the wolves would be safer. And now, at long last, there was nothing keeping me in the sector. I could leave with a clear conscience.

Even if I did nothing more, the pack would survive, if perhaps, not thrive. I still needed to figure out a means of escape though. And find a way of keeping the sector from falling to the Dark. Not to mention deal with the wyvern somehow.

I sighed. *Alright, maybe there is still a lot more that needs doing.* But even that knowledge didn't dampen my excitement. Because with my task from Duggar complete, I could finally seek out the pack again.

I rose to my feet. What time was it?

Assuming Nyzack had kept to his schedule, it had to be near noon. *Past time I left the safe zone.*

After cleaning up and munching through a hasty meal, I dashed out of the room. Keeping my face shielded, I padded noiselessly down the stairs, intent on hurrying through the crowded room unseen once more.

But when I reached the bottom, I froze.

The room was empty.

Or not quite. Benadean busied himself silently behind the bar and a single patron, staring straight at me, sat at one of the tables. It was Ultack.

The half-orc rose at my appearance.

Why was he here? And how had he known where to find me? There was no doubt in my mind that the Tartan recruit had been waiting for me. Feeling sudden trepidation, I nodded to Benadean in passing and approached Ultack slowly.

"The captain wants to see you," the half-orc said, his face expressionless.

I scrutinized his face carefully but caught no hint of his emotions. "What about?"

"About the Howlers... among other things," he replied.

I nodded slowly. I didn't have to go with him, of course, but I owed it to the captain to hear what he had to say and, if it came to it, to explain my actions in person. "Lead on."

Wordlessly, Ultack turned about and marched through the door. The streets proved as empty as the tavern. "Where is everyone?" I asked in surprise.

The half-orc glanced at me sideways as we passed through the silent village. "They all left. Not an hour ago, the players trapped in the safe zone decided to mob the gates. Eventually, they broke it down, only to find the fort abandoned and the Howlers vanished."

He eyed me again, a glimmer of suspicion in his gaze. "You wouldn't happen to know where they've gone, would you?"

"I do, actually," I replied easily, having no intention of keeping the Howlers' whereabouts secret. In fact, I was surprised the Tartans didn't already know.

My response seemed to catch Ultack off guard. Had the captain feared I had betrayed him entirely? It seemed that way.

"That's good," Ultack said after a moment's pause. "It's why the captain wishes to speak to you."

*　*　*

In contrast to the emptiness of the village, the Tartan barracks were a hive of activity with players rushing back and forth. I was escorted into the captain's chambers without fuss. There, another surprise awaited me.

Sturm had returned.

I nodded to the young player, standing at attention next to the seated captain. Seeing the pair together, their relationship was obvious.

"So, you made it back," I remarked casually, despite the tension I sensed in the room.

Sturm scowled at me. "No thanks to you!"

I shrugged and, without being asked, seated myself in the chair across from the captain. "I freed you, didn't I?"

"Then abandoned us in the middle of the forest, and at night too!" he growled.

I rolled my eyes and very carefully did not call him a pampered fool. I still wasn't sure what was going on, but Sturm was easy to read. He held himself stiffly and moved jerkily when he spoke. There was no doubt: the youth was angry.

Talon's own feelings were harder to decipher. Was he angry on his son's behalf? I couldn't tell. The captain was a pond of stillness, silently observing but giving nothing away.

"We could have died!" Sturm shouted, resuming his tirade.

"So?" I asked disinterestedly. "You're a soldier, aren't you? Surely a night in the forest didn't scare you."

Sturm's face turned red with outrage, but before he could yell at me again, the captain intervened. "Enough, boy," he said mildly.

His son's mouth closed with a snap.

The captain leaned forward and stared at me expressionlessly across the desk. "Sturm has told quite the tale."

"Oh?" I remarked. This meeting wasn't going the way I'd expected. Instead of grilling me about the Howlers, the captain seemed more interested in his son's unhappiness.

Talon nodded sagely. "First, you somehow managed to get the Red Rats to abandon their camp, then you slew two squads of elite goblin warriors all on your own, and finally, you traveled cross-country—alone and at night."

"All true," I said simply.

The captain's eyebrows tilted upward at my confirmation. "Sturm thinks you only accomplished all that because you're secretly an agent of the Awakened Dead."

I couldn't help it. I laughed. "Really? And what? I killed over a dozen Awakened Dead players and two of Ishita's sworn—" the captain's brows rose higher at that—"just to remain in character? That's ridiculous," I scoffed.

"It's not!" Sturm protested. "No one could have—"

The captain raised a hand, silencing his son. "Sturm, leave us."

The young recruit stiffened, but he didn't protest his father's orders as he marched angrily out the room.

"Ordinarily, I would agree with you, Michael," the captain continued without acknowledging his son's departure. "The idea seems far-fetched." He held my gaze. "But recent events have given me pause."

Ah, now we come to it. I said nothing, waiting for him to go on.

"Where is the Howler army?" Talon asked, his voice going cold.

"Marching north to do battle with the Red Rats," I replied evenly.

Some emotion, too quick to parse, flickered across the captain's face. "Why?"

He hadn't, I noticed, questioned the veracity of my statement. *Maybe because he already knows it's true.*

I shrugged. "I needed a means to win the shaman's trust, so I showed him Stayne's letter." I paused. So far, everything I said was true. *Now for the lie.* "His reaction was... unexpected. Hyek was outraged at Erebus' duplicity and wanted revenge."

The captain leaned back in his chair, steepling his fingers before him as he considered my words. "So the Howler shaman abandoned his fort and committed his people to a pitched battle against what is likely to be a combined force of Red Rats and Awakened Dead because of... a single letter?" Talon asked, his voice dripping with skepticism.

I shook my head. "No, not only. I also assured him the Tartans would support him."

The captain whipped forward so quickly I barely caught the motion, and instinctively my hands dropped to my blades.

Chapter 129: The Gift of a Blade

"You did what?" Talon whispered, staring at me from only a few inches away.

How had he moved so fast? The captain seemed unconcerned by my clenched fists wrapped around the hilts of my swords, and I had to remind myself we were in the safe zone.

"You asked me to secure the tribe's loyalty," I said, not backing away from the captain's frosty glare. "This was the only way how. Hyek has assured me that if your soldiers join the Howlers in battle, they will pledge allegiance to your god-emperor."

The captain said nothing, but he also didn't back away. Second by second, the tension in the room built up again as Talon scrutinized me intently. I kept my own face smooth and my gaze unflinching, waiting.

"You are certain of this?" he asked finally.

I nodded. "It was their only condition."

The captain sat back, frowning. "Volunteering my people was presumptuous of you."

I shrugged. "The decision on whether to uphold the terms I agreed upon is yours alone. If you do as the shaman requests, then he will make his pledge after the battle."

Talon's frown remained in place. "Why didn't you come to me earlier with his terms?"

I sighed. "As your son told you already, I traveled overnight across the length of the valley to get here and then had to fight two of Ishita's sworn." I lowered my gaze in pretended embarrassment. "I'm sorry, but I was tired. I planned on reporting as soon as I got some rest."

"What about that business with the mages?" Talon asked, not contesting my explanation. "You don't expect me to believe they just happened to visit the fort when you were there."

I smiled. "No, I had Hyek summon them to explain the killings in his barracks."

The captain stared at me. "It was *you* who killed the Howler goblins?"

I nodded.

"Sturm was right," Talon muttered. "You play your own game."

"I never concealed that fact from you, Captain," I replied evenly. "I'm not one of your god-emperor's soldiers. The ends I serve are my own." I paused. "But I've secured the Howlers' allegiance, if perhaps not in the manner you anticipated."

Talon sighed. "You've been more successful than I expected. And if I'm being honest, that you manipulated events to your liking isn't unusual. It is the rare Darksworn who isn't playing his own side-game." He paused. "Maybe you're more suited to the Dark than you know."

Before I could respond to that, Talon held up a hand. "But fair warning, Michael." He stared piercingly at me. "If you've betrayed me—*if* the shaman fails to live up to his end of the bargain—I will grant you no quarter. The Awakened Dead will be the least of your worries. Do you understand?"

I nodded mutely.

"Good," the captain said. Leaning down, he retrieved something from behind his desk and set it down on the table. "Now that that's settled, this is for you."

I glanced at the small leather satchel. "What is it?"

"Go on, open it," he replied.

Leaning forward, I unhooked the clasp and peered in. It was full of gold bars. Ten of them, to be precise.

"Each of those bars is worth one hundred gold. They're payment in full for Stayne's letter."

"Thank you, Captain," I said gravely before taking the satchel and wordlessly sliding the letter in question across the desk.

You have acquired 1,000 gold. You have lost Stayne's letter.

Your task, <u>Forging Dark Alliances</u>! has been updated. You have provided Captain Talon with definitive proof that Erebus is stymying the Dark's efforts to secure the sector. Optional objective completed.

The captain waved away my thanks and pocketed the parchment. "As for the second task, once the shaman completes his pledge you will get your payment."

"You will aid the Howlers in the battle against the Red Rats then?"

"I will. The players under my command here are already gathering. We will march out soon." Talon's lips thinned into a cold smile. "Erebus' restrictions be damned."

Your task, <u>Forging Dark Alliances</u>! has been updated. Captain Talon has agreed to the terms you've negotiated between the Tartans and the Howler Shaman Hyek. Objective one revised: wait for Hyek to uphold his end of the agreement and pledge allegiance to Tartar.

"You yourself will march out?" I asked, looking at him in surprise.

The captain nodded. "Stayne's letter has freed my hands. I finally have the proof my master needs of Erebus' duplicity, and I no longer need to abide by the Awakened Dead's rules." His eyes glinted. "There will be a reckoning." A moment later, he shook himself and turned back to me. "How shall I make payment?"

I stared at him blankly.

"Once the shaman pledges himself," Talon clarified, "how do you want your money? In gold bars again?"

I shook my head. "I may be gone from the sector by then," I said. "But you can deposit the money into a bank," I added and gave him the details of my Albion Bank account.

A frown flickered across the captain's face, but he didn't pry as to how I hoped to accomplish leaving the sector.

"Well, if that's all, I best be going," I said, rising to my feet and turning toward the door.

"There is one more thing," the captain said, stopping me.

I turned around and, to my surprise, saw hesitation cloud Talon's face as he stood up himself. Patiently, I waited for him to go on.

Withdrawing an elongated object from his desk, the captain placed it in front of me. It was a shortsword. "This is for you too," Talon said. "As repayment for saving my son."

Casting my gaze downward, I inspected the sword. Both the blade and the hilt were jet black. The blade had been forged from a metal with a dull obsidian sheen, while the handle was wrapped in scaled black leather.

It was a beautiful weapon and, from appearances alone, expensive. Probing deeper, I analyzed the shortsword.

This is the rank 4 soulbound shortsword: ebonheart. This item increases the damage you deal by 30% and bears the enchantment unbreakable. Neither its edge, blade, or hilt will ever fail you in battle. This item requires a minimum Dexterity of 16 to wield.

The ebonblades are weapons carried by the centurions of the famed Ebonguard Legion and are regularly farmed from the Twilight Dungeon by them.

Soulbound items are exceptionally rare. They will remain with a player even after death and cannot be stolen. The art of creating them is unknown to both players and Powers alike. These powerful artifacts are one of the few truly Game-created items and, once bonded, cannot be unbound. After a player's final death, it will be destroyed.

My gaze whipped upward to stare at the captain in shock. "Are you sure? This weapon seems priceless."

"I am," Talon replied. "I'm not ungrateful for what you've done for my son, you know." He smiled wryly. "And neither is Sturm himself, no matter how much it may appear that way. If Erebus' minions took him down into that dungeon, my son would never have returned to me, no matter how many lives he had left."

"But this... surely it's too much?" I protested.

Talon chuckled. "For my only son's life? Definitely not. And as valuable as the blade is, as soulbound weapons go, ebonheart is among the least of them. You will find many non-soulbound weapons that have better enchantments. But when you've lost everything else—and you will at some point—ebonheart will remain faithfully by your side." Seeing that I still hesitated, he added encouragingly. "Go on, take it."

I did as the captain bade and took up the blade in my hands.

You have acquired the rank 4 soulbound shortsword, ebonheart. This weapon is presently unbound. Do you wish to soul-bind this item?

"Ah," I breathed as I replied in the affirmative to the Adjudicator and felt bonds slip into place between the blade and myself.

You have soulbound ebonheart. From this point onward, this weapon cannot be wielded by any other, stolen, lost, or kept from your hands except by the strongest of enchantments.

The captain smiled on seeing my awed expression. "I can still remember my first ebonblade. May this one serve you as well." He sat back down. "Now, if you will excuse me, I must prepare my people to join the Howlers, and I'm sure you have things to do," Talon said in what was a clear dismissal.

I bowed to him, hand over waist. I wasn't sure when the captain and I would meet again, and I suspected when we did it would be on less friendly terms. Still, I wouldn't forget his generosity.

"Farewell, Captain," I said and left.

Chapter 130: Another Task Down

With ebonheart in one hand and the heavy leather satchel in the other, I hurried through the Tartan barracks, speaking to no one and ignoring the inquisitive stares directed at the black blade.

Once on the empty village streets again, I removed my secondary shortsword from its sheath and replaced it with ebonheart.

The captain's gift, no matter what he said, was priceless and left me feeling uncomfortable. I hadn't betrayed Talon's trust, not precisely—I didn't owe him any loyalty—but there was no doubt that I had twisted his ends to serve mine, accomplishing the letter of the task he'd given me while defeating the purpose behind it.

Because of me, the Howlers would ally with his god-emperor. But also because of me the Dark wouldn't claim the sector, at least not immediately.

I shrugged, setting aside my unease. What was done was done, and now it was time to look to the future. Looking upward, I saw that the sun had moved past its zenith.

I had one last bit of business to attend to in the safe zone before I could leave. *Or perhaps two*, I thought, considering the heavy satchel. First, though, I had to visit Gelar.

Reaching the alchemist's shop, I entered without knocking and found the gnome still busy. "Almost done," he called over his shoulder. "Make yourself comfortable on the couches and I'll be with you soon."

I sat down as instructed and while I waited thought about what the next two days would bring. Objectively, I was unlikely to survive—not without dying a couple of times.

I can't lug around all this gold, I decided. I would only lose it. *Better to spend it and perhaps buy myself some insurance in the process.*

"Do you have a pen and paper I could use?" I asked, a tentative idea taking root in my mind.

"Third shelf on your right, under that pile of books," Gelar replied without looking up from his brewing.

I dug around on the indicated shelf and, sure enough, found some blank sheets of parchment and ink to write with. Sitting down on the couch again, I began to compose a letter.

✳ ✳ ✳

"What do you have there?"

I blinked and shook my head, pulled out of my musing by Gelar's question. I had completed the letter some time ago and for the last few minutes had been staring off into space, wondering if sending it off was the right thing to do.

"Nothing," I replied and stowed the note in my pocket. I rose to my feet. "Have you finished?"

The alchemist nodded and held up a stone flask for me to see. "Here you go, one rank five antitoxin."

"Excellent," I murmured, taking the brew from his hand.

You have acquired a rank 5 antitoxin. This potion has been created from the essence extracted from a wyvern's venom and will cure nearly all known poisons.

"Now, you'd best be gone," Gelar said, shooing me toward the door, "before Ishita's dogs hear you've been here."

"Just a minute," I said. "I want those full healing potions."

The gnome shook his head. "You can't have them. I shouldn't have told you about them at all. I don't know what I was thinking. And now I hear the goddess is going to increase the bounty on your head." He scowled at me. "Dealing with you is becoming too dangerous. You're lucky I was honor-bound to complete our previous transaction. But I can't risk further—"

Extracting three bars of gold from the satchel, I handed them to Gelar. "I want them," I said firmly, "and any other useful concoctions you may have."

The gnome's eyes grew round at the sight of the money before his lips widened in what was the first smile of true pleasure I'd witnessed on him.

"Of course," he murmured. "Come this way."

✳ ✳ ✳

You have acquired 3 full healing potions.
You have acquired 5 fire bombs. Each bomb is highly combustible and will burst on impact, causing a small fire to spread outward.
You have acquired 5 smoke bombs. Each bomb contains a dense magical fog that will expand rapidly outward when released from containment.
You have acquired a rank 5 poison: refined wyvern venom.

I left the alchemist's shop a little later, three gold bars lighter. As expensive as my purchases proved to be, I was satisfied with them. It turned out that Gelar not only made regular potions but crafted incendiary devices too.

Instead of spending the money I budgeted on regular potions, I bought the gnome's little "infernos of destruction" as he fondly referred to the pellets. Each was no larger than my fist and weighed about as much as a small stone. The alchemist had assured me they would burst on impact after being thrown.

The last item I'd acquired was what little remained of the wyvern venom after Gelar had finished crafting my antitoxin. The alchemist had no use for such a small quantity and had been only too happy to sell it to me. As for why I purchased the poison, I wasn't too sure... it was a whim, no more.

Now to see to my final piece of business.

Hurrying across the deserted village, I returned to the tavern. Thankfully, despite it being empty of patrons, Benadean remained behind the bar.

"Oh good," I said. "You're still here."

The barkeeper gave me a morose look. "Where else would I go?"

I smiled. "That's what I've come to speak to you about."

He looked at me, baffled.

"You haven't changed your mind about selling the tavern, have you?" I asked obliquely.

He shook his head. "No, but the chances of selling it are looking more remote every day."

"How much?"

"How much what?" Benadean asked, looking confused again.

"How much do you want for this place?" I clarified.

Benadean leaned across the bar, looking suddenly eager. "Don't tell me you know a prospective buyer?"

I grinned. "Something like that."

The barkeeper pursed his lips. "Well, it cost me nine hundred gold to purchase, but considering the state of things at the moment, I'll settle for five hundred."

I laid my remaining seven gold bars on the bar counter. "How about seven hundred?"

Benadean stared at me for a moment before picking one up. "These are stamped with Tartar's mark," he whispered, turning it over in his hands. "Where did you get them?"

"Don't worry, they're not stolen. Well?"

The barkeeper blinked, seemingly still struggling to process my request. "*You* want to buy the tavern for seven hundred gold?"

I nodded. "More precisely, I want to buy the tavern *and* a favor."

Benadean's eyes narrowed. "What favor?"

I placed my scribbled note in front of him. "When you leave the sector, I need you to deliver this letter for me."

"To whom?"

I told him, and the barkeeper frowned.

"Can you do it? Will Ishita's sworn let you pass through the portal unmolested?" I asked.

Benadean licked his lips nervously but nodded. "I think so."

"Good, then will you do it?"

The barkeeper still looked hesitant. "Will it get me in trouble with the Dark?"

"Not if you don't read the letter." I paused. "Or tell anyone about it."

"Alright," Benadean said after a moment.

"Alright?"

"I'll do it."

I shoved the stack of gold bars toward him. "Then this is yours."

Mutely, Benadean retrieved the gold before reaching into his pocket and handing me an official-looking piece of paper.

You have acquired a bill of ownership for 'The Sleepy Inn' in the safe zone of sector 12,560.

All safe zone building bills of ownership are Game-created items that grant you full control over the building and cannot be stolen or lost, even

upon death. Note, if the building is unoccupied or unused for an extended period of time, ownership will revert to the Game.

This item must be freely gifted or traded to pass on to another. On final death, it will drop and be freely lootable.

"Thank you," I replied, storing away the item.

"When do I have to leave?" Benadean asked, still looking shocked at his rapid change of fortunes.

"Immediately." Rising off my barstool, I nodded at the letter. "I'd also appreciate it if you get that to its intended recipient as soon as you can."

"I will," Benadean affirmed.

I shook his hand. "Well, this is goodbye then I guess. Lock the door behind you, and good luck in your next venture."

"Wait," he called, stopping me on my way to the door.

I swung around to look at him.

"Why trust me with this?" he asked, waving my letter in his hands.

"Because there's no one else," I said, turning back to the door. *And sometimes you just have to take a gamble.*

✻ ✻ ✻

I left the safe zone immediately after that.

Just as Talon had said, the fort was abandoned. The entrances to the barracks and other buildings had been left wide open. Only the keep itself had been sealed shut.

It felt strange walking past the eerily silent buildings. Hyek had kept his word and hadn't left even a token force behind. To all appearances, it looked like the Howlers didn't plan on returning.

I wonder what the Awakened Dead are thinking now.

I chuckled in amusement at the thought. Whatever plans the faction had for the sector, it all seemed to be falling apart.

The outer gates had been left gaping open too, and I strolled through without pause. Then, increasing my pace to a steady jog, I headed northeast.

I had only a vague idea of where to find the dire wolves. According to the information Aira and Oursk had provided, the pack had taken shelter in a network of caves beneath the eastern mountain slopes. Getting there though would take me the rest of the day.

I jogged through the forest the entire afternoon without once being threatened by any of its creatures. I'd grown appreciably since my time in the valley, and now threats that had initially worried me—like packs of serlines and roving rhomodillos—didn't even give me pause.

I also didn't see any signs of goblins. From what I could tell, the Howlers had marched due north after leaving the fort and our paths had diverged long ago.

I reached the Long Fang encampment just as the last rays of the sun disappeared beyond the western horizon. The camp was located at the base of the eastern mountain itself, and I figured it would be a good place to start combing through the slopes.

The encampment was gutted.

I wrinkled my nose, struggling to breathe through the awful stench of death and rotting as I drew closer. The deep trench that had guarded the southern entrance of the Long Fang base was gone, filled in with corpses. Standing at the edge of the channel, I looked down.

The bodies were all Long Fangs.

The corpses bore testament to the violence that had been done upon them—wide, unseeing eyes, spilled guts and intestines, exposed bones, and mutilated faces.

My stomach heaved. I had dealt my own fair share of death since coming to the Forever Kingdom, but this was a massacre on a scale I hadn't witnessed before. Yet, it was more than that. The Long Fangs' death could all be attributed to me. I was the one responsible.

It will be worse when the Howlers and the Red Rats clash.

I shivered uneasily at the thought. But despite all the deaths left in my wake, I couldn't find it within me to regret my actions. They'd been necessary and the only way I could save the wolves. Still, I could never forget that what I did had consequences, nor dismiss the cost in lives.

Breathing in deeply to fortify myself against whatever else I might see, I skipped over the trench and entered the ruined camp. Corpses were strewn everywhere. Tents had been torn asunder, belongings were scattered about, and the little furniture the camp had housed lay broken and burned. Nothing of value remained.

The Red Rats had been most thorough in their destruction.

Padding through the area, I reached the base of the cliff at its far end, then stilled as I sensed a presence above. My head whipped upward.

A dire wolf sat there.

It was Duggar.

The dire wolf alpha stared down at me with an inscrutable gaze. *"Well met, human."* He swung his head from me to the dead camp and raised his snout to sniff at the air. *"And well done."*

CHAPTER 131: AMONG THE PACK

Day Five. Night.

"Hello, Duggar," I called back. My gaze drifted down the height of the cliff separating us. "How do I get up there?"

"We will guide you," he replied.

We?

"We," Duggar repeated, sounding amused.

My mouth dropped open. I hadn't projected the last thought, and I was sure the dire wolf alpha had just read my mind. *How did he do that?*

"There is much we can do that will surprise you," another voice responded.

I spun around. Less than three yards away, a dire wolf was sitting on her haunches with her tongue hanging out as she inspected me.

I bowed from the waist. It was Sulan. "Greetings, pack elder."

"You're still alive, I see." The white wolf's eyes gleamed. *"And growing fast too."*

"Where's Aira and—" I began, then broke off as more bubbles of awareness appeared in my mindsight. My head whipped around, searching for the other presences my mind insisted were a few yards to my left and right.

Sulan snorted. *"But still you remain a pup."* Before I could retort to that, she went on. *"Show yourselves, brothers and sisters. The wolfkin is too blind to see you."*

Shapes coalesced out of the darkness—from within leaping distance—and my heart thudded in sudden fear even though I knew I wasn't in any danger.

Five other wolves accompanied Sulan, all strangers to me. Despite my enhanced senses, I had detected none of them. How had they gotten so close? *Their stealth has to be damn high.*

I sensed Sulan's wince. *"Stop shouting, pup,"* she snapped.

"Sorry," I muttered, trying to make my internal thoughts small.

"Better," she remarked. *"But when we get back to the den, we'll have to teach you some control."*

"The den?" I asked in sudden interest.

"That's why you're here, isn't it?" the elder asked. *"To find out more about Wolf from the pack council?"*

I nodded in vigorous agreement.

Sulan rose to her feet and turned tail. *"Then follow us and try to keep up."*

✻　✻　✻

Sulan and the others led me deeper into the mountains, using forgotten goat trails and hidden paths. I scaled steep slopes, wormed through narrow crevices, and hiked across dry riverbeds. Thankfully, I had no problems following the wolves.

Despite me being unable to spot them while hidden, my night vision was keen enough to pick out their silent forms slipping through the fast-deepening night. Eventually, we came to a halt before a darkened cave mouth.

The den entrance, I presumed.

Duggar sat before it, his bulk filling nearly the entirety of the space. *"Come, wolfkin,"* he said. *"It's time you meet the council."* Turning around, he slipped into the cave.

I followed after him while Sulan brought up the rear. The other five wolves didn't follow. I paused in my steps.

"They will stay above, guarding the den entrance," Sulan said.

I nodded and hurried after Duggar. The pack leader hadn't waited. A small tunnel was situated at the rear of the cave and, going down on all fours, Duggar had crawled through.

It was a tight fit, even for me. I had no idea how the larger Duggar was managing. Thankfully, after a dozen yards the tunnel opened up and we were all able to walk upright again. A few minutes later, the tunnel spilled out into an underground cavern.

Stalactites grew down from the ceiling, glowing blue mushrooms sprouted out of cracks in the rocks, and a still, dark pond occupied the cavern's center. Gathered around it, at rest or at play, was the pack—nearly a hundred dire wolves of all ages—from newborn pups to graying elders.

It made for a picturesque scene, and I had to remind myself that this was a pack in exile.

"We have arrived," Duggar said, drawing to a halt and looking over his shoulder at me. *"This is the pack, or at least,"* he added, sorrow slipping into his mindvoice, *"all that remains of us."*

"How many have you lost?" I asked cautiously.

"We numbered more than three hundred before the goblins' coming," Sulan replied from behind me.

My eyes widened in empathy as I turned her way. More than two-thirds of the wolves had perished.

"Most of those who've fallen were among our best fighters, their lives stolen while protecting the pack," Sulan continued. *"Now wolves too young—like Aira and Oursk—have been forced to serve as our defenders."* The white wolf sighed. *"These are dark days for the pack."*

"But the Long Fangs are no more," I said in an attempt to reassure her. "Your persecution has come to an end."

"Or our troubles have just begun," Duggar interjected obliquely. *"Your coming will not be without cost."*

My brows drew down and I stared at him questioningly, but the alpha's gaze remained maddeningly opaque. *"Follow,"* he ordered, swinging around to advance further in the cavern.

My face still scrunched up in confusion, I turned to Sulan for answers.

The elder wolf sighed. *"We are not ungrateful for what you've done, Michael, but Duggar is right. You bring your own brand of danger. Now the pack must decide how much to risk on your behalf."*

I opened my mouth to question her further, but she slunk past me. *"Come, the council will explain everything."*

* * *

Duggar and Sulan escorted me across the cavern under the intense scrutiny of the rest of the Pack. While none of them spoke to me, they didn't bother shielding their thoughts. Emotions spilled into my mind: menace, anger, suspicion, and... fear.

I staggered under the mental avalanche, then stiffened my spine to walk with my head unbowed.

Not all the dire wolves exuded darker emotions though. Some—the younger ones especially—quivered with excitement and curiosity. Still, it didn't stop the tension from ratcheting upward, and while I wasn't exactly scared, I was grateful for the presence of Duggar and Sulan.

A yap of delight broke the silence.

My gaze swung to the left to see three shapes of black and gray streaking toward me. I barely had time to brace myself before they crashed into me.

My efforts were for naught though. Sputtering in helpless laughter, I landed on my rump, my arms full of the gamboling pups.

"It's good to see you guys too," I chuckled as the three tried to lick my face clean off.

"Well met, Michael," Oursk and Aira said in tandem.

Lifting my head, I saw the two approaching me more sedately than their excited pups. "Aira, Oursk!" I replied, struggling to contain my own relief. I hadn't realized how much I missed seeing them earlier.

Aira nipped gently at my hand in affectionate greeting while Oursk ducked his tail in a more dignified manner.

"We never doubted you would return successful," Aira said.

"Oh, I don't know about that," I replied with a laugh, "I had my own doubts."

"Yet you still freed us from the Long Fang's persecution," Oursk replied.

I was about to respond, then noticed an oddity. Both Aira and Oursk were broadcasting their words, and I realized the rest of the pack was listening intently to the pair and their three pups.

More remarkable still, the oppressive sense of mistrust and fear had vanished entirely.

My gaze darted to Sulan and Duggar and noticed both were watching the dire wolf family and me just as closely as the pack, and while both had their emotions on a tight leash, I sensed a trace of smugness about Sulan.

This was no chance-met encounter, I realized. This meeting had been staged to occur within the center of the pack.

"What's going on, Aira?" I asked softly across the thinnest mental link I could manage.

"All is well. The pack needed to be reassured," she replied, whisper-quiet. *"And now they are."*

Reassured? I wondered. It was obvious from the reactions I'd received that I unsettled the wolves, but why that was the case I still didn't understand.

"This was a test as much as a welcome, Michael," Aira said, *"The council will have observed the pack's reaction and will take it into account when making their decision."*

My consternation only grew.

Sensing this, Aira added, *"Follow Sulan's lead when you meet the elders. She will guide you true. Neither Oursk nor I will be allowed to accompany you."*

"It's time," Sulan said, gently pawing away the pups. *"We must go. The council grows impatient.*

✱   ✱   ✱

Beyond the large cavern sheltering the greater part of the pack was a smaller cave. Shepherded by Duggar and Sulan, I ducked into its narrow entrance.

Four other dire wolves waited there.

Their coats varied in color from dusty brown to charcoal gray, but like Sulan herself, each had graying muzzles. *They're old and past their prime,* I thought. *These must be the elders.*

Four sets of piercing gazes swung my way. *"That we are, impudent pup,"* the smallest of the four said—a brown-furred wolf. From the flavor of her mindvoice, I suspected she was female.

"Bah! Past my prime??" another growled. *"I'm not too old to fight—"* he bared yellowing but still sharp fangs—*"or to gnaw through your bones!"*

Oops.

I needed to learn how to conceal my thoughts better, or they were bound to get me in trouble among the pack. Before I could think about how to soothe the offended wolf's feelings, Sulan slipped into the cave behind me. *"Barak, you old dog, leave the pup alone."*

"Taken him under your wing already, have you, Sulan?" a wolf with a salt-and-pepper coat asked.

"I have, Leta," the white wolf at my back replied serenely.

The largest wolf in the cave, and the only one of the four to have remained silent, rose to his feet and limped toward me. By appearance alone, he was ancient. His coat lacked the healthy sheen of the others. Tufts of his fur stuck out in patches, his claws were ragged and broken, and both of his fangs were chipped.

The old wolf swayed slightly as he drew to a halt before me. Duggar padded forward to his side, letting the elder lean on him for support.

The rest of the council fell silent as the oldest among them studied me, shoving his muzzle inches from my face. *"So, it's true,"* he said. *"A scion of Wolf walks among us again."* For all that his body appeared to be failing him, there was nothing weak about the elder's mindvoice.

Seemingly satisfied with his inspection, the old wolf limped back to his former position and slumped heavily back to the ground. *"Enough chatter,"* he pronounced. *"Let's begin."*

"As you wish," Duggar replied in the most subdued tone I'd heard him use. He swung back to me. *"Wolfkin, we six form the pack council."* He gestured to the two as-yet-unnamed wolves. *"That is Suva,"* he said, pointing out the small female. *"And this is Monac, former alpha,"* he finished, sitting down beside the aging wolf.

I examined each of the council members surreptitiously.

The target is Duggar, a level 67 dire wolf alpha.
The target is Suva, a level 54 dire wolf.
The target is ...

...

Dire wolves, once a populous species in the Forever Kingdom, have been hunted nearly to extinction. In days gone by they were among the most respected and feared wolfkin, famed for their hunting prowess, size, and extraordinary mental feats.

These days, dire wolf packs only haunt the remotest regions and sectors. Alphas are pack leaders, responsible for the protection of their individual packs and for overseeing the interests of all wolfkin in their domain.

Unlike Aira and Oursk, who were only rank one creatures, the pack elders were rank five and rank six beasts. While I'd been examining the council, Sulan had joined the others to form a half-circle around me.

"Today we will sit in judgment of you," the white wolf said.

"Judgment?" I asked, trying to keep my voice even. Matters, I felt, were straying off course. I was here for one thing only: to find out about the path of the Wolf. Whatever the council was talking about, I didn't have time for it. "Erebus and his followers will be following on my heels soon. I have to leave—"

"We are aware of your time limit," Leta said.

"Nor will what we do here take long," Suva added.

"Besides, until you show yourself worthy," Barak interjected with what was undoubtedly a bloodthirsty grin, *"we can't let you go."*

"Can't?" I repeated, jutting out my chin aggressively.

"Can't," Duggar affirmed equably. *"The bloodline you bear is awakening, and for the good of the pack—all the packs—we must decide your fate."*

I stared hard at the pack alpha. I didn't understand half of what he had said, but the threat in his words was unmistakable. If the dire wolves thought I was going to lay down and let them pass judgment on me, they were sorely mistaken.

"I didn't come here for this," I said, folding my arms. "If you don't want to help—"

"Michael," Sulan interjected. *"Trust us. This is necessary."* She left it at that, saying no more.

I glared at the white wolf, still bristling with anger. I wanted to fling back her words at her, but I couldn't forget she had saved my life—and at great peril to her own.

My gaze drifted to Duggar. Nor could I ignore the danger the alpha had placed his people in to rescue me from the wyvern. And I also remembered that Aira—who I *did* trust—had advised me to follow Sulan's lead.

I let my shoulders slump and sighed heavily. "Alright, what do I do?"

CHAPTER 132: THE COUNCIL'S JUDGMENT

"For starters, you can seat yourself," Suva said.

Mutely, I sat down cross-legged on the cold hard ground as instructed. Now that I had decided to comply with whatever the council was planning, I saw no reason to drag this out any longer than it needed to be.

The quicker I get this done, the quicker I can leave, I thought, refusing to contemplate the possibility of needing to fight my way out.

"Tell us everything that's happened since you entered the Forever Kingdom," Leta ordered.

"And don't think to lie," Barak growled. *"We can sniff out any falsehoods you think about telling."*

I scowled at the brown wolf but didn't retort. Taking a moment to gather my thoughts, I began telling the council my story, embellishing nothing and making no attempt to conceal my motivations. But I had barely started my tale when I was interrupted.

"Why pick the scout Class?"

"Didn't you think of refusing the familiar?"

"Was it cowardice that stopped you from entering the dungeon first?"

"Why didn't you band with your fellow candidates?"

"Are you a murderer?"

Those were just the questions in the first five minutes. They didn't stop after that. If anything, the elders' queries only grew more expansive.

On and on it went as the wolves fired question after question at me. Initially, I could see no rhyme or reason to their interests.

Some questions I had to ponder deeply on and seemed to cut to the heart of my motivations.

"Why did you refuse Loken?"

"What prompted you to trust Ultack?"

"How did you know Gnat was false?"

Others were almost trivial—why did it matter when I'd eaten last?—but regardless of how inconsequential the questions were, I was closely scrutinized the entire time.

As the hours wore on, I finally noticed a pattern to the elders' questions. Unexpectedly, they had no interest in my prior interactions with Aira and Oursk's family—the subject I assumed would most concern them—but instead they focused primarily on my interactions with the Powers and factions I'd encountered: Loken, Erebus, Tartar, and even Arinna.

Why and for what purpose I didn't understand, but I was certain I was being assessed and my every response weighed. And not only my verbal responses but also the unvoiced thoughts that accompanied each of them too.

At times, I sensed the six wolves nipping at the fringes of my mind, tasting my emotions and the truth of my answers—both the words left unsaid and those I'd chosen to voice. It forced me to a degree of care I found draining, and by the end of the session I was drenched in sweat.

Finally, Monac, the only one who'd had no questions for me, put an end to the interrogation. *"Enough,"* he ordered. *"The wolfkin will do."*

I sensed surprise in the other council members at the aging wolf's pronouncement, but only Duggar was willing to question him. *"Are you certain?"* he asked softly.

"I am," Monac replied. *"He remains unbound, and for now that is all what matters. Tell him what he needs to know."*

The alpha didn't protest further. Glancing at Sulan, Duggar inclined his head. *"Go ahead."*

I sat up attentively. Finally, it seemed I was about to learn something of interest. I wasn't exactly sure what Monac meant by "unbound," but I suspected it was a reference to me being unsworn.

Sulan rose to her haunches while the others watched on silently. *"What you are about to hear, Michael, is forbidden knowledge, held secret from most players. The Powers have gone to great lengths to eradicate all traces of it. If you choose to share what we tell you among your fellow players, know that you will be endangering them, yourself, and the pack."* She held my gaze. *"Do you understand?"*

I nodded, sensing the seriousness of her tone.

"What do you know about evolutions?" Sulan asked.

My interest quickened. This was a subject of particular interest to me, and while Loken had told me a little on the subject and implied more, I still didn't understand enough on the matter.

"Not much," I admitted. "I know it's rare among players, and those who are capable of evolution use it to transform their Classes, seemingly for the better." I rubbed my lips in thought, then added, "I suspect, too, that it's my ability to evolve that has attracted the interest of the Powers."

The white wolf cocked her head to the side. *"Partially true."*

"Oh?" I said, wondering which part I'd gotten wrong.

"All players can evolve," Sulan said.

I sat up straighter. "What?"

"It is the ability to evolve that separates players from non-players. Only by evolving can players train skills and accumulate traits, feats, and Classes."

I nodded slowly. I didn't know enough to dispute Sulan's explanation, but one thing didn't make sense. "If that's true, if *all* players can evolve, why are the Powers interested in me?"

"While every player can evolve, not all can do so equally," Sulan said. *"Your own capacity exceeds most players. Where the average player's Classes are bound by their initial choices, yours are not, or at least not entirely."*

"I see," I murmured.

"In fact," Sulan continued, *"your ability to evolve is strong enough that, with time and effort, you may transform from player to Power."*

For a moment, I said nothing, having already suspected as much. "Does this mean Loken and Erebus were once players?" I asked quietly.

"Correct," Sulan said. *"It is how all the New Powers came to be."*

My eyes narrowed slightly. *"New* Powers?"

"We'll get to that soon enough," Sulan replied. *"Do you understand the implications of what I've said?"*

I nodded. "I understand why the Powers would want to keep knowledge of evolutions secret, but I knew—or suspected—the gist of what you told me already. There was no reason to interrogate me first you know," I finished somewhat grumpily.

Sulan chuckled, and I sensed amusement tinge the others' thoughts too.

"What's so funny?" I asked suspiciously.

"You are, pup," Sulan replied, still laughing. *"I have not come to the forbidden knowledge yet."*

I blinked. "You haven't?"

She shook her head, amusement fading. *"What the New Powers do not share freely, even among themselves, is what gives players the ability to evolve."*

I waited, sensing we were coming to the heart of the matter.

"It is what lies in your blood," Sulan said.

I stared at her. "My blood?"

The white wolf nodded. *"The blood of the ancients flows in your veins—and that of every other player."*

My bewilderment deepened. *Ancients?* What was Sulan talking about now?

"Millenia ago, even before the advent of the Game, the old Powers—the ancients—roamed the Forever Kingdom," she replied in response to my unspoken question. *"Unlike the new Powers, the ancients were true gods. Kill one and they would simply be reincarnated."*

I scratched my head, truly perplexed. "Alright, but what does any of that have to do with player evolutions?"

Sulan's tongue lolled out in a lupine smile. *"Before players became players, they were called by another name: scions, bearers of the ancient blood. When one of the ancients perished—whether through foul means or fair—the blood of the House's scions would awaken, beginning their evolution into the latest reincarnation of the deceased ancient."*

My mouth dropped open in shock. The pieces were beginning to fall in place. "Wolf was one of the ancients," I whispered.

Sulan nodded. *"He was. As was Dragon, Lion, Serpent, and many others."*

I pursed my lips, pondering deeply. "If all that is true," I said slowly, "why have I heard of none of them?"

"Because," Monac said, at last joining the conversation, *"all the ancients are dead. More than one thousand years have passed since the last was reborn."*

✳ ✳ ✳

I stared at the aging wolf and former alpha of the pack. "How is that possible? If, as you say, the ancients are immortal, then why haven't they reincarnated?"

It was Duggar who answered. *"For hundreds of years, none of the scions who awakened their blood survived long enough to transition into a Prime."*

I glanced at him. "And why is that?"

"The new Powers hunted them down," he replied with an angry growl.

"The new and old Powers warred among themselves?" I asked. "Why?"

"No one remembers anymore," Duggar said. *"Or if they do, they tell no one. What is clear, though, is that the war was lost by the ancients. And the new Powers are determined to keep it that way."*

"By preventing any of the ancients from being reborn?" I asked.

"Exactly," Duggar said.

"And now," Leta added, *"knowledge of the ancients is so suppressed that most scions who have the potential to evolve into Primes don't even know to try."*

"It is only us, the gatekeepers, who still remember the old ways," Suva finished sadly.

"Which brings us back to the subject of evolutions," Sulan said.

I turned back to her. "Meaning?"

"You are both scion and player and may walk a multitude of paths. If you choose to follow the new ways, you will, in time, evolve into one of the new Powers, be it of Light, Dark, or Shadow." The white wolf paused. *"But if you abandon new for old and walk one of the now-forbidden paths, you may eventually become a reborn Prime."*

There was that word again. "Prime? What does that mean?" I asked.

"It is what the old Powers called themselves," Duggar said, *"and refers to the title each held as the head of their respective Houses."*

I bowed my head and considered what I had learned. Around me, the wolves fell silent, giving me space to think.

I'd come to the pack to learn more about Wolf, yet I had discovered more than I'd bargained for. Now I also understood why the dire wolves were uneasy about me. If I truly possessed the potential to be reborn as Wolf Prime, and if the new Powers were indeed still at war with the ancients as the council implied, then my very presence among the pack imperiled them.

Yet they seemed willing to shoulder the danger.

"What is it you want from me?" I asked finally. I suspected I knew that already, but I sought their confirmation.

"You know already," Sulan replied gently. *"This pack cherishes the old ways. Our lore is full of tales of a better time under Wolf and his brethren, and we would see a return to those days."* She held my gaze. *"I believe it is your destiny to follow the way of the Wolf, Michael. And if you prove worthy, to become the Prime reborn."*

"Don't push him, Sulan," Duggar chided. He turned to me, his mindvoice grave. *"You are approaching a crossroads, wolfkin. Up until now you've been treading lightly across many paths—both old and new."*

The alpha's tongue lolled out in a rare smile. *"Like the nomadic wolves of old, you've refused to settle and have held yourself aloof from all the factions, binding yourself to neither Light, Dark, Shadow—or Wolf. But all your Marks are deepening, and whether of your own accord or not, you will soon find yourself bound."* He paused. *"Better you make the choice consciously."*

If I understood Duggar correctly, he was telling me I couldn't stay on the fence. I would have to choose a path. Hamish had said something similar long ago in relation to the Forces, but where he'd mentioned only three choices—Light, Dark, or Shadow—the wolves were suggesting there was a fourth choice.

"*So what will it be?*" Barak broke in. "*Will you become Lightsworn, Darksworn, Shadowsworn, or scion of House Wolf?*"

"*Choose carefully,*" Duggar said. He glanced sideways at Sulan, quelling whatever she was about to say. "*And remember, the choice of which path to walk is yours alone.*"

I closed my eyes and fell silent again, thinking.

Minutes passed, and seemingly no longer able to remain silent, Barak snapped, "*Enough dithering! What will you do?*"

I opened my eyes and scrutinized each of the elders in turn. My gaze rested longest on the oldest among them. Monac had said little and asked even less. And from his almost-bored countenance, the old wolf seemed to have no doubts about my choice.

And he isn't wrong, I thought wryly.

Despite still knowing little about Wolf, I felt an instinctive rightness about the path Sulan was urging me onto.

There was something of Wolf about me already. I had felt it numerous times already, prompting my actions and swaying my choices. It wasn't an alien force either. The wolf within me had always been there, I thought, and it was as much part of me as any other aspect of myself. Most of all, I couldn't deny that I yearned to awaken my Wolf heritage more completely.

Perhaps Sulan is right; perhaps it is my destiny.

"I will become a scion of House Wolf," I said at last.

DAY FIVE. NIGHT.

At my words, I felt excitement ripple through the minds of the others. My response was the one they'd been both hoping for—and dreading.

"Tell me what I must do," I said in the small silence that had fallen.

Sulan was the first to speak. *"To begin with,"* she began in a more animated voice than I'd yet heard her use, *"your Wolf bloodline must be fully awakened."*

"Left to its own devices, your blood would eventually awaken of its own accord," Leta added, *"but in these troubled times, that would be dangerous and leave you without the means to defend yourself."*

"Be warned, though," Suva said, *"once your blood is awakened, there will be no turning back. Any other bloodlines you carry will be subsumed as your Wolf bloodline rises to the fore."*

My gaze flitted between the three female wolves. "I carry *other* bloodlines?"

"Almost certainly," Leta answered. *"Over the years, the bloodlines of the ancient Houses have become so commingled that nearly every scion carries multiple strains. But this won't matter once your blood has been awakened."*

My brows drew down at the elder's answer, but I didn't pursue the matter further. "How will you awaken my blood?" I asked instead.

"We won't," Sulan said. *"You will awaken it yourself by completing the first Wolf trials."*

I waited for her to go on.

"Long ago, before the fall of his House, the Wolf Prime appointed our pack as one of his gatekeepers," Suva said. *"It is our sacred duty to guide suitable candidates to the First Trial."*

I frowned. "What is the trial? Some sort of dungeon?"

"Not quite," the white wolf replied. *"Dungeons exist only in the nether. The first Wolf trial is a closed sector in the aether."*

Sulan nodded to Suva, and the other elder grabbed something from the rear of the cave. Padding closer, she dropped it before me.

It was a metal object consisting of two large, interlocked rings, each inscribed with arcane symbols.

"This is a device used to open a portal," Sulan explained. *"With it, we will send you to the trial."*

A portal! It was potentially another means of escaping the valley. But I curbed my sudden spurt of excitement. I couldn't expect it to work, not given the shield woven over the sector by Ishita's sworn. Unable to resist further, I inspected the object.

The target is a Ring of Astral Walking, an artifact of unknown rank forged by the Wolf Prime Atiras himself. This item is a spirit portal device and may only be used by a circle of mind-linked dire wolves.

I glanced up at Sulan in confusion. "What is a spirit portal?"

"It is exactly what the name implies," Sulan said. *"A portal opened by this artifact will send your spirit to the first Wolf trial."*

"As for your concern about the Awakened Dead's shield," Leta chimed in, *"fear not, their shield will not interfere with the workings of this device."*

I nodded to the smaller wolf in acknowledgment, then turned back to Sulan. "Only my spirit?" I asked. "Why not the rest of me?"

"You are still new to the ways of the Wolf," Monac interjected. *"But in time, you will learn that Wolf is as much a stalker of minds as he is of prey in the physical realm."*

I rubbed at my chin, struggling to make sense of the old wolf's response. *Huh-uh, that's... cryptic.*

"The First Trial is that of the Mind," Sulan said, sounding amused again. *"To that end, you will undertake it without a body."*

I stared at her blankly for a moment. *I guess there will be no escaping the sector through the spirit portal then.* "What happens to my body while I'm in the trial?" I managed finally.

"It will remain here under guard by the pack," Duggar said.

I nodded slowly. "What challenges can I expect to face?"

"That we do not know," Sulan said. *"None of the candidates the pack sent through since becoming gatekeepers have ever returned."*

Urgh. This keeps getting better. "And how many were those?"

Sulan looked to Monac. *"Six,"* he said.

"But you are certain this trial will put me on Wolf's path?" I asked skeptically.

"You have already begun to tread the ways of the Wolf," Sulan assured me. *"Your Wolf Mark has been deepening, hasn't it? And if I'm not mistaken, your Mark has already had an impact on your Class. The First Trial will simply hasten your blood awakening and ready you for the next step."*

My brows rose at her words. It was true that when I'd fully configured my primary Class, it had evolved from scout to nightstalker, and in part that evolution seemed to have been a result of my Wolf Mark.

The Adjudicator had also referenced my Wolf Mark when I'd merged my primary and second Classes into the mindstalker bi-blend. *Sulan's right. I am already on Wolf's path.*

Which brought me to another interesting point.

I glanced at the pack's alpha. "You said the new Powers hunt down those who attempt forbidden evolutions, didn't you?"

Duggar nodded. *"I did."*

"Loken, Ishita, Erebus, and probably also Tartar and Arinna know that I'm a mindstalker by now," I said, turning back to Sulan. "Won't they already be hunting me?"

The white wolf shook her head. *"They will be wary of you certainly, but nothing more. As yet, you tread the path of Wolf only lightly and may still turn back. All that will change, though, once your blood is fully awakened and your Class evolves further. Then the new Powers will consider you and every wolfkin you come into contact with to be tainted."* She looked at me soberly. *"They will spare no effort in purging the taint."*

I swallowed, understanding the grave risk they took.

Duggar eyed me carefully. *"Knowing what you now know, will you still attempt the trial, wolfkin?"*

I nodded firmly. "I will."

Sulan rose to her feet. *"Then get some rest. Tomorrow we shall open the portal to the sector containing the trial."*

I shook my head. "No. I can't wait that long. I need to enter tonight."

"That is reckless," the white wolf scoffed. *"The trial should not be taken lightly. Death there is permanent. Your player lives will not save you."*

My eyes widened slightly at that, but as disturbing as this latest tidbit of information was, it didn't change my mind. "Still, I must enter now," I persisted.

"Don't be foolish, pup," Sulan growled. *"You* will *enter tomorrow."*

"Let the wolfkin do as he wishes," Monac said, unexpectedly intervening on my behalf.

Sulan spun around to stare at the former alpha.

"Sometimes," Monac said with a twinkle in his old eyes, *"we must bow to the wishes of the young—as foolish as we believe them to be."*

Sulan stayed stiff-limbed for a moment before bowing her head in submission. *"As you wish, Monac,"* she said. She glanced over her shoulder at me. *"Ready yourself, pup. Your trial is about to begin."*

*　　*　　*

It took the wolves only moments to prepare themselves. Suva set down the ring of astral walking in the center of the cavern. Then the six wolves lay down around it and closed their eyes.

I stood by the entrance, where I had been instructed to wait, and watched curiously. In my natural sight, nothing seemed to be happening. To all intents and purposes, the elders were asleep.

But in my mindsight, I saw something entirely different. Strands of psi spun out of the six and wove themselves together in an almost seamless circle of energy.

Then, from Duggar and Sulan—anchoring the circle from opposite ends—more psi reached out to the astral artifact and ignited it in violet fire.

The twin rings forming the device—that I would have sworn were indelibly fused together—separated and slid across the ground until they were about three feet apart.

A moment later, the arcane script etched on the rings' surfaces lifted to tear open the air into two rectangular portals of light, one above each metal band.

A Ring of Astral Walking has been activated. A spirit portal to the First Trial in sector 214 has been opened.

"Step into the portal," Sulan ordered, sounding strained.

I straightened from my slouch at the entrance, my gaze flickering between the twin portals. "Which one?"

"Either!" Sulan snapped. *"And hurry!"*

I dashed forward, not bothering to unequip any of my items. According to Sulan, they would remain behind with my body. Choosing the closest of the hovering rectangles of light, I stepped through without hesitation.

Entering the first spirit portal gate. Corporeal separation commencing...

A weird sensation rippled through my body, quite unlike what I'd experienced with any other portal. It was as if thousands of tiny knives sliced through my flesh simultaneously.

I screamed and almost retreated, but I knew that would be a mistake. Persevering against the pain, I pushed through the portal until I passed through its other end and stepped into the space between the two rings.

Astral release completed. Your spirit has been successfully untethered from your body.

I was in two places simultaneously. One part of me—spirit—stood erect, while the other part—unanimated flesh—fell to the ground.

I glanced downward.

Only one of my two forms responded, the one that was a ghostly shape of white light. It—or rather I—was unclothed spirit. My discarded body was heaped on the floor, unmoving and still.

"Well done, wolfkin," Sulan said. *"Now step into the second portal and enter the trial."*

"How will I get back?" I asked, only now thinking to ask this seemingly vital question.

"Should you complete the trial, the way back for your spirit will automatically open," she replied. *"Good luck, Michael."*

I stepped forward and my spirit form responded as my body would have. Standing in front of the second portal, I took a second to gather myself.

This is it. Time to write your destiny, Michael.

I took the next step.

Entering the second spirit portal gate. Astral transfer initiated...

...

...

Leaving sector 12,560. Entering the first Wolf trial.

Chapter 134: Atiras' Gifts

I landed on my feet, without fuss and without experiencing the transition at all.

One moment, I had been in the cave. The next, I was elsewhere. Behind me, the portal receded and then vanished entirely.

Before turning my attention outward, I considered myself. I remained a being of pure spirit and lacked a body. Still, my ghostly limbs responded to my commands in the same way my real ones did, and for now that sufficed. Pivoting around in a slow circle, I took in my surroundings.

I was in a crudely fashioned log cabin.

A closed wooden door was directly opposite, and behind me was a simple table and chair. A few objects lay on the table, but I ignored them as I took in the rest of the room. To my left and right lay two wide-open windows with sunlight streaming in.

I puzzled over that for a bit. It had been dark when I'd left the pack. Did that mean an entire night had passed during my transition to here—wherever this was?

I sincerely hoped not.

Multiple Game messages awaited my attention, and turning my focus inward, I scrolled through them.

Congratulations, Michael! You have discovered a secret location in the Forever Kingdom. Few have entered this closed sector, and even fewer have left.

You have entered the First Trial of Wolf!
Wolf is one of the most mysterious of the ancients. Where others revel in their power, Wolf keeps his own strengths concealed. Where others move openly, Wolf lurks in the hidden corners of the world, stalking his prey.

Wolf isn't the strongest foe or the most powerful, but he is renowned for his stealth, cunning, and hunting prowess.

The Wolf trials encompass each of the many aspects that make up Wolf. This, the First Trial, focuses on the Mind, the key to Wolf's much-vaunted cunning. Finish it, and you will leave with the tools crucial to your continued survival in the Game as you venture further down the path of Wolf.

On behalf of Wolf, the Adjudicator has allocated you a new task: <u>Pass the First Trial</u>. Your objective is to complete all four tests of Mind. Once you have done so, the trial will be completed and your Wolf bloodline will be awakened. This is a task only for those Marked by Wolf.

Warning: this task represents a major milestone in your player evolution. Completing it will have a significant and irreversible impact on your other spirit signatures.

Alrighty, I thought.

The messages were somewhat ominous, especially the part about "few" leaving. *But at least I know I'm in the right place.* I still had no idea what the tests were, though, or how I was expected to complete them.

Time to explore a bit further.

I swung around to face the table and advanced toward it. The motion felt less natural than I had become used to since entering the Game, and I frowned, trying to pinpoint the exact difference as I walked.

It came to me suddenly. My movements felt... cumbersome and absent of the lithe, deft motions I had grown used to since boosting my Dexterity.

It was almost as if I was normal again.

Sulan had warned me, but I hadn't really grasped the significance of her words. I realized now that without a body, none of the attributes boosts relating to my physical form would apply here.

Argh. My mouth twisting sourly. I also realized that I wouldn't be able to sneak or, for that matter, use any of the skills and abilities that relied on my body.

I would manage though. Somehow.

And I still have my mental abilities, I reminded myself, even if they were the least advanced of my skills.

I reached the table and looked down. On it were three books, each shimmering with a magical haze. Resting above the centermost book was a handwritten note. Focusing my gaze on it, I began to read.

Welcome, scion of House Wolf,

You have entered the first of my trials. I'm certain you know this already, but in case you don't, all my tests are fatal. Pass them, and you may move on. Fail, and well, your death will surely be no great loss to House Wolf.

Others among my kindred may favor a less drastic approach, but I do not hold with such. The path of Wolf is a difficult one. A single misstep could be your last, and if you mean to be my successor, it is best you prepare for your new life now.

Wolf cannot be weak.

Now, to more immediate matters. This is the trial of the Mind. During it you will undergo four different challenges, each testing a different mental aspect. You may use any abilities and skills you have at your disposal to pass each test, although I am sure you have already realized that your non-Mind skills and abilities are useless to you here.

Do not think either that, without a body, you are immune to physical damage. I've carefully chosen the constructs inhabiting this trial to be ones that cannot only see your spirit form but that can harm it too.

However, this trial is not only a test of your worthiness, but it is also a means of preparing you for your eventual crowning as Wolf Prime—assuming you live that long, of course. To that end, at the start of each test you will be afforded the opportunity to acquire one additional ability.

I caution you to make your choice wisely.

You will find that the abilities I offer you here are not widely available elsewhere in the Forever Kingdom. So without further ado, look to the three ability tomes on this table before leaving the cabin. Only the knowledge from one of them can be absorbed.

I read the message twice over to make certain I hadn't misunderstood its contents. If I wasn't mistaken, it had been written by a former Wolf Prime, and I could almost imagine him penning it. Turning my attention to the books, I analyzed the one on the left.

Or tried to.

Nothing happened.

Bleh. It seemed analyze wouldn't work here either. Left without a choice, I read the titles on the books instead. They were *Astral Blade, Puppet Master,* and *Terrifying Howl.* All were subtitled *"a basic telepathy ability tome."*

I pursed my lips as I considered the abilities. All three were suitable for my current skill rank. Was that a coincidence? I wasn't sure, but I suspected it wasn't.

The tomes' descriptions weren't much to go on, but I thought it was a fair bet that astral blade was a direct damaging spell, puppet master was a mind-control spell similar to charm, and terrifying howl was a crowd control spell of some sort.

Even not knowing what the upcoming tests entailed, I was fairly certain which ability I needed. It hadn't escaped my notice that without my physical skills, I had no means of inflicting damage on any enemies I would come across, and the Wolf Prime's note had been pretty explicit in that regard: I was certain to encounter hostiles.

Without further hesitation, I rested my hand on the ability tome titled *Astral Blade.*

Nothing happened.

I grimaced. *Just great. If I can't even interact with the tome, how do I absorb its knowledge?*

At the thought, a Game message dropped into my mind.

You have acquired the basic ability: simple astral blade. This is a mind spell that manifests a psi dagger in one of the caster's hands. It can be wielded by hand as a melee weapon or thrown like a projectile.

The astral blade is no ordinary weapon though, and it cannot be used to repel physical attacks. Its use is governed by the telepathy skill, and the damage it inflicts is psionic in nature.

The dagger will remain manifested for a maximum of 10 seconds or until it strikes a target. The effects of this ability may be overcome by mental resistance. This ability consumes psi and can be upgraded. Its activation time is fast.

You have 21 of 26 Mind ability slots remaining.

The other two tomes disappeared. I barely noticed, whistling appreciatively at my new spell's properties. It seemed especially potent for a tier-one ability—which was all well and good. Drawing on my psi, I cast astral blade.

It took only a moment for the dagger to manifest in my hand. I studied the slim shape of vibrant violet energy resting in my ghostly palm. It looked as lethal as any shortsword I'd wielded.

Perfect, I thought, grinning in pleasure.

I turned back to the door. It was time to exit the cabin and find out what the first test was about.

At first, I tried simply passing through the door as any incorporeal being would.

But despite my ghostly appearance, my spirit form had substance and met with resistance when it came into contact with the wood's surface. I sighed and, turning the handle, I opened the door like I would've ordinarily.

Exiting the cabin, I found myself on an elevated platform. More accurately, the building was a treehouse built in the upper branches of a tall redwood that rose a few dozen yards off the ground. There were other trees nearby, but all were shorter than the one in which I was located, giving me a panoramic view of my surroundings.

I was in a forest grove.

In the distance, I spied a lake and what appeared to be another log cabin resting on its shores. From where I stood, I couldn't make out the lake's far shores or what lay on the other sides of the forest grove.

Hmm... what now? I wondered.

A Game message dropped into my mind.

Your task, <u>Pass the First Trial,</u> has been updated. Revised objective: reach the second log cabin safely to complete the first test.

The cabin didn't look like it was too far away. By all appearances, it was only a few minutes' walk from where I stood—if I could get down from my elevated perch, of course. And assuming the forest held no danger, which I was sure it did. I glanced over the edge of the wooden platform.

There was no way down.

The platform surrounded the treehouse on all sides, and I walked a slow circuit around the entire perimeter but still failed to spot a means of getting to the forest floor.

Can't I just jump? I wondered. If I was corporeal, I would never have considered it, but I didn't have a body... *the impact shouldn't hurt me.*

Still, it would be foolish to try.

I eyed the tree's lower limbs. Leaping my way downward using one-step and the intervening branches to break my descent seemed possible. It would be tricky though.

I walked the perimeter a few more times, trying to figure out another way down, but after a while I gave up when I failed to spot a better approach. Sighing, I mapped a route through the branches, then dropped from the platform.

After a second of freefall, I cast one-step and flung myself at the closest branch, hands outstretched to wrap around its thick bough.

I mistimed my leap.

Arms windmilling, I grabbed for the branch but missed my grab by more than a handspan. *Uh-oh,* I thought with a sinking feeling.

It seemed I was taking the quick way down after all.

The first waypoint on my planned route down had been the simplest to reach, and I should've made it easily. But I'd forgotten that my spirit form wasn't as lithe as my physical one, and I was no longer capable of performing the acrobatics I'd grown used to.

I plummeted, jaw clenched to hold in the scream that threatened to erupt. On the way down, I bounced off countless branches and, despite numerous attempts, missed every grab.

I hit the ground hard, landing with a thud that would have been bone-jarring if I had a body to feel it. Then, the fall would have killed me for sure.

You have sustained zero damage. In spirit form, you are immune to physical damage.

I paid the Game alert barely any heed. For all that its message was welcome, it did nothing to alleviate the agony ripping through me. Even absent a body, I experienced pain.

Every square inch of me felt like it was on fire.

The bones I didn't have felt as if they'd been shattered, the limbs I was missing screamed that they'd been mangled, my eyes refused to see, and my fingers barely twitched. For an interminably long time the pain went on, not abating, and I lay stretched out on the forest floor—unmoving and vulnerable.

Eventually, the pain receded.

The unbearable whiteness that gripped my mind faded, and my thoughts began to work once more. *Gods, let's not do that again,* I gasped. Steadfastly refusing to dwell on the experience—if I tried hard enough, I was sure to forget it entirely—I lifted myself to my feet and glanced around warily.

The forest was eerily silent. There were no bird calls, buzzing insects, or cries from predators or prey. To my senses of sight and smell, the forest appeared empty of life.

I didn't believe it for a second.

Unfurling my mindsight, I reinspected my surroundings. Immediately two dark bubbles of energy made themselves known. They were inching closer, one on either flank. Given how they advanced and where I was, I had no doubt the pair were hostile.

I considered my options. I could make a dash for it and race to the second cabin at the lakeshore. Presumably it would provide me sanctuary, but there was no telling what else lay in the path between me and it.

And I couldn't forget I was many times slower now. It was possible—probable even—that my pursuers would run me down.

Best to deal with the threat here and now.

Remaining relaxed and betraying no sign that I'd spotted the incoming hostiles' stealthy approach, I took stock of my Mind abilities: charm, one-step, mindsight, and astral blade. My lips turn down unhappily. There were fewer than I liked.

I had two other Mind abilities—stunning slap and reaction buff—but both of those only worked in conjunction with my body and were no help to me in my present state.

I can make this work, I thought adamantly.

With affected casualness, I slid my gaze to the left, trying to uncover the hostile there, but whatever my foe was, it was too well concealed for me to spot, and with my insight skill inoperable I couldn't identify it with mindsight either.

I could still charm it though.

I set about doing just that. Using my mindsight to navigate to my target's consciousness, I sent tendrils of psi toward the creature and broke through its defenses with ease.

A level 28 burrower has failed a mental resistance check! You have charmed your target for 10 seconds.

My brows rose in surprise at my foe's description. *A burrower? Does that mean...?*

My gaze slid downward.

My charmed minion had stopped moving less than five yards away from me and in a spot that had no cover. It had to be beneath the earth. *So that's why I can't see them.* Ordering the creature upward, I swung around to face my second foe.

It hadn't stopped advancing.

With every second, the creature drew closer in the same slow and careful manner it had before. Originally, I thought this meant the hostiles had been sneaking up on me. Now I knew it was because they were digging through the soil.

I cursed softly. Until the creature emerged from below ground, there was little I could do to it. Setting myself to wait, I cast astral blade and slipped a psionic dagger into my hand. At the sound of a disturbance behind me, I swung around.

The bespelled burrower was surfacing.

And it was ugly as hell.

Part worm, part maggot, the burrower's outer covering was slimy, white, and translucent. It had no neck or limbs to speak of and seemed to propel itself by contracting and expanding its body. The good news was that its skin was paper-thin and should be easy to pierce.

The bad? The thing was huge.

The gaping hole that was its mouth could easily swallow me whole, and as for its length, the burrower still hadn't fully emerged from the earth, but judging from the size of its head I guessed the creature had to be at least a dozen yards long.

Fighting these things should be fun, I thought humorlessly, as I began to seriously reconsider the impulse that had urged me to stay and face the critters.

By all indications, the burrowers were slow-moving. Even without my Dexterity boosts, I should be able to outrun the pair. Worse yet, my charm spell was about to expire. I glanced over my shoulder. The second creature was still two yards away and hidden beneath the ground.

Fight or flee?

Flee, I decided. Fighting was unnecessary. Turning tail, I hurried in the direction of the lake.

You have lost control over a level 28 burrower.

Hard on the heels of the Game's message, the burrower lifted its head skyward and emitted an eerie howl, giving vent to its anger as the leash I'd slipped over its mind fell away.

The wave of sound rolled over me, unnaturally loud in the still forest.

Uh-oh. It doesn't sound pleased.

If the rage filling the creature's scream was anything to go by, it would pursue me relentlessly. It didn't matter though. I was out of the burrower's reach already and increasing my lead with every second.

A moment later, my mindsight lit up.

I skidded to a halt.

Another eight bubbles of darkness were converging on my position. Four of the creatures blocked the way to the lake. Two approached from the left and the last pair from the right.

I was surrounded. *Damn it!*

My latest foes were unseen. I *could* run over the ground concealing them, but that would risk an ambush from beneath. I spun around.

The original two burrowers were also closing in.

The second had emerged from the soil to join its fellow, the lengths of their slick bodies undulating as they wriggled in my direction.

I was wrong about their size too, I saw. The creatures weren't twelve yards in length. They were at least twenty. And even that estimate might prove wrong—parts of their bodies were still concealed beneath the ground.

I looked up. Without my increased Dexterity I wouldn't be able to traverse the treetops as I had in the wolves' valley. But I could still find shelter within the branches.

Darting toward the nearest tree trunk, I cast one-step and pulled myself onto a low-lying branch, then repeated the maneuver twice over until I was at least five yards off the ground.

Perched more precariously than I liked on a bough, I glanced down.

One of the burrowers had reached the tree and, wrapping itself about the trunk, was propelling itself upward.

Perhaps this wasn't such a good idea.

More burrowers were emerging from the ground to squirm around the tree's base. I was trapped.

What now, Michael?

✳ ✳ ✳

My first thought was that I should have chosen terrifying howl instead of astral blade. A nice crowd control ability would have come in handy just about now. But regret didn't help me at all, and while I sat dithering on the tree trunk, my situation only worsened.

The first burrower hadn't let up on its damnable shrieking, and every second more burrowers entered my mindsight's sphere of awareness—summoned by their enraged fellow.

Charming the creature had been a mistake, one of many I'd made already.

I squashed the renewed impulse to dwell further on my poor choices and forced my thoughts toward something more productive: what to do next.

Venturing further up wasn't an option. There were no other branches in reach. Likewise, returning to the ground was suicide. It boiled with squirming burrowers.

Multiple burrowers had wrapped themselves around the tree trunk and, wriggling all over one another, were making their way slowly but surely toward my position.

No choice now but to fight, I decided. *Let's see if I can't convince these worms that I'm not worth the effort.*

Casting charm, I targeted one of the burrowers wrapped around the tree. It fell under my spell as easily as the first had, and I ordered it to attack its closest fellow—another burrower squirming up the tree.

While I waited in anticipation of the outcome, I recast astral blade. After the purple dagger manifested in my hand, I turned my attention to the battling creatures.

The pair weren't fighting.

I frowned. Had my charmed minion refused my order? Turning my focus inward, I checked the leash I had around the burrower's mind. It was intact, and from the emotions I sensed roiling off the creature, it was doing my bidding.

So why weren't its jaws clamped around its companion? My frown deepening, I studied my minion and its target more closely.

The two creatures *were* battling, if only in an inept manner.

Each was constricting its body around its foe. My lips twisted sourly. The pair were attempting to strangle each other, and while one of the creatures *might* eventually kill the other, it would take far longer than the ten seconds allowed by my charm spell!

Charming the creatures is all but useless, I concluded in frustration. That left me with only one other means of hurting my pursuers.

Hefting the ethereal blade in my palm, I whipped my arm forward, launching the dagger at the closest burrower's head.

The luminescent blade flew through the air and struck its target dead center. But instead of tearing open the flesh around the burrower's head the way a normal dagger would, the blade formed from strands of psi expanded into a patch of violet that pulsed angrily before fading.

You have injured a level 26 burrower, inflicting psi damage. Nerves at the point of contact have been weakened. Inflict further psi damage to deaden them entirely.

Your telepathy has increased to level 37.

That's better, I thought, smiling grimly. The astral blade hadn't dealt the same amount of critical damage I was used to inflicting with my shortswords, but it had inflicted damage all the same.

I summoned another astral blade and struck the burrower in question in nearly the same spot again.

You have injured a level 26 burrower, inflicting psi damage.

Then I did it again and again, all while the creature and its companions climbed closer to my perch.

CHAPTER 136: A SPIRIT HARMED

You have inflicted irreparable nerve damage to a level 26 burrower. A burrower is brain dead. You have killed a burrower.

Multiple strikes later, the burrower finally died. Its head drooped and its body sagged, but wrapped around the tree, the creature remained anchored in place.

Sadly, the burrower's fate didn't deter its fellows, and they kept climbing. There were too many to kill before they reached me, but I didn't let that deter me.

Picking out another target, I unleashed another flurry of astral blades at it.

You have killed a level 29 burrower.
You have killed a level 27 burrower.
Your telepathy has increased to level 41.

I killed a second creature and then a third, but by the time I got around to attacking the fourth, the encroaching horde reached my branch.

A burrower's large head snaked around the tree trunk and advanced toward me, swaying slightly as it made its way along the branch I sheltered on. More of its companions followed in its wake.

I'd drawn as far back as I dared on the bough, and there was nowhere left for me to retreat. My face hardened as I studied my oncoming foes. *This is where I make my stand.* If I killed the creatures quick and fast, there was still a chance I could survive the encounter.

Summoning a dagger to my right hand, I flung it at the leading creature.

You have injured a level 26 burrower, inflicting psi damage.

My strike didn't even give the worm pause, and it kept coming.

I manifested a dagger in my left palm and threw it in nearly the same motion. Then I did the same with my right hand, my arms swinging back and forth in tandem as I attempted to keep an endless series of daggers hurtling toward my foe.

Unfortunately, given the burrower's swaying motion and the speed of my attacks, more than a few daggers flew off-target, striking either my foe's body instead of its head or its trailing fellows.

I was just about to adjust my tactics when the lead burrower stopped. It was less than two yards away from me. Raising its body off the bough, the creature stared down at me and opened its gaping maw.

I frowned. *What's it doing now? Is it going to try eating me?*

My hand whipped forward, releasing the waiting blade in my right palm.

A level 26 burrower has evaded your attack.

The burrower swayed out of the way and my dagger sailed harmlessly by. My left hand swung forward, but before I could unleash my next attack, the creature screamed.

An avalanche of sound descended on me.

The burrower's shriek wasn't the unfocused scream of rage I'd heard earlier. This shout was a high-pitched and focused squeal aimed squarely at the creature's target—me.

A burrower has injured you! Your spirit has taken damage. Warning: damage incurred by your spirit cannot be mended until you have been rejoined with your original host.

I staggered backward, slapping my hands to my ears to stop the agonizing sound. But it did no good. My spirit still writhed in the grip of my foe's piercing scream.

A burrower has injured you! Your spirit has taken damage.

Bloody hells! My foes had a sonic attack of some sort, and one that could injure my spirit form. *Why didn't it use it earlier?* As devastating as the assault was, I could think of no reason for the creature to hold back until now.

The burrower kept screaming. Its head swaying, the creature kept me pinned in the narrow cone of sound it was unleashing, and by degrees I felt myself fragmenting under its effects.

A burrower has injured you! Your spirit has taken damage.

I hunched over, cradling my head. At the edge of my vision, I spied another creature close to almost the exact distance as the first. It began to rear up, presumably to unleash its own sonic attack.

The attack must be short-ranged.

Hard on the heels of that realization came another. *If I stay here, I'll die.*

Without considering the matter further, I rolled off my perch and plunged down to the forest floor.

✳ ✳ ✳

I landed in a heap of twisting, slimy bodies, though I barely noticed as agony lanced through my being.

Wha... where...? How—move! Move! Move!

My thoughts were incoherent and my mind was dizzy with pain, but one imperative drove me: the need to escape. Among the burrowers squirming on the ground, I was in greater danger than I'd been above but, crucially, I wasn't trapped either.

But you will be if you don't bloody move right now!

I moved.

Squelching the desire to succumb to pain, I lumbered to my feet. Out of the corner of my eyes, I saw heads lifting among the bodies surrounding me.

The burrowers were about to scream.

I couldn't afford to be hit by their sonic attacks again. Diving forward into the coils of soft white flesh before me, I called a psi dagger to hand.

You have evaded a burrower's attack.
You have evaded a burrower's attack.

Twin sonic booms shattered the air, but I'd moved in time and dodged them entirely. The creature in front of me curled inward, trying to wrap its body around me.

I cut at it blindly and sent numbing trails of psi coursing across its surface. Ignoring the creature's angry hiss, I scrambled over its ample white folds.

More shrieks erupted. I threw myself forward, crawling beneath another wriggling torso.

You have evaded a burrower's attack. A burrower's attack has grazed you.

The hurtful howls passed me by. The first narrowly missed me, while the edges of the second caught me, scraping my eardrums raw.

I spun around and stumbled but managed to stay on my feet. Half-weaving, half-staggering, I fled, aiming for the single spot of greenery I spied between the heaving white bodies.

More attacks followed in my wake, but thankfully they fell short. New foes emerged from the ground ahead of me. Most were still too far to be of threat yet though, and I kept running.

With every step, the pain assailing my mind from my fall faded and my balance grew steadier. My focus improved. *I can do this.* Narrowing my gaze, I mapped a path through the creatures.

Six burrowers converged on me.

Drawing on psi, I charmed the closest, then, using its body to shield me, raced past the next few.

A patch of ground ahead of me heaved.

I flung a psi dagger at the spot and, not pausing, cast one-step, leaping over the burrower as it surfaced. The way ahead was clear. Dropping my head, I put all my effort into running.

One way or another, I planned on getting to the next log cabin.

✻　✻　✻

Nearly thirty minutes later, I reached the lake.

It had taken me much longer than I'd anticipated, mostly because the initial direction I'd fled had been the wrong one, but once I'd put enough distance between me and my pursuers, I cut a wide arc through the forest to return on course.

En route to the cabin, I had multiple run-ins with more burrowers, but now, more truly understanding their threat—and limitations—I avoided becoming entangled again.

And for all the downsides of not having a body, there was one benefit that served me well: I was tireless. Even after running flat out for half an hour, I felt like I could go on forever.

At the door to the cabin I paused, savoring the moment. No burrowers were in sight; I'd left them long behind. I'd done it. I'd passed the first challenge, if with more difficulty than I'd anticipated.

On to the next.

Turning the doorknob, I pushed my way inside. A Game alert dropped into my mind.

Congratulations Michael! You have completed the first test: Power of the Mind. You have gained experience and reached level 69!

Dismissing the Adjudicator's message, I inspected the room. It was nearly identical to the first, but this time the table lay in the center and a second door was positioned opposite the entryway of the first.

The way to the second test?

I advanced directly to the table and glanced down. Once more, it held three ability tomes. There was no note this time though. In its place was something equally interesting: a lesser attribute gem.

The gem alone made completing the first challenge worth it. With a pleased smile, I picked it up.

Lesser attribute gem used. You have gained 1 attribute point.

Next, I turned my attention to the three books, studying their titles. They were *Water Walking*, *Shadow Blink*, and *Levitate*. This time, all three were subtitled *"a basic telekinesis ability tome."*

The first thing that struck me about the books was the pattern I could see forming. In the first challenge, I'd been given a choice between three telepathy abilities, and arguably the test had been one of my telepathic abilities.

Did that mean the second test would focus on my telekinetic strength? It was a safe assumption that it would.

I glanced out the window at the still and dark lake. The cabin's second exit faced directly onto the water, and it didn't take any great genius to figure out that the second challenge would likely occur in the lake itself.

I rubbed my chin as I considered the three abilities offered to me. If I had to make my choice based purely on the forthcoming test, I would have no hesitation in acquiring water walking. And if not that, then levitate.

But outside of the trial, I could see little use for water walking, and while levitate would be more handy, it was shadow blink that attracted my interest the most.

Of the three abilities offered, it seemed the most combat-focused. If I was interpreting its description correctly, it was an ability that would allow me to move quickly in *and* out of combat using the surrounding shadows. Such versatility couldn't be ignored and would be priceless in future battles.

My decision made, I dropped my hand to the tome in question and willed my choice to the Adjudicator.

You have acquired the basic ability: short shadow blink. This mind spell allows the caster to teleport to any living entity within 9 yards, taking your shadows with you. If the caster was hidden when he used the ability, he would remain concealed after jumping to his target.

This ability consumes psi and can be upgraded. Its activation time is fast.

You have 20 of 26 Mind ability slots remaining.

I frowned, unsure whether to be pleased or worried by the unexpected manner in which shadow blink functioned.

The ability was limited *not* by available shadows but by available *targets*. On one hand that made it more versatile—I could use it in even the most well-lit environments—but also more restrictive: I *couldn't* use it without a creature to target.

I sighed. For better or worse, my decision had been made, and it was time to move on. Or almost.

Turning my focus inward, I meditated to recover my lost psi, then reviewed my skill gains from the first test and spent my attribute points.

Your telepathy has increased to level 43. Your telekinesis has increased to level 38. Your meditation has increased to level 43.

Your Mind has increased to rank 28.

Finally, I was ready.

Striding to the next door, I stepped through to see what awaited me in the next challenge.

Chapter 137: The Mind's Reach

Your task, <u>Pass the First Trial,</u> has been updated. Revised objective: reach the log cabin on the far side of the water to complete the second test.

Dismissing the Game update, I surveyed the scene in front of me. I'd been right, I saw.

The cabin door exited on a small wooden platform low enough for the lake's waters to lap over its edges. To my left and right, the lake disappeared into the horizon. However, the opposite shore—and the next cabin—were clearly visible.

About half a mile of lake separated me from the cabin. Like the one in which I stood, it sat on the water's edge, but behind it was a sheer cliff that marched all along the opposite shore, making the cabin accessible only by water.

I glanced to my sides again. To reach the cabin, I could walk along the shore to the opposite end and then try to make my way down the cliff, but given that I couldn't see the left and right borders of the lake, I had no idea how far they extended. For that matter, I also wasn't certain the waterway was indeed a lake and not a river.

I didn't have time for such explorations anyway. Every moment I spent in the trial was one less I had to escape Erebus' clutches. Crossing the lake directly seemed the only viable option.

Across the lake it is.

Crouching at the edge of the wooden platform, I turned my attention to the water itself. It was cold, clear, pristine and, at first glance, innocuous enough.

Then I saw something move.

You have detected a hostile entity.

A long predatory shadow cut through the water. It was big—four, maybe five times my own length. I could make out little else about the thing except that it had a triangular head, a whiplike tail, and was rapidly approaching.

I stepped hastily back from the edge, and about a foot short of the platform the half-seen shape spun around and swam away lazily before I could take any further action.

Alrighty, I thought, *swimming doesn't seem wise.*

How did I cross the water then?

The lake was deep enough that I couldn't see to its bottom, and I was sure it hid more predators. But the unknown creature that had slipped up to the edge hadn't approached me directly. A few feet from where I stood, the critter had zigzagged oddly... almost as if passing around an obstacle.

I studied the area in question intently and spotted a slight sheen as the water lapped back and forth. Narrowing my eyes, I took a step forward and looked harder.

The shimmer I spotted was from a rock. A black rock that glistened in the sunlight as the lake's gentle waves uncovered it. My interest was piqued. The stone lay close to the surface.

My attention skipped from the rock to the surroundings, and after another long minute of study, I spied another stone about two yards away from the first.

Was it part of a ford? A pathway across the lake hidden just beneath the surface?

Has to be. It made sense, too, for there to be a crossing, given my suspicion that the second challenge was a test of my telekinetic abilities.

I searched around again but didn't spy any more glinting shapes in the water. *That doesn't mean they aren't there, just that I can't see them from here.*

My gaze slid back to the first rock. It was close enough that I could reach it with one-step. *Time to move,* I thought, deciding to trust my instincts.

Advancing to the platform's edge, I stepped off and cast one-step. My left foot landed on solid air. Continuing to walk naturally, I stretched out my right leg and found the submerged rock with the tip of my toes.

The rock was slippery, and I swayed slightly as I brought around my left leg to stand still on my watery perch, but other than for that initial bobble, I had no difficulty retaining my balance.

I turned my attention to the next rock. It, too, was within reach. Beyond it I could just make out another stepping stone, but it was even farther away and would be harder to get to. Still, there was no reason I couldn't make it, even if it meant me getting a little wet.

I readied myself, then froze as my mindsight pinged suddenly.

One of the lake's predators was stealthily approaching. I'd anticipated it, however. Spinning psi, I cast charm. With barely any resistance from my target, I invaded its mind and extended my influence over it.

You have charmed a level 39 river crocodile for 10 seconds.

A crocodile, I thought, my brows lifting. The creature sounded surprisingly ordinary, but I was sure it was no simple beast. Like the burrowers, the crocodiles were sure to have a means of harming me.

This time though, I wouldn't try fighting it. And besides, I had a much better use for my charmed minion.

I commanded the crocodile to the surface. With a lazy burst of speed that had my eyebrows rising again, the beast positioned itself where I'd ordered—adjacent to the next rock in the chain of stones that made up the partially submerged ford.

I didn't hesitate. Only five more seconds remained on my charm spell. Targeting the crocodile, I cast shadow blink.

Psi rushed outward from my mind to encompass my form and, with breathless speed, pulled me from the physical realm and into the aether.

I stayed there for less than a fraction of a second though.

More psi rushed outward from me to tear a hole through reality for my form to re-coalesce on the crocodile's back.

You have cast shadow blink and teleported yourself two yards away.

Damnation, I thought, still dizzy from my abrupt translocation. There was no time to waste though. Stepping onto the rock, I commanded my soon-to-be-free minion away. Skimming along the surface of the water, it heeded my orders. The crocodile's back was ridged, armored, and uneven, but for all that, it had been a more stable platform than my current perch.

I grinned, suddenly envisioning using a combination of charm, blink shadow, the crocodile, and the rocks to skip my way across the lake. *This test may turn out to be easier than I expected.*

My mindsight pinged again.

Three more hostiles were homing onto my location.

I sighed, hopes dashed. *Why is nothing ever easy?*

✷   ✷   ✷

You have lost control over a level 39 river crocodile.

My spell lapsed before the three new hostiles could reach me, which was at least one bit of good news.

Ignoring the approaching crocodiles, I recast charm over my former minion. The beast was zipping through the water, heading furiously back my way—no doubt to wreak vengeance upon me.

Midway to me it crashed to a halt, bewitched again.

Then I shadow blinked onto its broad back. In my mindsight, I sensed the three submerged crocodiles pause momentarily at my sudden disappearance before reorienting themselves on my new position. They didn't speed up though, perhaps assuming I was still unaware of their presence.

At their current pace, it would take the three hunters a handful of seconds to reach me. *And even longer if my 'raft' flees.* Ordering my minion deeper into the lake, I scanned its depths for another stepping stone.

It didn't take me long to spot one.

Directing the bewitched crocodile toward it, I stepped off and commanded the beast deeper into the lake. The other three crocodiles hadn't surfaced and had slipped out of mindsight range entirely.

Good, I thought. It gave me time to repeat my previously successful maneuver.

Drawing psi, I readied my charm spell, then waited for my bewitched minion to shrug off my hold upon its mind. I fully intended to continue leapfrogging across the lake in the manner I had.

Who knows, with a bit of luck maybe I can complete the trip without mishap.

✷   ✷   ✷

Unbelievably, my luck held, and five minutes later I stepped off the back of the hard-working crocodile and onto the platform of the next log cabin.

During my trip across the lake, I'd sensed the approach of multiple predators. None had surfaced though, and none had gotten close enough to threaten my routine of charm and shadow blink. In the end, the journey across the water had proven uneventful.

Stepping up to the door, I considered the latest cabin. From the outside, its rear wasn't visible. The cabin's left and right sides disappeared into the rockface of the cliff at the back and had neither doors nor windows.

So, where is the entrance to the next challenge? I wondered.

Only one way to find out, I thought and stepped into the cabin.

Chapter 138: Mind over Body

A flurry of Game messages accompanied my entrance into the cabin. Halting in the doorway, I took a moment to peruse them.

Congratulations Michael! You have completed the second test, the Mind's Reach. You have gained experience and reached level 70.
You are now a rank 7 player. For achieving rank 7, you have been awarded 1 additional attribute point.
Your telepathy has increased to level 46. Your telekinesis has increased to 43.

Dismissing the alerts, I studied the room. It was dark, no light penetrating within except from the open door at my back. With night vision though I had no trouble picking out the shapes in the shadows.

The table lay in the room's center once again, and interestingly enough, a closed door was situated opposite me. It had to lead into an underground tunnel. But it wasn't the exit's placement I found most surprising.

It was what lay next to it: a humanoid entity.

Letting the entrance door close behind me, I advanced on the still and motionless form next to the exit. Though, as I drew closer, I realized that whatever was near the door wasn't alive. It was too still and motionless for one thing, and it also had no presence in my mindsight.

I stopped in front of the thing. *It's a construct,* I realized, studying it closely.

The construct was eight feet tall and had been molded from compressed sheets of metal—iron, I guessed. It had no facial features, and the digits of its hands and feet were short and stumpy.

I laid a hand on the construct, and a Game message unfurled in my mind.

Do you wish to possess an iron golem?

I responded in the negative to the Adjudicator and, with my mind buzzing with questions, turned to the table for answers. Its contents were familiar: three ability tomes and a lesser attribute gem.

I used the gem first and invested my new attribute points without having to give the matter much thought. Given where I was and what challenges I faced, Mind was my most critical attribute.

Your Mind has increased to rank 31.

I inspected the books—all chi ability tomes—next. They read *Hardened Body, Steel Fist,* and *Chi Heal.*

Well, I thought. *That explains the construct.*

The next challenge was obviously focused on testing my chi, which could only be used with a body. I didn't spend any great length of time considering the abilities on offer. As useful as two of them appeared, there was only one I simply had to have: chi heal.

Being unable to heal myself was my greatest weakness, and I could barely curb my eagerness to finally resolve that lack. Resting my hand on the tome, I willed my choice to the Adjudicator.

You have acquired the basic ability: minor chi heal. This mind spell allows the caster to mend his body using psi. This ability consumes psi and can be upgraded. Its activation time is very slow.
You have 24 of 31 Mind ability slots remaining.

I sighed as I saw the ability's activation time. It was too slow to be ordinarily of use in combat. Still, any healing spell—even one I couldn't use in battle—was better than none.

After meditating to recover my lost psi, I stepped back up to the construct and clothed my spirit in it.

You have possessed an iron golem. Abilities gained from the host body: none. Your physical skills are available once more. Note your Strength, Constitution, Dexterity, and Perception attributes are determined by your new host body as follows: Strength: 20, Constitution: 20, Dexterity: 5, Perception:5.
Warning: if this body is destroyed while you reside in it, your spirit will be torn asunder.

The golem's body felt strange.

Where my human form had been lithe and quick, the golem was clunky and slow. I willed my new body toward the door, and it creaked into motion with the sound of metal sheets screeching against each other.

Urgh. I wasn't going to be sneaking around anytime soon in my new body. Still, I would make do.

Yanking open the door, I stepped through and into the next test.

✳ ✳ ✳

Your task, <u>Pass the First Trial,</u> has been updated. Revised objective: defeat all enemies in the arena to complete the third test and reveal the exit.

I tensed as I read the message. It made clear that the next test was different, breaking the pattern established by the first two.

Warily, I scanned the darkness. No immediate threat made itself known. I still didn't move away from the door though. Summoning psi, I cast reaction buff.

Your Dexterity has increased by +2. Duration: 10 minutes.

The boost provided by the ability was small, but considering the low base Dexterity of my new body, the improvement was significant. I flexed my arms and winced as they squeaked. Possessing a metal body was more problematic than I imagined.

But despite the horrendous noise I'd made, nothing jumped out at me.

I was in an enclosed area. It was completely sealed without even an iota of light penetrating. That didn't bother me though. What did was the bareness of the space.

The so-called arena was box-shaped and about twenty yards long on each side. The floor, walls, and roof were all formed from granite, smooth and unadorned. There was no sign of the door through which I'd entered either. It had disappeared, leaving the wall to my rear seamless.

I didn't spot anything I could use as a weapon or any obvious threats. I frowned. *So, where are these enemies?*

I took a cautious step forward. Then another.

As I advanced further, I spotted a small white circle painted on the floor and about five yards away another one of darker red. I stepped onto the white spot.

A Game message opened.

Ready yourself, scion. Commencing the first battle…

I stilled, hands clenching into fists. In the exact center of the red spot, a shape appeared.

It attacked immediately.

I braced my feet and stretched out my hands. Whatever my foe was, it was fast. As it charged toward me, I glimpsed arms and feet tipped with claws, menacing yellow eyes, and a mouth stretched wide and filled with razor-sharp teeth.

Then it was upon me.

From two steps away, my foe hurled itself through the air. Crashing into me, it wrapped its legs around my waist. Despite the momentum behind my foe's charge, I didn't budge so much as an inch. My golem body was too-damn heavy.

Useful, I grunted and swung my arms forward.

But before I was halfway through the motion, my foe completed its own attacks. The claws of the creature's left and right hands raked down my metal chest, scoring deep furrows while its jaws clamped down on my neck.

A level 70 zombie has injured you!

An undead?

The zombie's opening assault had been fast and furious, a blitz series of attacks almost too quick to see. Helpless to evade or block my opponent, I did the only thing I could think of: I wrapped my arms around it.

Given the strength of my new body, my best weapons were my hands. Hugging the zombie, I squeezed.

You have injured a zombie.

Flesh compressed under my grip, bones cracked, blood—thick and congealed—broke free.

The undead though was unfazed and kept beating at me with rabid abandon. Dents appeared in my body, and slivers of metal flew off.

A zombie has injured you!
A zombie has injured you!

I wasn't sure who was doing more damage—me or the undead—but there was no reason I had to endure the zombie's own attacks, not when it was so helpfully pressed against me. I cast stunning slap.

You have failed to stun your target. Zombies are immune to all forms of mental assaults.

Well, damn.

If stunning slap had failed to work, then astral blade or charm wouldn't do any better. I had only one option now—to hurt my foe quicker than it was damaging me.

With me and the zombie still wrapped around each other, I took a step forward. Then another, building momentum. The undead was indifferent, the fury of its attacks not abating in the least to consider my actions.

I kept running and I kept squeezing. Careening straight at the closest wall, I crashed into the unyielding rock. The floor beneath shook, and if I had teeth, I was sure they would be rattling.

You have injured yourself!
You have critically injured a zombie!

I smiled in grim satisfaction at the Game alert. The damage to myself meant little in the face of the fine web of cracks that had appeared in the rear of the zombie's skull.

My foe had borne the brunt of the impact.

Time to do it again. Turning around, I aimed myself at the opposite wall. This, finally, gave the zombie pause, and for a moment it stopped its frenetic assault.

Then it squirmed, trying to wriggle free.

My grin widening, I tightened my grip and built momentum again, slowly but surely. The undead's attempts to escape grew more desperate, but it was no use. With all the grace of a lumbering ox, I plowed into the next wall.

You have injured yourself!
You have critically injured a zombie!

Once again, my foe was squashed between stone and my equally unyielding torso. I'd timed my second collision better too, ramming the zombie headfirst into the wall.

The crunch of its skull was audible.

For a handful of seconds, the undead didn't seem to realize its fate and its limbs continued to batter at me. Then the zombie stilled as what little intelligence animating it faded entirely, and it slid to the ground in an untidy heap.

You have killed a level 70 zombie.
Congratulations, scion, you have defeated the first challenger. Step onto the starting circle to commence the second battle.

CHAPTER 139: NEW CHALLENGES

Ignoring the Game message, I leaned heavily against the wall beside my defeated foe and took stock of the damage to myself.

Warning! Your health is at 40% and will not recover without healing.

"Wow," I murmured softly. I was more hurt than expected, especially considering I felt nothing, no sense of unease at all.

But then a construct doesn't feel pain, does it?

Gingerly, I ran metal fingers over the wounds the zombie had inflicted and felt jagged edges and crumpled metal. I closed my eyes. *Time to find out how well this healing works.*

Drawing from the well of psi in my mind, I sent it probing downward into my body. The energy rippled through me, identifying and analyzing the flaws in my form.

Then one by one, I began to rectify them.

Bent iron reshaped into smooth sheets, torn edges reconnected with their opposite ends, and missing pieces regrew entirely.

You have restored 10% of your lost health with chi heal. Your health is now at 50%.

Far too soon, the process stopped.

I grunted in disappointment. Minor chi healing, it seemed, worked only as well as a healing potion of the same tier.

Shutting close metal eyelids, I recast the spell five more times until my metal body was fully mended, then spent a few moments more meditating.

Your psi is now at 100%.

Finally, I recast reaction buff and heaved myself off the wall. With body and mind restored and buff cast, it was time to face the next challenger. Marching forward, I strode to the white spot and stepped onto it.

* * *

Ready yourself, scion. The second battle will commence shortly. Preparing arena...

My concentration was so focused on the spot where I expected my next foe to appear that I paid little attention to the Game alert. The resulting changes in the terrain, however, were impossible to miss.

The floor had begun to bubble.

What the-?

My neck creaked left and right. The once hard-packed granite rock of the arena was melting, transforming into thick, sucking mud.

My feet sunk, first an inch, then a foot deeper, until finally I was knee-deep in sludge. I groaned unhappily. My metal body was clunky enough already. Moving in the muck would be nearly impossible.

Glancing downward, I tried lifting my foot.

A level 80 shadow hunter has backstabbed you!

My head jerked upward and I swung around—or I tried to. With my movement restricted by the mud, I barely managed a half-turn.

It was enough, though, to glimpse my attacker.

At eye level with me was a creature hovering aloft on wings spanning eight feet. It was shaped less like a bird and more like a glider, with a triangular-shaped body that expanded outward from its elongated snout. The shadow hunter's hide was black and dull, toughened and aged like shoe leather, making it difficult to spot in the darkness.

Its eyes were the most disconcerting bit.

They shone red in the dark, bright and malevolent. Meeting my gaze, the shadow hunter hissed, revealing a sibilant tongue and snout filled with rows of sharp teeth.

I pulled my left foot free, intent on swinging all the way around to face my foe. But before I could complete the maneuver, the shadow hunter spun and glided silently out of reach.

Two yards away, the creature vanished from my sight. *It's hiding,* I thought and opened my mindsight. But it, too, was empty.

Huh? How could that be?

Stealth only concealed one physically—not magically. The creature couldn't have traveled out of mindsight range either, not in the scant seconds it had taken me to activate the ability.

That left only one possibility.

Its mind is shielded. That makes sense, given where I am. I should—

A shadow hunter has backstabbed you!

My thoughts broke off as the creature hit me once more. It had circled the room to strike at me from behind again. I clenched my fists in annoyance and turned around to face it.

This time, though, the creature didn't bother to taunt me and vanished into the darkness before I caught more than a glimpse of its rear.

The shadow hunter was going to strike at my unprotected back again. I just knew it. But I knew just as well that there was nothing I could do to stop it. Clenching my jaw in frustration, I waited.

Sure enough, a few seconds later the anticipated attack arrived as the shadow creature's sharp beak clamped down on my iron shoulder.

A shadow hunter has backstabbed you!

I didn't bother turning around again, confident now of my foe's tactics. Strike and retreat. That's how it intended on taking me down. The question was, what did I do about it?

I'd kept my mindsight open during the last attack, and it had confirmed what I had feared. Even when the creature was within a yard of me, it had been invisible to my mindsight—conclusive proof that the shadow hunter's mind was shielded.

Charm won't work against it. Will astral blade and stunning slap?

I dearly hoped so. Turning my attention inward, I examined the damage the shadow hunter had inflicted already.

Your health is at 90% and will not recover without healing.

Thankfully, the creature had barely scratched me. For all the suddenness and inevitability of the shadow hunter's strikes, each one had done little damage. *That means I have time, and if I want to live, I better make good use of it.*

Wading through the mud, I cast chi heal as I headed toward the closest wall.

✳ ✳ ✳

Every step was a battle.

The mud sucked at my feet, only reluctantly letting go each time and eagerly reclaiming them with every step. But slowly and surely, I inched toward the wall.

The shadow hunter flew lazy circles above me the entire time, swooping down and attacking unopposed. I ignored it, staying focused on my twin goals of reaching the wall and recasting chi heal.

Eventually, I reached my destination and planted my back against the cold granite. *Now that it can't backstab me,* I thought grimly, *let's see how it fares.*

I checked my health. Even with the constant healing, it had dropped below half. *It'll be enough,* I told myself. Banishing further doubt, I waited.

You have detected a hidden entity. A shadow hunter is no longer hidden!

About a yard away, my foe emerged on my right flank, its dark form a blur as it streaked out of the shadows and toward me. I raised my hands to intercept the creature.

I missed.

The shadow hunter nipped at my face, then angled away, deftly avoiding my reaching hands to vanish in the darkness again.

Refusing to be daunted, I reset my stance, adjusting the placement of my hands to where I expected the next assault to come from. Then I waited.

The attack wasn't long in coming.

You have detected a hidden entity.

The shadow hunter flew at me from the left, the same direction my hands were poised this time around.

The creature dove.

My hands rose.

Already, I knew I'd be too slow to stop the incoming attack. Still, I hoped to lay at least a finger on my foe before it could escape.

The shadow hunter ducked past my left hand and hammered its beak into my neck. Then it beat its huge wings to escape my upward-reaching hands.

That proved to be a mistake.

Its right wing clipped my slow-moving right hand. It was the moment of contact I'd been hoping for. Instantly, I released the psi I'd been holding ready and cast stunning slap.

A shadow hunter has failed a physical resistance check! You have stunned your target for 1 second.

Yes!

A heartbeat later, I reined in my jubilation. It was too early for celebrations. The shadow hunter plummeted, its limbs locked motionless. My head creaked downward following its fall, while simultaneously I dropped my right hand, trying to keep it in contact with the beast.

But the creature fell faster than I could follow.

A foot from the ground, the stasis imprisoning the shadow hunter unraveled, and in a sudden flurry of motion the creature flapped its wings to climb aloft again.

But momentum was against it.

Before the hunter's wings could gain traction, they hit the sludge at my feet where the mud—which was no kinder to my foe than it had been to me—promptly held the creature prisoner.

Now I can celebrate, I thought, grinning at my foe's squawk of protest. Bending down, I reached toward the frantically struggling beast with outstretched hands.

The shadow hunter hissed in dismay. But the tables had turned and, stuck in the mud, the creature was no more able to evade me than I had been able to stop its earlier attacks.

My hands wrapped around the hunter and pushed it deeper into the muck. The creature's struggles grew more panicked. I hung on, not yielding an inch.

Its death, I was certain, wouldn't be long in coming.

* * *

You have killed a level 80 shadow hunter.

Congratulations, scion, you have defeated the second challenger. Step onto the starting circle to commence the next battle.

With the shadow hunter's death, the mud vanished.

Straightening from my bent-over posture, I found myself standing on hard, firm rock again. I stamped my foot on the ground approvingly. *Much better.*

Before returning to the start position, I took the time to heal myself, regain my lost psi, and renew my reaction buff.

How many more of these battles will I have to fight? I wondered as I advanced back to the center of the chamber. *As many as necessary,* I answered myself and stepped onto the white dot.

Ready yourself, scion. The final battle will commence shortly. Preparing arena...

Final battle, I thought, suddenly feeling more enthused about the upcoming fight. Setting my stance, I waited.

Once more, the arena transformed around me. This time, the floor to my left and right retracted lower, leaving me standing on an elevated platform—*a rock bridge?*—that ran the length of the room and was just over a yard wide.

My foe hadn't appeared yet.

Not wanting to be caught by surprise again, I didn't take my eyes off the red dot where the final challenger was sure to manifest.

The seconds ticked by.

And still I waited with no opponent in sight. *C'mon,* I growled impatiently.

An ominous hissing filled the room. It was coming from the pits on either side of me. *What now?* Wrenching my gaze away from the red dot, I glanced over the bridge.

The pits were filling with a red liquid that bubbled and spat angrily. It was magma. *Falling will definitely not be a good idea.*

Out of the corner of my eye, I spotted a shape coalesce on the bridge and returned my attention to it, hands raised in guard position. What would it be this time?

An iron golem appeared.

I lowered my arms a fraction. *Why do I need another body?* I wondered. Then the golem shifted and I realized this one was already occupied. *It's my final challenger.*

The golem strode toward me. Deciding not to wait for its arrival, I launched a preemptive attack, casting charm.

You have failed to charm your target. A level 90 iron golem possesses no mind to subdue.

I took the spell's failure in stride and backstepped. Summoning an astral blade to hand, I flung it forward with the flick of a wrist.

You have failed to injure your target. An iron golem possesses no nerves or sensory organs.

That's two for two against me.

Would stunning slap work? I wondered. Given the failure of my first two spells, probably not. My foe drew closer. The good news was that it was slower than me. The bad news was that both its fists were glowing.

What spell is that? Steel fists? More than likely, I decided.

I suspected that if it came to a battle of blows, I would come off worse. *Best make sure it doesn't come to that then.*

I retreated faster, only stopping when my back hit the stone wall behind me. Glancing over the edge of the bridge, I saw the pits were half full with magma and still filling. I turned back to my foe. More than ten yards separated us now.

This should do.

Crouching down low, I extended my arms, palms up and fingers pointing to the roof. The iron golem ignored my strange pose and continued its relentless march forward.

I smiled in satisfaction and, drawing the shadows around me, faded into the darkness.

You are hidden. A hostile entity has failed to detect you!

Despite my disappearance, the iron golem didn't stop its advance, but I hadn't expected it to.

Timing my moment, I cast shadow blink.

A heartbeat later, I reappeared behind my foe, crouched and concealed. I'd executed my intended maneuver perfectly and caught the golem mid-stride.

Not hesitating, I shoved my arms forward, angling them a touch to the left. My flattened palms made contact with my foe's rear and pushed hard.

The iron golem, with one leg raised, was surprised by the unexpected shove and stumbled sideways. Its arms windmilled in slow motion as it tried to regain its balance.

I didn't give it the opportunity.

Lurching forward, I drove my shoulder into the golem's hips. It was enough. The construct toppled backward and, with a mighty splash, fell into the magma.

I rose slowly back to my feet, eyes never leaving my foe as its metal body melted away in the superheated liquid.

You have killed a level 90 iron golem.
Congratulations, scion, you have defeated the final challenger. Make your way to the exit.

I'd won, and the third test was over.
Only one more to go.

CHAPTER 140: STRENGTH OF MIND

The arena changed again.

The magma drained away and the pits filled with solid stone again. More importantly, a door appeared on the opposite facing wall.

I made my way toward it, then paused. My golem form was far too large to fit through. I grunted in dissatisfaction. *I guess I'll have to leave it behind.* In response to the thought, my spirit broke free from the metal body sheltering me.

You have de-possessed an iron golem.

In my more familiar spirit form, I opened the door, and as I crossed the threshold I was showered by the expected Game messages.

Congratulations, Michael! You have completed the third test, Mind over Body. You have gained experience and reached level 71.

Your chi has increased to level 45. Your meditation has increased to level 45.

Dismissing the alerts, I scanned my surroundings.

Once more, I found myself in a log cabin. But this time it lacked any windows and had an additional exit. One of the doors was carved with the symbol of a howling wolf. The other was unmarked.

Two doors? I wondered. *What's this?*

The familiar table lay in the center of the room, and eager to see if it held an explanation, I hurried toward it. A moment later, I slowed. Its contents were different too.

The table didn't contain the expected three ability tomes. Instead, there was only one book. Beside it was a lesser attribute gem—which I used immediately—and a note. My surprise mounting at the deviation from the established pattern, I read the message.

Congratulations, scion of House Wolf,

You have passed the first three tests of the Mind Trial. This is an achievement in and of itself. Suffice it to say, not many candidates make it this far despite extensive preparations.

However, you haven't yet faced the First Trial's true test. Everything you have undergone so far has merely been a precursor to the final challenge.

What awaits you beyond this cabin is probably the most important test, not just of this trial but of any trial. In the next chamber, your bloodline will be awakened—assuming, that is, you manage to survive the process.

But before you proceed further, there is some knowledge I must impart. Most of it you should know already, but given the gravity of the decision that awaits you, I feel it necessary to repeat some salient facts.

You hold within you an ancient bloodline, one potent enough to give you abilities beyond the norm. But no matter how concentrated the blood you carry may be, it is diluted and not as strong as it needs to be for you to evolve into a Prime.

Before your bloodline can be awakened, it must be strengthened. To do this, your blood will be infused with the spirit of fallen scions. This will be the first blood infusion you undergo on your journey, but hopefully not the last. Survive them all and you will become Prime and wield the power of your forebears.

The rituals you will undergo are ones every Prime since the dawn of time has gone through, and it is at the core of what makes us who we are.

A Prime is more than an individual.

A Prime wields not just his own strength but the spirit and power of his ancestors too. If you become Prime, it will be your duty to continue our sacred traditions and strengthen the Wolf bloodline before passing it on.

If you fail along the way... well then, know that your efforts would not have been in vain and that your spirit will strengthen the next scion who ventures down this path.

So, scion, you are faced with a decision.

There are two exits from this cabin. If you pass through the unmarked door, you will leave the path you are on and forevermore be barred from the way of the Wolf, but your spirit will remain your own.

If you go through the wolf-marked door, you will become an anointed scion eternally bound to House Wolf. On your final death, your spirit will not leave the Forever Kingdom but stay to strengthen the Wolf bloodline. Let me stress, fail or succeed on your journey to becoming Prime, once you are an anointed scion, you will be bound eternally to Wolf.

There is another consequence of binding yourself to House Wolf. Hopefully you know this already, but if you do not, be aware that all Primes straddle the Forces of Light, Dark, and Shadow equally.

We ancients do not favor one over the other like the so-called new Powers do. When you become anointed, any Marks of Light, Shadow, and Dark you bear will disappear—forever. To those who know the old ways, your absence of Force Marks will be telling...

Choose your course wisely, scion, and may darkness always shelter you.

Atiras.

I read the former Prime's message with something akin to disbelief. Walking the path of Wolf required greater sacrifice than I'd realized. And was more dangerous than I expected.

Doing this will bind me eternally to Wolf. Not just in this life, but forever.

The idea gave me pause but, surprisingly, didn't bother me. The truth was that as dangerous as it was, the way of the Wolf was the only path open to me if I wished to forge my own destiny in the Game and not become sworn to one of the Powers.

But even more than that, on some gut-deep instinctive level, the idea of becoming Wolf appealed to me. Maybe that was just my blood talking, but whatever the case, binding myself to House Wolf didn't trouble me. *Thank you for the warning, Atiras, I thought, but I'm doing this.*

Turning away from the note, I focused on the ability tome on the table. Its title read *Mind Shield, a basic meditation ability tome.*

My brows drew up at that. I hadn't known the meditation skill had any abilities. But considering that I hadn't been given any choices, it was likely that the skill didn't have many abilities. It didn't matter though. Dismissing further speculation, I laid my hand on the book.

You have acquired the basic ability: simple mind shield. This ability encapsulates the caster in a shell formed from psi. The shield protects you from all mental attacks, both those directed against your mind and those targeted at your nerves. While protected by a mind shield, you cannot use any psi abilities.
The damage that the mind shield can absorb is directly proportional to the size of the caster's psi pool. This ability can be upgraded, and its activation time is fast.
You have 23 of 31 Mind ability slots remaining.

I frowned as I absorbed knowledge of the ability. Not being able to use my own psi spells while shielded was a significant drawback and made me wonder if I would ever employ a mind shield.

I swung toward the exit doors. There was one more matter I needed to attend to before leaving. Turning my focus inward, I invested my new attribute points.

Your Mind has increased to rank 33.

With that taken care of, I strode to the wolf-marked door and passed beyond.

✳ ✳ ✳

You have gained the trait: <u>anointed scion</u>. This trait irrevocably binds you to House Wolf. Your Marks of Lesser Dark, Lesser Shadow, and Lesser Light have been stricken from your spirit signature.
Your task, <u>Pass the First Trial,</u> has been updated. Revised objective: enter the crucible and survive the mental assaults of the spirits of the fallen scions until the blood infusion ritual is completed.

I paused in the doorway as I considered the latest Game alerts. The new trait didn't surprise me, but the warning to expect mental assaults did. Was that why I had been given the ability?
Deciding it was better to be prudent, I cast mind shield.
The entire pool of psi at the pit of my subconsciousness rose out to reform into bands around my mind.

Your psi pool has been transformed into a mind shield. Psi abilities are unavailable.

Protected, I advanced further into the room and inspected my surroundings.
I was in a cavernous hall. Marble mosaics depicting wolves in various states of battle or play covered all four walls. Chandeliers hung down from

the ceiling, bathing the chamber in warm yellow light, and the floor was polished stone. It was a room fit for a king.

Or a Prime.

Despite the rich décor, the room held only a single object—an enormous ivory throne sitting in the exact center of the hall. *I guess that's where I'm expected to go.*

I strode silently through the chamber with only the floor's reflection of my ghostly visage to keep me company. Reaching the throne, I took a moment to study it. On closer inspection, I realized it was formed not from ivory but bone.

Wolf bones? I wondered, a shiver of unease passing through me.

Two lupine skulls, complete with menacing fangs, formed the chair's armrests. The eye sockets weren't empty either but glowed a magical sapphire that seemed to beckon to me. Feeling suddenly more anxious, I sat down on the throne, prompting another Game alert.

Commencing the Ritual of First Infusion...
Place your hands on the twin wolf heralds to begin the summoning.

Guessing the heralds to be the glowing skulls, I rested the palms of my hand on both.

Commencing summoning...
Warning: if you leave the bone throne or break contact with the heralds while the ritual is in progress, you will fail the First Trial.

I grimaced. The message was certainly ominous sounding. My trepidation increasing, I waited for whatever came next.

The seconds ticked by, and nothing else happened.

Then, the light in the heralds' eye sockets began to pulse, getting brighter with each beat.

The first fallen scion of House Wolf has answered the ritual's call. She will test you, and if she judges you worthy, she will gift you her essence to empower your blood.

A ghostly shape coalesced on the polished floor. I tensed, eyes fixed on the new arrival. It was a spirit. *A fallen scion.*

The spirit woman studied me as intently as I did her. She looked young, in her mid-twenties. Her features were sharp, her hair was plaited with military precision, and her eyes gleamed with intelligence.

Whatever she saw in me caused the scion's lips to turn up in amusement. Advancing lazily, she raised both hands. A psi dagger formed in each. Her wrists flicked forward, sending both hurtling my way.

I braced myself, not daring to move. Both blades struck me dead center.

A fallen scion has damaged your mind shield!
A fallen scion has damaged your mind shield!
You have lost 10% of your psi repelling the mental attacks. Your psi is now at 90%.

I flinched as I felt my defenses shudder.

The woman smiled and summoned another pair of daggers to hand. Continuing her advance, she flung both at me.

A fallen scion has damaged your mind shield!
A fallen scion has damaged your mind shield!
You have lost 10% of your psi repelling the mental attacks. Your psi is now at 80%.

My worry grew. How many attacks would the woman launch? At the rate my shield was weakening, I couldn't take much more of this.

But what could I do except endure?

Wrapped in a mind shield and forced to remain in the bone chair by the ritual, the only course available to me was to trust in my defenses.

Unless.... My shield was powered by my psi pool, wasn't it?

While I couldn't attack the woman in turn, I *could* work to regain my lost psi. Closing my eyes, I stilled my mind and began to meditate. My subconscious stirred, and energy flowed out of it and into the bands of psi around my mind.

You have replenished 4% of your psi. Your psi is now at 84%.

Another mental assault rocked my defenses.

You have lost 10% of your psi repelling the mental attacks. Your psi is now at 74%.

The attack almost broke my concentration, but with grim determination I kept myself relaxed and maintained the outward flow of energy from my subconsciousness.

Settling deeper into my own mind, I ignored my foe's further attacks and ever-so-slowly replenished my defenses.

You have replenished 4% of your psi. Your psi is now at 78%.
You have replenished 4% of your psi. Your psi is now at 82%.
You have lost 10% of your psi repelling the mental attacks. Your psi is now at 72%.

The fallen scion threw volley after volley at me, but as my focus deepened, the rate at which I recovered my psi increased. Soon I lost track of my surroundings entirely, barely feeling the bite of her blades as they struck my shield.

Eventually, though, I noticed a change.

The fallen scion's attacks had stopped.

Surfacing from the depths of my mind, I opened my eyes. The spirit woman was kneeling before the throne. A smile still played on her lips as she met my gaze and placed her hand on one of the heralds.

"Hail, scion," she mouthed.

Before I could think how to respond, the herald's jaws yawned wider and the woman's spirit was sucked within. The glow in the skulls' socket expanded to encompass her entirety and my palm, which had previously been resting lightly on the bone, was held fast by some unseen force.

Something—I'm not sure what—passed into me, and I could've sworn I heard a light, feathery laugh.

You have absorbed the essence of a fallen scion. Your blood awakening has begun...

Chapter 141: Gifts from the Fallen

The woman was only the first of many.

Dozens of other fallen scions followed in her wake. Some were as gracious as her in defeat, willingly offering their essence. Others fought to the bitter end, railing at me until they were entirely depleted of their energy and forcibly consumed by the wolf heralds.

With every infusion, I felt my awareness expand until my mind thrummed with energy. Some of the scions were deadlier than others, and many times—early on especially—I teetered on the edge of defeat.

But with every attack I foiled my meditation skill grew, and soon I made my mind an impenetrable fortress, replenishing its defenses faster than it could be damaged. Safe within it, I ignored the fury of my foes as they battered at me.

The scions were always summoned individually, but halfway through the process I felt a strange flutter at the edge of my mind, almost as if someone else was there, someone watching... and waiting.

With my mind shield up, I couldn't use mindsight to confirm if what I perceived was real or merely a figment of my imagination. And what with the scions' relentless assaults and the need to focus on my own meditation, I quickly lost track of the half-sensed presence.

Eventually, the last challenger fell, causing a flurry of Game messages to scroll through my mind.

Congratulations, Michael! You have rebuffed the challenges of the fallen scions and absorbed their essences, completing the fourth test, Strength of Mind. You have gained experience and reached level 72.

Your meditation has increased to level 67.

You have completed the task <u>Pass the First Trial.</u> Your blood is ready to be awakened. To determine the form its awakening will take, consult the Blood Talisman.

Your spirit signature has changed.

Wolf is an ancient god and has been many things in his multiple incarnations. Oftentimes, Wolf may favor one aspect of self over the other, sometimes becoming a consummate were-fighter, other times a fearsome wolven mage.

But one thing about Wolf has always remained constant: the Prime has always been a threefold being, equally proficient at wielding psi, mana, and stamina.

You have completed the First Trial of Wolf and demonstrated your skills in the aspect of Mind. Your performance has met with Wolf's approval, and your Wolf Mark has deepened.

You have accomplished the feat: <u>Realize your Lineage!</u> Requirement: Awaken one of the ancient bloodlines lying dormant within you. As the first

player in centuries to assume the mantle of Wolf scion, you have been awarded the trait: <u>Inscrutable Mind</u>. This trait increases your Mind by +8 ranks.

At the Adjudicator's message, I sagged wearily in my chair, mentally exhausted by the ordeal. *Finally, it's done,* I thought and raised my head.

Then I froze.

I wasn't alone.

Standing silently in front of the throne was another spirit. *A challenger?* I wondered. But no, this spirit was that of an older man with graying hair and a face deeply seamed with age. The fallen scions I had faced had been mostly youths full of fire and anger, players who had failed the First Trial, I suspected.

My visitor, by contrast, had eyes both ancient and somber, shadowed by the experiences of a lifetime—or many lifetimes. His back was unbent, and in his left hand he carried a staff that topped his own six feet of height.

I frowned at the staff. It was as ghostly as my visitor himself, but none of the scions had borne physical weapons of any kind.

What is he?

"What I am is not dead," the spirit said. His voice reverberated through my mind, not actual words but a form of mind speech.

My gaze grew sharp, and my hands tightened around the heralds' skulls. *How does he know what I'm—*

"And no, I did not read your thoughts," he added. *"Your mind shield is quite proficient for one so young."*

Was that a hint of approval in his voice? Or something else? Either way, I didn't care for my visitor's patronizing words.

I itched to summon an astral blade or prepare to defend myself in some other way. The test was over, and it was no longer necessary for me to remain confined to the throne. But the spirit in front of me appeared adept with mental skills, and I didn't dare lower my mind shield just yet.

"WHO ARE YOU?" I asked, attempting to forcibly project my words into my visitor's mind in the same manner he had.

The spirit winced. *"Your mind speech, on the other hand, could do with a bit of training,"* he murmured. He eyed me carefully. *"You know you could drop the shield around your mind halfway. If you do that, your thoughts will still be protected and you will also be able to employ your mental abilities. This is the trick all pups learn early. Unfortunately, it has limitations too. When your shield is configured that way, it will not stop incoming mental assaults."*

I said nothing. I wasn't sure I believed him, and I noticed he'd avoided my own question. Rising from the throne, I advanced on the unknown spirit, stopping less than a yard from him.

"Who are you?" I demanded again.

The spirit did not answer, studying me through lidded eyes. *"The more relevant question, boy, is who are you?"*

Not waiting for my response, he began to pace a slow circle about me, ignoring my clenched fists. *"That you have become a scion of House Wolf is clear. But what else are you? And how did you reach this trial?"*

I pivoted with the spirit, unwilling to allow him out of my sight. As I did, I noticed that a wooden table had appeared some distance behind the throne. Next to it was a shining rectangle of light. *The exit portal.*

"If you refuse to answer me, this conversation is over," I said harshly.

Following my gaze, the stranger spotted the open portal and came to a halt. He nodded equably. *"I am Ceruvax, the last living envoy of Wolf."*

My head jerked up in surprise. I'd half expected the spirit to name himself Atiras. Still, his claim was bold enough. *"You're an envoy? Then Wolf lives?"*

Ceruvax shook his head, sorrow darkening his face. *"No, my Prime is no more."* His gaze flitted to my own. *"But maybe the time of his return is at hand."* His expression cleared. *"Now, perhaps you will introduce yourself?"*

I hesitated, then seeing no harm in it, I told him, *"I'm Michael."*

"Michael," Ceruvax repeated. *"Just Michael? No last name?"*

I nodded.

"You are not a native of the Forever Kingdom then," Ceruvax said, rubbing his chin. *"You were summoned here?"*

I nodded again, growing more perplexed. How had he figured that out from just my name?

"That explains your ignorance," he murmured, speaking more to himself than to me. *"And why I did not sense you earlier."* He turned back to me. *"Which Power called you?"*

I folded my arms, ignoring his question. *"Why does me being an outsider surprise you?"* I asked, fielding my own question. *"I thought most players came from outside the Forever Kingdom?"*

A smile flitted across the envoy's face. *"Very few players choose to walk the path you have, and those who do are invariably ones whose family traditions still recall the ancient ways."*

I opened my mouth to ask another question, but before I could do so Ceruvax stopped me. *"Please, hold your questions for now. I have much to tell you, and there is little time."* His gaze turned inward. *"Already they hunt me."*

It was on the tip of my tongue to ask who hunted him, but I bit back the question. If the self-proclaimed envoy wanted to provide me with information, I wasn't about to stop him, no matter how much I might doubt his identity. *"Go on."*

Ceruvax nodded gratefully. *"As I told you, I'm the last envoy of Wolf. Ages ago, the new Powers imprisoned me in one of the dungeons they control in Nexus. For the last few hundred years, it has been my home."* He smiled grimly. *"Much to the Powers' disappointment, I've proved too powerful for their players to kill."* His grin grew feral. *"That has not stopped them from trying though."*

The envoy resumed his pacing. *"When the ritual of infusion began, I was surprised."* He chuckled. *"That's putting it mildly. It has been a long time since anyone has attempted these tests. I sensed the summoning and came here and found you: a young player, still half-formed."*

"Half-formed?" I couldn't help but ask.

Ceruvax nodded. *"You have yet to choose your third Class, and considering your ignorance, that is good."*

I opened my mouth, then closed it with a snap.

"*I'm guessing you started with some form of generic rogue Class and perhaps a simple psionic Class?*" he asked, his gaze passing over me in frank assessment.

I wouldn't have quite described my Classes that way, but choosing not to argue, I nodded simply in response.

Ceruvax turned away and continued his pacing. "*There is no getting around it: your first two Classes were badly chosen.*"

The envoy was facing away from me, so he missed what I thought of *that* pronouncement.

"*But a mindstalker,*" he mused, "*you didn't do half-bad by managing to achieve that bi-blend. And there is hope still that you can achieve a strong incarnation of Wolf.*" He swung back to me and scowled. "*And make no mistake, considering the forces arrayed against you, you will need to be mighty indeed. Strength, however, is not easily obtained. If you wish to become truly powerful, you must risk much. Are you ready to do that?*"

I held his eyes and said nothing. My actions to get here alone spoke of my willingness.

Seeming to read the answer in my gaze, Ceruvax nodded grudgingly. "*What do you know about Wolf?*" he asked.

"*Little,*" I admitted.

The spirit sighed. "*That's not unexpected, I suppose, but I'd hoped otherwise. There is too much to share at the moment, but what is most relevant for now is that to stay on the path of Wolf, your third Class must be mana-based.*"

Seeing my confusion, he explained further, "*Over the course of his many lives, Wolf has taken many forms, but in every incarnation, three aspects have always defined the Prime: mind, body, and magic. To be a true Wolf, you must be able to wield all three. Thankfully, you have already covered two of those aspects with your initial Class selections.*"

"*I see,*" I said thoughtfully. "*What does it mean for a Class to be mana-based?*"

"*It must contain an element of magic,*" Ceruvax clarified. "*A single magic or faith-based skill will suffice. It does not have to be entirely magic in nature.*"

That seemed simple enough to achieve.

"*But I would caution you against selecting just any magic Class.*" Ceruvax's expression twisted in disgust. "*Or buying one through a merchant. The best Classes are the ones no one sells and those you will only find in a dungeon. Unfortunately, the best dungeons to search are also among the most dangerous—for you in particular.*"

"*Which ones are those?*" I asked, curiosity piqued.

"*The dungeons of Nexus,*" Ceruvax replied. "*Their original purpose was to test scions and provide them with appropriate Classes. The new Powers have put a stop to that now though. And nowhere else is the concentration of new Powers and their sworn greater than in Nexus.*" His gaze turned serious. "*If you go there, you will risk death—or worse.*" He paused, seeming to wait on my response.

"*I'll consider it,*" I replied noncommittally.

The envoy sighed. *"Good enough, I suppose. And you will see once you inspect the Blood Talisman that there are ways to minimize the danger. Speaking of your bloodline, I'd advise—"*

Ceruvax broke off suddenly, his entire being stilling and his face twisting in a snarl.

"What is it? What's wrong?" I asked.

The envoy's gaze jerked to me, and I almost stepped back in shock.

Ever so slowly, Ceruvax's face was changing. His eyes were turning yellow, and his teeth were growing into fangs. And was it just my imagination, or was his nose lengthening into a snout too?

"The hunters are here," the envoy replied. *"We are out of time. I must go. If you ever journey to Nexus, seek me out in one of its dungeons."* He bared his lips in a distinctly lupine smile. *"If you dare."* His spirit began to dissipate, growing more ethereal with every passing moment.

"Wait! What about my bloodline? Can't you tell—"

"Goodbye, scion," Ceruvax broke in. *"And good luck. I hope we meet again."*

With that, he was gone.

Chapter 142: Blood Awakening

In the wake of the envoy's disappearance, two Game alerts buzzed for my attention.

You have been allocated a new task: <u>Find the last Wolf Envoy</u>. Your objective is to locate Ceruvax, the only remaining envoy of House Wolf. By your target's own words, he is presently trapped in one of the Nexus' many dungeons. Find him to learn more about the way of the Wolf.

You have been allocated a new task: <u>Stay True to Wolf</u>. Your objective is to acquire a mana-based Class for your tertiary Class to remain on the path of Wolf.

I pursed my lips as I considered both messages. They added weight to Ceruvax's own words. *So, it looks like he wasn't lying.*

Setting aside the matter for further consideration later, I stepped up to the table beside the still-open exit portal. It was almost time to leave, but I still had a few things to finish up first.

The table was empty.

I'd been hoping for another attribute gem, but alas, there was none to be had. However, carved on the table's surface, in glowing lines of silver, was an elaborate and intricate depiction of dozens of fantastical beasts.

On the left was a dragon captured mid-flight, toward the bottom was a writhing serpent, in the right corner a griffin dived downward, and in the center a hydra battled a snarling wolf.

But these weren't the only beasts depicted, only the largest. Intertwined around them were many others, including a two-headed lion, a unicorn, a manticore, and so on.

This must be the Blood Talisman. Without hesitation, I placed both my hands flat down on the table.

Contact established between anointed scion and Blood Talisman. Reading candidate's blood signature...

I waited patiently. After a drawn-out moment, another message unfurled.

Scion, the fallen of your House have gifted you their essences, and your bloodline is ready for its first awakening.

The blood of an ancient is a fearsome thing. Memories of traits, skills, and abilities lie long dormant within them. When sufficiently awoken, your blood can be made to 'remember' its ancient lineage and perform feats you had not thought possible before. It is up to you, with the aid of the Blood Talisman, to determine which of your blood memories will awaken.

Exploding blood: your blood can be weaponized. This blood memory will grant you the ability: exploding blood. It can be used once per day to destroy

all enemies lower leveled than yourself within a 9-yard radius. Its activation time is instantaneous. This is a generic blood memory.

Note: blood memories are powered by your blood itself and consume neither psi, mana, nor stamina.

Revitalizing blood: your blood can reinvigorate. This blood memory will grant you 4 abilities: recover health, recover psi, recover mana, and recover stamina. Each can be used once per day on yourself or another to fully restore any lost health, stamina, mana, or psi. Its activation time is instantaneous. This is a generic blood memory.

Secret blood: your blood can be used to conceal and deceive. This blood memory will grant you the trait: secret blood. It will hide every aspect of your ancient lineage—including Marks, Classes, skills, and traits—behind a false façade. Players and Powers alike will be deceived. The effects of this trait are untraceable and permanent. However, it will only apply to aspects related to your ancient bloodline. This is a blood memory unique to House Wolf.

My mouth dropped open in astonishment as I read the descriptions of the blood memories. All three were exceedingly powerful. *Which should I choose?*

Exploding blood was a combat ability I could see multiple uses for and was especially useful in that it would scale with my own level. Revitalizing blood could prove the difference between life and death in battle—literally—for me or an ally.

But despite the obvious benefits of the first two blood memories, my attention focused on the third. At first glance, what it offered seemed redundant. My deception skill allowed me to conceal more about myself and just as well—though only *after* I trained the skill sufficiently, which could take months to years.

Secret blood, on the other hand, was both permanent and untraceable.

As hunted as I am now, how much more so will I be once the Powers discover that I've awoken my Wolf blood?

I was certain, too, that Ceruvax had been referring to secret blood earlier. With my bloodline concealed, I could enter Nexus without fear of being hunted by any but the Awakened Dead faction.

Unless, I thought wryly, *I manage to make more enemies between now and then.* Which seemed entirely possible. Probable, even.

My humor fading, I refocused on the three blood memories and made my choice.

You have been awarded the trait: <u>secret blood</u>.

That quickly, I was done. The carving on the table stopped glowing, and I removed my hands. *Just one more thing to do.*

Turning my focus inward, I invested my newly earned attribute point in Magic. None of my other attributes needed urgent attention right now, and given that I would need to acquire a magic Class soon, I thought it prudent to begin improving my magic now.

Your Magic has increased to rank 1. Current modifiers: +2 from apprentice ring. Magic skills and abilities limited to rank 3.

I was finally done, and it was time to return to the Game. Approaching the exit portal, I passed through without breaking stride.

Entering spirit portal. Astral transfer initiated...
...

...

Leaving the First Trial. Entering sector 12,560.

✻　✻　✻

My spirit traversed the aether in the blink of an eye and, with shocking suddenness, I was sucked back into my body.

Astral recombination completed. Your spirit has been rehoused in its original host.

I groaned and dismissed the alert. More messages awaited me, but I ignored them. Something else consumed my attention.

The separation of my spirit and body had been painless. The same could not be said of the reverse. My head was pounding, and I felt lightheaded. My limbs were unresponsive, and each breath was a struggle. Far worse, though, was what I felt in my blood.

I was on fire.

Blood infusion initiated. Absorbing the first essence...
...

...

The Game message made clear the cause: the blood infusion ritual. Only now was I truly feeling its effects. The energy I'd siphoned from the fallen scions raged within me, an inferno that only gradually subsided.

Drip by drip, the fallen spirits' essences seeped into my blood. My nerves tingled in response, my skin was rubbed raw, and my organs expanded close to bursting.

Eyes squeezed tightly shut, I endured.

And after long minutes, the fiery sensations quieted.

Blood infusion completed.

Congratulations, Michael! You have awakened your first blood memory!

Blood memories are gifts from your forebears and contain the power of the ancients themselves. With each successive awakening, you will recall more powerful memories.

Your secret blood trait has been triggered! Your spirit signature has been etched with False Marks of Dark, Shadow, and Light, and your Wolf bloodline traits have been concealed.

All traces of your awakened blood have been successfully hidden.

I lifted my head and opened my eyes.

I lay in the center of the same cave, and surrounding me was the full dire wolf council. All but two of them slumped against the ground. The remaining pair—Sulan and Duggar—stared fixedly at me.

"Welcome back, pup," Sulan said. Her words carried an undertone of relief, carefully disguised, but I knew her well enough by now to recognize it beneath her seemingly casual air.

"Am I?" I asked.

I sensed her confusion. *"Are you what?"*

I pasted a sickly grin on my face—the best I could manage under the circumstances. "Am I still a pup? I passed the trial, after all."

Sulan chuckled, then inclined their head. *"I suppose you're not. Well done, wolfkin."* She paused. *"I never doubted you'd succeed."*

I felt more than saw Duggar roll his eyes at her. "Did *you* succeed?" the alpha asked. *"Is your blood awakened?"*

"It is," I replied.

The big wolf bowed his head. *"Then Sulan judged right,"* he murmured. He raised his head. *"Hail, scion of House Wolf. May darkness always shelter you."*

The alpha's words reverberated through the cave and the larger cavern beyond. He had projected his words to the entire pack, and I sensed their acceptance and acknowledgment of my place among them.

Now, I was truly one of the pack.

"Thank you, Duggar," I replied gravely, inclining my own head. I glanced at the slumped elders. They hadn't even stirred at the alpha words. "Are they alright?"

"They are," Sulan assured me. *"They have been worn out beyond their limits. Keeping the spirit portal open was... taxing."*

"It was more than that," Duggar added dryly.

I studied the pair more closely, only now noticing the weakness in their own limbs. Their eyelids drooped heavily, and their tongues hung out.

My debt to the pack had grown, I realized. I could only imagine what it must have taken to keep the portal open for as long as they had. "How long was I gone?"

"For the entire night and the better part of the morning," Duggar replied. *"It's almost noon."*

My eyes widened in alarm. "Noon?" That meant I had little more than a day remaining of my Pact with Erebus. Pressing my hands against the floor, I tried to lift myself up.

I failed.

My body was still too weak.

"You're not getting up just yet," Sulan said. *"Your body has been pushed past its limits."* She sat down beside me, resting her chin on my leg. *"Rest now. The pack will watch after you."*

"I can't. I have to—"

"Rest," Duggar commanded. *"For a few hours at least. I will wake you at sunset."* Slipping forward, he planted his own head across my chest.

Given no other choice, I closed my eyes and let sleep take me.

CHAPTER 143: SETTING MATTERS RIGHT

DAY SIX. NIGHT.

I found myself alone when I next opened my eyes.

It couldn't be too late—I trusted Duggar to do as he said—but time was short. I'd lost an entire day to the trial, more than I'd planned, and if I wanted to escape the sector, I needed to get going. First though, I had to attend to my body's needs.

Sitting up gingerly, I took stock of myself. The debilitating weakness in my limbs was gone, and my body felt rested—if starved. Right on cue, my stomach growled. I suspected it was my hunger that had awoken me.

Searching around, I saw my pack resting against one wall. Fetching it, I retrieved some rations and began to chew. While I ate, I turned my attention to the waiting Game messages.

You have fulfilled the first condition of your Pact with the envoy, Mariga. Leave the sector without revealing her identity to satisfy your Pact obligations in their entirety.

You have completed the task: <u>Goblin Wars</u>! As a result of your manipulations, the Howler and Red Rat armies have met in pitched battle.

You have completed the task: <u>Forging Dark Alliances</u>! Shaman Hyek has upheld his end of the bargain you struck with him and, on behalf of his tribe, has pledged allegiance to Tartar.

The Power Tartar has deposited 1,000 gold into your Albion Bank account. Your Pact with Talon is closed!

The Marks on your spirit signature have changed. By fomenting further discord between the sector's two largest goblin tribes, you made the valley safer for the brethren of House Wolf. However, all the good you accomplished through this has been undone by the alliance you negotiated between the Howlers and Tartar. The danger of the sector falling into the Dark's hands has increased.

While you have removed one threat to House Wolf's loyalists, your actions have also served to replace it with another. Wolf is dissatisfied, and your Wolf Mark remains unchanged.

Note, your Force Marks are no longer true Marks and will not shift with your actions.

I stopped chewing.

During my sojourn in the First Trial, two whole quests had been completed... with mixed results. I could almost feel the simmering disapproval of Wolf bearing down on me.

I'd known the potential consequences of my actions when I'd acted but had acted anyway. Because, quite simply, I had no other choices. To push the Howlers into a pitched battle with the Red Rats, I'd been forced to dangle Talon's offer before their shaman. Now, matters had played out and the Howlers had given themselves to Tartar—endangering the sector's neutrality.

But, crucially, the valley was still unclaimed.

While the Howlers were in the field and their fort remained un-garrisoned, there was still a chance to rectify matters. I already had a few vague plans on how to go about that. First, though, I needed to destroy the shield generator.

I sighed, regretting the lost day. I didn't think I had enough time remaining anymore, but I was determined to try—even if it meant staying in the sector to face the wrath of Erebus' followers.

I will set matters right, Wolf. I promise.

And the quicker I get moving, the quicker I can do that.

Setting aside the problem for now, I resumed eating while I turned my attention to my player profile.

<u>Player Profile: Michael</u>

Level: 72. Rank: 7. Current Health: 100%.

Stamina: 100%. Mana: 100%. Psi: 100%.

Species: Human. Lives Remaining: 3.

True Marks (hidden): Wolf-brethren.

False Marks (fabricated): Lesser Shadow, Lesser Light, Lesser Dark.

<u>Attributes</u>

Available: 0 points.

Strength: 2. Constitution: 14. Dexterity: 17*. Perception: 20. Mind: 41. Magic: 3*. Faith: 2*.

** denotes attributes affected by items.*

<u>Classes</u>

Available: 3 points.

Primary-Secondary Bi-blend: Mindstalker.

Tertiary Class: None.

<u>Traits</u>

Psi wolf heritage (hidden): +2 Dexterity, +2 Strength, +4 Mind.

Beast tongue: can speak to beastkin.

Marked: can see spirit signatures.

Nocturnal: perfect night vision.

Anointed scion (hidden): bound to House Wolf.

Inscrutable mind: +8 Mind.

Secret blood (hidden): conceals your Wolf bloodline.

<u>Skills</u>

Available skill slots: 0.

Light armor (current: 40. max: 140. Constitution, basic).

Dodging (current: 48. max: 200. Dexterity, basic).

Sneaking (current: 59. max: 200. Dexterity, basic).

Shortswords (current: 54. max: 200. Dexterity, basic).

Two-weapon fighting (current: 47. max: 200. Dexterity, advanced).
Thieving (current: 39. max: 200. Dexterity, basic).
Chi (current: 45. max: 410. Mind, advanced).
Meditation (current: 67. max: 410. Mind, basic).
Telekinesis (current: 43. max: 410. Mind, advanced).
Telepathy (current: 46. max: 410. Mind, advanced).
Insight (current: 60. max: 200. Perception, basic).
Deception (current: 55. max: 200. Perception, master).

Abilities

Dexterity ability slots used: 13 / 20.
crippling blow (Dexterity, basic, shortswords).
minor piercing strike (5 Dexterity, advanced, shortswords).
lesser backstab (5 Dexterity, advanced, sneaking).
basic trap disarm (Dexterity, basic, thieving).
simple lockpicking (Dexterity, basic, thieving).

Mind ability slots used: 8 / 41.
simple charm (Mind, basic, telepathy).
stunning slap (Mind, basic, chi).
one-step (Mind, basic, telekinesis).
minor reaction buff (Mind, basic, chi).
simple astral blade (Mind, basic, telepathy).
short shadow blink (Mind, basic, telekinesis).
minor chi heal (Mind, basic, chi).
simple mind shield (Mind, basic, meditation).

Perception ability slots used: 14 / 20.
improved analyze (5 Perception, advanced, insight).
lesser trap detect (Perception, basic, thieving).
conceal small weapon (Perception, basic, deception).
facial disguise (Perception, basic, deception).
ventro (Perception, basic, deception).
lesser imitate (5 Perception, advanced, deception).

Other abilities:
simple mindsight (Class, basic, telepathy).

Known Key Points

Sector 14,913 exit portal and safe zone.
Sector 12,560 nether portal and safe zone.

Equipped

spider's bite shortsword (+15% damage, webbed), concealed.
ebonheart (+30% damage), concealed.
common fighter's sash (+3 shortswords).
enchanted leather armor set (+20% damage reduction, −35% Dexterity and Magic).

slotted potion belt (2 minor heal, 4 moderate heal, 3 full heal, 1 antitoxin).
common thief's cloak (+3 sneaking).
apprentice's ring (+2 Magic).
acolyte's ring (+2 Faith).
troll's talisman bracelet (+6% damage reduction).
gift of the unbound ring (immunity to tier-1 and tier-2 entanglement spells).
band of stillness ring (immunity to tier-1 and tier-2 Mind spells).

<u>Backpack Contents (Key Items)</u>

<u>Money</u>: 4 gold, 6 silver, and 0 copper.
Loot (4 x enchanted rings, 2 x enchanted robes, 3 x spellcasters wands).
2 x iron daggers.
1 x alchemy stone (0 / 150 ingredients).
1 x common mage's cloak (+3 air magic).
1 x portal scroll.
1 x coil of rope.
1 x shortsword,+1 (+15% damage, +10 shortswords).
1 x rank 5 wyvern poison.
5 x smoke bombs.
5 x fire bombs.
1 x tavern bill of ownership.

<u>Alchemy Stone Contents</u>

None.

<u>Bank Contents</u>

<u>Money</u>: 1,046 gold, 4 silver, and 9 copper.
2 x full healing potions.
2 x basic steel shortswords.

<u>Open Tasks</u>

An Alchemist's Bounty (kill the wyvern mother).
Find the Last Wolf Envoy (hidden) (find Ceruvax).
Stay True to Wolf (hidden) (acquire a mana-based Class).

"Ah," I murmured, pleased with my growth. I had advanced significantly during my time in the valley and when I left would do so with a wealth of abilities.

Now to make certain I can actually leave. Despite all my planning, I knew that escaping the sector still wouldn't be easy. Especially with the need to ensure the pack remained safe.

"Do not worry about us. The pack will survive," a voice intruded. *"We have for centuries."*

I turned toward the cave entrance. Duggar stood there.

"You heard me?" I asked.

"Not entirely," the alpha said. *"I only caught the tail end of your thoughts as I walked in."*

"Night has fallen?" I asked.

"*It has.*"

Popping the last ration cube in my mouth, I rose to my feet. "Where are the others?"

"*Still resting,*" Duggar answered. He watched me pick up my pack and check my weapons. "*You're leaving?*"

I nodded. "I must. My Pact with Erebus is about to expire, and soon his followers will begin hunting me in earnest. Before that happens, there's much I still need to do."

"*We will help,*" Duggar said, sitting down on his haunches.

I shook my head. I had already involved the pack too much in my own troubles, and they had suffered enough grievous losses of their own. I couldn't imperil them again. "No," I said. "I have a plan."

"*But you are uncertain if it will work,*" Duggar stated.

I looked at the alpha in surprise. He was still reading my thoughts.

"*You may have become one of House Wolf's anointed,*" Duggar said, amusement tracing his voice, "*but you still have much to learn.*" He paused. "*Your thoughts are unshielded, wolfkin, and for those who know how, they are easy to read.*"

I should do something about that. Recalling what Ceruvax had told me, I constructed a half mind shield about my thoughts.

It was easier than I'd expected, and in the future I would have to remember to keep it active. "Better?" I asked, looking at Duggar.

"*Better,*" the alpha agreed. "*Now, how can we help?*" he asked, serious once more.

His offer was heartfelt, I realized. "Why?" I asked, staring at him searchingly. I was certain he knew better than me the peril he would be placing the wolves in by aiding me. "You've seen my thoughts. You know my actions have endangered your people already. Why help me now?"

"*You are pack,*" Duggar answered simply. "*And the pack is all.*"

He had not, I noted, mentioned my new status as a scion of House Wolf. It seemed to mean less to the alpha than it did to Sulan.

"Alright," I said. "This is the plan..."

✴   ✴   ✴

I left the dire wolves' hideout accompanied only by Duggar and Sulan. Both elders had wanted a larger contingent of wolves to accompany us, but I had refused. It was enough that I was risking two of the pack's most senior wolves. I wouldn't endanger the pack further.

The three of us traveled swiftly. Our destination, of course, was the wyvern's den on the western rim of the valley. Before I could do anything further, I had to find and destroy the shield generator.

But to do that, I first had to deal with the wyvern mother. Somehow.

Despite my growth and even with my companions' assistance, I was certain slaying the wyvern was beyond us, and truthfully I had every intention of trying to avoid a fight if I could help it. It was less risky for me to sneak in and destroy the generator while Sulan and Duggar distracted the beast.

The two wolves set a hard pace, running tirelessly through the forest. Jogging behind the pair, I did my best to keep up. The hours passed quickly, and close to midnight we neared the center of the valley.

Suddenly, both my companions stopped short.

I slowed to a halt behind them. *"What's wrong?"* I asked, using mind speech.

Sulan slunk lower. *"Goblins ahead,"* she said in a clipped tone.

"Lots of goblins," Duggar added, his gaze filling with predatory intent. *"A few hundred at least."*

"Goblins?" I tilted my head to the side and listened intently. No revealing sound carried to me on the night air, but then again, the wolves' senses were sharper than my own. *"We must be near the site of the battle,"* I murmured.

Following the direction of the wolves' pointing snouts, I gazed to the north and deliberated with myself for a moment before coming to a decision. *"Wait here. I'm going to check it out."*

"Why?" Duggar asked, sounding perplexed.

I wasn't entirely sure myself. I doubted there was anything I could do to manipulate events further—especially if players were present. But knowing how much longer the battle would drag out would be useful. If nothing else, it would tell me how much time I had before the Howlers returned to their fort. *"I won't be long,"* I assured the pair.

"We'll come with you," Sulan said.

"No," I said. *"There's less chance of me being detected alone, and while I may not be as good as you two yet, I'm no slouch when it comes to sneaking."*

The dire wolves were silent for a moment. *"Very well,"* Duggar said. *"We shall wait."*

✳ ✳ ✳

Wrapped in shadows, I crept through the forest foliage, following Duggar's directions to the goblins. It took far longer than I'd expected for me to reach them.

Exiting the tree line, I found myself in a large glade—the same clearing where I had fought the wyvern hatchling a few days ago, in fact.

Many more corpses littered the clearing today.

The battlefield was quiet and abandoned, but scores of goblins had died here earlier. Their bodies lay where they had fallen. As far as I could tell, there were as many bearing the insignia of the Red Rats as those wearing the garb of the Howlers. I tiptoed through the bloodied grass and tangled limbs. Here and there, I spotted the odd non-goblin.

Players have fought in the battle too.

While the number of dead was high, they didn't account for the greater part of the Red Rats and Howler forces. Lifting my head, I studied the surroundings and, through the trees, spotted campfires on my left and right.

The camps of the two opposing armies.

Do they mean to resume battle tomorrow? It seemed that way.

Picking a direction at random, I edged closer.

The camp I ventured toward had been established among the trees, and straight away I could tell it belonged to the Howlers.

The perimeter was too well guarded for me to penetrate it easily. Scaling a nearby tree, I perched on a bough to observe the occupants. The goblins sat around their campfires, ten or twenty to a group, eating and talking animatedly. They appeared in good spirits.

That must mean they're winning.

I didn't spare the goblins further notice though as my attention was snatched by a more arresting sight. Strolling at ease between the Howlers' tents were dozens of black-garbed figures. Each was armored for war and bore items that proudly displayed the insignia of a raging bull.

Tartans.

So, Talon's people are here, I thought, wondering if the captain himself was close by. As little as I feared the soldiers under Talon's command, the captain himself was something else altogether. *Best I don't attract his attention.*

Deciding to withdraw, I paused when I noticed a concentration of torches and magelights not too far from my present position. *What's going on there?*

The temptation to investigate further was too great to resist. Skipping lightly from tree to tree, I edged around the perimeter of the camp.

As I drew nearer, I saw that the ruckus was centered around a crowd of players. Their body language suggested the air was fraught with tension. Curious, I crept closer.

There wasn't one group of players at the spot in question, I realized, but two. The first was a company of Tartan soldiers. The second was a mob of Awakened Dead players.

And at their fore was Stayne.

I stopped dead, clinging to my treetop perch. *What is he doing here?* I wondered even as my pulse quickened. I was still too far to hear what was being said, even with my sharp hearing, but was wary about venturing any closer.

Stayne was in full battle dress, armored from shoulder to foot in sleek, shining, black armor. Only his distinctive skeletal head was uncovered.

Facing off against the undead player was Captain Talon. Dressed no different from when I had seen him in the safe zone, the Tartan envoy appeared calm and in control. Stayne, by contrast, leaned forward, red eyes boring into the captain and arms gesticulating wildly while he spoke.

There was no doubt Erebus' henchman was angry.

I bit my lip. Getting any closer was risky, but I desperately wanted to listen in on the pair's conversation.

I edged closer.

But I had taken no more than a dozen steps when the captain turned around and—almost idly—ran his gaze along the treetops.

I froze, not deceived by the casual manner of Talon's scrutiny. Even though I was still many yards distant, the captain had sensed something amiss.

It's not worth it. I couldn't risk being found out, or worse yet, being detained, not when I was so close to escaping. Retracing my steps carefully, I backed away.

My curiosity would have to remain unsatisfied.

Chapter 144: A Reckoning

Day Six. Midnight.

I made it safely away from the Howler camp without being detected.

While I made my way back to the wolves, my mind picked at the unexpected turn of events. That Stayne and Talon had been talking worried me. Would they compare stories and uncover the web of lies I had woven? And if so, could I expect imminent pursuit? *Damnation!* Hurrying my steps, I raced to rejoin my waiting companions.

A hostile entity has detected you! You are no longer hidden.

I stilled.

Standing not three yards away was Captain Talon.

How in the hells did he get ahead of me? I checked my mindsight, but it was empty. So not only had Talon somehow teleported himself directly to my location, he was shielded from detection too.

"I should kill you," the envoy said conversationally.

My gaze flitted over the surrounding foliage, but I spotted no one else. The captain was alone. Despite this, with his hands folded behind his back, he appeared completely at ease.

I eyed the sheathed blade at Talon's side. "And why is that?" I asked casually.

"Still playing games?" Talon remarked. "It's no use. The shaman told me everything."

Ah. "So you know," I said, deliberately relaxing my own stance. If it came to a fight, I doubted I would survive long.

"I do," Talon said evenly. "I know it was *you* who told Hyek to attack the Red Rats. And I also suspect it was you who convinced the Red Rats to march on the Howlers."

I said nothing, not denying the accusation.

"Why did you do it?" Talon asked.

"I told you, I play my own game."

The captain nodded. "You did," he agreed.

Talon shifted. One moment he was standing calm and relaxed. The next, he was inches from my face holding a bare blade to my throat.

My eyes widened. I hadn't even seen the captain move. *Damn,* I thought. *I'm even more outmatched than I suspected.*

"Are you Light's lackey?" Talon whispered.

I blinked. "Of course not! That's preposterous. What would make you think that?"

For a drawn-out moment, Talon said nothing. "Is what happened at the fort your doing too?" he asked, ignoring my own question.

I frowned. "The fort? You mean the killings in the barracks? I already told you I did that."

"Not that."

I stared at him blankly. "Then what?"

He didn't answer.

"What's happened, Captain?" I tried again.

Once more, Talon paid my words no heed. "Do you know who the Light spy in the sector is?"

I kept my face smooth, betraying no reaction. Talon's phrasing made it clear he knew there *was* a spy. How had he figured that out? Was it something to do with what had happened in the fort? *And what could that bloody be?*

"It's not me, if that's what you're thinking," I said after a heartbeat.

Talon studied my face intently, then drew back, sheathing his sword in the same motion. "If you aren't a soldier of Light, why did you manipulate the goblins? Of what benefit is a war between them to you?"

I exhaled a relieved breath at Talon's withdrawal and laid a tentative hand on my throat. The skin was whole and unbroken. I turned back to the captain. "The war was not of my making."

Talon's face hardened, but before he could speak, I held up my hand for patience. "I didn't lie to you about the Red Rats. They *were* ordered by Erebus to raid the Howler patrols. And if the shaman really has told you everything, then you know the Howlers had the same orders from Ishita. This war is the Awakened Dead's doing, not mine."

"That may be true," Talon said, "but it is you who forced the two tribes into a pitched battle, and you still haven't told me why."

"Because having them war with each other served my own ends." I sighed. "You want the truth, Captain? The truth is I don't want this sector to fall to the Dark." I held his gaze. "Be it into the Awakened Dead's hands or yours."

"And why is that?" Talon asked softly.

"I don't trust Erebus," I said bluntly, then stared unflinchingly into the captain's eyes again. "*Or* his allies."

"Tartar is nothing like Erebus," the captain said, his own voice harsh. "And our alliance with the Awakened Dead is one of convenience. I told you—"

"No offense, Captain," I said, interrupting him, "but in my short time in the Game, I've had more than my fair share of run-ins with the Powers, and nothing I've experienced would make me put my faith in any of them. They are *all* untrustworthy."

Talon stared at me for a second. "I can see that you truly believe that." He blew out a frustrated breath. "And sadly, I can't say I blame you, Michael. I've received reports of Erebus' treatment of his so-called candidates. What goes on in that dungeon of his..." The captain shook his head in disgust. "It's unforgivable."

"Then you understand," I said.

"I do," he said heavily. For a moment, the captain said nothing more, then one side of his mouth twisted upward. "And besides, matters in the sector have turned out better than I could have hoped for."

I couldn't hold back a start of surprise at that.

Talon chuckled at my expression. "I have proof of Erebus' treachery," he said, ticking off points on his fingers. "I have secured the alliance of one of the largest goblin tribes for the god-emperor, and most importantly—" his face widened into a genuine smile—"the Tartan legions can now move openly against the Awakened Dead. And for all that I have you to thank."

"So you're not angry then?" I quipped.

"Oh, I'm angry. Both at your betrayal and your manipulations," the captain said, his eyes taking on a dangerous hue. He paused, letting the moment draw out.

A bead of sweat dripped down my brow. I ignored it. *Damn, am I going to die here after all?*

"But I won't kill you," Talon finished finally. "In the end, you've served Tartar just as well as if you had done what I'd asked."

I nodded slowly, if a bit uncertainly. Despite all my machinations, it did seem like I'd only furthered the god-emperor's own ends. Had everything I'd done been for nothing?

No. The captain may have gotten what he wanted, but so had I. There were just two things left undone.

I snuck a glance at the captain. The ominous gleam had faded from his eyes, and he was smiling again. Seeing that, I questioned him on a matter that had been troubling me. "What is Stayne doing here?"

Talon pursed his lips as he considered whether to answer me or not. "He came to broker a truce between the tribes."

My eyebrows lifted at that.

"Shaman Hyek and I refused."

I chuckled, imagining how well Stayne had taken the news. "What will happen now?" I asked.

"War. War will happen," Talon said with obvious relish. "Tomorrow, the Red Rats and Stayne shall feel the wrath of the Tartan legions, and by week's end, I expect this sector will be free of the Awakened Dead's scourge."

"Now, that's an outcome I can live with," I said with a smile of my own. "Does Stayne know about my involvement?" I asked, wondering if I could expect a bigger bounty to be placed on me.

Talon shook his head. "He doesn't. Nor will he learn the truth from me."

I inclined my head. The captain was doing me more favors than I had any right to expect. "Why?" I asked.

Without being told, the captain seemed to understand the thrust of my question. "There is something about you, Michael... I believe you will survive your current vendetta with the Awakened Dead. One day, I suspect, you will be a great player, and when that day comes, I hope to make better use of you."

"So what? I'm an investment?" I joked.

"Yes," Talon said bluntly. "When that day comes, I expect you to remember this moment." Reaching into his pocket, the captain pulled out something and tossed it at me. I caught it automatically.

Glancing down, I studied the object in my hand and saw that it was a coin stamped with the symbol of the Tartan legion.

You have acquired a token of Tartar. This item cannot be stolen, traded, or lost, even upon death.

"What's this?" I asked.

"It's a token of goodwill from the legions and the next best thing to bearing a Mark of Tartar," Talon said. "Show it to any of the legions anywhere in the Forever Kingdom, and it will earn you a hearing at least from their commander."

"Thank you," I said gravely.

"You best be gone then," Talon said. "I have a war to oversee."

"Goodbye, Talon," I said and turned around.

"Oh, and, Michael, one more thing," the captain said.

At his words, I paused in my step and glanced over my shoulder. "Yes?"

Talon held my gaze. "A final word of warning. If I see you again in this sector, I will kill you—without hesitation and without warning. Understood?"

"Message received, Captain," I murmured as I disappeared into the trees. "Message received."

Chapter 145: Into the Viper's Nest

Day Seven. Dawn.

The rest of our journey was thankfully without incident, and when dawn broke on my seventh day in the sector, the jagged mountain cliffs that bordered the western side of the valley came into sight.

Today was the last day of my Pact with Erebus, and while some of my urgency to escape had dissipated, I still wanted to leave the sector quickly.

"I can smell the beast," Duggar said, hackles raised. *"She is up there now."*

I glanced from the alpha to the mountain ahead. The three of us were standing at the edge of the tree line, which ended less than fifty yards from the cliffs.

Before us, the mountain rose up in a vertical wall of rock that outstripped even the forest's tallest trees. The roof of the cliff was flat, almost as if it had been sheared off. Near the top, I also spied a series of darkened holes that seemed large enough for the wyvern mother to pass through.

"Are those caves I see up there?" I asked.

"Indeed," Duggar replied. *"The pack has observed the wyvern and her hatchling enter and leave them on multiple occasions."*

"Which cave is she in now?" I asked.

"We can't tell from here," Sulan said. *"It's too far for even us to sniff out the exact location of her scent."*

I pursed my lips thoughtfully as I measured the height of the cliff. It was considerable. "How do we get up?"

"Through that tunnel," Duggar said, gesturing at the base of the rockface. *"The inside of the cliff is riddled with tunnels. That particular one winds through the rock and connects with the caves above."*

I looked where the alpha pointed and, sure enough, spotted a darkened entrance half-hidden by shrubbery. The hole appeared small. It would be a tight fit, especially for Duggar, the largest member of our party. "You're sure it goes all the way to the top?"

"Yes," he replied.

"Alright, let's go," I said.

"I'll go first," the alpha said, and before I could stop him the big wolf faded into the darkness and padded toward the entrance.

"You better hurry," Sulan said from behind me, *"or he will leave you."*

I dashed forward, slipping into the cliff's shadows and following in the alpha's wake.

✳ ✳ ✳

I was right, the tunnel was a tight fit, and the three of us were forced to travel single file. I was in the center, Sulan brought up the rear, while Duggar remained on point.

At first the tunnel delved horizontally through the rock and navigating it was easy. But after a few dozen paces, the passage turned sharply upward, going through a series of twists and turns that, at times, compelled us to leap, climb, or contort ourselves weirdly. Fortunately, though, the wolves and I were agile enough to manage the challenge.

Still, it was rough going.

We had been in a tunnel for twenty minutes already, and I judged we were less than a third of the way up. Realizing this wouldn't be a quick journey, my thoughts began to drift.

I wondered how the wolves found this tunnel. Had they found an occasion to sneak up on the wyvern before? They must have. But more concerning than this idle speculation was my growing worry as to the shield generator's location.

As pocketed as the cliff was with caves and tunnels, I realized Ishita's sworn could have concealed the shield generator in any one of its many nooks or crannies.

God, I hope they haven't hidden it. Otherwise, I may never—

"Stop!" Sulan ordered abruptly, interrupting my musings.

I stilled, as did Duggar ahead. *"What is it?"* the alpha asked tersely.

"There's something ahead," Sulan said, sinking down to all fours.

My brows furrowed. If there was danger, Duggar, the one on point, should have detected it first. Reaching out with my mindsight, I probed the tunnel ahead, but except for the three of us, it was empty. My frown deepened.

"I see nothing," Duggar said, sounding just as perplexed. He sniffed the air. *"I smell nothing either."*

"They are concealed," Sulan said. No doubt tinged her mindvoice. *"The cloak around their bodies is too well woven for me to penetrate, but the shields surrounding their minds are less well-crafted. I can discern their minds' absence in the aether."*

"They?" I asked sharply, picking out the most important bit of the information Sulan had imparted. *"How many are we talking about?"*

Sulan was silent for a heartbeat. *"I count twenty, less than two dozen yards ahead."*

Twenty was a sizable number. And if they were hiding so well that Sulan barely sensed them—and Duggar and I not at all—those ahead couldn't be here by happenstance. Once more, I opened my mindsight and searched the area. But again, I detected nothing out of the ordinary.

Still, I didn't doubt the dire wolf elder.

There were enemies ahead. Ones well equipped and prepared for us—or rather, me. *"What can you tell me about the tunnel ahead?"* I asked Duggar.

"It turns sharply a few yards from here, then widens for a short stretch," he replied. *"That's where they must be."* He glanced over his shoulder at me. *"Wait here. I will go take a closer look."*

I hesitated, wanting to assume the risk myself, but Duggar had demonstrated time and again that his own stealth was superior to mine, and against hostiles of unknown capabilities, he was the better choice of scout.

"Go," I said. *"But don't be long."*

* * *

The alpha was gone for five long minutes.

He had vanished so completely into the darkness that I got no whiff of him either with my mindsight or my physical senses. But Sulan assured me Duggar was alright, and I schooled myself to patiently wait for his return.

"Sulan was not mistaken," Duggar said, emerging out of thin air less than three feet from me.

I nearly jumped in fright at his sudden appearance, much to the amusement of the two dire wolves. *"Tell me,"* I said with a scowl at the laughing wolf.

"Just like Sulan said, there are twenty of them. Ten on either side of the tunnel. Their shielding is almost perfect," he added with grudging admiration, *"but from up close, I was able to see beneath their cloaking."*

"Who are they?" I asked, suspecting goblins. Only the Howler shaman had known of my eventual destination. Had Hyek betrayed me?

"Players. They're well-armed too, wolfkin," the alpha said, his tone grave. *"Two are mages. The rest are heavy fighters dressed in full plate mail."* He shook his head ruefully. *"I fear neither tooth nor claw will penetrate their armor. We will not be of much use to you in this fight."*

Players. That was more worrying. With the goblins, at least I knew what I was up against, but against players, I had to be ready for anything. *"Is this the only way up the cliff?"*

Sulan bobbed her head. *"It is the only quick route. The other way will require us to travel aboveground, over the mountain itself, and that will take days."*

So. Not only had my foes guessed my destination, but they had figured out the route I'd take too. *They must be Awakened Dead players.*

The question was, what did I do about it? I couldn't turn back. There was no other viable way up. That left only one option: fighting.

I turned back to the patiently waiting wolves. *"Here's what we do..."*

* * *

I crept forward alone, every motion made with deliberate care and pausing between each step.

My abundance of caution was perhaps unnecessary. Not even the smallest sliver of light alleviated the darkness in the tunnel, making it perfect for sneaking. But I wasn't about to underestimate my foes. They had known enough to prepare this much, so I could expect them to be ready to combat those of my abilities that were common knowledge.

A few yards ahead the passage twisted abruptly, revealing the widened stretch of corridor Duggar had spoken of. I stopped, studying the area intently.

The tunnel section ahead was about three yards across and mostly level with only a slight upward slant. It continued in this manner for about ten yards before narrowing again and twisting sharply out of sight. My gaze roved the darkness, trying to pick out the hidden figures the dire wolves had spotted.

I failed.

Hmm... I inched forward again, each foot meticulously placed. Step by step, I drew closer to the ambush spot until, finally, I entered the widened tunnel section.

You have failed a magical resistance check!
An unknown hostile entity has failed to detect you! You remain hidden.

Mid-motion, I stilled as I considered the strange Game alerts. I'd failed a magical resistance check? Did that mean I'd been attacked? Suspecting a trap of some sort, I extended my senses and cast trap detect.

You have failed to spot any traps.

My brows crinkled in confusion as I uncovered nothing out of the ordinary. *What does it mean?* I had no idea, but the important thing was that I was still hidden.

And truly, I had no choice but to proceed. I took another step.

An unknown number of hostile entities have failed to detect you!

This time the Game message was comfortingly familiar, and I ignored it while I listened intently. Almost, I thought, I heard the faint sound of breathing. Was I close enough to my targets? I couldn't be sure. Tightening my grasp on the object in my hand, I took another step.

Then another.

An unknown number of hostile entities have failed to detect you!

I paused. My foes still hadn't revealed themselves, and the prudent course would be to act now while I remained undetected.

But I was still less than a yard into the ambush spot, and when the time came, I wanted to clear the widened tunnel section in a single shadow blink. The spell's range was only nine yards, after all.

I crept forward again. *Nearly there.*

You have failed a magical resistance check!
You have passed a mental resistance check!
A hostile entity has failed to detect you. You remain hidden.

There it was again. Another strange series of Game messages, and this time one even more confusing. I bit my lip, wondering what to do. *Proceeding further will be foolish, but I have to—*

"Something's wrong," an unseen voice whispered.

I froze, my gaze locking onto the spot where it had originated. There was nothing there. Or so my eyes told me.

"What?" hissed a second voice.

I knew *that* voice. It was Forsyth, the spellsword and leader of the gang that had attempted ambushing me in the Howler fort. *So, he's decided to try again. Not much good it will do him.*

Though, I had to concede the spellsword was better prepared this time around. I could no more detect him than I could the first speaker.

"Something tripped my ward," the first said.

Ward? What ward?

I tensed in concern. Was that what had prompted the strange Game messages? *It must've been,* I thought, worrying suddenly that I'd underestimated my foes.

Biting back the temptation to act—whether by fleeing or attacking—I stood completely still. If the players hadn't detected me yet, there was still a chance they wouldn't. And if I kept listening, maybe I could learn more of their ward's nature.

"Quiet then! Or you'll scare him off!" Forsyth snapped.

"What do you take me for?" the first said, sounding offended. "I've cast a spell of revealing already. It found nothing. Whatever tripped my ward, it wasn't our quarry," he finished confidently.

I swallowed. The revealing spell must've been the second magical resistance check I'd failed. But despite failing to avoid it, my presence had still not been uncovered. Was that because I'd passed the mental resistance check?

"Cast a magelight," Forsyth ordered abruptly.

"A magelight?" asked the first, sounding startled. "Why?"

"He has high stealth, you fool!"

I could delay no longer. I had to put my own ploy into motion before I was uncovered. I inched closer. Judging from where the two spellcasters' voices had originated from, I guessed they were positioned at the rear of the ambush party. *Perfect.* I took another step forward and wound back my right arm.

Forsyth's companion was still arguing. "I think you're overreacting—" he continued derisively.

I didn't wait to hear him finish. Whipping forward my arm, I flung a fire bomb into the corridor.

It was time for more mayhem.

Chapter 146: A Flaming Mess

Day Seven. Morning.

The crinkle of shattering pottery echoed loudly in the tunnel's silence. Still hidden and poised on the balls of my feet, I waited.

A heartbeat later, flames roared out of the activated projectile. Shooting upward, they fell back down to envelop everything within a six-yard radius.

You have ignited a fire bomb, injuring fifteen hostile entities. An unknown number of hostile entities have failed to detect you!

I grinned. Crouched down outside the range of the bomb, I was untouched. Fortunately, I'd made certain to get detailed information from Gelar on his creations and had gauged my throw accurately. Even better, I'd chosen my target location well enough to hit the majority of my ambushers.

Meanwhile, pandemonium had broken out.

"Find him!"

"Don't let him escape!"

"Down your darkvision potions, now!"

Many players cried out in alarm, pain, or questions, but more importantly, they *moved*, breaking the cloaks of concealment woven around them.

Two seconds later, the bomb's flames vanished. But that mattered little. It had done what I'd intended.

You have detected a hidden entity.
You have detected a hidden entity.

...

You have detected a hidden entity.

A full twenty such messages scrolled through my vision, pinpointing the location of each of the ambushers.

Excellent.

Not delaying, I targeted the rearmost player—Forsyth—and shadow blinked behind him.

A hostile entity has failed to detect you!

Clearly, the spellsword hadn't downed his own potion yet. Or if he had, it wasn't helping him much. Whatever the case, the mage was oblivious to my presence at his rear. Nor did I alert him.

As tempting a target as Forsyth's broad back made, I let the opportunity pass by and silently withdrew a second object from my pocket.

"God damnit, Zeera! Summon a bloody magelight!" the spellsword roared. "And the rest of you, drink those damn darkvision potions already!" he finished before muttering under his breath, presumably to complete a casting of his own.

Unfortunately for my hunters, I'd anticipated their next move—the magelights, not the potions—and had a counter ready. Hurling my arm forward again, I released the bomb in my hand.

You have ignited a smoke bomb, creating a smoke cloud.

Thick plumes burst out to blanket the tunnel in dense gray clouds, instantly blinding everyone caught in its grasp. The smoke bomb's radius was twice that of the fire bomb, and this time there was no escaping it.

I made sure to shut my eyes before the cloud rushed past my own position. My night vision wasn't proof against the smoke, and it would blind me as completely as it had the ambushers, but I didn't need to see for what I planned next.

Keeping my eyes shut, I withdrew my other four fire bombs and tossed them blindly one after the other, transforming the tunnel into a killing ground.

You have ignited a fire bomb, injuring twelve hostile entities.

You have ignited a fire bomb, injuring eighteen hostile entities. Two unknown players have died.

You have ignited a fire bomb, injuring five hostile entities. Eight unknown players have died.

You have ignited a fire bomb, injuring six hostile entities. Four unknown players have died.

In a matter of moments, nearly three-quarters of the ambushers died. I'd spent my fire bombs lavishly to accomplish that much, but the enemy had given me no choice.

The player party had been too big for the wolves and me to handle, especially considering how well prepared they'd appeared to be.

My work done, I swung around and, using my hands to guide me, fled further down the passage. Once I exited the smoke, I drew my blades and turned.

Only six of my hunters remained alive and, as shellshocked as they must be from their sudden transition to prey, I was sure most were only thinking of escape.

A second later, a coughing and red-eyed figure stumbled toward me.

It was Forsyth.

Flowing forward, I cut downward with ebonheart while thrusting forward with spider's bite.

You have killed Forsyth.

The mage's mouth opened in a silent O of surprise as he died. Letting the corpse slide off my blade, I reset my stance and waited.

Another figure emerged from the smoke. An armored brute. Before he could spot me, I shadow blinked behind him and drove my sword straight through his torso while simultaneously casting piercing strike.

You have backstabbed your target for 100% more damage! You have killed Terry.

The fighter died with as little protest as Forsyth. Leaving him where he had fallen, I returned to my original position and readied myself again.

* * *

No other players came through.

A minute after the last wisp of smoke disappeared, Duggar and Sulan emerged. "How many did you get?" I asked the wolves.

"Four," Duggar replied.

I sheathed my blades. "Good. Then that's all of them. Will you two stand guard while I loot the bodies?"

At the pair's nod of acquiescence, I slipped past them to check on the corpses. Those that had been caught in the raging fire had been burned nearly to cinders. Little remained of them except scorched pieces of plate armor, all of which were too heavy for me to lug around.

More surprising, none of those who made it out of the flames carried anything of value either. It was almost as if the ambushers had prepared for the possibility of defeat.

I smiled wryly. *I guess that means they're taking me more seriously now.*

As I walked back to the wolves, I attended to the waiting Game messages, investing my new attribute points in the process.

You have reached level 74!

Your sneaking has increased to level 61. Your two-weapon fighting has increased to level 48. Your light armor has increased to level 41. Your telekinesis has increased to level 45.

Your Magic has increased to rank 5 (+2 from item).

"Now what?" Duggar asked as I rejoined them.

"Now we find the wyvern," I replied. "And hopefully the shield generator."

* * *

It took us nearly an hour to traverse the remainder of the tunnel and reach the larger caves at the top of the cliff. While we journeyed through the rock, I worried at the mystery of finding Forsyth and his ilk here.

How had they known I'd be here?

Hyek could have told them, but I didn't think that was likely. From what Talon had said, it seemed clear that the Howlers had broken all ties with the Awakened Dead and thrown in their lot with the Tartan legion.

Worca, I decided. *It had to have been her.*

I had questioned the elven mage about the generator's location, and Ishita's sworn must have set up the ambush on the off-chance I would discover its location.

Pity they didn't come themselves. I would have enjoyed killing more of the Power's lackeys.

"Wolfkin," Duggar said, drawing my attention. *"We're here."*

I blinked, turning my attention outward again. The narrow winding passage we'd been traveling through had come to an end, terminating in a t-junction. The new tunnel, stretching away into the distance to my left and right, was many times larger.

Big enough for even the wyvern mother to fit through.

"Something isn't right," Sulan said.

I glanced at her. *Another ambush?* "What do you mean?"

The white wolf sat down on her haunches, her eyes darting back and forth down both ends of the corridor in a troubled manner. *"I sense too many life signs."*

I straightened, hand unconsciously dropping to my blades. "More players?" I asked.

"Likely," Sulan pronounced. *"But there is no immediate danger,"* she said, sensing my tension. Jerking her head to the left, she said, *"Far down that way, there are four minds concealed in the same manner as the players we encountered below."* Gesturing to the right, she added, *"And about the same distance that way, there are two consciousnesses. One is the wyvern mother. Even from here, I can sense the power of her mind."*

Two minds? My brows furrowed. "What's the other?" I asked, looking to the right.

"I'm not sure," Sulan admitted.

My frown deepened. "Could it be a hatchling?"

Sulan shook her head. *"No, the other mind is definitely no wyvern. Their minds are distinctly... serpentine."*

"I see," I said. The white wolf's revelations were troubling, and as grateful as I was to her for them, our time together had come to an end. I realized in the tunnels' confines that my original idea of using the wolves to distract the wyvern was too risky. I would have to uncover the mystery on my own. I glanced at Duggar. "This is where you must leave me."

"Are you sure, wolfkin?" he asked. *"We can aid you further if you allow us."*

"It's too dangerous," I said. "You have done more than I could have hoped for by bringing me this far, and I am grateful, but now it's time for you and Sulan to turn back. The rest is up to me."

"Don't be foolish, pup—" Sulan began.

I slashed my hand downward. "No, Sulan. This time I will not allow myself to be swayed. The wyvern mother is too grave a threat."

"You think you can face her alone?" she retorted.

I shook my head. "I don't. But if I die, I will be reborn. You will not."

Sulan growled deep in her throat. *"Still, this is—"*

"Leave him be, Sulan," Duggar interjected. *"He's right. And besides, this is the scion's decision to make."*

In the face of her alpha's childing, the white wolf subsided. Duggar turned to me. *"This is farewell then."*

I nodded. *"But we shall meet again, I promise."*

The pack leader turned and slipped back into the small tunnel. *"We shall, scion, and good luck."* Without further ado, he disappeared.

Sulan waited a moment longer. *"Do not disappoint us, pup,"* she said. *"We are depending on you."*

"I'll make sure the wyvern doesn't threaten the pack again," I assured her.

"I'm not referring to the wyvern mother, foolish human," Sulan said, holding my gaze. *"You are more important to the pack than that. You carry with you the promise of Wolf. Only you hold the key to the ancients' return."* She turned and slipped into the tunnel, following in the wake of her pack leader.

"Don't disappoint us, pup," the white wolf repeated. *"Remember, we are counting on you."*

Chapter 147: The Gang of Four

I followed Sulan with my gaze until she vanished entirely but didn't immediately move on. Crouching down low, I examined the passage in both directions. To the left it sloped gently downward, and to the right it angled upward.

The darkness in the tunnel wasn't absolute either. There were cracks in the ceiling through which light filtered in. Recalling the glimpse I'd caught of the cliff from outside, I realized the tunnel must run along the surface of the clifftop.

Which direction to explore first?

Left, I decided. Before tackling the wyvern herself, I needed to know what other surprises lay in the tunnel complex. Fading into the darkness, I crept through the pools of shadow, deftly avoiding the beams of light shining down.

My mindsight was open, and my attention was fixed on what was before me. Every so often, I stopped and slowed my breathing to listen intently. I couldn't afford to be caught off guard by whatever lay ahead, and without Sulan's sharp senses, I had to make do with my own less-capable ones.

It almost made me regret sending the wolves away, but I wouldn't subject the pair to the same risks I took with my own life.

As laborious as my advance was, I persisted in the same stop-start manner for the next twenty minutes.

Eventually, my abundance of caution paid off.

During one of my periodic stops, while crouched down behind a large rock and straining my ears, I picked out the faint thread of a conversation.

"... should go..."

The voice echoed weirdly as if coming from far off. Judging it safe, I crept out from behind the rock and into the center of the tunnel.

"... why do... have to guard it."

The speakers were still too indistinct to identify clearly. Deciding the risk was worth the gain, I advanced silently forward.

"... the shield generator... too important... the likes of... to protect."

I kept going.

"... stop panicking. Nothing is out there."

I drew to a halt. I'd finally drawn close enough that the voices were fully audible, and I'd recognized the last speaker too. It was Worca.

Ishita's sworn were here. *All of them?* I wondered.

"... my ward activated!"

That was Ishan. Also talking about a ward. *What are those bloody things?* More worrying still: if I *had* tripped a ward again, why had the Game not provided me with a warning message like it had earlier against Forsyth's group?

"Relax, it's probably just the wyvern," Lutra said, sounding bored. He was the other human mage.

"It can't be the beast," Ishan insisted. "It's him! I'm telling you! *All* of my wards were tripped this time."

"*If* it is him, you've likely already given away our position with your chatter," Worca said wryly.

"And I told you, you set too many of those damn wards," Lutra chimed in. "Why in bloody hell would we need *three* detection wards?"

"Easy for you to scoff," Ishan muttered. "*You* aren't on your last life."

"Lutra is right," another interjected. That was Xrex, the leader of the four. "It must be the beast roaming the tunnels again. Just be thankful you haven't drawn her attention again, Ishan. Do I need to remind you how well it went the last time she came here?"

"But—"

"Enough, you imbecile!" Xrex hissed. "I swear if you don't still your tongue, I will strangle you myself!

Xrex's scolding worked. The human must have believed the lizardman, because he spoke no more. *Poor Ishan,* I thought, almost feeling sorry for the mage.

"Besides, there's no need to worry," Lutra added soothingly. "I don't care how good a sneak that bastard is, he ain't getting through my paralyzing wards."

Crouched in the center of the tunnel, I very carefully did not move. Fear urged me to flee, but I stayed in place, waiting to hear what else the four mages would reveal.

Unfortunately, it appeared their conversation was over. Realizing there was nothing more to gain, I retreated to plan my next move.

❊　❊　❊

I returned to my starting point.

Sitting cross-legged in the t-junction, I considered what I'd learned. All four of Ishita's sworn were here, and only one thing could have drawn them this far out of the safe zone: the shield generator.

It must be in the same cave they're in.

If not for the fragments of the conversation I'd overheard, knowing that much would have caused me to rush in. Despite being alone and unaided, with darkness on my side I fancied my chances against the mages.

But.

But the repeated reference to wards gave me pause. I hadn't detected any of Ishan's wards in the passage, despite activating trap detect on my way back to the t-junction.

The wards were either not considered traps or beyond my ability to detect.

Either way, I couldn't afford to charge the mages, not when they had prepared the ground to their benefit already. I shuddered, imagining being paralyzed and at the mercy of the four.

304

I have to find another way to get to them. My lips pursed, I gazed up the right tunnel. *Perhaps...*

I rose to my feet.

It was time to find the wyvern mother.

✻   ✻   ✻

I slipped into the shadows as I crept up the tunnel.

Keeping my mindsight open, I moved cautiously, though I wasn't overly concerned about being detected. I'd successfully hidden from the wyvern in the forest, and this time around my sneaking was higher and the environment more conducive.

Nearly one hundred steps later, the tunnel began to brighten. I was close to the cave mouth, I realized. I slowed my advance but kept going.

A little later, I arrived at a second t-junction. To my right was blue sky and bright morning sun—the cave opening set in the cliff face—while to my left was darkness—the wyvern's lair.

Turning left, I slid along the side of the tunnel as I advanced into the beast's den. In a few dozen yards, the shadows in the passage became comfortingly thick again, and not far off I could hear the sound of dripping water. Beneath that, there was another noise as well.

The sound of heavy breathing.

The wyvern mother.

Pressing my back against the rock, I cocked my head to the side to listen.

The wyvern's breathing sounded harsh and guttural. Rising and falling in an even tempo, it sent faint vibrations rippling through the ground on each crescendo.

Is she... snoring?

It certainly sounded that way.

My confidence buoyed, I crept further down the passage. With each step, the beast's snores grew more distinct. I kept going. I had the vague inkling of a plan, but I needed to set eyes on the wyvern before I could determine how viable it was.

A minute later, a bright, burning ball appeared on the edge of my mindsight. The wyvern mother was close. A yard ahead, the tunnel turned sharply downward, hiding what lay beyond. Both the sound of running water and the beast's breathing had increased too. Stretching flat across the ground, I slid forward.

Cresting the top of the tunnel slope, I glance down.

Below me, the tunnel widened into a cavern. A gurgling stream flowed directly through its center. Curled up on the ground, with her head lying in the water, was the wyvern mother.

The beast's eyes were closed, and her wings were tightly furled against her side. Like this, she seemed almost peaceful and no threat, but I wasn't deceived.

If the beast awoke, she would kill me in a heartbeat.

Staying where I was, I let my eyes rove over the area. Unlike the rest of the tunnel complex, the wyvern's cave wasn't barren. Shrubbery, glowing mushrooms, and even some flowers peeked through the rocky outcroppings. Maybe it was the presence of water and the weak light filtering down from the roof that allowed them to grow so.

Why did the wyvern choose this cave in particular? I wondered in idle speculation as I continued to scan the surroundings. *Is it the greenery that—*

My thoughts broke off.

Beyond the beast's dominating bulk, I spotted a smallish body stretched out across the moss-covered ground.

Is that... a person?

From this far away I couldn't tell, but the shape did look humanoid. Whatever it was, it was outside the range of my mindsight, and I wasn't about to risk venturing into the cave itself.

It has to be a person or at least something living. Sulan did say she sensed two minds in this direction.

But why would the wyvern mother tolerate anything—much less a person—to live in her den? *Only one way to find out.* Reaching out with my will, I analyzed the unknown figure.

The target is Saya, a gnomish alchemist. She is a player and bears Marks of Lesser Dark.

My brows drew down in consternation. What was a player doing here? *And one without a level.* I paused as I realized the importance of my last thought.

If the *gnomish* player didn't have a level, that meant she was a civilian. Furthermore, I'd met only one other gnome in this sector, and it couldn't be a coincidence that it was the selfsame gnome who had taken out a bounty on the wyvern mother.

Whoever this Saya is, Gelar knows her. He must. But if he did, why hadn't Gelar told me?

And more importantly, what did I do about it?

Chapter 148: An Unlikely Pair

Day Seven. Morning.

Temporarily setting aside the mystery of the gnome, I cast analyze on the beast.

The target is a level 198 green wyvern.

I gulped. The bounty notice had been correct. Given that, I wasn't about to attempt taking on the wyvern mother myself—even if she was asleep and seemingly vulnerable.

I'd planned on luring the beast to Ishita's sworn. Much better that the wyvern was the one to trip the mages' wards. Still, the plan carried significant risk. Not least of all because of the creature's hate for me. She had my scent, and I worried she might ignore the mages entirely in favor of killing me.

I bit my lip. *So what now?* My gaze drifted to the gnome again. Was she sleeping too? *I need to investigate further before acting.*

Glancing up at the light filtering down from the cavern's roof, I realized there was a safe way—or *safer* way, anyway—to do that besides sneaking past the wyvern. Shuffling backward, I retreated into the tunnel and made my way to the cliff face.

✳ ✳ ✳

Bright sunlight was streaming through the cave mouth when I reached it. The morning was advancing, and I had to hurry. Soon I could expect the wyvern to awaken.

Standing at the edge of the entrance, I looked down. The cliff fell away sharply. Thankfully I appeared to have a head for heights and suffered no vertigo. Leaning forward, I craned my neck and peered upward.

Just as I'd thought, the clifftop wasn't far away. It was a climb of less than three yards, and I could manage that easily. Or so I hoped.

No sense in delaying.

Stepping up to the left side of the cave mouth, I swung myself out and onto the cliff's face. *Just don't look down,* I thought dryly, starkly aware I had no safety net.

I turned my face up and scanned the rockface, adamantly *not* thinking about slipping. There were plenty of handholds, and reaching up, I grabbed the nearest. *Easy does it,* I thought and hauled myself a foot higher.

I kept going, moving with spider-like precision.

A little later, I reached the top. Pulling myself over the edge, I rolled onto my back and stared up at the bright blue sky while I took a moment to catch my breath.

That wasn't so bad. I climbed back to my feet. But all the same, I would rather not do it again.

Turning full circle, I examined my surroundings. The mountaintop was flattened and barren, with even the hardiest plants struggling to grow on its surface. It was cold up here too, despite the morning sun. Leaving the cliff edge behind me, I strode inward, mentally following the path of the tunnel beneath.

When I estimated I was above my target, I opened my mindsight and, sure enough, felt two bubbles of awareness below. One was large and bright—the wyvern mother—and the other was small and contained—the gnome.

Excellent. Opening my eyes, I scanned the rock at my feet. *Now to find a way down.*

Given the amount of sunlight I'd observed in the cavern, I was sure there were plenty of fissures that led down from the clifftop. My task was to find one large enough to squirm through.

There were dozens of fractures.

Few cut a straight path down, and though most contorted wildly through the six feet of rock separating me from the cavern, many remained navigable.

I chose the one to use with care. The fissure I eventually judged suitable was positioned almost directly above the gnome and kept me about as far as I could hope to remain from the sleeping wyvern.

Before slipping into the crevice, I uncoiled the rope I'd taken from the Howlers and attached it firmly around a nearby rock outcropping. If I needed to retreat, the tethered line would be my way back out.

With the other end of the rope in tow, I approached the fissure. Now came the riskiest part.

I crawled in.

The crevice's walls were smooth, likely worn away by centuries of water running off the clifftop, and almost immediately I realized it would be a tighter fit than I expected.

There was no room to stand or even turn around and barely enough leeway for me to wedge my hands under my body and worm my way through. *I'm definitely not making a quick getaway out this way.* If things went wrong below, I would have to find another way out.

Despite my discomfort though, I navigated the crevice without mishap, and a little later I spied its other end. Wriggling toward the opening, I peered through.

The fissure ended in nearly the highest point of the cavern's roof and the ground was some seven yards distant. My lips turned down. I would need the rope to get down.

The good news, though, was that despite the convoluted path the crevice had cut through the rock, it opened at nearly the same point it had started above, and my quarry was almost directly beneath me.

My gaze shifted to the wyvern mother. She snored on, six yards away from the gnome. But from this vantage point, the distance separating the two was less comforting than I thought. Would the beast sense me when I reached the gnome?

I grimaced. It was too late for second thoughts. I was already committed. *Let's do this.*

Tugging on the rope, I lowered it bit by bit in the cavern, my eyes not straying from the wyvern. *She's not going to wake up,* I told myself. Even saying it, I wasn't sure I believed it. Still, time was passing, and every moment the risk grew greater.

The rope end reached the cavern floor with the wyvern none the wiser. Now, there was only one more thing to do.

Without further hesitation, I wormed the final bit of the way out of the crevice and swung onto the hanging rope.

A hostile entity has failed to detect you! You are hidden.

The tethered line swayed at my sudden weight but held without further protest. Clinging on, I waited for the motion to peter out.

Then I silently slipped further down.

A hostile entity has failed to detect you! You are hidden.

I touched down noiselessly on the moss-covered floor and dropped immediately into a crouch while I scanned the cavern again.

Only six yards separated me from the wyvern mother, and from this close her menacing presence was unmistakable. But thankfully, she slept on blissfully.

My gaze shifted to my quarry. The gnome was less than a yard away and, like the wyvern herself, hadn't stirred. I crept closer to the player, one eye on the wyvern all the while.

A hostile entity has failed to detect you! You are hidden.

The beast slumbered on, oblivious. Reaching my target, I examined her intently.

The gnome wasn't asleep. She was unconscious.

One of the alchemist's arms was strapped and bound in a makeshift sling. Her clothes were torn in places, and her legs were puffy and swollen. She also bore a host of other smaller injuries.

Reaching out, I laid a light hand on her forehead. The gnome was burning up too. I reinspected the alchemist, this time querying her health status.

The target is Saya. She is severely injured.

Damn. There was no way I could risk waking the gnome in her condition. Her cries of pain alone would give me away.

I'll have to use a potion. A full healing one. There was no way for me to gauge the extent of the alchemist's injuries more accurately, and I didn't have time to mess around. Unclipping the potion, I placed it on the unconscious gnome's lips and dribbled the contents into her.

As usual, the potion worked instantly.

The gnome's eyes snapped open in shock. Anticipating her reaction, I clamped a hand around her mouth before she could voice the question in her eyes. Moving slowly and not breaking eye contact, I raised a finger to my lips and jerked my head in the direction of the wyvern.

Saya's eyes grew wider, if that was possible, as she took in the beast's sleeping form.

I waited for a few drawn-out seconds. I had no idea why the gnome was in the cave, and I couldn't ignore the possibility she might be working for—or with—the wyvern, absurd as the notion seemed.

When the alchemist made no attempt to struggle or call out in warning, I carefully unwrapped my hand from her mouth.

Saya exhaled silently, her eyes not leaving my own.

I rose to my feet. "Can I help you up?" I mouthed soundlessly.

The alchemist nodded, her gaze darting nervously to the wyvern. The gesture alleviated my own worries. Whatever was going on, it was obvious Saya was afraid of the beast. *Small chance she's here willingly then.*

Bending down, I helped the smaller player up. The gnome weighed hardly anything and moved without clumsiness. It eased my mind further. I hadn't planned on any sort of rescue operation, but that seemed exactly what I was in the middle of now. That Saya was both mobile and seemingly agile made things simpler.

Leaving the trembling gnome to wait awhile, I studied the cave anew. The safest way out, I realized, was the same way I'd come in. I turned back to Saya and placed my mouth against her ear. "Do exactly as I say, and we'll get out of here alive," I whispered. "Can you do that?"

She nodded emphatically.

Placing my hands on the gnome's shoulders, I turned her to face the rope. "You see that? Head toward it," I said, still whispering. "Don't rush, and be careful where you place your feet."

The alchemist took a step forward, moving with exaggerated caution under my vigilant scrutiny. She was light on her feet though and didn't stumble.

I followed on her heels, and with painful slowness we made our way back to my dangling rope. When we got there, I tied the end around Saya's waist.

The climb to the top would be harder than the way down, and I couldn't expect the gnome to manage it. Leaning forward, I whispered into her ear again. "I'll climb out, then pull you up. Don't panic, and don't make a sound."

Saya's trembling intensified, and her face whitened in fear. But as much as the idea of remaining alone in the cave seemed to disturb the gnome, she didn't protest.

Getting herself under control faster than I expected, Saya nodded, if not firmly, then gamely in response to my instructions.

I squeezed her slim shoulders once, then, without further ado, scaled the rope and pulled myself up, quickly and without fuss, to the tune of the wyvern's snores. That was the easy part.

Next, I had to get Saya out.

Chapter 149: The Lost Alchemist

Reaching the crevice opening, I looked back to see how the gnome was doing.

Her face upturned, she stared at me fixedly. Giving Saya a thumbs up, I ducked into the fissure, hoping she continued to remain calm when I disappeared from sight.

I wriggled out of the fissure as fast as I could while listening intently for signs that the wyvern was rousing. Happily, I made it all the way through without Saya panicking. Squirming out of the hole, I whipped around and hauled on the rope. I couldn't see the gnome, but at this point I had to trust she'd continue to keep her composure.

It was slow going as, inch by inch, I pulled Saya upward. As nerve-racking as it was, though, I didn't dare yank too hard at the rope.

Eventually, my arms began to burn with the strain. The gnome was light, but Strength wasn't my best attribute. Still, I didn't utter a sound, and neither did the alchemist slowly being hauled aloft. After what felt like forever but objectively was less than five minutes, the rope went slack.

Saya had reached the fissure.

I sat back, panting in relief. While I massaged my arms, I followed the gnome's progress through the crevice with my mindsight.

Being nearly half as wide as me, the alchemist sped through the fissure, making it look easy, and in no time at all her head popped out of the hole. Placing a finger to my lips to remind her to be silent, I led her away.

It was time to find out exactly who and what she was.

✳ ✳ ✳

I didn't let the gnome talk, not until I'd put enough distance between us and the cave below. Finding a heap of gigantic boulders, I pulled the alchemist into their shadows.

"Alright, this should be far enough," I said. "Who—"

I got no further. The gnome flung herself forward and wrapped her tiny arms about me. "Thank you! Thank you! Thank you!" she whispered in an excited and fervent voice.

I patted her awkwardly and extricated myself. "You're welcome," I said. "But we're not out of danger just yet. The wyvern mother could wake up at any time."

Saya shook her head. "We have hours yet. She often sleeps past noon."

I studied the gnome carefully. She sounded certain. "You've been there for a long time then?"

Saya nodded vigorously. "She captured me weeks ago. I've been trapped in that awful cave since then."

I frowned. "The wyvern mother took you prisoner? Why would she do that?"

Saya sighed. "She figured out I was an alchemist—if only a half-trained one—and put me to work."

I blinked, not sure which part of her statement I found more surprising. "Put you to work...?" I repeated slowly.

"Harvesting mushrooms and cave moss for her," she said with a wan smile. "Apparently, Besina considers them to be quite the delicacy."

"Who is Besina?" I asked, confused.

"The wyvern," Saya said simply.

Of course. Why it surprised me that the wyvern mother had a name, I wasn't sure, but it did. More surprising, though, was that the gnome knew it. "So you've... talked to her?"

Saya's face twisted in remembered pain. "Well, I'm not sure if you could call it *talking.*" Unconsciously, she rubbed at her temples. "Besina transmitted her demands by dropping images in my mind. At first they were difficult to understand, but over time they grew easier to interpret. And when I talked, she understood me."

"I see," I said. "What can you tell me about the beast?"

For a long moment, Saya remained quiet, dark emotions flitting across her face. "Besina is old," the apprentice said finally. "She has laired in these mountains for a long time and knows them well. Many of the tunnels below are either of her own making or have been widened by her over time." She met my gaze, her own serious. "Don't try hiding in them from her."

I nodded thoughtfully. "Go on."

"Don't underestimate Besina either," Saya continued. "She's no dumb beast. The wyvern is cunning. And sadistic." The gnome's chin trembled and she raised her left arm, still covered by dirty bandages. "A few days ago, I tried escaping. Besina caught me easily, of course, then proceeded to teach me a lesson." She shuddered. "I will never forget what she did."

I shifted from foot to foot, made uneasy by the pain haunting the gnome's eyes. I didn't know how to comfort her, so I did the next best thing. I changed the topic. "I take it you work with Gelar?"

My awkward attempt worked, and the melancholy vanished from Saya's face. "No one works *with* Gelar," she said, eyes twinkling. "I work *for* him. I'm his apprentice."

"Ah," I said, pleased by her suddenly happier countenance. Whatever Besina had done to the little gnome, she hadn't broken her spirit.

"Did he send you to rescue me?" Saya asked eagerly, her entire face lighting up.

I hesitated, then shook my head and told her the truth. "No, he didn't tell me about you at all." I paused. "But he did send me to kill the wyvern."

"Oh," Saya said, deflating. "He must think I'm dead then."

I shrugged. I had no idea what Gelar had been thinking, but it seemed his reasons for posting the bounty weren't as straightforward as I'd originally assumed. "Will you tell me how you ended up here?" I asked quietly.

"Of course," Saya said, somewhat absently. I could see she was still upset by the notion that her mentor had abandoned her for dead.

"I was out into the forest gathering materials—" she began.

"Alone?" I asked sharply. "Gelar sent you out alone?"

Saya hung her head, not meeting my eyes.

"Why would he do a fool thing like that?"

The gnome's gaze flitted to mine, and seeing the look of disbelief on my face, she explained, "It's not unusual. I've often gone out on my own to collect ingredients." She lowered her eyes. "But I don't think I'm cut out to be an alchemist. I mean, it's not like I mind a bit of danger, but after Besina—" her word dropped to a barely perceptible whisper—"I'm not sure I can do it anymore."

I stared at Saya with renewed scrutiny.

The gnome was scrawny, her head appeared overlarge, and her features were sharply defined, almost as if her face hadn't grown to fit them yet.

I was no expert on gnomish physiology and had initially thought her somewhat odd appearance a result of her captivity. Now, I wondered.

"Saya, how old are you?" I asked suddenly.

The apprentice preened slightly. "I'm eighteen," she said proudly. "I reached adulthood three months ago, achieving full player status."

I didn't say anything, but in the privacy of my mind, I was cursing Gelar. *She's barely more than a child, and a civilian player to boot.* Why had the alchemist let her loose in the valley, alone and unaccompanied?

"What do we do now?" Saya asked, unaware of the train of my thoughts. "Do we flee over the mountains?" She bit her lip. "I warn you, I don't think we'll get far. Besina is an excellent tracker, and I don't think she'll just let me go..."

I refocused on the gnome. "Unfortunately, Saya, my business here isn't done yet. Before we can leave, there's something else I must do in Besina's lair." I hesitated, considering the youth again. Could I trust her? I thought so. "Alchemists are magic users, aren't they?"

Saya shrugged. "I don't have any spells, if that's what you're asking."

"But you have access to your mana?"

The apprentice nodded.

"Can you use a spell scroll?"

"If it isn't combat-oriented," she allowed cautiously, "then, yes, I can."

I withdrew the portal scroll from my pack and handed it to her. "Then you hold onto this. I'm going to go back into the tunnels below. If I'm not back in an hour, or you see the wyvern emerge from her lair, use this. It won't take you out of the sector, but it should return you to the safe zone."

You have lost a portal scroll.

Saya took the item curiously. A moment later, her mouth dropped open in shock as she realized what she held.

"Can you use the scroll?" I asked gently.

She nodded emphatically.

"Great," I said with a grin. "Then you wait here. I'll be back in an hour. And if I'm not, well, you know what to do." Turning, I began retracing my steps to the cliff's edge.

"Wait!" Saya hissed.

I paused and swung back to her.

"What do you need to do in the lair?" the apprentice asked in a low voice.

I stayed silent for a moment, then shrugged, seeing no harm in telling her. "Do you know what the shield generator is?"

Saya nodded.

"I'm going to destroy it."

The gnome's eyes widened. "But Ishita's mages are guarding it!"

I raised an eyebrow. "You know about them?"

She bobbed her head. "They arrived early yesterday morning, and since then Besina has been in a foul mood. Their presence grates on her."

"She knows they're in the tunnels then?"

"Besina attacked them yesterday." Saya frowned. "But I think the mages got the better of her and she was forced to retreat. She wasn't happy."

I smiled. "That's good to know. Thank you." I prepared to leave again.

"Is there anything I can do to help?" Saya asked, stopping me once more.

I shook my head. "It's too dangerous—"

"It can't be any more dangerous than trying to escape Besina, surely," she said with a grin.

I winced at the comparison. The truth was, I could see a way for the gnome to help, but I didn't want to entangle the youth in my own affairs. "It will be a bit more dangerous than that," I murmured. "And you'd be helping me against Ishita's sworn. If they discover your involvement, the Power won't look kindly on you."

"Pfft, who cares about Ishita," Saya said. But despite her brave words, she sounded suddenly less enthused. "Are you sure you want to tangle with the goddess?" she asked a moment later. "*She* is even scarier than the wyvern."

"Her people have left me no choice," I replied. "But you don't have to help. You can stay here and wait for me to return."

Saya's spine stiffened. "No. I want to." She paused. "But I won't need to fight, will I?"

"Not at all," I assured her. "If you really want to help, I won't stop you. This is what I need you to do..."

CHAPTER 150: A RUNNING BATTLE

It took me only a few minutes to position Saya and a little longer to explain what I intended. After that, I returned to Besina's cavern.

I felt a little guilty about using the young gnome, especially after mentally chiding Gelar for sending her into the forest alone, but Saya's part in my plan, while crucial, would be small and without danger.

I was sure of it. Or almost.

She'll be fine, I told myself. *And certainly in less danger than if she fled unaccompanied to the safe zone.*

Refocusing on the matter at hand, I stared downward. Once more, I was crouched atop the crest of the tunnel leading into Besina's lair.

This time, I'd taken the long way around to approach the wyvern. Lowering myself down the rope had been nerve-racking enough before, and besides, for what I intended, I needed to be near the cavern's entrance.

The beast was still asleep, and I mentally reviewed my plan. Once I set my scheme in motion, things would progress quickly, and I would have to act without hesitation.

I took a deep, calming breath. It was time. I knew the plan backwards already and was ready.

Sinking deeper into the shadows, I drew on my psi and cast astral blade. From where I crouched, Besina made for an unmissable target. Taking aim at the wyvern's forehead, I whipped my hand forward, releasing the purple dagger.

The magical projectile flew through the air and struck the beast dead center.

Your astral blade has failed to harm Besina. Green wyverns are immune to all forms of mental assaults! Your attack has been detected!

My lips twisted down sourly. The lack of damage was unsurprising; I'd known enough to expect it. Still, it was depressing to see how futile my attack had been.

Besina has failed to detect you! You remain hidden.

The wyvern's eyes had snapped open. I smiled grimly. Awakening the beast had been the true purpose of my attack. There was no turning back now.

Casting ventro, I projected my voice to a spot just inside the cavern and about five yards from my actual location. "Well, ugly, it looks like I found where you've been hiding," I said sneeringly. "This place is a real dump."

The wyvern mother's neck jerked erect, and her nostrils flared as she tasted the air. "You!" she hissed. With startling quickness, Besina's gaze fixed on the spot from which my voice had originated.

Besina has failed to detect you!

Knowing what came next, I slid down the slope, retreating silently while still throwing my voice forward. "Me," I agreed. "I've already rid the valley of your hatchling. Now it's time I put an end to you too."

I heard the slap of wings on water and the thud of feet as Besina heaved her bulk upward. The beast was moving.

Right, that got her riled up. My own pulse quickening, I hastened my retreat through the shadows.

A heartbeat later, jets of green, acidic spittle exploded across the top of the tunnel.

Yikes. "Haha, you missed me," I yelled gleefully, still using ventro to disguise my true position.

Besina herself appeared on the crest. Eyes narrowed and brimming with rage, she scanned the tunnel ahead of her. But by now I was further down the tunnel and well-concealed.

Besina has failed to detect you!

"You dare attempt your childish tricks on me, human? They will not save you," the wyvern hissed. "I will find you and kill you slowly. I shall feed off your bones, bit by bit. You will die, and horribly," she promised with menacing certainty.

I reached the t-junction and stopped. With the sunlight streaming in from the right fork, this was the brightest spot in the tunnels and I couldn't tarry long, but I still had time for another quip.

"Oh, I'm sure I will die," I said through ventro before slipping into the darker tunnel leading toward Ishita's sworn. "One day, I surely must, but that day isn't today. Today that honor is reserved for you." I paused. "I will make it quick, I promise."

I was keeping a vigilant watch through my mindsight so I didn't miss my foe's sudden re-entry in range as she rushed to the t-junction.

Besina has failed to detect you!

"Show yourself, worm," the wyvern screeched in frustration when she found the crossing empty.

I chuckled. "Now, why would I do that?" I asked, hurrying down the tunnel. Taunting the wyvern mother was probably not wise, but the angrier she was, the better my chances were of getting her to act without considering the consequences.

If she balked, it could prove disastrous.

"Where is my pet?" Besina asked abruptly, ignoring my own response.

"Pet?" I asked with feigned disinterest.

The wyvern didn't answer immediately, and when she did, her voice was flat, stripped of its earlier rage. "The alchemist."

I opened my mouth to retort, then paused as my senses prickled. Besina had fallen out of range of my mindsight and hadn't reappeared, so I wasn't worried she was close.

But something wasn't right.

Frowning, I listened keenly. At the edges of my hearing, I heard the faint scrape of claws on stone.

You have detected a hidden entity!

The wyvern had changed tactics and, under cover of our conversation, was stalking me!

Based on the half-heard sound, I placed Besina's position at less than eight yards away. She had shielded her mind too, which was why I wasn't seeing her in my mindsight.

Bloody cunning.

My lips thinned. *But you're not catching me that easily.*

I'd hoped to draw out my game of cat and mouse with Besina a bit longer, but that was looking too dangerous now. Pulling an object from my pocket, I slipped further away.

"Oh, you mean Saya," I said casually, resuming our conversation as if it had never faltered. "You don't have to worry about her. She is safely in the custody of Ishita's mages now."

Besina didn't reply, and I sensed she was done talking. Sure enough, a second later her large form rushed into sight. She was charging me.

You have detected a hidden entity. Besina is no longer hidden!
Besina has detected you. You are no longer hidden!

Well, damn. Ignoring the wyvern's hurtling shape, I smashed the smoke I held into the ground at my feet.

You have ignited a smoke bomb. You are hidden once more.

Turning tail, I rushed blindly through the thick plumes of smoke. My eyes were squeezed shut, and my left arm was extended so that my fingers brushed the tunnel's sidewall.

Behind me, I heard Besina pull to a stop and hiss in frustration as she lost sight of me again. It didn't stop her from retaliating though, and a moment later a lance of acidic spittle cut through the smoke cloud.

You have evaded Besina's attack.

The lethal jet of acid splashed into the rock less than a yard behind me. It had missed me more by happenstance than by design.

That was too close, I thought, wiping beads of sweat from my brow. *Time for a little more deception.*

Recasting ventro, I taunted my pursuer, "What happened to killing me nice and slow? You've reconsidered, I take it?"

My only response was another stream of acid. It was fired randomly and missed me by a long shot. Besina was clearly no longer interested in talking.

Grimacing, I burst through the smoke field and, foregoing any further attempt at stealth, sprinted through the tunnel to my next waypoint.

A few seconds later, Besina appeared behind me.

Knowing the wyvern was quicker than me and expecting her to reach attacking range soon, I began bobbing and weaving to spoil her aim.

A jet of acid splashed against the tunnel wall, inches to my right. Not slowing, I glanced over my shoulder. Besina had paused to launch the attack, opening the distance between us slightly.

Good, I thought. *That will help.*

Casting one-step, I added to the randomness of my flight, jinking up and down as well as left and right now.

You have evaded Besina's attack.
You have evaded Besina's attack.
You have ...

Head down, I kept running, steadfastly ignoring the slew of acid projectiles falling in my wake. I only had a little further to go to reach my next waypoint and, to my great relief, I got to it without being struck.

My hand whipped forward, releasing another bomb.

You have ignited a smoke bomb. You are hidden once more.

Safely concealed, I took a moment to gasp silently for breath while I recovered.

Behind me, I heard Besina slowly pick her way through the billowing clouds, while from further down the passage fresh voices carried to me.

"... hear that?"

Lutra groaned. "Please, Ishan, not this again."

"Quiet, Lutra," Worca snapped. "I hear it too this time."

With a tight smile, I felt my way to a small nook I'd picked out earlier and wedged myself into it. I'd advanced as far into the tunnel as I'd dared, and Ishita's sworn—and their mysterious wards—weren't much farther away. At my rear, I heard Besina draw closer.

It was time to play my final card.

Projecting my voice as far forward into the tunnel as I could, I shouted, "Xrex, Worca, help! She's on my tail. Get ready, we can finally kill this beast!"

Behind me, Besina snarled in rage. She'd heard me alright. Opening my mindsight, I watched the wyvern draw closer. Whatever shield Besina had woven around her mind had dissipated, and she hadn't bothered replenishing it. Abandoning her careful approach, the wyvern was charging blindly through the smoke now, ignoring her many collisions with the sidewalls.

Ahead, the four mages were yelling in confusion.

I smiled. *Perfect.*

Focusing on the only other bubble of awareness in my mindsight—Saya, strategically placed on the clifftop above my current position—I made my escape.

You have cast shadow blink and teleported yourself eight yards away.

Now, the fun begins.

Chapter 151: A Battle of Titans

Saya's eyes rounded in shock at my sudden appearance. "It's done?" she gasped.

"It's done," I confirmed. "Or it's begun," I amended. Through my mindsight, I still watched the wyvern in the tunnel below. She rushed past my position without pause, none the wiser about my escape.

I couldn't sense the mages themselves. They were either too well-shielded or out of range. But right now, I expected they were fleeing or preparing to meet the enraged beast.

Rising to my feet, I headed south, walking in the direction I had sensed the wyvern mother go. As fast as she had been moving, she hadn't stayed within range of my ability for long.

Saya followed in my wake. "Where are they?"

"I'm not sure yet," I replied absently while I searched for the beast again. "Besina was traveling this way."

Nearly twenty yards later, almost at the limit of my mindsight range, I found the wyvern and blew out a relieved breath. One of my biggest concerns was that the cave sheltering the mages would be too deep for me to sense the combatants from the clifftop. If that was the case, I would've had to alter my plans. Fortunately, that wasn't necessary. The wyvern mother was beneath me, just under nine yards away. I inspected her, querying her health status.

The target is Besina. She is barely injured.

The wyvern was no longer moving. *Trapped in Lutra's paralysis field?* I wondered. I couldn't sense the mages themselves, though they had to be around.

"Why have we stopped?" Saya asked. "Is the—"

I raised a hand, silencing her. "Ssh, I'm listening."

Were those voices I heard at the edges of my hearing? I couldn't be sure. But the wyvern mother still wasn't moving, and I recast analyze upon her.

The target is Besina. She is lightly injured.

"Ah," I breathed, observing the drop in the wyvern's health. "The battle has started," I murmured to Saya.

"Who will win?" she asked in fascination.

"It's too early to tell," I replied. "But I expect whoever does will be gravely weakened." I smiled. "Then, it will be my—"

In my mindsight, I sensed the wyvern mother dart forward, and in the wake of her abrupt movement, the faint noises emanating from below increased in volume.

Stretching out flat down on the ground, I placed my ear against the rock and listened intently.

"... kill her...!"

"... damnit, Lutra..."

"Idiot!"

With a satisfied grin, I rose back to my feet and tracked the wyvern to her new position. She hadn't moved far off, and I guessed she was within the cave holding Ishita's four sworn.

I studied the surrounding area. The ground underfoot was more solid here, and there were no cracks or crevices leading down.

My lips turned down in disappointment. That made what I needed to do next harder, but not impossible. I still had a way down. Drawing another smoke bomb from my pocket, I readied myself.

Saya walked up to me. "What do I do next?"

I smiled at her eager expression. "Nothing. Your work is done. All that remains is for me to finish matters below."

"Oh," she said, shoulders sagging in disappointment.

With another grin, I turned my attention downward and reinspected the wyvern.

The target is Besina. She is moderately injured.

It was almost time. Bouncing lightly on the balls of my feet, I readied myself and, second by second, checked on the wyvern mother.

The target is Besina. She is moderately injured.

...

...

The target is Besina. She is severely injured.

...

The target is Besina. She is near death.

That's it. The moment I'd been waiting for had arrived.

Spinning psi, I shadow blinked into the battle.

✳ ✳ ✳

I landed on my feet behind Besina.

Through a split-second glimpse, I took in the tableau in the cavern.

The wyvern was still and unmoving, held in place by some sort of magical leash. Her head bent, Besina gnawed at the magic tether around her neck. Arrayed in a circle around the beast were Ishita's sworn—unhappily, all four were still alive. The mages had their staffs and wands pointed in Besina's direction while they unleashed a storm of magic down upon her.

At my arrival, the wyvern's head jerked up. She'd sensed me.

Quicker than thought, she whipped her tail at me. But I was already moving. Backflipping, I dodged the appendage's deadly arc and dropped my bomb.

You have evaded Besina's attack. You have ignited a smoke bomb. You are hidden.

Smoke billowed out to wrap the entirety of the cavern in dense, gray clouds, blinding all the combatants. Predictably, bedlam ensued.

"Did you see that?" Ishan yelled.

"He's here!" Worca gasped.

"Forget *him,* god damnit! I've lost sight of the wyvern," Lutra shrieked. "She's broken my spell's hold!"

"Quick! Kill her!" Xrex ordered.

Eyes shut and moving blindly, I backpedaled quickly through the smoke, opening the distance between me and the battle.

Five hostile entities have failed to detect you!

Through my mindsight, I watched Besina whip about and search for me, but as wrapped in smoke as I was, there was little chance of her finding me.

Almost as if she came to the same realization herself, the wyvern spun around and charged at something—one of the mages.

Ishan has been critically injured.

A piercing shriek split the chamber. "Aargh! She got me!" Ishan cried.

The back of my shoe hit something. Reaching backward, I blindly felt out my surroundings and found solid rock behind me.

I'd reached one of the cave's walls. *Perfect.*

Drawing my twin swords, I crouched down and waited. It was still too early for me to intervene more directly in the battle.

Lightning ripped through the cave, burning away everything in its path— including the smoke. I wasn't sure if the bolt had been aimed at Besina or me, but it harmed nothing except the smoke cloud, and only temporarily at that. The hole left by the lightning was quickly filled in as more dense clouds rolled back in.

"Don't cast blindly, you fools," Xrex hissed. "Dispel the smoke cloud first!"

My head turned Xrex's way, and I fixed the lizardman's position in my mind by sound alone. I still couldn't see the mages in my mindsight, so I had to depend on other means to locate them.

I heard someone mutter to my right. Lutra, by the sounds of it. He was incanting the words of a spell. Realizing what he was doing, I wrapped myself in shadow. A moment later, the gray clouds were swept away.

A smoke cloud has been dispelled. Five hostile entities have failed to detect you! You remain hidden.

Unfortunately, Lutra's spell worked as much against Ishita's sworn as it did for them.

The smoke dissipated to reveal Besina hovering over Ishan. She was still trying to get to him. Much to the beast's annoyance, her jaws kept bouncing away each time she tried to snap at the downed mage. Ishan, I suspected, had triggered his dark repulsion spell, if a moment too late to save him from the wyvern's initial attack.

But the moment Besina regained her sight, things changed.

Abandoning her injured prey, the wyvern spun around, her malevolent gaze searching for another victim.

"Quick, Lutra, hold—" Xrex began.

He was too late. Besina had found a target. Hurtling across the cavern, the wyvern charged straight into Worca's stygian shield and, with a speed that left me breathless, cracked it open.

The elven mage's mouth opened in wordless shock, but before she could give voice to her fear, Besina trampled her underfoot.

Worca has died.

I gulped. Three seconds or less. That's how long it had taken—from start to finish—for Besina to kill the mage. *"Damnation,"* I mumbled in awe, doubly glad I'd chosen not to entangle with the beast myself.

"Freeze her in place again!" Xrex ordered.

"I'm working on it," Lutra yelled, sounding harried.

The lizardman lowered his own staff and sent a bar of liquid flames racing to the wyvern, striking her on the back of the head.

It was a brave, if somewhat foolish move, since it attracted the wyvern's attention.

Hissing in fury and pain, Besina lifted her head to bare jagged teeth, reddened with blood, at Xrex.

Xrex flung another flame bolt, but before the projectile could land Besina dove with catlike reflexes, slipping under the attack.

Then she flew forward.

The lizardman retreated a step backward, raising his staff in a warding gesture, but halfway to Xrex the wyvern made an abrupt half-turn and launched herself at the still-chanting Lutra instead.

The human mage's defenses were made of sterner stuff than his dead companion's though. Where Worca's shield had cracked, Lutra's didn't. The violence of Besina's charge flung the mage backward. Despite this, Lutra kept chanting, his concentration uninterrupted. The wyvern darted forward, intent on following up with a second attack.

Lutra didn't afford her the opportunity.

Before his foe could close in on him, icy blue lines of frost shot from the mage's hands to engulf the wyvern.

Besina has been frozen.

"Excellent," Xrex cackled. Lowering his staff, the Ishita sworn hurled a trio of flaming bolts at the wyvern.

The magical projectiles proved enough, and with a forlorn hiss, the wyvern mother slumped to the ground.

Besina has died.

Cloaked in shadows, I barely had time to notice the beast's passing, though her death triggered an unexpected cascade of Game alerts.

You have completed the task: <u>An Alchemist's Bounty!</u> As a result of your efforts, the wyvern mother, Besina, has been slain. Return to Gelar to claim your bounty.

The Marks on your spirit signature have changed. You have removed another significant threat to House Wolf's adherents, and this time you accomplished the deed without introducing further threats into the valley. Wolf is pleased, and your Mark has deepened.

Congratulations, Michael! Your Wolf Mark has advanced. You now bear the Mark: <u>Pack-brother</u>. As an anointed scion of the House, your new Wolf Mark gives you the option to evolve your mindstalker Class.

Do you wish to change your Class to that of a mindslayer? Doing so will cause your Class traits and abilities to advance. Note, the mindslayer Class is only available to scions of House Wolf.

Chapter 152: Death to my Enemies

For a second, I could only gape at the Game messages.

The Adjudicator was offering me a Class evolution? And *now*, in the middle of a battle? It couldn't have come at a worse time.

I knew I didn't have time to ponder the choice, but at the same time, I realized I couldn't pass up on the opportunity either. Not hesitating further, I replied in the affirmative to the Adjudicator's query.

Your Class has evolved! You are now a mindslayer!
Your secret blood trait has been triggered!
To conceal your bloodline, your Class will be reported as being that of a mindstalker to other players and Powers.

More messages vied for my consideration, defining the exact changes made to my Class, but I had no time to spare them. Ishita's sworn demanded my attention.

Remaining crouched near the cave wall, I eyed the three surviving mages.

"Finally!" Xrex exclaimed, eyes fixed on the dead wyvern. Striding toward it, he spat on the corpse. "And good riddance. Now, find that damn thief. I want his head!"

On my left, Ishan groaned and rolled onto his back. "Xrex... help me!" he gasped. "I'm... dying."

The lizardman ignored him. Turning around in a slow circle, he scanned the darkness.

My gaze shifted to Lutra, and with a start I realized that during my moment of distraction the human mage had begun another spell. Whatever it was, it couldn't be good for me.

I can't afford to let him finish. Spinning psi, I blinked into Lutra's shadow.

You have teleported yourself six yards away. Three hostile entities have failed to detect you!

Lutra was still chanting. Not waiting for him to finish, I dropped my last bomb at his feet.

You have ignited a smoke bomb. You are hidden.

As more clouds billowed into the chamber, Xrex spun in my direction. "Lutra, he's—"

I stopped listening. I was safe from the lizardman's attacks for the time being. Raising my swords, I assaulted the human mage's shields.

I struck hard and fast, attacking first with ebonheart, then with spider's bite. I empowered both blades with piercing strikes, and even though I hit out blindly, I didn't miss.

You have attempted to backstab Lutra. Backstab failed! The damage has been transferred to the target's shield. Three hostile entities have failed to detect you!

You have attempted to backstab Lutra. Backstab failed! The damage has been transferred to the target's shield. Three hostile entities have failed to detect you!

I felt Lutra's shield—already weakened by Besina—tremble under the pressure of my devastating twin blows. Even better, with the smoke concealing me, I remained hidden.

I repeated the combo, quicksilver fast. Both hits landed.

Lutra's chanting faltered. "Xrex... do something!" he shouted. "I can't hold him off much longer."

Ignoring the mage's outcry, I hit his shield again with piercing strikes.

"I can't see him!" Xrex hissed in frustration.

Lutra was done waiting. In a flat panic, he fled blindly. I kept up with him easily, tracing his flight by the sound of his footsteps alone.

On the run, I struck again. Once. Twice. That was enough.

Lutra's frost shield has been destroyed!

"No!" the mage exclaimed. "Ishita, help—"

He got no further. Following the sound of his voice, both my blades flew forward to slash at his face.

As powerful as the mage's shield had been, his body was equally frail.

You have killed Lutra with a fatal blow. You have slain a sworn servant of Ishita, increasing her ire toward you!

With a last whimper, the human mage crumpled to the ground.

✳ ✳ ✳

I rolled away from the corpse, senses alert for the one threat remaining: Xrex. Clouds still lay heavy in the cavern, and the lizardman, unhelpfully, had gone quiet.

Xrex was stalking me just as I was him.

Placing each foot with care, I padded through the cavern, listening intently, but other than Ishan's harsh breathing, I heard nothing. My foe was better at remaining quiet than I'd expected.

For Xrex, it was a waiting game. Once the clouds dissipated, he would have clear line of sight to me. For me, though, the passing seconds were precious.

Let's see if I can't lure him out.

I cast ventro, disguising my location. "Not suddenly scared, are you, Xrex?" I mocked.

There was no response.

"Don't tell me the high and mighty sworn of Ishita is afraid of a meager thief?" I jeered.

Still nothing.

"What will your goddess say? Mind you, her intelligence is questionable, and I wouldn't blame you if you didn't place much—"

A bolt of light cut through the smoke, shattering a harmless piece of rock. I grinned. I had the lizardman's location now.

I chuckled. "Touched a nerve, did I?" I quipped as I rushed through the gray smoke where I knew Xrex was.

Perhaps, realizing his error, the lizardman didn't respond. But it was too late for him to hide now. I had gotten close enough that the sound of Xrex's shallow breathing carried clearly to my sharp ears.

Accelerating suddenly, I rammed my shoulder into where I estimated the mage's shield to start.

I hit him head-on.

Xrex hissed as he stumbled backward. I didn't let him break contact. Keeping one hand outstretched and touching his shield, I fell with him. A bolt of fire burst from the mage, striking me on the arm. Intense pain rippled down the limb, but I ignored it.

I had my foe pinned under me, but I was running out of time.

I raised ebonheart and hacked at the lizardman. Another spell shot out from Xrex, this one striking me in the shoulder.

Xrex has cast stonegrip on you.
Spell failed! You are immune to tier-1 and tier-2 entanglement spells.

I laughed. Ironically, it was Xrex's dead companion's item that had saved me. Beneath me, the lizardman cursed as he realized his spell had failed. Ignoring his sputtered words, I kept raining down blows on him.

After a moment, Xrex grew tight-lipped again and returned to using damaging spells. I wasn't sure why he didn't try other castings. I suspected it was because his sight was too impaired to target me properly.

Whatever the case, from then on Xrex only threw fire bolts at me. Some hit me fully, a few missed entirely, and many only grazed me. Xrex was casting blindly—and ineffectually. My own attacks were more accurate. Every blow landed, and every blow ate at his shield.

Bit by bit, I wore Xrex down.

It wasn't pleasant or elegant, and halfway through I had to down a healing potion, but finally I broke through my foe's defenses.

Then, without hesitation, I plunged both my blades into the lizardman.

✳ ✳ ✳

Xrex took longer to die than Lutra, but after four successive blows, he stopped moving.

You have killed Xrex with a fatal blow. You have slain a sworn servant of Ishita, increasing her ire toward you!

Panting heavily, I rolled off the corpse. I didn't bother to move further. Smoke still clouded the cave, and the only one of my foes still alive didn't sound like he had long. Eyes closed, I cast chi heal and mended my body from the burns the mage had inflicted.

It took a while, and by the time I was done the air was free of smoke. Using my swords to support me, I rose to my feet. I was fully healed but remained weary.

I surveyed the cave, ignoring the corpses as my gaze fixed on Ishan. Miraculously, he was still alive. Moaning and mumbling to himself, the human appeared to be in the throes of agony.

Sheathing my blades, I walked over. Ishan's eyes widened at my approach, but he didn't stop muttering under his breath.

He's not muttering. He's chanting.

Suddenly wary, my hands dropped to my blades, ready to whip them out.

A heartbeat later, I paused as I noticed an oddity. Some of Ishan's wounds were closing. It was in response to his spell, I realized. I grinned as understanding dawned. "That wyvern's poison is no joke, is it?" I asked conversationally.

Ishan glared at me but didn't break off from his chanting. Reaching out with my will, I queried his health status.

The target is Ishan. He is severely injured and infected by a wyvern's toxin.

I shook my head in pretended sorrow. The mage was barely holding the toxin at bay, and all too soon I expected it would overcome him.

Deciding to let Ishan be for now—he was certainly no threat—I pivoted in a slow circle, searching the cave for what I had come for.

It didn't take long for me to find it.

In a tiny alcove, set in the rock wall behind where Xrex had fallen—*had the lizardman thought to guard it?*—was a tall cylindrical object with a dull red sheen.

The shield generator.

Walking over, I inspected the area intently for traps. As far as I could tell, there were none. Nervous suddenly, now that my goal was almost within reach, I lifted the object out of the alcove and inspected it.

The target is an Aether Cloaking Device, an artifact of unknown rank forged by the Power Ishita. Items of this type generate a sector-wide cloaking field and are often used to hide sensitive locations from hostile eyes.

I hefted the object in my hands. It was surprisingly light and seemed to be formed from multiple small crystals intricately fused together. But for all the importance of the artifact, it looked fragile. "Huh," I grunted, then, whipping my arm forward, smashed the shield generator against the ground.

You have destroyed an Aether Cloaking Device. Congratulations, Michael, you've shattered the shield woven around sector 12,560. This sector's aether coordinates are no longer hidden.

You have destroyed an artifact of Ishita, increasing her ire toward you!

That was easy.

With a pleased grin pasted across my face, I turned around to look at Ishan. He was staring at me aghast and even went so far to break from his chanting to hiss at me. "You idiot! Do you know what you've done?"

I nodded. "Sure I do," I replied easily, walking back to him. "I've opened up the sector for my escape." I smiled. "And I suppose for anyone else who wishes to enter."

Drawing to a halt before the mage, I crouched down. There was no doubt he was dying. The pallor refused to leave his face, and his limbs had begun to tremble. If Ishan could have healed himself of the wyvern poison, he would surely have done so by now. "Tell your goddess when you see her that her monopoly in this sector is over." I paused theatrically. "Oh wait, you're on your last life, aren't you? I guess you won't be seeing Ishita again after all."

Ishan glared at me. "She won't stop hunting you for this," he said between chants. "Before you die, you will be made to regret this."

I shrugged. "I don't fear your spider goddess." I stared at him thoughtfully for a moment, then withdrew a full healing potion from my belt and dangled it in front of his face.

The moment he realized what it was, Ishan couldn't tear his gaze away from the flask.

"Take it," I said, almost gently.

Naked disbelief crossed the mage's face.

"Go on, it's no trick. I want to talk to you properly, and I can't do that if every second you break off to chant a spell."

Ishan stretched out a trembling hand. Quivering with eagerness, he gulped down the flask's contents and squeezed his eyes shut as the potion's life-giving energy washed away the wyvern's toxin's effects, if not the toxin itself. A moment later, his eyes snapped open to feel ebonheart resting under his chin.

"Feeling better?" I asked.

He nodded slowly.

"Good. Now we can talk," I said and gestured to my blade. "Think of this as insurance so there are no... accidents. Chant again and you die. Got it?"

Ishan nodded again.

"Alright, in return for my generosity, you will answer a few questions."

The mage sneered. "And why should I? I'm still a dead man. The healing potion won't save me."

"It won't," I agreed. I held out a second potion. "But this will."

Chapter 153: A Toxic Interrogation

Ishan's eyes narrowed as he analyzed the potion in my hand. The next moment, he gasped and snatched desperately for the flask. It was laughably easy to pull it out of his reach.

"An antidote! Gimme!" the mage demanded.

"Tsk, tsk," I said, shaking my head. "Not so fast. Tell me what I want to know first."

Ishan's eyes darted from me to the potion, and I could see he wasn't convinced yet.

"You're on your last life," I said by way of encouragement. "This is it for you. Despite how much you fear or love your goddess, if you die now, you're gone for good. You don't want that, do you?"

Ishan licked his lips, then gave in to temptation. "What do you want to know?"

"Why do the Awakened Dead want this sector?"

"For access to the Nethersphere, obviously," Ishan sneered.

"Obviously," I agreed. "But that can't be all. There must be more to it."

The mage remained stubbornly silent.

I shook the antidote in my hand. "Do you want this or not?" I asked impatiently. "That healing potion I gave you won't last forever. I will *not* waste another on you. Now, are you going to talk or not?"

Ishan nodded reluctantly. "It's for the dungeons. The chain of dungeons accessible through the nether portal in this sector are no ordinary ones," he said at last.

That made no sense. I'd been in the dungeon. There had been nothing unusual about it. I threw Ishan a hard look. "Don't lie to me. I've been there, remember?"

Ishan snorted. "You're referring to Erebus' candidate dungeon?"

I nodded.

The mage guffawed. "That's only the *first* dungeon sector. It was cleared ages ago and, for obvious reasons, was configured to look normal. Erebus made certain it was reseeded with ordinary creatures."

I frowned. "The goblins, you mean?"

"Yes, like the goblins," Ishan agreed. "The candidate dungeon is just the start. Beyond it are many more dungeon sectors. Ones overflowing with high-leveled creatures, loot, and items beyond your wildest dreams."

I stared at him. "I don't understand."

The mage laughed. "That's because you're still a noob. Not all dungeon sectors are equal. Some are more prized than others, some more difficult and some wealthier. The region of the Nethersphere this sector's portal leads into is rich in loot and experience—richer than any other known dungeons in the Forever Kingdom. Enough to boost the level of every Awakened Dead player by many ranks."

"I see," I said, rubbing my chin. "And that is what makes controlling the valley vital?"

Ishan nodded.

"Then why force the goblins to fight each other? Why not fortify the sector heavily instead?"

"That's the last thing we'd want to do," Ishan said. "The moment the other Dark factions realize what lies beneath the valley, they'll all want a piece of it too. And we don't want to share."

I stared at him in consternation. "Wait. Are you saying the rest of the Dark doesn't know about these... rich dungeons?"

"Of course they don't!" Ishan scoffed. "If they did, do you imagine the valley would remain a backwater? The moment our discovery becomes common knowledge, players will flood this sector." Ishan's eyes slid to the broken artifact. "And now that you've broken the shield generator, that's likely to happen anyway," he finished bitterly.

I barely noticed, my mind preoccupied with something else. Hadn't Talon told me the nether portal led to a Dark-controlled region of the Nethersphere? Had he lied? I turned back to Ishan. "How can the Tartans not know about the rich dungeons? Doesn't the valley's nether portal connect to underground sectors controlled by the Dark?"

"Tartans," Ishan sneered. "What do they know? Bloody smug-faced bastards. They think they're better than everybody, but soon, very soon, they'll find out the Awakened Dead are not to be trifled with. We will teach those scum what—"

"Ishan," I said sharply, putting an end to his tirade.

The mage closed his mouth with a snap and looked at me. He was breathing heavily, and his face was flushed. *He must really hate the Tartans.*

"Just answer the damn question," I said.

For a moment Ishan remained rebellious, wanting to resume his rant, then he bowed his head. "That was unfortunate," he said.

"What was?" I asked in confusion.

Ishan looked up. "Finding a path connecting *our* dungeon sectors with Tartan ones," he clarified. "It complicated matters."

I stared at him blankly. "You're going to have to explain further."

The mage sighed. "The plan—the *original* plan—had been to tell no one outside of the faction of our discovery, and at first that worked well enough. Then, by accident more than anything else, an Awakened Dead scout team, venturing through a dungeon exit portal, found themselves in a Tartan-controlled sector." He shrugged. "After that, it was too late to keep the valley's existence secret. We were forced to scrub the dungeons between this sector and the Tartan ones underground and give the other Dark factions limited access. But we told no one of the other, richer dungeon sectors."

"Hmm," I mused, processing the mage's somewhat convoluted story.

Ishan, meanwhile, was shooting me dark glances. "This is all Erebus' fault," he muttered.

I glanced at him. "What do you mean?"

"If he hadn't insisted on locating his experiment here, we wouldn't be having this conversation now, would we? The goddess tried to tell him it was a bad idea, but Erebus wouldn't listen." The mage shook his head. "Bloody Power. Always thinks he knows best."

I hid my amusement. Ishan seemed to hate everyone but himself and his goddess. "By experiment, you mean the candidate dungeon?"

The mage nodded. "That was another damned hair-brained scheme. Why, he—"

I raised my hand, cutting him off. Ishan, I feared, was about to begin another tirade, and I didn't have time to listen to him rail again.

"So, Erebus *deliberately* started a war in the valley," I said, bringing the conversation back on track. "You're saying he would rather risk losing the sector than share in the spoils with his *allies*?" I asked dubiously.

Ishan glowered—still angry at me for silencing him, no doubt. "Yes," he replied in a clipped tone.

I shook my head at the Power's folly but then set it aside for future consideration to think through the rest of the puzzle. "So... by having the Howlers and Red Rats fight each other, Erebus and Ishita delayed the goblin alliances and gave themselves an excuse for not providing the other Dark factions full access?"

"You've got it," Ishan said. "And about damn time too," he added under his breath. The mage's gaze drifted back to the antitoxin in my hand. "Now I've told you what you want," he said more loudly. "Give me what you promised."

I considered the sworn servant thoughtfully for a moment. Despite his less than gracious attitude, Ishan *had* told me what I wanted to know, and the state of affairs in this sector was finally beginning to make sense. "Alright, I—" I began.

"Not so fast," a voice called out from behind.

I whipped around, my blade flying outward to point unerringly at the approaching figure.

The newcomer was far from perturbed by my reaction and continued to stride nonchalantly toward me. Eyes narrowed, I studied the figure.

He was clothed in a tight-fitting garment patterned with black diamonds. On his head was a black-and-white striped cap. Completing his outfit was a pair of black shoes and a white face mask.

I lowered my blade. I knew him, of course.

It was Loken.

✳ ✳ ✳

"You!" I heard Ishan gasp behind me. "What are—? You shouldn't—"

Loken waved his hand and an impenetrable white dome sprang into existence to surround the hapless Ishita sworn.

My gaze flickered back to the Shadow Power. He had come to a stop before me, standing casually with his arms folded and the fingers of one hand tapping against his face. "What did you do to him?" I asked while weaving a mind shield tightly around myself.

Loken's painted black lips spread in a wide grin. "What, no 'hello'? No, 'thank you, Loken,' or 'oh my gosh, Loken, how did you get here?'"

I rolled my eyes.

The Power sighed dramatically. "It's so hard to get proper appreciation these days," he lamented.

"Enough with the antics, Loken." I gestured to the corpses littering the cave. "I did this all on my own. I have no need to thank you. You haven't done anything to help me."

Leaning forward, the Shadow Power pressed one manicured forefinger against my chest. "Not yet, dear boy. Not yet." He cocked his head to the side, eyes wide and inquisitive. "But it *is* to help you that you've called me, isn't it?"

I bowed my head. "An impulse I'm already regretting," I muttered under my breath.

"I heard that," Loken said sharply.

I inclined my head in apology. "Sorry, I'm still a bit on edge from the fight."

The Shadow Power waved his hand negligently. "No matter, my boy, all is forgiven." Swinging away, Loken tiptoed around the cave, idly inspecting each of the bodies. "You do good work," he pronounced approvingly.

Ignoring the Power's remarks, I asked, "So I gather Benadean managed to deliver my letter after all?"

"He did," Loken said, turning to face me. "Quite a gamble you took, sending it to the Hamish and Spuren Trading Company. How did you know I was keeping an eye on the little gray merchant's correspondences?"

I shrugged. "I didn't. As you say, I took a gamble."

Loken, of course, had been my backup plan.

I'd known my schemes in the sector could go disastrously wrong, and if that happened, I had wanted someone whom I could rely on in my corner.

Well, "rely on" was maybe an overstatement. Loken wasn't the dependable type, but I knew enough of the Power's own goals to know he would gleefully wreck any of Erebus' plans if he could. Which was why I had written to Loken about the nether portal in the valley, the shield woven around the sector, and my intention to destroy the artifact keeping it up. I'd *also* urged the Power to find me as soon as the shield was down.

What I *hadn't* counted on, though, was being the scion of a fallen House when he arrived.

If I had known about my ancient bloodline when I sent the letter, I would never have risked entangling with Loken again. The capricious Power was too damned perceptive, and I most emphatically did not trust him with knowledge of my Wolf ties.

Damnit, I hope he doesn't start to suspect anything.

Reminded by Loken's visit that there were still several crucial Game messages awaiting my attention—not the least being the ones related to my Class evolution—I turned my eyes inward and ran a cursory gaze over my player profile. A more detailed review of the Adjudicator's messages would have to wait until later—when I had a moment alone.

<u>Player Profile: Michael</u>

Level: 76. Rank: 7. Current Health: 100%.
Stamina: 30%. Mana: 100%. Psi: 70%.
Species: Human. Lives Remaining: 3.
True Marks (hidden): Pack-brother.
False Marks (fabricated): Lesser Shadow, Lesser Light, Lesser Dark.

<u>Classes</u>

Available: 3 points.
Primary-Secondary Bi-blend: mindstalker (fabricated), mindslayer (hidden).
Tertiary Class: None.

Nothing seemed out of the ordinary. Thankfully, the secret blood trait was doing its work well. *That's a relief.*

"HELLO?" Loken called out. "Anyone there?"

I refocused on the Power. "Sorry. I got distracted for a moment."

"Is this really the time to be checking your player profile?" he asked in exasperation.

"I said I was sorry," I muttered. "What were you saying again?"

"I was congratulating you on your gambit," Loken said, sounding miffed at having to repeat himself. "It was well-played. Congratulations." The Power's eyes drifted slowly from my face downward and then back up again. "You've grown too," he said at last.

I nodded, remaining silent.

"But no third Class yet I see. Still only a mindstalker then." There was a hint of a question in Loken's voice, and I strove hard not to react to it. Had I done something to rouse his suspicion?

"Like I've had time to go around hunting Class stones," I scoffed, with what I thought was admirable conviction. "I've spent nearly every moment of every day trying to escape this damn sector."

"You're desperate to escape Erebus' grasp, I imagine," Loken said with a sly smile. "What with your non-aggression Pact about to run out."

I scowled, less at his words and more to conceal my relief at the shift in topic. "How do you know about that?"

"I know far more than you believe, boy," the Power replied with a chuckle.

Again, there was a dark undertone to Loken's reply. Were his words a veiled threat?

"Why don't you—" The Power broke off, his head jerking upward to stare at the roof. "Can you please do something about that gnome?" Loken asked plaintively a moment later. "I do so hate being listened in on."

My gaze tracked Loken's, unsurprised that he had sensed Saya on the clifftop. In all the excitement, I'd forgotten about the youth. "Let me fetch her," I said. "Then we can get down to business."

DAY SEVEN. MID-MORNING.

A few minutes later, I was back in the tunnels with a reluctant Saya in tow.

On my way to fetch the gnome, the thought had occurred to me to ask Saya to teleport me somewhere else—anywhere else. But there were still some things I had left undone in the sector, and as appealing as the idea of fleeing Loken's oh-too-inquisitive presence was, I suspected doing so would accomplish little.

The Power had found me frighteningly quick after the shield generator had broken, and I still worried about how he'd managed the feat so fast. If I left, it was more than likely he'd find me again.

"I don't want to meet him," Saya whispered furiously to me again for what felt like the hundredth time. "Why do I have to meet him?"

"There's nothing to be afraid of," I said, tugging on her arm once more when she balked at entering the cave.

"Easy for you to say," she retorted. "You're no civilian." A moment later, she resorted to begging again. "Please. It's not for the likes of me to mingle with Powers."

"Don't worry," I said soothingly. "He won't—"

Loken popped into existence behind the gnome. "I don't bite, you know."

Saya shrieked, jumping up in terror. If I hadn't thought to keep a firm grip on her arm, I was sure she would've fled.

The Power's face transformed into a mask of dejection. "Don't you like me?"

Saya's mouth worked wordlessly as she tried to figure out a response to that.

I sighed. "Don't toy with the girl, Loken. She's been through enough already."

The Power pouted. "You're no fun, Michael. But I think you're right." His gaze slid back to the alchemist. "My dear, if you don't mind, can I place you in a stasis bubble? I promise you won't be harmed, but you also won't hear anything... dangerous."

Saya bobbed her head emphatically. "P-p-please do."

Loken waved his arm again and the gnome disappeared under a silver bubble. "There you go. Now we can talk," he said lightly.

I eyed the dome around Saya suspiciously. It was a twin of the one Loken had placed Ishan in.

"Don't worry, she's alright," Loken said, catching my look. "I'm a Power, and she is a player, and by the rules of the Game I can't do anything to harm her. I've only placed her—" Loken pointed to Ishan—"and him in temporary stasis. Once we're done, I'll release both."

I nodded reluctantly.

Loken clapped his hands together. "Brilliant. Now tell me why you called me here." He gestured toward the corpses. "It was certainly not to help you slay your enemies. You seem more than capable of doing that on your own."

"You read the letter, didn't you?" I asked.

"I did," Loken said, "but as fascinating as I found some of your terms, I'm afraid I cannot agree to all of them."

I scowled. "You're not trying to wriggle out of our deal now, are you?"

"I've struck no 'deal' with you," Loken said primly.

Which was true enough, but I wasn't letting him off that lightly. I raised the palm of my hand and began ticking off points on my fingers. "I reckon I've done a lot to aid Shadow's cause here. One, I've helped you find the location of this sector—which I'm sure you've been trying to find for ages. Two, I've destroyed the shield generator, allowing any Shadow agents you care to send to enter."

I gestured to Ishan. I was sure Loken had eavesdropped on my interrogation of Ishita's sworn before showing himself. "And three, I've even uncovered the Awakened Dead's schemes for the sector." I glared at Loken. "Surely all of that is worth the paltry sum of one thousand gold?"

I hadn't written to Loken simply to ask for help. I suspected the Power would have ignored such a one-sided request. Instead, I'd dangled the mystery of the Awakened Dead's machinations in front of him and, in exchange, demanded payment—in the form of one thousand gold and something else equally valuable.

Loken shrugged airily. "But you've done all that *already*. And while I'm sure you had to work hard to accomplish everything you have, it's in the past. Done and dusted and all that. Why do I have to pay now? After all, it's not like you can undo any of it, can you?"

Dumbfounded, I scowled at Loken.

Does he really mean to...?

The Power bent over and clutched at his sides as he burst out in laughter. "Oh, Michael," he gasped. "Your expression... it's priceless."

I stared at him in consternation.

If anything, Loken's amusement only grew.

Fuming, I waited him out.

Eventually, Loken straightened, his mirth subsiding. "You really are a gambler, Michael," he said, still grinning. "And for that reason, if nothing else, I *will* pay what you've asked. But let this be a lesson to you. In the future, don't trust in a Power's generosity."

I grunted. I didn't. And despite how Loken was twisting matters, I wasn't depending on his generosity. Still, there was no need to appear ungracious. "Thank you," I said grudgingly.

"You're welcome," Loken replied solemnly. He paused. "But before I can pay you, there is one more thing I need you to do for me."

I bit back a sigh. *Here we go again.* "What?" I asked evenly.

Loken raised his arm and traced a slow circle around the cave until his fingers came to a stop pointing at Ishan. "Give him to me."

"What?" I asked, perplexed. Was Loken joking again?

"I want you to give me Ishita's sworn servant," the Power said without any trace of a smile.

I eyed him suspiciously. "What do you want with Ishan? And I thought Powers couldn't harm players?"

"We can't," Loken agreed. "That's why I need *you* to give him to me—" he paused—"or, more precisely, to one of my envoys."

My mouth worked in confusion. "How do I give Ishan to your envoys? Is one of them in the sector?"

Loken shook his head. "Sadly, I have no agents here." He pulled out an object from one of his many pockets. It was a silver bracelet, ordinary-looking. "But with this, you can send Ishita's sworn on his way. Wrap it around his arm and press this button," the Power said, indicating a small emerald stud on the center of the bracelet.

"What will that do?"

"It will teleport Ishita's agent to one of my holding cells in a sector belonging to Shadow."

I frowned. "You still haven't said why you want him."

"What do I want from one of Ishita's sworn?" Loken asked, amused again. "Why, information, dear boy. I suspect that mage over there will be a fount of information. There is a lot I hope he can tell me about those rich dungeon sectors." The Power grinned, baring gleaming white teeth. "He will be especially useful since Ishita will not know I have him. His companions will all think he's died his final death."

"You believe him then? You think Ishan was telling the truth about the wealth in those dungeons?"

"I do," the Power replied. "It ties in with other things my agents have observed." He rubbed at his chin. "For a long time now, I've been receiving reports of dramatic improvements in the levels of some Awakened Dead players, leaps in ranks that you wouldn't ordinarily expect in a short span of time. Then, too, there are the rumors of the powerful items seen in their possession." Loken glanced at me and shrugged. "When you put that together with what the mage told you, it all makes sense."

I nodded thoughtfully.

Loken looked at me expectantly again. "So, can I have him?"

I owed Ishan nothing other than what I promised him—the antidote. And if the tables were turned, I was sure the sworn servant would have no compunctions handing me over.

"Alright," I said slowly. As Loken's grin began to widen, I added, "but I want something additional too."

The Power sighed. "Of course you do," he said faintly. "Go on, I'm listening."

"I want an explanation," I said. "I thought I understood how dungeons in the Game work, but if Erebus went to all this trouble of deceiving his own allies just to control a few dungeon sectors—" I shook my head—"then maybe my understanding isn't as complete as I'd thought."

Loken chuckled again, seemingly happy with the smallness of my request. "And that's all you want?"

"That, my thousand gold, *and* the teleport out of the sector that I asked for in my letter," I added, not wanting to give him any wriggle room again.

"Of course," the Power murmured.

"Then do we have a deal?"

Loken nodded gravely. "We do."

✳ ✳ ✳

You have sealed a Pact with the Shadow Power, Loken.

Before Loken and I could see to the conclusion of our Pact, the Power left to scout the sector, promising to take no more than an hour. I gladly acquiesced to the delay, having some of my own matters to attend to.

After Loken vanished, I approached Saya. The Power had released her from stasis before going.

The gnome stood shivering in the center of the cave. Her arms were wrapped tightly about herself, and her eyes were downcast. It wasn't cold though, and I realized it had to be bodies strewn around her that were affecting her so.

Walking up to her, I laid my arms on her shoulder. "Saya, can I ask you for a favor?"

The gnome blinked and, tearing her gaze away from the dead Worca—Besina had savaged her badly—stared at me vacantly. "Yes?"

I gestured to the wyvern mother's corpse. "Do you think you could harvest her remains?"

Saya's gaze flitted between the beast's remains and me. "Besina was almost rank twenty," she squeaked. "Harvesting her is the job of a full-fledged alchemist. And you want *me* to do it?" she finished, sounding half-strangled at the end.

Some of the pallor coloring her skin had disappeared, I noted. I shrugged. "I don't have one of those hanging around," I said dryly. "You'll have to do. Will you do it?"

"Of course!" the apprentice replied, her excitement shining through clearly now. But a moment later, her shoulders sagged. "Oh, but I don't have anywhere to store the ingredients."

I retrieved the alchemy stone from my pocket and handed it to her. "Will this do?"

"Yes!" she exclaimed, eyes widening. "Where did you get that from?"

"From Gelar." I guided her to the wyvern. "Go ahead. And when you're done, we need to talk."

She nodded and got to work. Leaving her to it, I turned my attention to the other bodies in the cave.

It was time to loot them.

CHAPTER 155: INVESTING WISELY

DAY SEVEN. MID-MORNING.

The three dead mages—Ishan was still locked inside his bubble—carried a treasure trove of equipment. Unfortunately, most of the gear wasn't suitable for me.

Still, among the ones I could use, there were a few gems that had me all but rubbing my hands in glee. Laying out the trophies I'd recovered on the cave floor, I inspected each item in turn.

You have acquired 12 gold and 3 silver coins. Total money carried: 16 gold, 9 silver, and 0 copper.

You have acquired 5 full mana potions and 8 major mana potions.

You have acquired 3 invisibility potions. Each potion will completely hide your presence for 1 minute. Taking hostile action will break the enchantment.

You have acquired 9 enchanted rings, 3 enchanted bracelets, 2 mages' robes, 3 pairs of enchanted boots, and 5 spellcasters' wands.

You have acquired a rank 2 medallion of the stygian brotherhood. This item has an enchantment that allows the user to summon a stygian beast from the void. Note, unless the caster is a member of the brotherhood, the called creature will be hostile to the caster. Its enchantment can be replenished with mana. This item requires a minimum Magic of 8 to use.

You have acquired the wayfarer's boots. This item is indestructible and part of a legendary set. Find more pieces in the set to increase the benefits received. The wayfarer's boots increase the Dexterity of the wearer by +4 ranks and allow him to soundlessly traverse even the noisiest surface.

You have acquired a small bag of holding. This item contains an enchantment to store medium-sized and smaller objects. Courtesy of the enchantment, the bag itself and all the items stored inside are weightless. Only inanimate materials may be kept in the bag. Currently stored items: 0 / 50.

The mana potions were nice, but the invisibility potions were more fascinating and better suited for my own combat style.

The stygian medallion was another interesting item. Worca had been carrying it, which explained why it hadn't been used. Besina had killed the elven mage too fast. I couldn't use the medallion just yet, but given that I would have to invest further in my Magic attribute, I expected to be able to use it in the not-too-distant future.

The bag was easily the most useful find. It would make lugging around all the loot I seemed to find easier. It had contained an assortment of other items—junk to me mostly—which I'd promptly discarded.

By far the biggest and most noteworthy find was the wayfarer's boots. Xrex had been wearing them, and I could attest that they really made the user's footfalls whisper-quiet. They offered a nice Dexterity boost too, but what I found more fascinating was the implication that there were more wayfarer pieces to acquire—pieces that would increase the buffs I received. I would have to find them.

The rest of the loot was an assortment of gear that, while valuable, was unsuitable for me or had prerequisites I couldn't achieve. They all went in my new bag of holding to sell at a convenient time.

After I was done looting, I glanced at Saya. The apprentice was still busy with the wyvern, which gave me time to finally address the long list of Game messages requiring my attention.

Sitting down with my back against the cavern wall, I called up the waiting Game alerts.

You have reached level 76!

I'd gained two levels from the battle, which considering the ranks of my foes, wasn't much. But then again, I was sure it was the mages who had reaped the benefit from slaying Besina, not me. As for myself, I'd killed only two foes—Xrex and Lutra.

My skills I didn't bother reviewing; they'd increased only slightly. My new attribute points I invested in Magic.

Your Magic has increased to rank 5. Current modifiers: +2 from apprentice ring and -1 from light armor. Magic skills and abilities limited to rank 6.

Lastly, I turned to the most intriguing Game messages—the ones relating to my Class evolution.

Your Class has evolved! You are now a mindslayer!
The mindslayer is a master-ranked Class and unique to those with awakened Wolf blood. It is a path that embodies some of the most feared aspects of Wolf. A mindslayer doesn't just stalk his foes' minds and the dark corners of the world, he can act against them too: striking unseen, without warning, and often with fatal consequences. It is a Class that made the assassins of House Wolf some of the most feared in the realms.
Your Class base trait has changed from psi wolf heritage to <u>slayer's heritage</u>. It increases your Dexterity by +2 ranks, your Strength by +2 ranks, your Perception by +4 ranks, and your Mind by +4 ranks.
Your Class trait, nocturnal, has changed to <u>nightwalker</u>. Wolves don't just live in darkness, they thrive in it. This trait improves not only your sight but all your senses—including smell, hearing, touch, and taste— when in darkened surroundings.
Your Class ability has changed from mindsight to <u>slaysight</u>. The slayer cannot only detect the unseen minds around him, he can manipulate them too.
Slaysight is an improvement of the mindsight ability in every way. Where all tiers of the mindsight ability provide only passive benefits, slaysight allows the caster to enact progressively more powerful manipulations against his targets with every tier the ability is advanced.
Simple slaysight is an activated ability that allows you to sense every unshielded consciousness within a 10-yard radius and <u>blind</u> one to your

presence for 10 seconds or until you take hostile action against the target. This ability consumes psi and can be upgraded with Class points. Its activation time is fast. This is a Class ability and does not occupy any ability slots.

My mouth opened in a soundless O of amazement. My second Class evolution was nothing like my first—from scout to nightstalker. This time, the benefits were palpable.

Avidly, I read over the messages twice more, making certain I understood the changes to my new *master* Class. Studying its details, I was left in no doubt that master-ranked Classes were powerful. Both the slaysight ability and the nightwalker trait were a significant step up from their predecessors, and I could see multiple ways I could've used them in previous encounters.

Maybe it's time I spent those Class points I've been holding in reserve, I mused. There were definite benefits to improving slaysight in particular. What would happen if I invested all three of my Class points in the ability and advanced it to tier four? I rubbed my hands together in excitement. *Alright, let's try—*

"Michael?"

My attention snapped outward to find Saya standing in front of me. Mutely, she placed the alchemy stone in my hand.

You have retrieved an alchemy stone. New ingredients acquired: 25 x vials of beast blood, 25 x heaps of ordinary bonedust, 9 x sacs of wyvern venom, 1 x set of wyvern fangs, 1 x wyvern heart, 2 sets of wyvern claws, and 48 x wyvern scales.

The stone was brimming with components. The gnome had done a good job, harvesting more from the wyvern than I could've managed myself.

"Thank you," I said gravely and banished further thought of my player progression from my mind. It would have to wait for later.

Rising to my feet, I drew the apprentice into the tunnel and away from the scavenged remains. "We must talk about where you go from here, Saya."

"Oh?" she asked.

I remained silent for a moment, gathering my thoughts. My brief time alone had given me space to think, and I'd come to the realization that I had to leave the sector—and immediately.

While the risk of the Talon and the Howlers marching back to the fort and claiming the valley remained high, I could see no way to stop them on my own, and truthfully, I wasn't sure that was necessary anymore.

With the shield generator down and the interests of both Light and Shadow roused, I suspected the other Force factions would have more luck in stopping Tartar than me.

I turned back to Saya. "I'm leaving the sector. Traveling back to the safe zone over land alone is too dangerous for you to attempt. So, you have two choices. One, come with me, or two, go wherever you want with the portal scroll."

The apprentice looked at me in confusion. "But if you give this to me, how are you going to leave?"

"My *friend* will teleport me out."

"Your friend—?" She gasped. Her voice dropped to a breathless whisper. "You mean the Power?"

I grinned and nodded. "What will it be then? Where will you go?"

Saya bit her lip. "I'm not sure... I don't have anywhere to go."

I raised one eyebrow. "You don't? The scroll will take you anywhere, even back to the safe zone of this sector." I paused. "You could always return to Gelar, you know."

Saya hung her head. "I can't," she whispered.

"Why not?" I asked gently.

"Gelar didn't send me out to the forest," Saya admitted. "I don't know why I let you think that." She sighed. "I suppose it was easier than the truth. I went out on my own because..."

The apprentice fell silent, and I waited patiently for her to go on.

Saya raised her head and met my gaze almost defiantly. "I went to the forest alone because I'm a failure. Gelar was about to kick me out. He said I was worthless and that I'd never amount to anything as an alchemist. I had to prove to him I wasn't." Her chin trembled, and water formed in the corner of her eyes. She wiped them away. "Whole lot of good it did me. Anyway, he won't take me back in."

It seemed I'd done Gelar a disservice, if only in my thoughts. He hadn't endangered his young apprentice. She'd done that all on her own.

My gaze flitted over the despondent gnome, considering her thoughtfully. I sympathized with Saya's plight but wasn't so sure she was right.

From what little I knew of Gelar, he seemed the acerbic sort and not one to display affection. But he *had* placed a bounty on Besina, and that must mean that—in some sense, at least—he'd cared for his apprentice.

Still, I didn't think Saya would believe me if I told her as much. *And perhaps Gelar is right. Perhaps, she isn't cut out to be an alchemist.* Whatever else he was, the gnome was a master at his craft.

I rubbed my chin. "Maybe there's an alternative."

Saya stared at me with reddened eyes. "What do you mean?"

"What do you know about running a tavern?"

✳   ✳   ✳

By rights of your bill of ownership, you have appointed the player Saya as the tavernkeeper of 'The Sleepy Inn' in the safe zone of sector 12,560.

After I described to Saya what I meant, she was downright enthusiastic about the idea. Brewing drinks, she told me, was more exciting than harvesting ingredients, and she didn't need to be much of an alchemist to create alcohol.

For my part, I was more than happy to employ Saya as a tavernkeeper and let her keep a share of the profits. I'd purchased the building less because I wanted to run the place and more because I needed Benadean to leave the sector and carry my message.

I'd never expected to recoup the money I'd invested and was only too glad Saya was willing to take over running of the tavern. Given that the sector was now open to everyone and seemingly home to a sought-after series of dungeons, I expected business would pick up significantly—which would benefit both the gnome and me greatly.

And truly, even though I planned on moving on from the sector, I wasn't done with it. The valley was home to the dire wolves, and one way or the other, I would return here.

I wonder what Benadean will make of this.

The unfortunate barkeeper was sure to think I'd swindled him. But I couldn't help that.

"Alright," I said to Saya after we'd gone over all the details, "you're sure you remember everything?"

She nodded.

"Good," I said. "Then you better be on your way. And don't forget to claim the bounty reward from Gelar on my behalf. That note I gave you should be enough to convince him. The money will help you get the tavern going."

"I got it, promise," Saya said. Stepping forward, she wrapped her arms around my legs. "I won't forget this, Michael."

I grinned. "You make a success of that place, and soon it'll be me who's thanking you."

Smiling, Saya stepped back. "Maybe," she said. She waved a final goodbye, then, unrolling the portal scroll, began to read from it.

A moment later, she disappeared.

CHAPTER 156: ANOTHER ENDING

"You're full of surprises, Michael," Loken said, appearing behind me the moment Saya was gone. "I never thought to see you become a merchant."

I chuckled. "I didn't either."

"Are you ready to talk?" Loken asked as we strode back into the cave.

I nodded. "What did you learn from your jaunt through the sector?"

Loken's face took on an unwontedly serious cast. "Matters here are more... interesting than I expected. It's strange to find two goblin tribes in a sector, much less three. Although, someone went to a lot of trouble to see one of them destroyed."

He looked at me questioningly, but I remained silent. I hadn't told Loken *everything* in my letter. And the less he knew of my abilities, the better.

With a smile, Loken went on, "Then there is the presence of the envoys. For three of them to be here, in an—"

I stopped short and stared at the Power. "Did you say three?"

He nodded.

"Who?" I demanded.

Loken arched one eyebrow at my tone but didn't remark on it. "There's the Tartan captain, Talon, for one. He's a well-known figure in the realms, and while I've never had the pleasure of meeting him, he is reputed to be more diplomatic than his fellow legion captains. Tartar usually dispatches the good captain on missions when a more... deft touch is required than the heavy-handed hammer he normally employs to resolve problems."

I nodded thoughtfully, surprised the simple-seeming captain I had met in the safe zone was a respected figure in the Game. "Go on."

"Then there is Amgira," Loken said as he resumed walking.

I frowned.

At my look of confusion, Loken smiled. "She went by the name Mariga in this sector, I believe."

"Ah," I exclaimed.

"You've heard of her, I see," Loken said. "Finding her here was truly a surprise."

I was more impressed by Loken's ability to uncover the druid's identity so quickly. He hadn't been gone *that* long. "What do you know about her?" I asked casually.

"She is an envoy of Arinna and one of the wiliest players around."

There was no mistaking the admiration in the Power's tone. Clearly, even Loken, a master of deceit himself, was impressed by Mariga's—I suppose I should be calling her Amgira now—skill at deception.

"She left quite a mess on her way out too," Loken added.

"Oh?" I asked as we came to a stop before the silver bubble encasing Ishan.

"Oh, yes, she destroyed the Howler fort around the safe zone yesterday, not leaving even a single stone standing, and she did it while in her true form." The Power smiled. "That's how I knew it was her. The players in the village could talk about nothing else except the mysterious winged woman who rained down fire from the sky."

I blinked. *Destroyed the Howler fort?*

The news was both astonishing—and pleasing. With neither a fort or a shield generator, the Dark was even less likely to claim the sector now.

No wonder Talon was upset.

The captain must have already known about the fort's destruction when we had spoken, I realized, and suspected I had something to do with it.

"Who is the third envoy?" I asked absently, still preoccupied with Loken's revelation.

"Stayne, of course."

I stared at the Power. "*Stayne* is an envoy? How—"

I broke off. *Of course he is.* I should have caught onto that fact much sooner.

Loken chuckled at my expression. "You didn't know? Well, make sure you stay away from him. You're nowhere near ready to cross swords with someone like Stayne."

I nodded. For the time being, I had no intention of going anywhere near the undead.

"But as I was saying," Loken continued, "to find three envoys in any sector, much less one as out-of-the-way and small as this one, is nothing short of miraculous." Loken gestured to the stasis bubble. "As for why they're here, Ishita's follower has already told us that."

"The dungeon sectors the Awakened Dead discovered," I stated.

"Exactly," Loken said, rubbing his palms together. "I can't wait to explore them myself."

"You still haven't told me what's so valuable about them," I pointed out.

Loken sighed theatrically. "Ah yes, I almost forgot about our deal. Well, let's get it over with. Sit down and let me explain," he ordered, seating himself on the floor.

Sinking down into a cross-legged stance opposite him, I waited for him to go on.

"What do you know about the nether, Michael?" Loken asked.

I scratched my chin while I thought. "I know that it houses the Game's dungeons." I paused. "And that it's difficult to travel there. There is also no way to teleport into a dungeon sector the way one can into a Kingdom sector."

"Both those things are true, but not the entire truth," Loken agreed. "The aether and nether have existed as long as the Game has. Both are voids of nothingness with little pockets of land—that we call sectors—floating inside them. Despite these similarities, though, the aether and nether are very different from each other. The aether is a bright void, shiny and easy to see through. Its sectors are easy to reach—" Loken's voice turned dry— "assuming, of course, they aren't shielded."

I nodded, having understood this much already.

"The nether, on the other hand, is murky," Loken continued. "Its sectors are hidden and impossible to get to without using the network of ley lines connecting them."

"Ley lines?" I asked, vaguely recalling mention being made of them before.

"Ley lines are what allow the nether portals to exist. They are magical threads stretching through the void to form a bridge between sectors. Most scholars believe the leys were formed during the long-ago cataclysmic event that led to the Forever Kingdom's dissolution into isolated pockets of land. Why they only originate from nether sectors though, no one knows."

"I see," I said.

"If you recall, you traversed a ley twice already. Once to enter this valley, and before that to reach the dungeon where we first met."

I nodded. "Got it."

"Do you see now why control of the ley lines and the sectors anchoring them—like this one—is crucial for any faction wanting to delve into the nether?"

"I do," I replied. "But I still don't understand why the nether is so important."

"I'm getting to that," Loken said primly. Lowering his head into his hands, the Power paused to gather his thoughts. "Do you know what the Game's purpose is?" he asked finally.

I stared at Loken, perplexed by the strange detour in the conversation. "Uh... no."

"Power," Loken said. "At its heart, the Game is about gathering power. Do not forget that." He smiled wryly. "It's why we have named ourselves such. We 'Powers' fancy ourselves as being at the pinnacle of power in this world." Loken looked away for a moment, his gaze going distant. "Although sometimes it does not feel that way..." he whispered so faintly I barely heard him.

Catching me leaning forward, the Power shook himself and refocused on me. "Where was I? Oh yes, power. The essence of the Game is about gathering power. Call it what you will: progression, evolution, leveling. They are all the same thing."

Loken paused to meet my gaze again. "I can see you're still wondering what this has to do with dungeons."

I nodded.

"Simply put, there's nowhere else in the Forever Kingdom where a player can gather power as quickly as he can in a dungeon. The Game has specially designed them for that purpose. Of course, not all dungeons are equal. Some are meant for low-leveled players, still early in their evolution. But others— like the network of dungeon sectors the Awakened Dead seem to have discovered here—are meant for elite players. And they can conceivably elevate a player to godhood."

I stared at him, "Godhood?"

Loken nodded gravely. "Of course, not every player can reach such heights, but it doesn't stop most from trying."

I frowned. "I still don't understand. The dungeon I passed through—that you yourself saw—was nothing remarkable. Why would—"

I stopped short as I saw Loken shaking his head.

"The dungeon you went through, Michael, was a reseeded one."

"What does that mean?"

"The sector was already cleared by the Awakened Dead, then reconfigured for their own purposes—supposedly to train Erebus' candidates. It is the wild sectors of the Endless Dungeons, the ones seeded by the Game itself, that are desired by those who aspire to become Powers in their own right."

I bowed my head and fell silent while I pondered on that.

"It seems the Dark was lucky twice over with their find in this sector," Loken mused. "Not only did they find a ley line leading to a section of elite dungeons, but they also discovered a hereunto unknown connection to their own Dark-controlled nether sectors. That makes this valley doubly important."

The Powers gaze drifted to the silver bubble. "Questioning Ishita's sworn is bound to be interesting," he murmured, almost to himself. After a moment, his gaze refocused on me. "Have I satisfied my end of the bargain? Do you understand the importance of dungeons now?"

"I do," I said.

Loken rose to his feet and tossed me the amulet. "Then put this on the prisoner and I can send you on your way too."

The silver bubble around Ishan disappeared, and I kneeled beside the mage. His face was a picture of befuddlement. "What happened?"

Withdrawing the antidote from my potion belt, I held it out to Ishan. "Here. This is yours, like I promised."

Loken looked at me questioningly but didn't interfere as the mage downed the contents of the wyvern antitoxin.

"You're letting me go?" Ishan asked in surprise, his gaze darting from me to Loken.

"In a manner of speaking, yes," I murmured. Before the mage could protest, I slapped Loken's amulet on him and pressed the emerald stud.

In a blink, the mage vanished.

You have fulfilled your Pact obligations to Loken.

The Power chuckled. "Well done. And as promised, here's your money." Pulling out what looked like the very same keystone he'd shown me in the dungeon long ago, Loken laid his palm across its sigil-carved surface.

The Power Loken has deposited 1,000 gold into your Albion Bank account.

"Done," the Power said, smiling in satisfaction. "Now, to see to your own transportation." He bowed elaborately. "Where to, good sir?" he asked mockingly.

Ignoring Loken's antics, I answered, "Nexus."

Whatever he was expecting, it wasn't that. "Nexus?" Loken asked in surprise. "Why do you want to go there?"

"I'm tired of rattling around at the edges of this world," I lied smoothly. "I want to see what sits at the heart of the Game." I paused. "Besides, I'm rich now, and it's time I properly equipped myself." I grinned. "Where better to do that than in the biggest market this world has?"

Loken tilted his head to the side and studied me the way one would a strange puzzle. "A bold, if somewhat reckless move," he remarked finally. "Are you *sure* you want to go there?"

Was it just me, or did the Power seem reluctant? I nodded. "I am."

"As you wish," Loken said—somewhat curtly, I thought—and waved his arm.

A portal sprang open before me. I stepped toward it but paused just before entering. "Oh, there's just one more thing."

The Power looked at me questioningly.

"I've been meaning to ask: how did you find me so quickly? I expected you to take longer to reach the sector, much less my own location."

Loken smiled. "I suppose I shouldn't be telling you this, but if you're going to Nexus, you'll discover the truth soon enough on your own," he said cryptically.

I waited patiently.

The Power held up the keystone. "When you touched this in the dungeon, you didn't just consent to opening a bank account but also to the tracking spell I placed on you."

I gaped at him. "You did what?" I asked in a half-strangled voice.

"Once the shield dropped, I knew your location instantly," Loken finished with a cheerful grin, ignoring my look.

"Remove the spell," I demanded.

Loken's smile widened. "No. That wasn't part of our deal now, was it?"

I stared at the Power for a drawn-out moment, then sighed. It was my own fault, really, for trusting the self-proclaimed trickster. I would just have to find a means of removing his spell myself. I spun around to face the portal again.

My work in the sector was done, and I had a lot to think about. Now it was time to look to my own future and maybe, just maybe, evolve into something greater.

"Farewell, Loken," I called over my shoulder. Before he could respond, I stomped toward the portal and, without further ado, stepped through.

Transfer through portal commencing...

...

...

Leaving sector 12,560. Entering Nexus!

Loken has fulfilled his Pact obligations to you. Your Pact with Loken is closed!

You have fulfilled all your Pact obligations to the envoy, Amgira. The Power Arinna has deposited 1,000 gold into your Albion Bank account. Your Pact with Amgira is closed!

*   *   *

THE END.

Here ends Book 2 of *The Grand Game*.
Michael's adventures will continue in **World Nexus**.
<u>Get it here</u>!

I hope you enjoyed the story! If you did, please leave a review and let
other readers know what you think.
<u>Click here to leave a review.</u>
Happy reading!
Tom Elliot.

MICHAEL AT THE END OF BOOK 2

<u>Player Profile: Michael</u>
Level: 76. Rank: 7. Current Health: 100%.
Stamina: 100%. Mana: 100%. Psi: 100%.
Species: Human. Lives Remaining: 3.
True Marks (hidden): Pack-brother.
False Marks (fabricated): Lesser Shadow, Lesser Light, Lesser Dark.

<u>Attributes</u>
Available: 0 points.
Strength: 2. Constitution: 14. Dexterity: 21*. Perception: 24. Mind: 41.
Magic: 6*. Faith: 2*.
denotes attributes affected by items.

<u>Classes</u>
Available: 3 points.
Primary-Secondary Bi-blend: mindstalker (fabricated), mindslayer (hidden).
Tertiary Class: None.

<u>Traits</u>
Slayer's heritage (hidden): +2 Dexterity, +2 Strength, +4 Mind, +4 Perception.
Beast tongue: can speak to beastkin.
Marked: can see spirit signatures.
Nightwalker (hidden): improved senses in the dark.
Anointed scion (hidden): bound to House Wolf.
Inscrutable mind: +8 Mind.
Secret blood (hidden): conceals bloodline.

<u>Skills</u>
Available skill slots: 0.
Light armor (current: 42. max: 140. Constitution, basic).
Dodging (current: 50. max: 200. Dexterity, basic).
Sneaking (current: 61. max: 200. Dexterity, basic).
Shortswords (current: 55. max: 200. Dexterity, basic).
Two-weapon fighting (current: 49. max: 200. Dexterity, advanced).
Thieving (current: 39. max: 200. Dexterity, basic).
Chi (current: 47. max: 410. Mind, advanced).
Meditation (current: 67. max: 410. Mind, basic).
Telekinesis (current: 46. max: 410. Mind, advanced).
Telepathy (current: 46. max: 410. Mind, advanced).
Insight (current: 62. max: 240. Perception, basic).
Deception (current: 57. max: 240. Perception, master).

<u>Abilities</u>
<u>Dexterity ability slots used: 13 / 20.</u>
crippling blow (Dexterity, basic, shortswords).

minor piercing strike (5 Dexterity, advanced, shortswords).
lesser backstab (5 Dexterity, advanced, sneaking).
basic trap disarm (Dexterity, basic, thieving).
simple lockpicking (Dexterity, basic, thieving).

<u>Mind ability slots used:</u> **8 / 41.**
simple charm (Mind, basic, telepathy).
stunning slap (Mind, basic, chi).
one-step (Mind, basic, telekinesis).
minor reaction buff (Mind, basic, chi).
simple astral blade (Mind, basic, telepathy).
short shadow blink (Mind, basic, telekinesis).
minor chi heal (Mind, basic, chi).
simple mind shield (Mind, basic, meditation).

<u>Perception ability slots used:</u> **14 / 24.**
improved analyze (5 Perception, advanced, insight).
lesser trap detect (Perception, basic, thieving).
conceal small weapon (Perception, basic, deception).
facial disguise (Perception, basic, deception).
ventro (Perception, basic, deception).
lesser imitate (5 Perception, advanced, deception).

<u>Other abilities:</u>
simple slaysight (hidden): (Class, basic, telepathy).

<u>Known Key Points</u>

Sector 14,913 exit portal and safe zone.
Sector 12,560 nether portal and safe zone.

<u>Equipped</u>

spider's bite shortsword (+15% damage, webbed), concealed.
ebonheart (+30% damage), concealed.
common fighter's sash (+3 shortswords).
enchanted leather armor set (+20% damage reduction, -35% Dexterity and Magic).
slotted potion belt (2 minor heal, 3 moderate heal, 1 full heal, 1 full mana potion, 3 invisibility potions).
common thief's cloak (+3 sneaking).
apprentice's ring (+2 Magic).
acolyte's ring (+2 Faith).
troll's talisman bracelet (+6% damage reduction).
gift of the unbound ring (immunity to tier 1 and 2 entanglement spells).
band of stillness ring (immunity to tier 1 and 2 Mind spells).
wayfarer's boots (legendary item, +4 Dexterity).
backpack, small bag of holding, alchemy stone.
medallion of the stygian brotherhood (summon stygian beast).

Backpack Contents

<u>Money</u>: 12 gold, 9 silver, and 0 copper.
20 x field rations.
1 x flask of water.
2 x iron daggers.
1 x bedroll.
1 x goblin writ of safe passage.
1 x bounty letter authorization.
1 x coil of rope.
1 x shortsword,+1 (+15% damage, +10 shortswords).
1 x tavern bill of ownership.
1 x Tartan token.
4 x full mana potions.
8 x major mana potions.

Miscellaneous Loot

13 x enchanted rings, 5 x enchanted robes, 8 x spellcasters wands, 3 x enchanted bracelets, 3 x enchanted boots.

Alchemy Stone Contents

(111 / 150 ingredients stored).
25 x vials of beast blood.
25 x heaps of ordinary bonedust.
9 x sacs of wyvern venom.
1 x set of wyvern fangs.
1 x wyvern heart.
2 sets of wyvern claws.
48 x wyvern scales.

Bank Contents

<u>Money</u>: 3,046 gold, 4 silver, and 9 copper.
2 x full healing potions.
2 x basic steel shortswords.

Open Tasks

Find the Last Wolf Envoy (hidden) (find Ceruvax).
Stay True to Wolf (hidden) (acquire a mana-based Class).

Books by the Author

By Tom Elliot

The Grand Game (series page)
Book 1: The Grand Game: ebook | audiobook
Book 2: Way of the Wolf: ebook | audiobook
Book 3: World Nexus: ebook | audiobook
Book 4: House Wolf: ebook | audiobook
Book 5: Wolf in the Void: ebook | audiobook
Book 6: A Scion's Duty: ebook | audiobook
Book 7: Ancient Debts: ebook | audiobook
Book 8: The Lost Reclaimed: ebook (coming soon)

The Grand Game Box Set (series page)
Book 1-3: Birth of a Player: ebook.
Book 4-6: Rise of the Elite: ebook (releasing 31 December 2024)

The Grand Game, Elana (series page)
Book 1: Empyrean's Rise: ebook
Book 2: Empyrean's Flight: ebook

By Rohan M. Vider

The Dragon Mage Saga (series page)
Book 1: Overworld: ebook | audiobook
Book 2: Dungeons: ebook | audiobook

The Gods' Game (series page)
Crota, the Gods' Game Volume I
The Labyrinth, the Gods' Game Volume II
Sovereign Rising, the Gods' Game Volume III
Sovereign, the Gods' Game, Volume IV
Sovereign's Choice, the Gods' Game Volume V

Tales from the Gods' Game
Dungeon Dive (Tales from the Gods' Game, Book 1)

AFTERWORD

Thank you for reading the Grand Game!

If you enjoyed the book, please consider leaving a review on Amazon [click here]. I'm already working on Michael's next adventure.

If you have any questions, comments, or want to support my writing, please feel free to contact me through my site, TomLitRPG.com or Discord.

Alternatively, if you wish to learn more about the world of the Forever Kingdom, understand the system of the Grand Game better, or are just looking for the latest news on the Grand Game, please visit my site at TomLitRPG.com or signup up here for my: Newsletter.

Regards,
Tom
Support my writing on **PATREON**
Amazon Author page | Goodreads | Facebook | Reddit | Discord |

DEFINITIONS

alchemy stone: a device used to store alchemical components.

ancient: old Power.

anointed scion: a scion who has bound himself to a bloodline.

ascendant undead: term the Adjudicator used to describe Stayne, meaning unknown.

blended Class: a combined Class.

blood awakening: the process of recalling blood memories.

blood infusion: the absorption of the essences from former scions.

blood memories: gifts from your forebears containing the power of the ancients themselves.

bi-blend: a combination of two melded Classes.

bloodline: reference to the ancient the player descends from.

civilian player: a player without a Class or combat abilities. Civilians do not have a player level.

closed sector: a landmass that does not physically border another, making the area inaccessible except by portal.

controlled sector: a sector owned by a faction. Ownership of a sector gives the faction's players increased privileges in the region.

Class: a defined path or vocation that gives a player access to specific skills.

Class evolution: the advancement of a Class, generally to a better-ranked one due to particular traits, skills, or Marks acquired by the player.

Dark: one of the three Forces.

Darksworn: a player pledged to the Dark who values the self over the collective.

ebonblade: soulbound weapons found in the Twilight Dungeon.

envoy: a trusted representative of a Power, authorized to speak on their behalf.

Endless Dungeon: a section of the Nethersphere where dungeon mechanics are active.

evolution: the advancement of a player's core characteristics.

follower: a player who has pledged themself in a binding vow to a Force or Power.

Force: Light, Dark, Shadow. The building blocks of the cosmos and energy in its rawest form.

Forever Kingdom: the world of the Nethersphere and Kingdom.

Game: refers to the Grand Game.

gatekeepers: holder of ancient lore, guardians of the ancients' trials.

House: House of the Ancient.

House of the Ancient: a grouping of followers pledged to one Prime.

Kingdoms: the sectors located in the aether.

ley line: magic threads connecting nether sectors.

Light: one of the three Forces.

Lightsworn: a player who champions the cause of the many, even to their own detriment.

meld: the process of combining multiple Classes into one.

neutral sector: a sector unowned and unclaimed by any faction or Force.

Nethersphere: the sectors contained in the nether.

new Power: one of the Powers who usurped the ancients.

Pact: a binding enacted between a Power and player, overseen by the Adjudicator.

Power: an evolved player.

Prime: head of ancient bloodline. An ancient.

scion: one bearing the blood of an ancient.

soulbound: an item that remains with the player after death.

sworn: as in sworn servant. A sworn is a follower of a Power who has sufficiently deepened their binding Mark.

Tartan: the faction of Tartar, the god-emperor.

Tartan legion: the military forces of Tartar.

trials of the ancients: tests created by the Primes for their successors.

tri-blend: a combination of three melded Classes.

wolf trials: ancient trials created by Wolf Prime.

wolfkind: used interchangeably with wolfkin.

KEY CHARACTERS & FACTIONS

DRAGONKIN

wyvern mother: Besina. In dire wolf valley, level 198.
wyvern hatchling: killed by Michael, rank 4.

GOBLINKIN

Fangtooths: broken-off section of a goblin tribe.
Grul: apprentice witch doctor, Long Fangs, level 41.
Howlers: goblin tribe, one thousand members, in fort around the safe zone.
Hyek: shaman, Howlers' leader.
Klaxis: shaman, Red Rats' leader, level 71.
Long Fangs: goblin tribe with a two-hundred-strong delegation in the valley's east.
Nyzack: shaman apprentice, Red Rats' new leader.
Red Rats: goblin tribe, two thousand strong in a crater to the north.
Sstak: apprentice witch doctor, Long Fangs, level 35.

HOUSE WOLF

Atiras: dead Wolf Prime.
Ceruvax: last envoy.

OTHERS

Albion Bank: major non-aligned bank in the Forever Kingdom.

Amgira: Arinna's envoy.
Benadean: tavernkeeper.
Cecilia: level 29 elven player.
Forsyth: human, Ishita follower, level 67.
Gelar: alchemist.
Henry: bounty hunter.
Ishan: human mage, Ishita sworn.
Knorl: bounty hunter.
Lutra: human mage, Ishita sworn.
Mariga: dark druid, envoy.
Michael: protagonist.
Saya: apprentice alchemist.
Stayne: Erebus' henchman.
Sturm: the captain's son, born in the Forever Kingdom.
Talon: the captain, envoy.
Ultack: half-orc player.
Worca: elven mage, Ishita sworn.
Xrex: lizardman mage, Ishita sworn.

Powers & Factions

Arinna: Light Power.
Artem: Shadow Power. Goddess of nature.
Awakened Dead: A Dark faction.
Axis of Evil: An alliance of Dark factions.
Erebus: Dark Power, leader of the Awakened Dead faction.
Ishita: Spider goddess, Dark Power, member of the Awakened Dead.
Loken: Shadow Power.
Tartar: Dark Power, also known as the god-emperor.

Wolfkin

Aira: dire wolf dame, level 14.
Barak: dire wolf elder.
Duggar: dire wolf alpha, level 67.
Oursk: dire wolf sire, level 19.
Leta: dire wolf elder.
Monac: dire wolf elder and former alpha.
Sulan: dire wolf healer, level 51.
Suva: dire wolf elder.